PRAISE FOR K

"K. Bromberg always delivers intelligently written, emotionally intense, sensual romance."

—*USA Today*

"K. Bromberg makes you believe in the power of true love."

—#1 *New York Times* bestselling author Audrey Carlan

"A poignant and hauntingly beautiful story of survival, second chances, and the healing power of love. An absolute must read."

—*New York Times* bestselling author Helena Hunting

"A home run! *The Player* is riveting, sexy, and pulsing with energy. And I can't wait for *The Catch*!"

—#1 *New York Times* bestselling author Lauren Blakely

"An irresistibly hot romance that stays with you long after you finish the book."

—#1 *New York Times* bestselling author Jennifer L. Armentrout

"Bromberg is a master at turning up the heat!"

—*New York Times* bestselling author Katy Evans

"Supercharged heat and full of heart. Bromberg aces it from the first page to the last."

—*New York Times* bestselling author Kylie Scott

"Captivating, emotional, and sizzling hot!"

—*New York Times* bestselling author S. C. Stephens

RESIST

ALSO BY K. BROMBERG

RESIST

WICKED WAYS, BOOK ONE

K. BROMBERG

Montlake
Romance

Published by Montlake Romance, Seattle
www.apub.com

Amazon, the Amazon logo, and Montlake Romance are trademarks of Amazon.com, Inc., or its affiliates.

ISBN-13: 9781503905306
ISBN-10: 1503905306

Cover design by Letitia Hasser

Cover photography by Wander Aguiar

Printed in the United States of America

RESIST

CHAPTER ONE
Vaughn

Carter Preston jolts when I shove the adjoining door open and take the room by storm. He's wearing nothing more than black dress slacks, his untrimmed physique on display from the belt up, and his eyes widen when he sees me.

Not Lola, who he was expecting.

Just me.

"What the hell—"

"You." I point a finger at him, fury on heels, as I make my way across the elegant hotel room. But all I can picture is the image of mascara-laced tears staining Lola's cheeks. The bruises on her upper arms. The ripped lace of her lingerie. "You put your hands on her."

"Well, that's the point, isn't it? My hands on her? My dick in her?" His chuckle is like sandpaper to my eardrums, and his eyes are lasers of suggestion as they take me in. I can see the minute it registers that I'm not here to replace Lola. "Ah, the queen has left her throne."

Queen? More like madam.

"You broke the agreement." I stand my ground despite how his eyes scrape over every part of my body. How they study me. How they want me.

His head angles to the side, and his smile slides arrogantly onto his lips, putting the thousands he's spent on cosmetic dentistry on display. "What a good boss. Coming to fulfill what your employee failed to finish?"

"Not a chance in hell."

"I want what I paid for," he says cavalierly, as only a person born into money can.

"You got what you paid for."

"See?" He chuckles and takes a step toward me. "That's where we disagree. Lola ran next door before anything happened . . . so from where I stand, I was shortchanged and overcharged." I control the hitch of my breath when he reaches out and traces a finger down the side of my cheek. "Unless, of course, you'd like to take her place."

My body revolts at the thought.

"Lola ran next door because being rough with her wasn't the agreed upon terms of your contract."

"A little spanking isn't rough." He waves his hand at me in dismissal.

"What you wanted was a lot more than spanking. I have girls willing to do that, but not Lola. There is such a thing as consent, and you clearly didn't get it, nor did you ever ask for it."

"Is this an escort service or a day care?"

My smile is lethal and laced with sarcasm. "You know what this is, and you signed an acknowledgment of the rules and requirements ahead of time." I quirk a brow as I find my footing despite the absolute discord I feel at the moment. "Like I said, I require consent, and you didn't get it."

"I didn't get much of anything"—he runs a hand over his face, and the sound of it scraping over his stubble fills the room—"least of all what I paid for."

"You did get what you paid for. A dinner date."

His chuckle is low and unforgiving. "I paid for a hell of a lot more than—"

"Stop," I shout, needing to cut him off as the realization hits me that this could be a complete setup.

It could, couldn't it?

I stare at him and try to gather my wits in spite of the adrenaline rushing through my veins. Thinking on my feet has always been a strength of mine, and I need it to be right now as well.

Repeat the company line, Vaughn. Tell him what he knows just in case he's recording this to use against you later.

"You paid for companionship. A woman to spend time with you. All money was exchanged ahead of time, so anything agreed upon after the fact was between the two of you," I explain. And yes, I just contradicted myself. I just said that sex wasn't paid for, when moments before I was telling him I required their sex and his need for roughness to be consensual. Lucky for me, he's so distracted he doesn't call me on it.

Our eyes meet. Hold. "Cute. That's how you want to play this?"

"I'm not playing anything," I assert.

"We both know what this transaction included." He takes a step toward me, the shock at my presence now giving way to anger. His sneer turning into an elitist smirk.

"Companionship," I state evenly, although my insides feel like a kick drum is pounding in my veins.

"You think that will fly when I make a phone call to the attorney general about a certain woman named Vee who seems to—"

"Let me stop you right there," I say and lift my hand up to prevent him from speaking and to thwart him from stepping too close to me. "There won't be any phone calls to anyone."

"Then that means either Lola *or you* will be providing the services I paid for."

"I don't think you're listening to what I'm saying, *Senator.*"

"I'm hearing you all right. It's you who isn't listening." He begins to unbuckle his belt as panic reverberates through me. "I think you forget who you're dealing with here. Don't you know who I am?" A goading

3

smile. A condescending chuckle. "Don't you know I could ruin you? You're nothing but a two-bit whore, Vee, and I'm—"

"Uh-uh-uh," I warn, needing to toughen up despite his words hitting me harder than they should. "You broke the terms of the contract you signed. You're required to pay for the damages."

"I'm not paying you a dime more. In fact, I want a refund or the services I paid for. Besides, it's a bullshit contract."

With my eyes locked on his, I pull my phone from my pocket. "Then that must mean these photos are bullshit too. Right?"

He visibly jars at my words as his eyes flicker down to where my thumb scrolls across the screen of my phone. "I don't play games," he grits out.

I take my time finding what I need despite knowing exactly where the images are stored. I don't hide my wince when I open the folder marked "Carter Preston" and the first picture fills the screen.

"Neither do I," I murmur as I turn the phone around and show him the image of him with his pants around his ankles in front of an unknown female. A female who definitely looks underage.

His face pales and his eyes widen. The sudden panic that flickers through his expression is fleeting before he puts his practiced politician's face back on so that the righteous sneer owns his countenance again.

"That doesn't show anything. Nice try, though. You might want to tell whoever you pay to collect your dirt that they need to do a better job."

He says the words nonchalantly, but the forced bob of his Adam's apple tells me all I need to know. I've got him right where I want him.

"Do you actually think that's the only image I have?" It's my turn to chuckle as the tables begin to turn. Affluence often comes hand in hand with a false sense of invincibility, and I'm going to have so much fun yanking this rug out from under him. "There's at least fifteen more where this came from, and your face is clear as day in those. I'm smart enough not to show my ace the first hand I play . . . but I forgot, what did you call me? Just a two-bit whore while you're a Harvard-educated prick?"

"You bitch."

"*Thank you* for the compliment." My smile taunts him in response.

"Sex scandals are a dime a dozen, Vee. You're not successful in politics unless you've had one."

"So your wife won't mind. Other senators? Voters? You think they'll applaud you for fucking underage girls?"

"I'm not scared of you."

We stare at each other like dogs circling, each trying to gain the upper hand. Both trying to find a foothold in the situation.

"Then don't pay for the damages, and we can test your theory." My tone drips with saccharine. "Simple as that."

"Try posting that photo, and I'll bury you with everything I have." He shakes his head and starts to pull his shirt on as if this conversation is over. *Arrogant prick.*

"Number one rule: always know who you're working with, *Senator.*"

Carter falters with his arms halfway in his sleeves and meets my gaze. There's a hard glint to his eyes that tells me he revels in playing dirty, and hell if I just didn't bring a dump truck full of dirt to roll around in.

"I wouldn't push me," he threatens.

"Then I guess you better pay up."

"So you have a private investigator, do you?" he asks, changing the subject and leaving me to unscramble where he's going with this. "You think you're the only one in this situation who has information to hold over the other one's head?" He quirks an eyebrow, and a smarmy smirk fails at lighting up his features. "Number one rule and all that."

My nerves rattle violently beneath the surface as our eyes hold and his threat takes hold.

He's bluffing.

He has to be.

No one knows who I am. Where I'm from. What I have at stake here.

There's no way he can know.

Panic like I've never felt before claws over my throat and threatens to siphon off its air. I tamp down the anxiety and know the only shot I have at putting him in his place—fearful of what I can do to him and his career—is to use my trump card. To play the unexpected information that was emailed anonymously to my PI days ago.

Here goes nothing.

"Bribery and swing votes seem to be all the rage this congressional session, now don't they?" I lift a single brow and let him know I'm ready to play.

"And?" His voice may be unaffected, but the quick dart of his tongue to his bottom lip says plenty.

"It would be a shame if the documents I had in safekeeping somehow made their way into the hands of the right people."

"You're lying!" His voice thunders into the room, but the gray pallor of his skin tone tells me I've struck enough fear into him to gain a little more security.

"But am I?" I bat my lashes, the picture of innocence.

"You don't want to fuck with me." He seethes. The tendons in his neck strain, and the muscle in his clenched jaw tics. Even now, there's a manicured attractiveness to him. Too pretty. Too polished. And with an underlying callousness to him.

"But it's so tempting," I say sarcastically. "Here's how this is going to go—"

"This conversation is over." He cuts me off and stuffs his wallet into the back of his slacks without looking at me.

"With so much at stake too . . ." My voice is singsongy as I play with fire.

"I'm not a man who'll kowtow to bogus threats and be led around by the balls."

"Seems to me I have both of your balls firmly in my grasp," I say.

Without warning he strides across the room—shirt unbuttoned, muscle in his jaw pulsing—and steps into me. I retreat, my breath hitching ever so slightly when my back bumps up against the wall.

Don't panic.

But I do.

My pulse thunders as the awareness seeps into every part of my being—that if he could leave those marks on Lola in the pursuit of sex, I can't imagine what exactly he'd do to someone when his temper was sparked.

Carter stands close enough that our bodies brush against one another. I can smell the whiskey on his breath. The subtle mix of sweat and cologne. I can feel the heat of his body.

"Oh, this could be so much fun, Vee."

A man who gets off on making a woman scared. *The worst kind.*

Beads of sweat appear on his temple. I meet him stare for stare as he squares his shoulders and stands to his full height, his physical presence more than dominating the space and dwarfing my five-foot-five frame.

Needing to de-escalate the situation—to get his focus off me—I draw in a measured breath. "You laid your hands on Lola."

"She liked it."

Asshole.

"You left marks on her. That's unacceptable. You didn't pay for that right. In fact, in doing that, you've cost me more than a pretty penny because I can't send her out on any more dates until she's healed."

"Not my fucking problem."

"Oh, but that's where you're so very wrong." I angle my head to the side and purse my lips as I draw out the pause. "Per our contract, you will pick up your phone and deposit an additional ten thousand dollars in my account to cover the loss of income I will be incurring because you couldn't act like a gentleman and treat a lady kindly."

"You're out of your fucking mind."

"Maybe I am, but I'm thinking the *New York Times* would love these photos . . ." I hold up my phone as spittle forms in the corner of his mouth when he opens it and then closes it again, at a loss for words. "And then once they post them, and the attention is front and center on you, we can follow them up with the coup de grâce . . . I'll leave what that might be up to your imagination."

"You bitch."

"I believe we've already established that." I quirk an eyebrow. "I hear your seat is being highly contested this midterm election with the supposed blue wave and all. I'd hate to see the favored senator have some problems that might cause him to lose those votes he so desperately needs."

"Like playing with fire, do you?"

"Only when it's someone else who's going to get burned." Our eyes hold, challenge, as silence filters through the room and we each consider our next move.

He lowers his face so that his mouth is near my ear and murmurs, "You're a real ballbuster, and it's such a goddamn turn-on."

"At least a ballbuster doesn't use their fists. Transfer the funds, Carter," I demand, stilling when he reaches out and runs a hand down my arm.

I don't react.

I can't.

Showing him fear is not an option right now.

"I'm going to have you. You know that, right?" I snort at his words, and he emits a guttural groan full of suggestion, his erection bumping against my thigh. "It's inevitable that I will. I love showing a woman who thinks she's in power just who really is."

He draws in a breath as I attempt to even mine out. "I'll say it again: *transfer the funds.*"

"This is fucking extortion," he says with an exaggerated sigh as he steps away from me, and I feel like I can breathe for the first time since I entered the room.

"Nah. It's called protecting my investment." I chuckle. "And preserving your candidacy hopes."

There's a split second where I fear I've pushed one too many buttons. It's in the stiffening of his body. The clench of his fists. The glare in his eye when he turns around and meets my stare.

"All it takes is a push of a button to transfer the funds . . . or to send the pictures . . . and that vice president opportunity is down the drain."

"Fucking cunt." He sneers as he stalks full force toward me, anger emanating out of his every pore.

I don't swerve. I don't call chicken. Instead, I stand my ground as he gets within an inch of my face.

"I'll give you what you want this time, Vee. *Only once.* After that, make no mistake that I'll get what I want from you or one of your girls. No one says no to me or threatens me—*no one*—without serious consequences. The customer is always right, after all, and you stepped way over the fucking line."

My throat is dry. My palms are sweaty. My voice hard to find.

But I find it.

"I know where the line is. It's protecting my girls." *And myself.*

Leave it to a man to make sex messy.

CHAPTER TWO

Vaughn

I push through the door to the adjoining hotel room, click the lock when I shut it, and head straight for the bathroom, slamming the door behind me.

It's only then that my every nerve is overcome with the fear that owned my body over the past fifteen minutes.

My legs feel like rubber, and my hands tremble so harshly that I fumble to pull a Kleenex from the box by the sink. Bracing my hands on the counter, I hang my head to catch my breath, which sounds just as shaky as I feel.

Thank God I was close by. Luckily I was in the city meeting with a new potential hire and was able to get here quickly.

I allow myself a moment. One to be scared shitless that I just faced down a very powerful senator of the United States and held my ground when I didn't have a leg to stand on. And another to allow the tremors and the doubt and the fear and the *holy shit* to own every part of my body and mind so that I'm the real me—the woman terrified this will all fall to shit—instead of the ball-busting bitch I just pretended to be.

But it's when I look up and meet my eyes in the mirror—light aqua framed by a black wig—with impeccable makeup and clothes expensive looking enough to rival Carter's that I see both. The normal woman living behind this ruse I've been portraying.

I have a clean record thus far. No assholes roughing up my girls. No jerks thinking they get more than what they've paid for. No texts from my girls saying Mayday because they need help.

But you did get one tonight, I tell myself as I recall the panic I felt when I received the text earlier. *And you challenged him and stood your ground, and hell if it didn't feel good to wipe that arrogant smirk from his face.*

Because money may grant you many things in life—privilege, material items, reputation, power—but it never gives you the right to harm another person.

With a deep breath and a quick once-over of my appearance, I prepare myself to be the woman I'm not and open the door.

Lola is across the room. She's sitting in her Agent Provocateur lingerie set, her mile-long legs are crossed at the knee, and a highball glass filled with vodka is in her hands. Even with the tearstained cheeks and bruises blossoming on her biceps, she's stunningly gorgeous.

"That was bullshit, Vee," she says before I can speak.

"You okay?" I ask.

She nods emphatically, a sure sign that she's shaken. "Nothing I can't handle." Her foot bobs up and down as she brings the drink to her lips with an unsteady hand. I fight the urge to comfort her further, the natural instinct to make sure she truly is okay.

Because I can't.

The touchy-feely territory is a no-go between me and my girls. I am their boss. That's it. If I look to them for friendship or approval, I'm only setting myself up for trouble. Emotions are the downfall of anyone in my position.

Always.

They make you drop your guard, and when your guard is down, anything can happen.

"I'm pissed. Angry."

"As you should be."

She pushes up from her chair and stalks from one end of the room to the other, her heels thumping on the thick carpet, the champagne color of the decor a soft hue against the dark lace of her outfit and her hair. "But he paid *a lot* of money."

I cringe at her words. "And? That doesn't give him the right to lay a hand on you. He paid for companionship, Lo. A date to be at his side through his dinner function. That's it. Whatever—"

"Whatever happens after the exchange of money is up to me." She mimics the one line I repeatedly drill into my girls' heads. The one caveat that might save my ass jail time if anything with Wicked Ways goes sideways.

"He still in there?"

"Probably."

Her back is to me, her silhouette against the darkened sky beyond the window, and I thank God that if this were to happen to any of my girls, it happened to Lola. Feisty, defiant Lola.

"You know I used to think you were ridiculous for making us book two rooms per gig. I used to be pissed at how much of my cut was being spent on a room I'd never set foot in . . ."

"The client more than covers the cost. That's why it's in the contract."

"True, but I'd gladly take that wasted money to pad my own pockets instead. At least that's how I used to look at it: cash I was leaving on the table." She blows out a breath. "But now I get it. Now I understand. Getting through that door to a safe space was all I could think about. Telling him I had blindfolds and bindings in here that he could use on me was the only way I was able to get him to give me a moment." She falls silent as she relives it, and I can only imagine what she's remembering. "I apologize for fighting you so harshly on it in the past."

A rare contrition from my most sought-after girl . . . and the one who I butt heads with. I nod, even though she can't see it. "Your safety is my number one concern."

She laughs softly. "Well, that and money. Let's be real here, Vee—we're not doing this for our health now, are we?" She turns to look at me, lips turning up into a soft smile to hide the shadows of earlier.

I nod again and then force a smile in return when I still feel like a riot of chaos inside. "Exactly, and that's why the senator has paid me for your time off for the next few days."

Lola's full lips slide into a grin that contrasts with the smudged mascara and her bloodshot eyes. "I knew it was a good choice switching agencies."

"I promised I'd take care of you."

"You just did."

All is now right in her world.

While mine is still on shaky ground.

CHAPTER THREE
Vaughn

S-E-X.

Three letters that spell one very powerful word. And an even more potent act.

Sex. It's something many want. It's something some would risk everything for. It's something men have staked their empires on.

In all reality, it's two people coming together in the most primal of ways. A pleasurable act for some. The way others display their affection.

For me, it's none of that. It's not pleasurable. It's something that gets screwed up when emotion is thrown into the mix. It's definitely not something I think about in the contextual sense.

Sex is about power, just like money is. And when one pays money for sex, it's a transaction. Quite simply, it's a temporary exchange of power.

Sex.

On paper and in public, I sell dates.

In reality, I sell sex.

And I'm damn good at it.

I sigh and walk toward my desk—my itemized lists dotting every surface—and know right now I need to be even better at it.

Ryker Lockhart.

He's the reason why I need to up my game.

He's the man Lola was supposed to meet for the first time tonight, and no thanks to the senator, now she can't.

He's the key to reaching the next level in this business.

And damn it to hell if he isn't gorgeous as well.

Lowering myself into my desk chair, I study the striking image on my computer screen of Ryker Lockhart staring back at me.

Dark hair with salt and pepper at the temples that adds a distinguished air to him. His hair has a wave to it that he's tried to control with product. His eyes are captivating. Intense. Their light-brandy color and the look in them hold my attention much longer than they should.

"Why do you need an escort?" I murmur, curious why a man that handsome has any problem getting a woman.

He must be a jerk.

Or be horrible in bed.

But even jerks and guys who are selfish in the sack get women when they look like him.

With a shake of my head, I turn to his profile and reacquaint myself with it, even though I know every detail by heart, as is my habit. I skim over it. Ryker Lockhart, age thirty-five. One of New York's high-powered divorce attorneys with a net worth astronomical enough to keep him in luxurious penthouses and lavish cars for more than a lifetime.

Too bad all that money and status can't buy the man some favor, because anyone I know who's gotten close enough to even call him an acquaintance says he's so aloof that you can't figure out if he's really an asshole or just playing the part.

I study his image longer than I should.

Definitely a legitimate asshole.

Good thing for me I have enough to keep him in line. Just like all of my clients, Ryker has a skeleton or two in his closet that I'll keep close to my vest for safekeeping should the need to use it arise.

I flip through his completed profile questionnaire. His likes and dislikes in a woman are pretty typical—nothing one of my girls can't provide for him. The only difference from my other clients is his stipulation that, in not so many words, requires his chosen girl to jump when he snaps his fingers.

Most men would like to think that's how women react to them but deep down know otherwise.

Ryker Lockhart actually made me put it in his contract.

One woman. Available to him at all times.

Easy enough in my line of business. Not so easy when his chosen escort is the now-bruised Lola.

But I agreed to the add in the contract because I've learned men are simple creatures. Either they want the same woman time and again so they feel like she adores them and wants them, and it builds their ego, or the man wants multiple women. A new date each time to feed their insatiable sexual appetite, while at the same time wanting anyone who sees them out and about to equate numerous gorgeous women with their status as players.

Both reasons are screwed up.

Both reasons are why men and sex and the interconnection of the two are nothing more than something to manipulate to my benefit.

But now I'm the one who's screwed.

Ryker's a new client. One I've wooed my way after hearing through the grapevine that he was in the market for a service. Funny thing is, I thought he was reaching out to me in the hope of helping his affluent clients. Men who have more money than they know what to do with and are feeling a little reckless now that they've gotten rid of the old ball and chain after so many years with it cinched tight. What better way to celebrate your divorce than with some great, no-strings-no-emotion-in-the-way sex?

So I threw the kitchen sink at Ryker. A few extras, a couple of discounts . . . and a lot of promises. Little did I know that the first client he was going to throw my way was *himself*.

And now I'm backed into a corner. Now I have to make good on all of my promises, and the first one out of the gate—that Lola is going to be his companion for the night—isn't going to happen.

I look down at my phone and fire off a quick, cowardly text to him and prepare to kiss all of his influence and referrals goodbye. Because making Ryker happy would mean getting more clients. More clients would mean more income. And more income would mean I could pay off this looming debt quicker. Then I'd be able to sell my list of contacts to a rival escort service, allowing me to be free and clear of this realm I've unexpectedly found myself immersed in.

Running Wicked Ways was always supposed to be a means to an end. A fast-track means but a means nonetheless. Too much risk can catch up with you, and after everything with the senator last night, it's now more apparent than ever that I'm threading a needle I don't want to sew with.

Please don't screw this up for me. Please be understanding.

I close my eyes for a minute, willing this to be true as the soft New York breeze blows in through my open windows. The kids are out playing their daily game of baseball in the street, their "Hey, batter, batter" hitting my ears every now and again.

When I open my eyes, they find the picture on my desk that takes me back to my own childhood, where we played games on the sidewalks till the streetlights came on. The image is grainy, but I am standing beside my sister, Samantha. Her arm is slung over my shoulder, and our mother is standing behind us, smile wide just above our heads. Happier times. Times when giggles were free, love was constant, and our mom's hugs were given out no matter the problem.

Back before her accident.

The picture makes me long to see Lucy, her smiling face and bobbing pigtails, again. She's the only family I have left, and even though it's only been a few days since I last saw her, I can't wait to wrap my arms around her.

17

My love for that little girl is fierce.

But she's part of my other life. The life I hope to be able to settle into once I put this all behind me.

One day soon . . .

And that's why I need to focus on work—on my newest client, on getting Lola better—so that I can provide for Lucy and prove that she's meant to be with me. That she belongs here.

I startle when my work cell rings. *Speak of the devil.*

"Mr. Lockhart, to what do I owe this pleasure?" I ask in a throaty voice as I slip into the role and act as if the text I sent, telling him to pick another girl to meet his needs tonight, wasn't something out of the ordinary.

"I'm a little confused here, Vee." His voice cuts through the line, its tenor deep and its authority unmistaken.

"Yes?"

"I'm looking at a text from you saying Lola is no longer available for my event tonight."

"Correct. She—"

"These aren't exactly the terms I was promised when I signed on with you."

"Sometimes things happen that are beyond my control," I say placatingly, but his low rumble of a chuckle tells me he's not buying it.

"And you knew my demands." His words settle on the connection as I take a deep breath and try to figure out how to assuage his needs and ego simultaneously. "For the thousands I'm paying per night, I'm sure you can make these issues within your control."

"As you know, sometimes things come up. Lola was injured. That's not exactly something I can control." I lean back in my chair and close my eyes. "Surely you're a reasonable man who can understand that."

That chuckle again. The kind that would perk the ears of most easy women and catch the attention of those who play hard to get. For me, though, it does nothing more than scrape over my nerves. "*Reasonable* isn't exactly a word many would use to describe me."

"I wouldn't know."

"I would think a woman in your position would *make* it your business to vet your clientele," he says, challenging me.

It's my turn to laugh, low and knowingly. "I always know more than people think I do. No worries there, Mr. Lockhart."

"Ryker."

"And your point, Mr. Lockhart?" I reiterate to let him know I don't take direction from him.

"My point is that this could be a very valuable relationship between us. I have a lot of men who want companionship without complications, and you have the means to provide it."

"No one said I needed more clients," I lie, loathing the arrogance in his tone.

"There is no such thing as *too many* clients. Nice try, though. I can see this game you're playing quite clearly, Vee. I tell you to do something. You do the opposite of what I say to assert that you're the one in charge in this situation here. We talk a bit more before the cycle begins again. I think what you're forgetting in our little exchange is that without someone like me, you're nothing. I have the money. I have the contacts. And while selling sex is one of the oldest professions known to man, you're forgetting that it just takes one bad step to ruin that reputation you're crafting . . . so we can keep playing this game your way, or we can just get down to business with a mutual understanding that neither one of us will be abdicating any power to the other."

Silence weighs heavily between us as I straighten my shoulders and fight the urge to hang up the phone. It's the first time since I've started Wicked Ways that I've been made to feel like the girl I once was—powerless and trapped despite being surrounded by riches.

I clear my throat and shake off the sudden inferiority his words brought on.

"I have a catalog of other highly skilled, equally gorgeous women—"

"I've looked through them all already."

"—who would be more than willing to fulfill your needs, Mr. Lockhart."

"I have a lot of needs," he murmurs, and something about the way he says it makes me shift in my seat.

"Yes, the needs were clearly outlined in your dossier. One woman who is yours when you need her to be." The snap-my-fingers-my-ego-is-too-big syndrome.

"Consistency is what I need. She's more than able to make her own money when I don't need her, but when I do, I expect her to be there. No scheduling conflicts. No ifs, ands, or buts. My job, my reputation, is based on many things, and a woman causing trouble for me isn't one of those."

"As you've stated previously. And as I assured you, that shouldn't be a problem."

"Ah, but now it is a problem because the one woman I wanted is the one woman you're telling me I can no longer have."

"I have many others who meet your requirements." I pause and scroll down his profile. "She needs to come off well educated. Classy. Current on politics and world events. Able to play the part." I say the words but know that I don't, in fact, have that. My ladies aren't exactly giving up jobs as doctors and astrophysicists to be escorts.

"Lola was screened for me."

The damn blood tests. God, how he made a fuss about wanting a woman with a clean health check because if he was going to pay $4,000 for a night with a woman, he sure as hell wanted to feel her, skin on skin. Add to that the terms that Lola signed in return stating that she was on birth control, and if she were to have other companions, all sex must be protected or else risk a lawsuit of ridiculous monetary value.

"She was, just as all of my girls are screened."

"But she was by *my* doctor. *For me.*"

I nod my head, even though he can't see it, and roll my shoulders. This was one point he was adamant about, and as much as I wanted to strangle him for the hoops he required me to jump through, I can't blame him for it.

"I'd be more than happy to direct you toward some of my other girls who can meet your needs—and your medical requirements," I say to direct the conversation back to the matter at hand.

"And that means they wouldn't be able to meet *my needs* this evening as I previously scheduled with Lola." I hear what I think are his fingers drumming on his desk. "What exactly do you plan to do to fix that?"

I scan the calendar of my planner and see that every single girl I have who could possibly fit the bill until Lola recovers is otherwise occupied. *Shit.* This is not what I need right now.

"What about you, Vee?"

I almost ask him what he means when those four words break through my thoughts. And then I laugh.

"I'm not for hire."

"Anyone's for hire if offered enough. What exactly would your amount be?"

I'm not sure why the simple question flusters me when I've been asked more obscene things in my life, but it does. My brain's not functioning properly, and rather than just flat out tell him he's crazy, I open the door by giving the lamest of excuses.

"I haven't been medically screened."

His hum slides through the line. "You and I both know that's not true. A woman like you is meticulous in everything she does. Details, semantics . . . everything matters. You wouldn't be able to run your operation if they didn't. So let's cut the crap and not pretend like you don't go and get tested every single month just like you make your girls do because you're a set-the-example type of boss."

"And who said I haven't had unprotected sex since then?" I ask to throw him off like his accurate assessment has done of me.

It's that murmur of his—the one that's laced with just the right amount of amusement—that tells me he likes this challenge. "Because you haven't. You can pretend that you have, but we both know you haven't. A woman like you is too busy running her empire and too disconnected from what sex actually involves to ever care to have it."

I stare at his picture on the computer screen in front of me and curse him.

He's wrong.

Dead wrong.

Jesus Christ, he's right.

"And the silence says it all," he says, making me grit my teeth.

"You're wrong."

"Let me guess. You're one of those self-proclaimed feminazis who can go on and on about equal pay for equal work, and yet when it comes down to it, you exploit women for a living."

Screw you. Irritation has me biting back my temper out of professionalism only. "I do no such thing."

"Then why don't you put your money where your mouth—or other areas of your body—is and step in for Lola tonight."

There's something about the directness of his tone that makes me feel vulnerable—like he's watching me through my windows somehow—either that or he has me on the stand during cross-examination, and despite every part of me wanting to hang up the phone and return the money he's already transferred to my account, I don't.

Because $4,000 a night for a girl is a lot more than I can take in normally.

"Not going to happen."

"Why not?"

"I could be hideously unattractive."

"I doubt it."

"You said you wanted one woman only. Lola will be better in a few days. You could wait—"

"I don't like to wait."

"Mr. Lockhart—"

"What's the problem, Vee? You afraid a man like me might ruin you for other men? I assure you I'm more than capable of making you forget your own name."

Arrogant asshole. And men wonder why some women think they're better off with battery-operated toys and their own fingers?

"Charming." No wonder he needs Wicked Ways. With lines like that, the prick wouldn't even be able to catch a cold if he tried.

"Isn't that the bonus of hiring an escort service? I don't have to be charming or put on an act. There is no need for niceties. Getting laid is a foregone conclusion."

"You're paying for her companionship . . . anything after that is between you and your date. Getting laid is never a foregone conclusion."

"So says the woman who sells it." This time when he laughs, it makes my hands clench into fists. It angers me that his words have somewhat gotten to me when I am rarely fazed by anyone other than Lucy. "A real boss knows she has to get her hands dirty when need be . . . and *I'm all for dirty*, Vee."

"Peer pressure won't work with me," I say, hating that my mind goes there and wonders what exactly his definition of *dirty* is. "You might be able to coerce others—women who'd die for the chance to be on your arm—but not me. I'm not interested."

"Mmm." That sound irritates and provokes all at the same time. "You say that, but right now you're shifting in your chair, wondering what those women know about me and how far they'd actually go to be on my arm . . . or other places on me."

I start to shift in my chair and then stop myself when I realize he's right, and I hate him for it. "Mr. Lockhart . . . I appreciate the hard sell here, but I assure you it's not going to work. *A*, I'm not your client.

B, I'm behind the scenes. *C*, I rarely meet clients. *D*, I don't sleep with clients."

"I'd love to know what *F* is," he says putting emphasis on the letter *F*.

"A repeat of *D*—I don't sleep with clients."

"Ever?"

"Ever." I grit my teeth.

"What if I were to pay you double? Could I have you?"

"This is not a negotiation, Mr. Lockhart."

Did he really just offer eight thousand dollars for a night with me?

"Everything in life is a negotiation, Vee." There's that chuckle again, but this time the suggestion in it causes chills to chase over my skin.

"Not for me." I clear my throat, needing to get on with this conversation before my mind agrees to do things it shouldn't even consider. "I have someone for you," I lie, just to stop him from relishing a fantasy that isn't going to happen.

"But what if I want you? With a voice like yours, I'm certain—"

"I have a girl for you. Her name is . . ." I struggle to think up a name for whoever I'll find in the next few hours to take care of him. "Saxony."

"Saxony?"

"Mm-hmm. She's college educated. Drop-dead gorgeous. Is familiar with the power players in New York."

"And has many other skills?" Suggestion laces his tone.

"Of course."

"Why haven't you mentioned her before?" he asks.

"Because she's new to the agency, and I didn't want to give you a new girl without vetting her . . . but her previous agency has a list of reviews on her—many men of your stature—who all have decided to follow her over to Wicked Ways." The lies continue to roll off my tongue, and of course I have no idea where in the hell I'm going to come up with a Saxony to fill this bill. "While I can't get her health screen in time, I'm sure you can wear a condom just this one time since she meets all of your requirements and—"

"And she's not you."

"Correct. While I appreciate your more-than-aggressive debating skills, save it for the courtroom—you have zero jurisdiction over me."

"Can't blame a man for trying."

"Can't fault a woman for saying no," I counter.

Silence falls on the line, and his resignation is in his sigh. "She's not going to let me down and in turn let you down, is she?" he asks.

"I told you, Wicked Ways is a professional organization. You've seen the referrals. You've read the reviews in the confidential company profile I sent you. I don't think you have to worry about being let down, Mr. Lockhart."

"You don't let up, do you?" His question throws me momentarily. The admiration in his voice even more so.

"I'm not like most women, Mr. Lockhart. I'm not one to be impressed by a smooth-talking man or a large bank account."

"Then what is it that would impress you?"

The unexpected.

The thought flickers and fades through my mind, and I hate that it does, because it's true. Men are predicable, they are creatures of habit, and I've yet to meet one who does anything more to me than make me wonder how much he'd be willing to pay.

But he's talking to Vee. A madam. A woman who is strong, experienced, and a ballbuster.

"What would impress me? *Nothing.*" My voice is even when I speak. "Is that so?"

There is an edged silence as we feel the other one out. Men like to play with power. Who has it. Who's willing to cede it. Who's willing to fight for it.

I'll give him none of that.

I'm in control.

That's how this relationship works.

"I'll have Saxony at the agreed-upon place and time. Good day, Mr. Lockhart."

And before he can argue or question me, I end the call, lean back in my chair, and blow out a sigh.

Yet when I give myself a small moment to breathe before the panic sets in because Saxony doesn't exist, all I can think about are the words he said. How well he has me pegged.

And how every part of me would love to prove him wrong.

CHAPTER FOUR
Vaughn

"This is the stupidest thing you've ever done," I mutter to myself as I put one last finishing touch to my lipstick.

Exploit my girls, my ass.

Who did he think he was talking to? I don't exploit them, and I damn well could step into their shoes if need be, although it is breaking my cardinal rule number one when it comes to running an escort business: never—ever—sleep with a client.

I stare at myself in the mirror. I look like me.

But not like me.

And that's a good thing because what I'm about to do crosses every boundary I've ever made for myself when it comes to Wicked Ways.

Every single one.

I close my eyes and shake off the frustration of the day. The mad dash to find a new girl who was available and who fit Ryker's criteria. The phone calls to a few of my current girls asking them if they could cancel their plans with regulars and take up a new client in their place. Their refusals because existing customers mean steady income while a new one could mean a one-time-and-done situation . . . even though I explained to them that the unnamed client might be lucrative in the long run.

Then the resignation that I was going to let Ryker down and all of the connections that come with him. I shouldn't have offered him Saxony. I should have just said no.

And losing his connections is not something I can afford right now as I try to grow my clientele. A larger clientele means I can make money faster so I can pay down my debt and get out of this business as soon as possible.

Add to that Ryker's words ghosting through my mind every chance they had, sowing doubt about my abilities as a boss and making me wonder why I couldn't step in for Lola and save my own ass instead of relying on someone else to.

His challenge settled in my craw and baited me to go against my hard-and-fast rule.

"It's just sex," I murmur as I sweep the wand of mascara over my eyelashes. "In. Out. Done."

An act.

It's not like it's ever done anything for me before. Maybe my cold heart and ability to remain impassive will serve me well in this endeavor.

Because screw Ryker Lockhart. *Literally.* I'm a good boss. I can do what my girls do and do it damn well if need be.

And I can do it without forgetting my name, as he so claimed.

Screw the rule . . . just this once.

Your stubborn streak always did get you into trouble. I can hear my sister's voice clear as day in my head, and I close my eyes and smile bittersweetly, thinking about what she would say to me right now if she knew what I was about to do.

When I open them back up, I force myself to look in the mirror. Wash away the guilt. The doubt. The *holy shit, this is stupid.* And then get prepared.

Gone is the jet-black wig my girls know me in. Gone is the all-black ensemble I typically dress in when they have met me: black pencil skirt, black jacket with lace camisole underneath. No black Jimmy Choos.

No lace stockings with the seam running down the back of my legs. No dark and sophisticated red lipstick.

Instead, I'm me.

Soft blonde hair set in curls falling a bit below my shoulder blades. Natural makeup—nude lips, light blush—with a smoky eye.

I look like me. And that almost makes this even harder to do—to face—because I don't have my facade, any armor, in place to hide behind.

Tonight there will be no hiding.

I'm meeting Ryker as myself, not Madam Vee, because I can't take the chance that one of the few people in my very small "escort" world would see Vee with him tonight and approach us.

I'm meeting Ryker as myself because the obstinance in me stupidly wants to prove him wrong and in turn break every parameter I set for myself when creating this business.

But a boss has to do what a boss has to do.

"Deep breath, Vaughn," I mutter to myself as I smooth down the burgundy dress I have on. "Here goes nothing."

The lobby is elegant, with its large chandeliers, but they're kept dim so as to allow each of its patrons some privacy. Almost as if they know I'm trying to hide some from the rest of the room for a bit. Soft classical music flows from the overhead speakers as people mill about in evening wear. There are hugs given among people, and laughs echo off the walls and marble floors.

I stand in the corner, surveying the crowd as nerves I don't want to admit to run a riotous act within, and my mind tries to grapple for the nth time with what I'm about to do.

You're keeping your reputation intact.

That's how I have to look at this. That's how I have to justify this.

Just like that, my breath catches when Ryker Lockhart waltzes into the lobby. I'm rarely affected by a man—sure, I can say one is handsome or sexy or gorgeous, but rarely does a man really catch my eye. Seldom does one make me wonder if there's something wrong with me since sex isn't the be-all and end-all *for me*.

But there he is . . . standing in the middle of the lobby, surveying everyone around him, making my pulse race.

This is a bad idea.

He's tall, his shoulders are broad, and there's an air about him that screams *authority* while a magnetism about him makes people look his way.

And he hasn't even spoken a word to anyone yet.

Such a bad idea.

He's in a well-tailored tuxedo, everything black save for the crisp white dress shirt beneath it. His hair is styled, and an expensive watch glints at his wrist when he holds it up to look at the time.

Of course, that's my cue that I'm not there exactly on time, but I give him a few more seconds to make him wait.

It's all about power, even when I'm in a different pair of shoes.

With a deep breath, I walk toward him, shoulders square, head high, and remind myself that I'm not Vee right now. I can't act like we're on an equal playing field.

He has hired me.

I am his.

CHAPTER FIVE
Ryker

Of course, she's late.

I shouldn't expect anything less from a woman . . . but this is a woman I paid for. The least she could do is be prompt.

Time is fucking money.

Impatient and already irritated, I glance at my Rolex. *Ticktock, sweetheart. You're supposed to already be on my clock, and if there's one thing I hate, it's having billable hours wasted.*

She gets two more minutes before I pick up the phone and let Vee know she just seriously fucked up by not keeping me happy.

If old man Kavinsky hadn't already put me in a shitty mood when he canceled our dinner meeting tonight, then I'd have more patience.

That's a lie. I never have patience. Life's too short to have an iota of it.

"Ryker?"

The voice—sultry and throaty—catches my attention immediately, but when I turn toward the woman standing before me, a whole lot more than my ears stands at attention. Her dress is a deep burgundy and perfect for the dinner meeting that just was canceled: elegantly sexy with a hint of cleavage and a road map of curves. Completely not what I expected and everything I wanted.

"Saxony?"

Her smile is wide, her body language tentative, her eyes incredible. She nods, and I narrow my gaze to study her.

"You're late."

She chuckles, and Jesus Christ, my balls draw up at the sound. "In many parts of the world, it's acceptable for a man to wait for a few minutes for a woman."

"In my part of the world, 'if you're five minutes early, you're already ten minutes late.'"

"Last I checked, you weren't Vince Lombardi," she says, shocking the shit out of me and earning her major points for knowing who said the mantra I live by.

"A football fan?" I ask.

"No. Just a woman who knows a lot of things about a lot of topics." She lifts a perfectly shaped eyebrow and purses her lips as if to challenge me and see if I'm going to question her further.

Maybe I will. Maybe I won't.

I take a moment to try to place why I feel like we've met before and draw my gaze over the total package. Blonde hair styled flawlessly. Makeup that says she's not trying too hard. A trim physique with defined arms that says she works out but doesn't go overboard.

"You'll do," I murmur nonchalantly when I damn well know she'll more than do.

"Excuse me?" She stutters the question.

"Vee was right. You'll do fine. Ryker Lockhart." I extend my hand. "Nice to meet you."

She stares at my hand and then with a slight lift to her chin gives me the same languorous appraisal I gave her before meeting my eyes. "Saxony . . . and I guess you'll have to do too."

I chuckle. I do love my women feisty. Vee definitely nailed that aspect.

"Good to know you approve," I murmur and wonder what in hell I've gotten myself into with that blatant defiance warring in her aqua-colored eyes. "Shall we get a drink?"

Her eyes flit around the space. She's either nervous or making sure she doesn't know anyone else here.

Gentlemanly protocol says if you see your escort out with another man, you don't approach them. So that means she's afraid of seeing someone who knows her outside the business.

Interesting. She frequents these places often, then.

"Saxony?" I ask.

"Huh?" She gives a little shake of her head and then a quick smile that clears the caution from her eyes. "Yes. Of course."

When I place my hand on the small of her back to guide her through the lobby, she startles ever so slightly at the touch, and a part of me wonders if I'm being played.

I used Wicked Ways so I wouldn't have to teach someone the ropes of how this all works. If Saxony is in fact a newbie, that negates the point, and I was way overcharged. I could snap my fingers and have a date, but I'd have to worry all night whether the right words were going to come out of her mouth in front of clients or whether she's going to have proper manners.

That among a long fucking list of other things I'd rather not think about.

But she flinched.

And now my mind is stuck on that.

I shove the thoughts away as we walk across the lobby toward the bar. A few men are less than subtle when they look at her, and I give them a tight smile to let them know that yes, she is in fact with me.

The question is . . . what am I planning on doing with her?

We find a seat at a table in the back, and once we have our drinks in hand, I lean back and study her again, her own gaze waiting for mine when it looks up to her eyes.

"What is it you do for a living, Mr. Lockhart?" she asks, when I know she's read my profile already and is just doing this to let me pound my chest and throw my testosterone around.

I'm not a man who has to boast to feel good about myself.

"It's Ryker," I murmur as I lean forward and place my hand on her knee. Skin and silk and a perfume that's subtle but sexy. "And we both know what I do, but thanks for asking."

"Let me guess—you're not one for small talk." She takes a sip of her wine and meets my eyes above the rim.

"Depends on what the topic is."

Her eyes question me, but her lips don't utter the one she wants to know the most: Why did I hire an escort?

"What is your meeting about?"

"It's been canceled," I say, her eyes flashing up to meet mine at the unexpected change of plans.

"Then shall we head upstairs?" She starts to stand, and my hand reaches out to stop her.

"What's the rush? It's not like we don't have all night."

CHAPTER SIX
Vaughn

Down-payment sex.

That was the first thought I had when Ryker informed me his meeting was canceled. Lola's crass terminology flitted through my head, and all I could think about was how I was going to escape this evening unscathed—except for a quick bout of meaningless sex.

The sex no doubt would consist of me lavishing undeserved praise on Ryker—*oh my God, it's so huge, you're so amazing, you're the best I've ever had*—all the while wondering myself, *"Is it in yet?"* This would be followed by a few grunts and groans on his part as I would lie there like a human pincushion before he would roll on his back and fall asleep, with me no worse for the wear except for needing a shower to wash his scent off me.

Definitely down-payment sex—a quick lay that would net me enough for a down payment on a car.

Yes. I could do this.

Those were my defining thoughts in that split second before standing and before Ryker grabbed my hand to stop me.

You know what they say about best-laid plans.

Because now brandy-colored eyes stare at me from across the dimly lit dining room where we sit in a back-corner booth. They judge and question, but no words fall from his lips, where his fingers are running back and forth absently over the rough cut of his jaw.

Sex I'll be able to handle, no problem.

Small talk is a torture all in itself, unbeknownst to me.

Unnerved by his sudden attention when I shouldn't be—because isn't that how a normal date works?—I glance around the restaurant. It's high-class swank like I've never seen before . . . and it's definitely more of an old boys' club. Dark-red booths with high-backed seats to secure privacy for the customers.

"Do you come here often?" I ask, more than grateful for the other patrons who have stopped by to say hi to him, saving me from having to maintain any real flow of conversation between us.

"When it suits me." He goes back to eating his filet while I move my vegetables around on my plate and think about the room upstairs we'll head to next. The senator and last night flash through my mind. The image of Lola, battered and bruised, standing at the window, not far behind it. The notion that if something goes wrong with Ryker like it did for Lola, I don't have anyone to call to come and save me. I have no one I can text Mayday to.

Just breathe, Vaughn. You can do this.

It's only once. Nothing is going to happen to you. Ryker is a well-respected, sought-after, high-powered divorce attorney. Not like that matters, though. My only saving grace is my rock-solid research. If he had any dirty secrets—any hidden fetishes—beyond the ones I already know, they'd already be out in the air somehow.

It's just sex.

I study him as he cuts his meat. Refined yet rugged. Polite but with an edge. Handsome but not pretty.

And private.

Talking to him is like pulling teeth. Or maybe it's just me. Maybe I'm not doing the slithering up to a man properly. Maybe I'm not stroking him enough verbally and making him feel manly enough. Hell, maybe I'm going to lose him as a client regardless, and so this whole charade I'm putting on is fruitless on all fronts.

Including my own damn ego.

His hands still, and when I look up to see why, his gaze is on me. "Yes?" he asks with a look that tells me my scrutiny is unwelcome.

"Why are we here if you're not going to talk at all?" I ask the obvious.

"Because it's been a long damn week, and last I checked, it's not a crime to enjoy a nice meal with a beautiful woman."

I nod my head slowly, his words surprising me.

"Ryker Lockhart? No fucking way," a voice booms to our left, and we both turn our heads toward its owner. *Wow*. It's my first and only thought when I take in the man striding our way. He's tall with dark hair and green eyes. There's light stubble on his jaw and a swagger that the expensive suit he has on can't hide. "I thought that was you!"

"Colton Donavan?" Ryker stands automatically and is shaking the man's hand instantly. The name rings a bell, but I can't place it. "No shit."

"You don't call. You don't write," Colton says with his hands out and a killer smile on his face that has a lone dimple winking on one side. Boyish charm exudes from an absolute grown-man's body.

"Like you're one to talk," Ryker says through a laugh.

"What's it been? Five years?"

"At least." They man-pat each other's shoulders. "What are you doing in town?"

"Sponsorship stuff for the team and a little side trip with my wife."

"Wife?" Ryker sputters with eyes wide and a hand coming up to cover the cough he gives in disbelief.

"Wife," Colton says with an unabashed shrug and no-holds-barred grin, and the way that Ryker just stares at him tells me this news is definitely a shock.

"You're giving me a heart attack here," Ryker says through a laugh and pats his chest.

"Even the most stubborn of us fuckers fall one day. Just you wait."

"Nah. Not me. You know me better than that."

"And you sound just like I used to."

Ryker stares at him for a beat, grin widening and head shaking as if he can't believe it. "How? When? Never mind—I'm happy for you if you're happy."

"It's almost been five years, and it was close family at the ceremony. Sorry there was no invite. You know how it goes."

"The goddamn paparazzi."

"Exactly. But yes, very happy."

"Is she here? When do I get to meet the woman who tamed Colton fucking Donavan?"

"You actually think I'd let her near you?" he jokes and then blanches when Ryker shifts some and he notices me. I can see the word *fuck* glance through his eyes when he sees me there and realizes what he just said. "I'm sorry." He takes a step toward me and extends his hand. "Colton, nice to meet you."

I fumble over the right name. The *V* is on my lips, but I catch myself before *Vaughn* falls out. "Saxony. Nice to meet you."

We shake hands, his smile genuine if not a little bit embarrassed for insinuating that Ryker is a player when he's unaware of the state of our relationship.

"First date," Ryker says as Colton winces with the knowledge that he might just have fucked things up for his buddy.

At least the man has manners.

"What's she doing with you?" Colton laughs. "This guy's a pain in the ass."

"I'm learning," I murmur as I bring the glass of wine to my lips and watch them above the rim.

"I'll leave you two, but it was great meeting you," Colton says with a nod.

"Likewise."

"So, wife? Do I get to meet her?" Ryker asks as they step a few feet away toward Colton's table.

"She's not here," Colton says, but then I can't hear the rest as they finish their conversation.

But I watch them. Where Ryker is refined yet rugged, Colton Donavan is refined but edgy. It's like a battle of sexiness with the two of them standing there, and hell if any woman would complain about which man won the fight.

"Next time you're in town . . . ," Ryker says.

"Yeah, yeah." Colton flashes a grin and shakes his head before turning and walking away.

Ryker heads back to our table and sits down. "Sorry about that. Just an old friend."

"No worries," I say. "Good friend?"

"Something like that." Ryker picks up his glass and takes a sip. "See? I am talking."

I snort and roll my eyes. "To everyone else, yes."

But when he just eyes me and then begins to eat without furthering the conversation, my frustration gets the better of me. Wasting my time annoys me.

I lean forward and lower my voice. "If I'm only here for one thing, then why don't we do that one thing, and you can then come back down here and chat up your friends."

"Chat up my friends?"

"Yes. Your friends. Acquaintances. Whatever they are . . . because it's not like you're including me in any of your conversations with them, so it seems I'm not needed here."

He sets his fork and knife down and leans back in his seat, those eyes of his back on mine again as he weighs whatever it is that he wants to say. "Friends? Acquaintances? I wasn't aware that our date meant I had to fill you in on every person who stops by. That was an old friend of mine," he says with a nod to where Colton walked off to. "Colton's a race-car driver. You might have heard of him before. But it doesn't matter if you have or you haven't because he's my friend, in town for a few nights, and it wasn't like I was inviting him to join us."

"That's not what I was implying," I say, frustrated with him for not understanding what I mean and wanting to do a double take in the direction of Colton now that I know who he is. "I meant—"

"You're pretty forward for a woman in your position." There's a bite to his voice, annoyance lacing its edges and matching how I feel.

"My position?"

"Am I boring you, Saxony?"

"No, but let's just say the fact that you're not paying me for conversation is overly apparent . . . as is what you think of me, and so I was just thinking we could cut the pretenses and awkwardness."

Careful. You're sounding way too much like Vee. A madam and not an escort.

"And what is it that you think I think of you?" he asks.

"You tell me."

He laughs. It's a low rumble that vibrates in the tense air between us. "That's not how this game works, Saxony."

"I wasn't aware we were playing a game."

"Isn't everything a game, though?"

It's my turn to hesitate in response, and then I decide to be honest. "I think you see a woman who you can't figure out. You assume she's uneducated, uncensored . . . and unrefined. She has no self-worth and therefore turned to this profession to make a quick buck doing the only thing she's good at until she can wrap her tiny brain around what else she can do better."

With our eyes still locked on one another's, he picks up his tumbler of whiskey and takes a sip of it. There's something about the intensity in his eyes. They make me feel like they can see right through this lie when I know there's no possible way he could know.

None.

His nod is even and measured. "And I think you're wrong. We all choose our careers for certain reasons. I spend hours trying to make men happy. I pore over their history, their assets, their everything and try to find a way to extricate them from their marriage with the least amount of collateral damage to themselves and their financial well-being. You spend hours trying to make men happy too. The way I look at it, we're no different. We're both getting paid very well to screw one person to satisfy another."

"That's an interesting way of putting it."

"Would you rather I sugarcoat it?"

"No." I look down to my steak, barely touched, because while I may be fine with having sex with him later, it doesn't mean I'm not nervous about it.

"Both are business transactions with our endgames in mind."

"And what's your ultimate endgame?" I ask, curious if it's to win the case. Make millions. Or I don't know, gain satisfaction knowing he's screwing over women.

"I could ask you the same question."

Our eyes meet—hold—until we both realize that neither of us is comfortable answering that question just yet. I glance down to where my fingers are running up and down the stem of my wineglass before looking back at him.

"You said *men*. Do you always represent the men in your cases?"

"Yes."

"Even if the divorce is their fault?"

"How would it be their fault?" he asks and angles his head to the side.

"Like if they cheat."

"No matter how you look at it, a spouse doesn't cheat if the marriage is a good one."

"And you're wrong."

His laugh is loud and boisterous, and I can't tell if it's because he's not used to being told he's wrong or if it's because he flat out disagrees with me. "How so?"

"Because some men are just bastards. Just like some women are assholes. Not everyone is good in this world."

He stares at me longer than normal and nods slowly, conceding without admitting it verbally. "Yes, I always represent the husbands . . . bastards or not."

"Why?" I'm fascinated.

"Because I understand men. Their motivation. Their positioning in social circles. The appearances they need to uphold. I also understand women too. More than I'm ever given credit for . . . and it comes in handy during negotiations."

"Do you use a private investigator?"

I can see the sudden jolt of surprise at my question and the ghost of a smile. It's conniving . . . a bit dangerous, and tells me everything I need to know—yes, he'll have no hesitation trying to look into me, *Vee*. Or maybe he already has. "Of course I do."

"Have you ever lied in court to get the judgment you want?"

His eyes darken for the briefest of moments as he purses his lips. "Why the twenty questions?"

"I like to know what I'm working with."

"What you're working with?"

"Character matters," I state.

"Everyone lies in some form or another. Some people drive a car more expensive than they can afford to look the part. Others tell their spouse they satisfy them and then hire an escort to take care of their darker needs on the side. Some lie to get ahead at work. Everybody lies,

Saxony . . . the question you need to ask is why the person is lying. That will tell you about their true character."

I hate that every point he makes feels like it has a double meaning, like I'm the one sitting in the jury box during his closing arguments as he drives home a conclusion he wants me to figure out on my own.

"Is this your full-time job?" he asks, the sudden change of topic unexpected, seeing as we were just speaking about lying.

I proceed with caution, wary that I'm falling into a trap he's set.

"No."

"Do you mind me asking what else it is that you do?"

"Only if you mind me asking why you're using a service when I've clearly seen every woman in this restaurant glance your way more than once." I offer a tight smile as he chuckles, evidently not surprised by my forwardness.

He leans closer, his voice low. "Some things are better left unexplained."

I'm uncertain what he means, and we both stare at each other for a few moments in a break from our combative conversation. He leans back, elbow on the arm of his chair and thumb and forefinger running back and forth over his jaw.

"Is there something you want to ask?" I finally voice when our plates have been cleared but his eyes haven't left mine.

He purses his lips and angles his head to the side. "Just trying to figure you out is all."

"I wasn't aware I need to be figured."

"That's what I do for a living."

"And what is it that you've figured out?"

"I'm not quite sure. You're smart, obviously educated, well mannered . . . and arguably stunning . . . but there's something I can't quite put my finger on that tells me this"—he flicks his hand in between us—"isn't you."

Making sure my breath remains steady, I try to move this evening to where it needs to go. Onto him and off me. "I think it's time we move on to dessert."

And without saying another word, I slowly slide out of the booth with our eyes locked and make my way toward the front of the restaurant, curious how long it will take for him to follow suit.

The sooner this is over, the better for me.

CHAPTER SEVEN
Vaughn

When we were having dinner, a small part of me forgot what was supposed to happen next. Surprisingly, I was enjoying his company, our banter, the conversation with an intelligent adult, and so for that brief moment, I lost track of what this was.

That I was playing a role and he was paying for my time.

He charmed me when I'm rarely charmed.

He wined and dined and enchanted me, and now I have to take my clothes off and give him my body.

And now the one part of the evening I was more than certain I could handle feels off.

The sound of him moving around the suite at my back makes this more real than I expected—the clink of the decanter lid hitting the edge of the glass is like a reminder that I have a job to do.

Disconnect. Close your mind. Shut everything down.

It's just sex. Just an exchange of power. It's just an act like it's always been before.

When I turn to face him, I don't expect him to be standing there in the dim light of the room with his shirt unbuttoned and his tie resting loosely around his neck. I don't expect to see that look in his eye and to suddenly realize how damn attractive he is.

Unsure what to do only because I've never been in this situation before and nerves have taken hold, I begin to shrug out of the arms of my dress and let that part pool around my hips. No fuss. No frills. Just get to the endgame.

"Mmm. Not so fast," Ryker murmurs. His eyes darken as he sets his glass down on the console beside him before taking a step into me. "I'm a man who likes to take his time."

I almost laugh. Those words coming from a man are like an oxymoron and just the words I need to hear to calm me down and remind me what this is. Who this is.

So when he stands inches before me, his eyes on mine and our lungs breathing the same sexually charged air, I'm far from prepared for what I feel.

I expected indifference.

What I got was anticipation.

It's something I've never felt in the moments before a kiss. It's something I never wanted in the brief meeting of lips. But in those few seconds between him stepping forward, his hands touching my bare arms, and him leaning into me so his chest brushes ever so slightly against mine, I feel it.

It's foreign to me. And for the briefest of moments I attempt to fight it, but the thought is erased the moment his mouth meets mine.

Gone is the awkwardness I expected there to be. The sex will be casual, yes, but the attraction is mutual, and that's something you can't fake. That's something hurried words or soft caresses can't make up for.

Our lips move.

It's a soft sigh of a kiss. A tender brush of lips on lips as the heat of his body begins to warm mine up against the chill of the air-conditioned room.

I taste the whiskey on his tongue. Feel the softness yet adeptness of his lips as they move against mine. Feel the scrape of his evening stubble against my chin.

Our hands move.

Cool palms and anxious fingers slide around my waist and rest on my bare skin. They then move up the plane of my back to frame the sides of my face as his tongue coaxes mine. Chills chase over my body as the slow ascent of arousal begins to burn into desire.

I want him when I typically don't want.

The single thought staggers me in a way I never expected it to.

And then it's swept away when Ryker's mouth slides down the line of my neck, placing open-mouthed kisses there while my hand reaches out to cup the cock that's all but bursting from his pants.

He moans, his teeth nipping my collarbone when I do.

There's a greed on his part after that. It's tangible. In the way he unzips the rest of my dress so it falls to the floor. In the way he pushes me against the wall behind us. In the antagonistic groans in the back of his throat as he palms my breast through the lace of my bra.

My eyes flutter shut as my head falls back against the wall behind me when his fingers slide down my torso and find their way beneath the small fabric swatch of my panties.

His cock, now free of his slacks, is thick and hard against my hip. His mouth—wet and warm—closes over the peak of my breast. His fingers, adept and resolute, part me and slide through the wetness to find me aroused.

And just as his fingers push their way into me and his lips close over mine, his tongue darting to meet mine with a touch more urgency this time, my world spins, tilts off its axis, and comes crashing down around me.

Memories I don't recall. Sensations I don't remember. They slam into me unexpectedly. *Him* being on top of me the most prevalent of all of them.

The shock hits me and knocks the breath out of me.

I must freeze . . . or shout or push Ryker away or . . . I don't know, because he steps back with a strange look on his face—confusion mixed with a healthy dose of arousal, disbelief, and anger.

His hair is mussed from my fingers in it; his eyes are dark with desire, his body taut with need.

I violently try to shake the vile memory from my thoughts. Try to tell myself that going through my sister's journals has messed with my mind. From the shock of falling into Ryker's unexpected kiss to the sudden flashlight of my childhood recollections shining right into my eyes and melding the past and present together as one when they clearly are not.

Confused and lost in a memory that only presents as a stomach-churning sensation I can't solidify, I know the best way to forget about it is to lose myself with the man in front of me.

To use him just as he is using me.

I step back into Ryker, fight the sudden revulsion roiling inside me, and try to use his lips and his body to stanch it.

"Saxony?"

Ryker looks at me with concern in his eyes, and it takes me a second to realize he's saying what he thinks is my name. "What?"

He reaches out and cups the side of my face, thumb brushing over my jawline. I tell myself to shake his hand off—that the touch is too intimate for a woman like me—but I'm paralyzed by the look in his eyes.

"You look like you just saw a ghost," he says.

"I'm fine," I assert as my stomach pitches, only serving to encourage me further. I step into him again, but this time he bats my hands off his chest.

"Terrified sex isn't my thing," he says as I stare at him.

Lips lax, heart pounding, embarrassment swelling. *What is wrong with me?*

"Sorry, but I'm not into the rape-fantasy thing." He takes a step back, hands held up in surrender.

My pride wars against shame as desperation edges the vulnerability I feel standing here before him, prompting me to lash out.

"Well, fumbling egomaniacs who want to be stroked and praised for their shitty kissing aren't my thing either." I shout the baseless lie at him. Those words stop him in his tracks as tears I don't want to shed well in my eyes. My heart pounds like a freight train in my ears as adrenaline just adds a kick to it.

And then I see it. The transformation of his expression from annoyance to shock to fury. "You're a fucking *virgin*, aren't you?" He takes another step back, with his hands running through his hair and his exasperation so tangible it's rolling off him in waves and slamming into me. "Jesus Christ. What the fuck?"

"I'm not," I tell him, my head shaking back and forth just as vehemently as the shame that's suddenly beginning to swamp me. I'm a woman who's always in control, and right now I can't control anything, including the emotions swirling around inside me. "I'm not a virgin."

"Are you out of your goddamn mind?" he shouts at me.

"Apparently." My confusion and embarrassment morph into mortification and anger. "I thought I could do this with you . . ." He stalks back across the room, body primed for sex, face a mask of fury. "But you're just . . ." I shudder in revulsion that's in no way because of him. "I can't."

Something alights in his eyes at my veiled insult. At the disgust my face reflects that's misdirected at him. Something dark and dangerous, and I take a step back so that I bump into the wall he had me pressed against moments ago.

"Get out!" he shouts, his finger pointing to the door.

His rejection stings. Not having to do this is the one thing I've wanted since I talked myself into being Saxony, and now that I have it, it stings. Pride has me warring some to save face. "Your previous girls were right—you're a lousy lay." I lash out with another lie to twist the blame of this disaster back on him.

No one's told me that. And we didn't sleep together, so how could I know? But the words do the trick, igniting his temper and pushing him over the edge.

"Get the hell out!"

"Gladly."

CHAPTER EIGHT
Ryker

What the actual fuck was that?

The fear in her eyes is burned into my mind.

And the taste of her kiss is seared into my goddamn memory.

I pace back and forth across the lush carpet and expansive suite. I'm amped on adrenaline, horny as hell, and confused as fuck.

A quick glance at the door she just rushed from tells me, *yep*, it sure as hell did just happen.

But the question is what is it that happened?

The highly recommended escort who is a really virgin?

The Saxony who isn't really a Saxony. Her hesitation to respond every time I said her name tells me that.

And why does that bug me? Why does not knowing more about her infuriate me?

Did Vee really think I wanted to deflower a fucking virgin? Did she think when I said I wanted someone who was experienced that I was playing a goddamn game?

I may be a callous fucker, but I'm not heartless. Scratch that—I am heartless, but even I have my limits. Even I have a conscience when it comes to taking the one thing from a person you can never give back.

"A fucking virgin." I scrub a hand over my jaw, and fuck if the smell of her pussy isn't on my fingers still. I must be a masochist because I inhale—take in the scent—and then laugh into the empty room.

There's no way she could have been a virgin. No goddamn way.

Then what was it? What am I missing?

"Give it a rest, Ryk," I mutter as I grab the decanter and, with a heavy hand, pour myself some more whiskey.

Amped up, I move to the floor-to-ceiling window of the bedroom and look out to the city's lights beyond. To the million people living their lives. Fucking someone. Cheating on someone. Loving someone.

And here I am in a hotel room screwed . . . and not in a good way.

CHAPTER NINE
Vaughn

Shame.

It coats my skin in an impermeable layer as I enter my bathroom.

It became heavier on me with each step home.

Out of the hotel. Finding a cab. The long drive to the house. The fumbling to unlock the door. The discarding of clothes piece by piece as I trudged through the family room and into the hall.

The shame is tinged with a confusion that makes me physically ill as I repeatedly try to recall what it is that my memory blindsided me with.

My uncle James. The man who took care of us after our mom died.

That's all I know.

All I can remember.

It somehow had to do with him, and the grotesque feeling in my stomach tells me more than I need to know.

I stutter to a stop in the hallway. The box of my sister's things calling to me from the closet. Telling me the answer's in there when I've already looked through everything before.

But this time, maybe I'll see something different. Maybe this time, I'll understand what she said, what she did, and why she did it a little bit more.

Bile rises in my throat as I dare to think the truth. That my sister protected me from him by using herself.

Because I would remember if it had been me, right?

I double over and retch at the thought, running to the bathroom, but nothing comes up. Nothing purges to make me feel better.

Unwilling to look at myself in the mirror right now, knowing I'm a mess of ruined makeup and hair tousled by his fingers, I turn on the shower. I crank it as hot as it will go and then hiss when the frigid water hits my skin.

But I don't move. Not when the cold water turns lukewarm. Not when it bleeds into scalding hot. Not when my skin turns bright red from its punishing cadence.

I let the water sluice over my skin and use its scorching temperature to erase everything from tonight. The colossal error in judgment I made thinking I could pretend to be one of my girls. The mistake in thinking I actually liked Ryker, actually found him attractive. The vile memory that hints at the corners of my mind that as much as I want to know the whole of it, I'm afraid to . . .

If only I didn't go tonight. If I didn't let Ryker's words, his challenge of what a good boss would do take hold. If I didn't have so much pride . . .

"Shit," I groan.

Uncertain and lost to the confusion, the mortification, the unknown . . . I scrub my body with the loofah as hard as I can, knowing no amount of soap is going to wash away whatever was in the past.

And fully aware that something was different for me with Ryker.

I've had sex before. With men I liked. With men I wasn't sure I liked. But each time, it was more about going through the motions. For me, orgasms were few, far between, hard to come by, and only when brought about by my own hand . . . but it's not like the men I slept with ever noticed.

Sex had been monotone for me. A sacrifice of my body. Knowing what actions and reactions were expected. Is that because of the memory? Was that my body and my brain's way of protecting me from the truth?

Does everything stem from that?

But tonight . . . with Ryker . . . we didn't even get to the sex part—only the kissing—but this time it wasn't monotone. This time it was a Metallica song played at the highest decibel, bright and with a throbbing beat that was so loud I needed to cover my ears but couldn't.

Tonight, when I was supposed to be numb, to tune out, to be how I normally am, I felt things—sensations—and I wanted *more*.

Then a switch was flipped, the memory. The flash of my uncle's face right in front of mine. Knowing what he did without being able to remember the details, only the ghosts of them.

Is this the reason—is *he* the reason—that I'm so guarded? Is he why I've always felt so indifferent when it comes to sex compared to every other female I've known?

And for the first time, I let the tears come.

Huge, racking sobs that are so violent my whole body shudders from their force.

But I don't cry for me. How can you cry for the loss of something you never even knew was missing? How can you long for something to be like *before* when you didn't know there was a *before*?

No. I cry for my sister.

Because for the first time since her suicide, I don't hate her for it. For the first time since I received that call telling me she was gone, so many things make sense.

For the first time, I want to apologize to her and tell her I didn't know.

CHAPTER TEN
Ryker

"Did you hear a word I said?" The voice on the other end of my speakerphone snaps my attention back to the task at hand. My job. And screwing over the soon-to-be former Mrs. Martin Hinkle.

"Yeah. Yes. Sorry. My assistant brought in something while you were talking, and I got distracted. What did you say again?" I lie.

My mind is in a goddamn fog. I glance down to my call log on my cell and shake my head at the name Vee and how many times it sits on the list.

Each one either dialed and then ended before the call went through . . . or dialed and left unanswered.

"Mm-hmm," I murmur to Marty as he drones on, repeating the same shit he says each time he calls.

"I don't want her to get a goddamn penny is what I said. Fifteen years stuck with her and probably a total of fifteen blowjobs to go with it. Do you know what it's like to be a man and have to beg your wife to get blown on your birthday? Add to that she's off spending money left and right every time I leave for work. She's bled me dry already with her Chanel and Givenchy and whatever you call it. She doesn't deserve another dime from me."

I clear my throat and think of the photographs in the file beneath my fingertips of his version of "at work." Martin entering a hotel with a buxom blonde two days of the week and then a sexy redhead on two others.

"I've got you covered, Marty. I have records, and Stuart has been digging around—"

"Stuart?" he asks.

"My private investigator." Never leave home without one. "He's been hard at work. I'm more than certain that she'll agree to mediate the terms before we ever approach trial. I doubt she'll want all of her friends hearing about how half of her shit is knockoffs and how all of the hours she's told them she's spent donating her time is all a bunch of bullshit."

It sounds like he smacks his hands together on the other end of the line and rubs them in anticipation. "I can see her face now."

"Good. Keep thinking about that. And make sure to keep your distance from your"—I clear my throat—"*friends* for the time being. We were watching her long before you asked for the divorce. That's the only reason we have dirt on her. I'm sure you're being watched now."

"Definitely. Definitely," he says before ending the connection, and I know he's already trying to figure out how to sneak out and get some. *Prick.*

But a wealthy prick indeed, whose $500,000 retainer sits paid in my account.

An incoming email dings on my laptop, and I'd much rather stay distracted by looking at it than deal with my crappy day. First, Judge Marcos denying my motion in one courtroom and then being on the losing end of a rather shitty decision on another one across town.

Still thinking about the money I'm out from Wicked Ways and the lack of response when I call is just icing on the fucking shit-cake I don't want to deal with.

Because it's not the money I give a rat's ass about . . . not in the least.

Maybe it's my wounded pride from the insults she hurled at me. I know they're bullshit, but still . . .

Stop caring, Lockhart.

I click to open the email just as my receptionist buzzes the phone on my desk.

"Mr. Lockhart?"

"Not now, Bella."

The first picture opens on my screen.

"But—"

"Not now."

I jab the intercom button on my phone and hang up on her as I stare at my screen and the images Stuart just sent over.

They're grainy and taken at night, but there she is. I stare at the black-and-white image of the woman I know only as Vee. Scroll through the photos, one after another—my eyes squinting, my mouth twisting in thought. Her hair is jet black and cut into a severe angle at her cheek, her clothes are expensive yet understated in black to match her hair, and even without color, I know her lips are a deep red.

Not blonde like I'd expected.

I zoom in on the screen as if that will help with the image quality so I can see if that unique-looking birthmark on Saxony's wrist is there, but the photos aren't clear enough.

Grabbing my cell, I have Stuart on the phone in a second.

"Where did you take these?" I ask in greeting, but he doesn't hesitate to answer. He's used to me by now.

"It was across town a few weeks ago."

"Why?" For a quick second, jealousy roils inside me as I wonder if Stuart has met her.

"You asked me if I'd heard of her, and so I figured you needed to know for a client. I asked around, knew she was meeting with someone . . . I made a point to get some shots for you."

"Who was she meeting with?"

"Fuck if I know."

"Where did she go after?"

He chuckles. "That's the funny part. She went into the hotel and never came back out. Either that or she did come back out, but dressed as someone else."

"Hmm. Did she—never mind."

"Is there a problem, Ryk?"

"Nah. Just trying to figure something out." And not sound like a crazy man asking if he noticed a dark-red birthmark on the inside of her wrist.

"She's hot . . . in a dominatrix kind of way."

"That she is." And my mind immediately veers to her other look. The soft blonde hair and pale-pink lips. Equally as hot.

"Do you want me to do the usual workup on her for you?"

I stare at the picture a bit longer. "No."

"No?" There's surprise in his voice that matches how I feel.

"No. Thanks, Stu."

I hang up and wonder what it is about her that has me holding back when normally I could know the answer to my question in days. If she's one and the same woman. Where she lives. What color her goddamn kitchen counter is, for Christ's sake.

It's that voice of hers. It's distinct, with a hint of rasp and a whole lot of sexy, and there's no mistaking that voice no matter how hard she might try to disguise it.

With a sigh, I scroll through the pictures a few more times. The two women couldn't look more polar opposite, but there's something about the images. Something I notice as I flip through them, study them, scrutinize them that tells me I just might be right about my hunch. She might not have blonde hair in the photos, but my hands were on those curves the other night. A man doesn't forget curves like that.

"Who are you, Vee?" I murmur as I sink back into my chair, my anger at being left high and dry slowly morphing into a small sense of satisfaction that I was wrong. She did get her hands dirty.

But then that creates a whole other list of questions. Number one being what the hell happened in that hotel room the other night, because judging by how wet she was, she wasn't just going through the motions.

Hell no.

So what the fuck put the fear in her eyes?

The intercom on my desk buzzes again. "Mr. Lockhart?"

"What part of *not now* do you not understand, Bella?"

"Mr.—"

"Bella."

"Someone is here—"

"I'm not taking any appointments right now," I snap.

"Your mother is here wanting to see you."

Fucking perfect.

I hang my head and close my eyes with a sigh. If Bella's telling me this, then that means she's already tried every way imaginable to get rid of her to no avail.

"Fine."

"I'll buzz her in."

With a sigh of resignation, I stand up from behind my desk, more than aware that my shitty day just got crappier.

"Mother," I say when she walks in bathed in some cream-colored designer ensemble, fur stole hanging over her shoulders, dark sunglasses still on her eyes, and skin with the shine that says it's been sucked and tucked and Botoxed more than any person's hide should ever be.

Vivian Lockhart-Stein-Bismark-Whatever-Husband-Number-Four's-Last-Name-Is always knows how to make an entrance.

"Ryker, dear!" she says as I step to her to kiss her cheek and am handed her Birkin to take care of in return. "How are you?"

"Fine. And you?" I place her purse on one of the chairs in front of my desk before moving to take the fur resting on her shoulders and laying it over the back of the chair.

Just going through the motions.

"That woman out there is simply dreadful. How can you stand letting her be your assistant? She guards you like she owns you. Doesn't she know I always get a free pass to come back here, regardless of your schedule? She should be fired for how she tried to tell me you were in meetings."

"I was in meetings, Mother. And Bella does the job I tell her to do. I can handle my own employees, thank you."

She makes a show of patting down her perfectly styled silver hair before removing her sunglasses and taking a seat.

Three. Two. One.

She sighs.

And there it is like clockwork.

"You haven't come to see me lately."

"I've been busy. There are a lot of people getting divorced these days—shocking, I know—and so I all but live here."

"That's not healthy."

"I'm fine with it."

"Well, can't you take a break to come visit me?"

"We're visiting now." My smile is tight as I lean my ass against my desk a few feet in front of her.

"Such a handsome man I made."

"I do believe my father had something to do with that," I say wryly.

Her expression goes hard momentarily before she waves a hand in dismissal. "Tell me, where are the women in your life?"

"I keep them hidden so you don't scare them off."

"Shush." She rolls her eyes and swats a hand at the air. Her way of disagreeing when she knows I'm right. "And your father? He's well?" I nod. "I'm sure he is. He always is."

"You say that like you're angry at him."

"Of course I am. If he hadn't left me destitute and—"

The derision lacing my laugh cuts her off. "Getting ten million dollars in a divorce settlement is far from destitute," I say, wanting to nip this in the bud and forgo the *woe is me* bullshit. "How about you, Mother? How are you and . . ." *Hank?* No, Hank was number three. Niels, I think?

"Niels and I are . . ." She shrugs with a shake of her head like I've seen way too many times before. "You know how it goes."

Jesus. *And another one bites the dust.*

"What's wrong this time?" Has the money run out? Has his health declined? Did he sell the villa in France—*God forbid?* And yes, that was sarcasm there.

"Oh . . . you know."

"Of course. I'm sorry," I say, when I'm indifferent about the whole thing. I know she has an ironclad prenup to protect all of the money she's taken from her other husbands in divorce settlements. I know because I wrote it.

"Come have lunch with me." She reaches her hand out and squeezes mine as she rises from her chair.

"It's three o'clock. I've already eaten." Another lie. Let's hope my stomach doesn't rumble to tell her otherwise.

"Then we can have an early dinner."

I feel like an ass when I shake my head after hearing the excitement in her voice over the prospect of a dinner date with me. It's amazing how even the notion of being in the right social circles can lighten her mood instantly. "I can't. I'm scheduled out for the rest of the afternoon."

"C'mon." She tugs. "Play hooky."

"Another time."

"Don't you have time for your mother?"

"Always." I lean forward and press a chaste kiss to her cheek. "But I also have to make time for my clients."

"You haven't been out to the island in a while. This time of year, you're always there."

"No, I'm not." My house in the Hamptons is calling me, but not with my current schedule.

"I stopped by the house when I was there last weekend, and those lovely people who care for the place said you hadn't been out in some time."

"As I said, I'm swamped here."

"Take on a partner."

"A partner is fine, but it's me people want to hire."

"The Lockhart name is well known." She smiles proudly.

"Look, when you get home, send me your schedule, and we can find time to have lunch."

She pats my cheek, and eyes that reflect the same color as mine light up. "I'll look forward to it. I love you, sweetie."

"Love you too, Mother."

Another kiss to her cheek as her sunglasses slide back on, and her heels click on the slate floors of the hallway as she leaves.

With a sigh and a roll of my shoulders, I head back to my desk, determined to finish my prep for the start of my trial tomorrow.

But when I take a seat, there are the images on my screen of Vee.

They steal my thoughts and promote procrastination.

Fuck. I need to get laid.

CHAPTER ELEVEN

Vaughn

The smell of the strawberry shampoo in her hair and the grip of her arms around my neck is exactly what I needed.

I breathe Lucy in. The soft hum she emits when she's happy. The copper-colored Brushfield spots lighting up the irises of her pale-blue eyes. Her always-smiling face. Her constantly cheery demeanor, even after everything she's been through.

I love absolutely everything about her.

Even her extra chromosome 21 that's given her Down syndrome.

"I missed you like crazy, Luce!" I murmur into the top of her head when I press a kiss there, tears unexpectedly burning the backs of my eyes as I fight them back.

"I missed you more." She kisses the palm of my hand. "I was waiting and waiting for Tuesday. 'Cause you always come on Tuesday, right? I'm so ex-excited you're here!"

"Not as excited as I've been all morning." Her smile widens, and I see my sister in her expression. It hits me harder than I expected this time around. Harder because I know the answers have to be in her journals, and yet I can't bring myself to face them just yet. "I have so many fun things planned for us today."

"Like what?" Her fingers link with mine out of reflex, and we swing our arms as we walk in the outdoor common area of the facility where she's staying.

"I was thinking a carriage ride in Central Park." The quick tightening of her fingers and high-pitched squeal tells me that idea went over well. "I mean, a princess needs her carriage, right?"

"Yes."

"And then maybe story time at the library."

"Is it a princess book?"

I twist my lips in pretend thought. "Of course!"

Her grin widens. "Can I bring my crown?"

"Only if you have one for me too!"

She chatters incessantly as we make our way back across the lush grounds to where her quarters are. Clinical halls decorated to disguise the fact that this is a community residence where little kids with disabilities are housed while their guardianship is settled in court.

Soon, baby girl. If I have my way, I'll get you out of here soon.

"Be right back!" Lucy says as she heads to her room to grab her costume. Most likely it will be the yellow Belle one because that's her favorite this month.

The tears threaten again as I watch her bound down the hall with energy and excitement.

Get a grip, Vaughn.

But that's what I'm doing, right? I'm trying to ground myself by spending the entire day with the only person who matters to me. The one person I'm doing all of this for.

What happened with Ryker knocked me back some. Sure, it was two nights ago, but the more I think about it, the worse it seems. The more I know what a fiasco I created.

I spent all day yesterday trying to compartmentalize everything.

The result? I've written off Ryker Lockhart.

Maybe it's easier to write him off so that I'm not worrying about the loss of possible income his referrals could bring and the funds I have to return to him. If I'm obsessed with the stress of how he'll most likely ruin the reputation I've worked so hard to build, then maybe all of that will overshadow the truths hiding just beneath the surface.

The way my mind keeps wandering to memories I have of growing up while questioning the legitimacy of every single one of them.

Compartmentalize. So much easier said than done. Hell, I can talk a good game—I can convince myself that I can do just this—but when I close my eyes, I can still taste Ryker on my tongue, I can still see that look in his eyes . . . I can still remember how he made me feel when I didn't want to.

And I can still feel that blinding panic over something I can't completely pull from the depths of my mind.

No matter how much I tell myself it doesn't matter because I've been better off living all this time and not remembering, it still does.

"I thought I was dropping her off at your house today?"

I startle at the sound of Joey's voice but am more than grateful for the reprieve from the noise in my head. My smile is wide when I turn to face Lucy's favorite counselor here. "I couldn't wait that long. I was missing my girl. How's she doing?"

"Very well under the circumstances. We just keep telling her this is like a fun camp and she'll get to go home soon." His soft smile says, *Let's hope* home *means going home with you.*

"At some point, she's going to ask why *soon* seems to be lasting month after month. She needs to be home. She needs to be—"

"You're preaching to the choir, Vaughn. If I could speed up the process somehow, you know I would. Just know I'm taking care of her as best as I can while she's here."

"Thank you," I murmur. "Has he been here lately?" I ask of Lucy's father, and even that term is putting it loosely.

"Not since last week, no."

"Hmm." It's all I say as a hundred questions flicker through my mind. *Did he take her somewhere? Did she seem like she had fun with him? Did he seem sober this time? Was she as excited to see him as she is for me?* But I don't utter a single one because I know social services can question Joey at any time as well.

"She was better after the visit than she normally is, if that's what you're asking."

"I don't know what I'm asking . . . ," I confess, but my smile returns when I hear her voice down the hallway ordering someone around.

"Not the Snow White one. The Belle one. 'Cause Belle likes books like me."

Little Miss Bossy Pants.

"She misses you in between your visits," Joey says with a lift of his chin in her direction. "Misses the routine she used to have, but you know her. She's like a ray of sunshine—always happy, always eager, always wanting to try."

Pride fills me at the truth in his statement. "She definitely is, and I could use a huge helping of her sunshine right now."

"Social services still giving you grief?"

My shoulders sag some at the question. "I'm getting good at jumping through hoops, but man, they're particular with what they want."

"You wouldn't believe some of the shit I've seen."

"Let's hope I don't see—or experience—any of it either. Fingers crossed I can comply with their demands sooner rather than later."

"That bad, huh?"

"Not bad . . . it's just taking too long. This is a kid we're talking about—does the red tape have to be everywhere when another life is involved?"

"I'm rooting for you," Joey says and pats my shoulder in support.

"There's my beautiful princess," I exclaim when Lucy rounds the corner, decked out in head-to-toe princess garb: yellow sparkly dress, tiara to match, and a smile so wide I don't think it can get any bigger.

My heart swells with love.

Yes.

She is exactly what I need right now to center myself. To bring me back to normal.

To remind me why I'm fighting so hard.

For her.

It's all for her.

CHAPTER TWELVE
Vaughn

My smile is permanent and my spirits are high from my afternoon with Lucy as I flit around the house picking things up. Always on the ready for social services to stop by unannounced, I try to keep the place clean and orderly, reflecting a home that would be suitable for Lucy, all the while making sure any hint of Wicked Ways is nonexistent.

Grabbing my dry cleaning from the kitchen counter where I laid it when I walked in, I separate out my day-job uniforms from my "Vee" clothes and begin putting them away when the distinct ring of my Wicked Ways cell phone echoes through the house.

"Yeah, yeah," I mutter before picking it up and sighing when I see the number. The same number that has called me numerous times in the past forty-eight hours that I've yet to have the courage to answer.

But I need to. I'm the boss he's calling, not the escort who insulted him and ran out without giving him what he paid for.

Now or never, Vaughn.

With a straightening of my shoulders, I sink down onto the edge of my bed and then stand back up, figuring this is a job I need to do while on my feet.

Here goes nothing.

"Mr. Lockhart. What a pleasure to hear from you," I greet him, my voice smooth as silk and brimming with professionalism while my insides are suddenly a bundle of nerves.

"Is it? I'd think by the way you're avoiding my phone calls that you're busy figuring out what to say to me or how to explain why I was left high and dry and completely unsatisfied."

"Not avoiding you, no," I say as the grate of his voice rumbling through the phone gives my body a visceral reaction. My pause is unexpected. I've tried to figure out how to play this a million times and never decided how. Now that we're talking, I decide honesty is the best way. Well, almost honest. "Actually, I'm rather embarrassed about what happened and have been busy trying to figure out how to make it up to you. We are a professional company, and what Saxony did—or rather, what she told me happened, as I'm fairly certain there is more to the story from your end—is unacceptable to me."

When in doubt, stroke a man's ego, and if you stroke it long enough, he'll come to the conclusion that you're wrong and he's right even when you never utter the words.

"As it should be."

"Would you mind giving me your version of events, Mr. Lockhart, for her employee file?" I ask.

"No."

"No?"

I picture him sitting behind some big desk somewhere with the night skyline stretched out in front of him while he runs his hand over his jaw and contemplates my words.

"No," he answers resolutely, leaving no room for question.

"May I ask why not?" Curiosity gets the better of me.

"Because it's my understanding that I've paid for companionship and that nothing else is included in the price." There's a hint of amusement in his voice as he reiterates the point I drive home to all my clients. "Whatever happened was part of that *nothing else.*"

I walk over to the window and look at the swing set in the backyard and wonder how long it's going to sit here before Lucy will be able to come home to use it.

"Is that so?" I ask, wondering why he's giving me a break when he could deservedly be a real asshole.

"That's so."

"While I appreciate your understanding of the situation, I still feel the need to refund you your full payment as well as offer you a night with another one of my girls on the house as an apology for the mix-up."

"Mix-up?" He chuckles, and I swear I can all but feel it tickling over my skin. "Is that what we're going to call what happened?"

"What would you like to call it, then?"

"A refund won't be necessary," he says, disregarding my question.

"I insist."

"What if I want to see Saxony again?"

I jolt at his question, unsure how to respond. *"What?"*

"I asked, What if I want to see Saxony again?"

"I heard you. What I meant was . . . *why?*"

"Maybe she intrigued me."

My throat feels like sandpaper when I try to swallow. "She no longer works for me. After what happened, I let her go." I say the words because it's the right thing to do but am confused knowing that a little part of me wonders why he'd want to see me again.

"Why would you do that?"

"It seems pretty self-explanatory to me."

"I want to see her again." His tone is more adamant this time.

"Mr. Lockhart," I say to try to bring him back to reality. "Like I said, she no longer works for Wicked Ways."

"Yes, she does—I'm speaking to her right now."

I open my mouth, but no words come out as his comment shocks every part of my system. I laugh in disbelief, and then it takes me a few seconds before I can respond. "That's funny."

"I make a living out of observing people, catching nuances, Vee . . . or is it Saxony? Which name do I call you?"

"This is Vee. I'm not sure what—"

"You're talking about," he finishes for me. "But you know exactly what I'm talking about, don't you?"

"Mr. Lockhart—"

"So official sounding now when it was nothing but *oh, Ryker* the other night."

"As I said previously, *Mr. Lockhart*, feel free to revisit my website and pick a date of your choosing. An evening with her will be on the house."

"And I already told you who I wanted."

I end the call.

It's hasty and chickenshit, but I didn't know what else to do because I was getting flustered, and now I'm staring at my cell wondering why I just fucked this whole situation up even more.

And to make matters worse, why did I want to tell him yes?

This time when I sink down onto the edge of my mattress, I stay there, flop back, and grab a pillow to put over my face.

Maybe if I hold it here long enough I'll put myself out of my own misery.

CHAPTER THIRTEEN

Ryker

Exhaustion owns every part of my body. My hands hurt and my arms feel like jelly, but I punched and kicked and dodged and weaved my way out of my sexual frustration with my boxing workout only to step into the lobby of my building and face a whole different kind of sexual frustration.

I take her in. Auburn hair pulled back in some kind of sophisticated twist at the back of her neck. Green eyes that already beg and plead for my time—my forgiveness—before I even say a word. A body made for sin that's covered in some exercise outfit made to sweat in that I'm sure is worth more than most people's car payments.

A body made for sin that I've sinned with.

"Roxanne." It's the only thing I'll give her as I take a step back when she tries to kiss me in greeting.

"I've missed you." Her words are soft, timid, after my subtle rebuke.

"Don't you have some function to be at? Some cause that needs to be championed while drinking one-hundred-dollar glasses of champagne and pretending to care?" My smile is tight, my eyes lasers of distrust.

"I deserve that," she murmurs, willing to be compliant with my insults so long as she gets to see me.

"Why are you here?" I glance over to the doorman across the lobby greeting someone who just walked in. My hand is on her arm, not so gently guiding her to a small alcove for privacy.

"Ryker." My name is a plea—for what, I can only guess. Her bottom lip quivers, and she bites it to fight the emotion.

"I asked you not to come here anymore. We can't be seen together."

"Then let's go upstairs," she says softly.

"No. This is over. It was over the minute I found out you were married." *More so when I realized the man who'd just hired me for representation in his divorce was the husband she was married to.*

"I've told you . . . I didn't know—I didn't mean for this to happen." She twists her fingers together and stares at them for a beat before lifting those eyes back up to mine. Eyes that for the first time in a long time belonged to a woman who I thought I could trust. A woman who might have actually owned a little piece of my cold heart.

"It doesn't matter how it happened, Rox. It just—"

She emits an audible sob at the sound of her nickname and covers her mouth to bite it back. An unintentional gaffe on my part. *Shit.*

I run a hand through my hair and walk a few feet away from her to gain my composure. I liked her. Really fucking liked her . . . but just as with all women, I should've known better than to trust her.

"You lied to me." I turn back around to face her, my words causing her to force a swallow. "We met. We had fun. We had incredible sex. Not once did you tell me you were married. Not once did you tell me that your husband was some Nobel laureate who was off on sabbatical. Not once did I know the man who'd hired me to divorce his adulterous wife wanted representation against the same woman I was sleeping with." Every word I utter drips with venom.

"I love you."

"No you don't. You love the idea of me, Roxanne. The thrill of the cheat. The *fuck you* you feel because you're sticking it to your husband, who loves his work more than he loved you."

Tears well and one escapes and slides slowly down her cheek. "I love you, Ryker. Just give *me* a chance. Give *us* a chance." She grips her hands onto my biceps, and the only reaction I give her is the tic of the muscle in my jaw. "I won't fight the settlement terms of the divorce if you do. I'll just take whatever he gives me, and then once the papers are signed, we can be together." Hysteria bubbles in her voice, and the tears she fought are now streaming down each cheek. "No one has to know. We can be happy. I know we can. I just want you, Ryker. I love you."

I give her the moment to say what she wants to say. The same moment I've given her too many times to count so far. My generosity only has so many lives, though.

"I can't do this, Roxanne. *We* can't do this. I'm going to ask you again, as nicely as possible, if you would please leave."

"Just like that, you're going to throw us all away?" She shrieks as her hands go from gripping my arms to hitting against my chest.

"Stop. You're making a scene." It takes me a second and a few slaps to my chest before I can get my hands around her wrists to stop her. The doorman glances my way, eyes asking if I need help, and I just shake my head no, firing off a warning glare. He's the one who let her in here in the first place. Besides, a scene is the last thing I need right now. I look back to her, some hair falling out of her twist now, makeup streaked with mascara, and desperation in her eyes.

"Ryk."

I push her away from me to gain some distance. "Stop begging, Roxanne. Have some dignity." My voice holds zero sympathy or compassion.

And this time she finally hears it.

The expression on her face slowly changes. Muscle by muscle. Emotion by emotion. Her eyes glint with steel, and her lips curl up in something akin to the anger I feel toward her. For being here. For putting me through this. For reaffirming why I won't make this oversight again.

"You're making a huge mistake," she grits out between her teeth, mirroring my thoughts.

"I already did. That's why we're here." My compassion has given way to exasperation.

She takes the words in stride, her anger now fueling her emotions. "You're going to regret this. I'm going to fight David for every penny he has. I'm going to take every one of his skeletons out of the closet and take him for all he's worth."

"To spite me?" I ask with a chuckle, glad to help add kerosene to her temper so she hates me and leaves me alone. "Whatever happens, happens. You taking David to the cleaners doesn't affect my paycheck."

"I'm going to ruin you, Ryker. Your reputation. You. I'll let everyone know you sleep with clients' wives. You'll look like the slimy bastard you are so that no one will ever use you again because they'll think you're incompetent."

"Then I guess they'll question your judgment in turn." I don't quite enjoy watching her flail around like a fish out of water, but I've been patient long enough.

"Do you think I care?" she shrieks.

"I think you're forgetting one thing, Roxanne," I say with the smarmy smile I've perfected over the years and step closer into her. When I speak, my voice is low, even, threatening. "Your prenup is rendered invalid in the case of adultery. You and I both know the answer to that, so if you want to come at me . . . come at me. I promise you the cost you'll face is much worse than the one I will." I take a step back and shrug, knowing from the look on her face that I've just delivered the coup de grâce. "We're done here."

She sputters a litany of things as I skirt around her and head toward my elevator. I push the button and wait.

"Ryker," she calls just as my door dings, and I step inside.

When I turn to face her, I see it in her eyes—the fact that she still loves me despite her venomous words—just before the door closes to separate us one last time.

I sigh in frustration and lean my head back against the wall as it begins to ascend, my mind already on the whiskey I'm going to pour the minute I walk in the door.

And I pour it too. Three fingers' worth of a serving.

It sure as shit doesn't do anything to complement the workout I just did, but it helps deal with the shit in my head.

First my mom.

Then Vee.

And now Roxanne.

But it's only one of them I'm thinking about now as I let the alcohol burn the back of my throat and slowly begin to unwind after a long day.

It's only one of them who has piqued my interest enough that I want to know more.

And of course it's the one woman I should probably stay as far away from as I possibly can . . . but for some reason I can't get her out of my goddamn mind.

Not even after she lied to me earlier today.

A woman who lies is one I stay away from. I chuckle to my nonexistent company because that means I better steer clear of all of them since they all lie.

Every damn one of them.

So why is it Vee's lies are the ones I want to understand? Why is it her lies that make me want to know more about her? Why is it her goddamn trap I want to fall into?

Another sip. A little less of the burn. A whole lot of exhaustion.

I see the desperation in Roxanne's eyes. I remember the taste of it in Saxony/Vee's kiss. Two women. Two completely different reactions elicited from me.

"Christ." I run a hand through my hair, knowing the only thing I need desperately is a shower.

But I don't move. Instead, I sink back into my chair and prop my feet up onto the railing of my outdoor terrace. The sounds of a city's nightlife starting to come alive filters up—horns honking, laughter faint but there, music from several directions—while I'm up here in my tower removed from all of it.

Thinking of a particular woman when there are hundreds of others out there. Wondering if it's a simple case of wanting what I can't have. Is that the uncomplicated truth? That I'd rather waste my time thinking about her when I should be working on a brief simply because she's a challenge to be conquered?

Fucking women.

No matter how good a relationship starts, it always turns to shit. Always. And then they'll take you to the cleaners—financially and emotionally—until you've got nothing left.

Nothing.

CHAPTER FOURTEEN

Vaughn

"Lola? Is everything okay? I was just running out the door," I lie into my cell phone as I slip on my heels in the empty locker room at work.

"Yes. Fine. Sorry, I didn't mean to scare you. I'm healing quickly. The bruises are fading."

"That's great news." I glance around the room to make sure I'm alone, never knowing what my conversation might hold.

"I ran into a friend of yours last night," she says.

"A friend?" I ask cautiously. Vee doesn't have many friends.

"Archer."

I pause midmotion with my purse halfway in my locker in reaction to the name of the only person who knows me, who knows the truth . . . about everything.

"Oh," I say to buy time as my mind spins, wondering if she's calling to tell me she has me all figured out. That this is all over for me.

"Such a nice guy. We were in a club, and I handed him one of my cards—"

My laugh cuts her off.

"Yes, I now know he's gay and isn't interested in female anatomy, but it doesn't hurt."

"It wouldn't be the first time a woman came on to him."

"He's gorgeous—I can see why." She clears her throat. "Anyway, he said he knew you when."

"He said *me*, specifically?" I ask, paranoid about how much information has been divulged.

"No. Jesus, Vee. He's not going around saying he knows who you are by name. He just said he knew the owner of the company on my card, and that was that."

I feel my shoulders sag. *Paranoid much, Vaughn?*

I think of Archer. Tall. Handsome. Knower of everybody in this town who needs to be known. And the one person who helped me get Wicked Ways set up and my name out there to the silent masses.

Confidentiality agreement or not, it still worries me sometimes.

"Archer is a sweetheart."

"Seems like it. How did the other night go? Did you find someone to fill in for me?"

"Yes." *No.*

"Okay." She draws the word out, and the resignation in her voice tells me she knows she missed out on a big client and is pissed about it.

"You know you'll be the first person I call if the client decides to look for someone else."

"Oh." She stretches the sound out as if she hears my unspoken words that the customer wasn't 100 percent satisfied. "You know I'm here."

"I do." I glance at the clock on the wall. "Look, I've got to go, but I'm glad you're feeling better."

"Everything okay?" she asks.

How do I tell a girl who works for me that I'm at my day job? That I waitress at a high-end club so that the social worker handling Lucy's case sees a hardworking woman trying to do the best to provide for her niece. It also helps to explain where the money is coming from to pay down the debts I have looming over my head from trying to take care of my sister.

"Yeah, everything is okay. Thanks for asking."

We say our goodbyes, and I hang up my cell and place it in my locker with my purse and jacket. Drawing in a deep breath, I shake my head and laugh at this ridiculous situation I'm in.

There are so many lies to keep straight. So many covers that I have to shift and finagle so often that if I survive long enough to accomplish my goal, I might die from the sheer exhaustion when all is said and done.

The door opens and then closes. A fellow server, Melissa, comes in and throws a smile my way as the speakers on the other side of the wall throb a dull beat.

"It seems like it's a busy night out there," I say as I double-check my uniform: emerald-green bustier, black skirt—short and tight—nylons with the seams up the back, and black high heels. The kind that are so comfortable to walk around in all night long, said no one ever.

"Let's hope that means we get some serious tips." She winks as she steps up beside me to the mirror and pulls out a tube of red lipstick to reapply to her full lips. She's petite, with her strawberry-blonde hair in a pixie cut, and has a killer personality that helps to earn her those tips.

"Tips are always welcome."

"You're in the west pods tonight," she says, referring to my area assignment for the night. Looking her way, I raise an eyebrow because I typically work in the south pods.

"Why the change?"

"Someone in yours requested me tonight."

"Lucky you." A requested server usually means it's a repeat customer, and repeats always spend money like water and make tips fall like rain. But while that may be good for her, that means I'll be stuck in a different section with people who might be all new.

And all new means you never know what you're going to get.

"Yeah, yeah. Lucky me that the tips are good, but fuck if this guy isn't handsy as hell." Melissa rolls her eyes and lifts her hands up to mock a man grabbing a woman's breasts. "He comes here, gets all horny with me because I giggle and swat his hands away, and then probably goes home and disappoints his wife because he's so drunk he can't stay hard."

"Sounds about right." I glance up at the clock on the wall. "Time for me to clock in."

"Have a good shift," she says as I open the door.

"You too."

I walk onto the floor of Apropos. The light is dim and filtered a pale blue. It's crowded tonight for a Thursday. Some women dance on the floor while men sit around the outside near the bar area, unwinding after a long day, wondering if they have a shot at a one-night stand with any of them. Their ties are pulled looser, sleeves are rolled up some, and jackets are hung on the backs of barstools.

I move up the stairs to the pods where I typically work. The top tier overlooks the dance floor, but it is divided up into twelve private areas called pods. Each server is responsible for three pods at a time. These areas are reserved in advance and are typically booked by repeat customers here to relax under the guise of a business meeting, almost always to cater to their clients' needs that they don't always subscribe to themselves personally. Either that or to screw around on their significant others.

Privacy and service is what they pay for.

Privacy and service is what I give them.

Moving into the Seven Pod, I assess the two men in deep conversation, one obviously angry despite the two women fawning all over him, and the other one more smug. I gather the glasses, empties left behind still half-full with a complete disregard for the wasted money spent on expensive alcohol. Living life in excess. A quick meeting of eyes with the smug one, and the quick shake of his head tells me *not now*.

The Eight Pod has been hard at work drinking, but judging by the women milling around in the private space versus the three men huddled over something at the table, it's the women who are consuming the alcohol.

The lighting is faint in this pod, the couches a dark-blue velvet, the view of the rest of the club unhindered. Keeping my eyes averted, I look down to the dance floor below. Hips are swinging, and the soft lights illuminate their movements. The music isn't obnoxiously loud like at other clubs as the owners of Apropos know business is being conducted, wheeling and dealing commenced, and they like to keep their customers happy so they come back and rent these pods at their ridiculous price tags.

I pick up all the empties I can access on the periphery and place them on the tray just inside the pod where a dumbwaiter will move them to the kitchen two floors below for cleaning. It's when I turn my focus to the gentlemen in discussion that I'm completely knocked off my stride.

The three men are still sitting on the couches, heads down in discussion over something on a mess of papers cluttering the tables in between glasses dripping with condensation, but even before the one sitting in the middle lifts his head, I know *it's him*.

And just as the thought crosses my mind, the man looks up.

Ryker Lockhart must feel the weight of my surprised stare—or maybe he's just thirsty—but when he lifts his eyes and locks with mine, I feel like we both stutter to a halt.

Him for obvious reasons: the escort who insulted and then ran out on him—the one he accused of also being the madam—is now standing in front of him dressed in the unmistakable Apropos server's uniform.

And me, because this is me here. I am Vaughn Sanders. Just an everyday woman at work, trying to make a living, who isn't hiding behind a black wig or a sultry voice on the phone. A woman who, regardless of any of that, freaked out on him over sex and is now standing before him with nothing to mask her emotions or her true identity.

In that split second, the small world I live in suddenly just closed in on me. My decision to meet with Ryker as a version of myself instead of in disguise just became ten times worse.

How did he find me? Is he here to out me? To get his revenge for the things I said to him?

Recognition fires in those brandy-colored eyes of his, but when he opens his mouth to speak, for some reason he thinks better of it and closes it in favor of simply staring. His eyes scrape over my outfit. His tongue darts out to wet his bottom lip. He angles his head to the side, making no effort to hide how he studies me.

His sudden absence from his conversation pulls his counterparts' attention, and they both lift their heads, look at him, and then turn to see what he's staring at.

Emotions are a turbulent ocean inside me. Everything I've worked so hard for, everything I want so desperately, is suddenly at stake in a way I naively never thought possible.

The music switches to a softer, subtler beat that is no match for the blood whooshing through my eardrums right now.

"Drinks?" Ryker asks with a lift of his eyebrows, irritated impatience in his voice despite the curiosity owning his eyes. So . . . he's not going to *out* me? *Is this really just a coincidence?* "Another round perhaps? Or are you just going to stand there and stare all night?"

I ignore the chuckles of the women around us, whose only thoughts likely center around how I'm one less woman in their line of competition to bed him.

"Yes, of course. I didn't want to interrupt your meeting. Sorry." Clearing my throat, I take a step forward and offer a tight smile. "What can I get you, gentlemen?"

Each man places an order. A double scotch on the rocks for the dark-haired gentleman of Asian descent named Ken on Ryker's right. An old-fashioned for Gene, the gray-haired gentleman on his left. And a gin and tonic for Ryker, even though I notice the one in front of him still sits barely touched.

Feeling like I've been dismissed, I lean forward to pick up their empties to give them more room on the table and notice the scribbles in red ink on what certainly looks to be legal documents.

"We're celebrating," Ken says.

"Is that so?" I ask with a soft smile. "What are we celebrating tonight, gentlemen?"

"How much of my money my wife *isn't* going to get when this shark of a lawyer here is done with her." He reaches his glass out and clinks it with Ryker's still sitting on the table.

My immediate reaction is disgust, as my need to side with another woman when it comes to a man and relationships is inherent.

Don't judge, Vaughn. You don't know the whole story.

But I avoid looking toward Ryker. Instead I smile. "Sounds like a good enough reason. I'll get fresh drinks out to you in a few minutes. My name is Vaughn . . ." My words drift off as I realize that my canned response to customers just became so much more personal tonight.

"Vaughn?" Ryker asks as my own thoughts stumble over one another.

I straighten my spine and keep the smile plastered. "Please let me know if there's anything else I can do for you."

The minute I exit the doorway and am out of sight, I sag against the wall of the darkened hallway, lean my head back, and close my eyes.

Ryker is here. At my work. Holy shit.

Every part of me wants to bolt. Head down the stairs and walk out of this job—a job I have simply to prove that I'm a responsible adult— and never look back . . . because he's too close. Way too close. And no matter how many ways I try to dice it, this spells disaster.

Huge freaking disaster.

"You okay, sweetie?" a woman asks as she walks by.

"Yes. Thanks," I say softly, suddenly embarrassed that I'm acting this way when I don't let men affect me like this. Ever.

But at the same time, this man in particular knows too much about me. He sees me too well. He makes me feel when I don't feel.

I push away the crushing pressure in my chest. A reminder of the other things Ryker Lockhart has triggered in my life. The memories I can't escape but can't exactly remember.

Get to work, Vaughn. This isn't a big deal. He isn't a big deal.

But deep down I know it is. I know that there's something about Ryker that affects me in ways no one has before.

I'm on autopilot, my mind reeling in ways I don't want to comprehend, as I head to the bar, their drink requests on repeat as a way to calm my nerves. No sooner do I type their orders into the computer than the bartender, Ahmed, presses a kiss to my temple as he scoots around me to his perch behind the bar. "Hi, love. You doing okay?"

"That's debatable." I lean my hips against the counter and look his way. As always, he's dressed sharply: dress shirt, tie, black slacks. The women who come here love him, and he has no problem charming the pants off them more often than not—literally.

"Nine Pod is asking for drinks," he says as he shakes a martini canister.

"Yeah. Yeah. I'm getting there."

"Just letting you know."

But I don't move. My feet refuse to trudge back to my pods because all I keep thinking about is how to avoid going back to the Eight Pod where I have to face Ryker.

"You have to switch back with me," I say to Melissa the minute she walks behind the bar to the computer.

"Hell no." Her laugh floats above the beat of the music. "Any other time I'd say yes, but not tonight. Not only do I have my highest tipper in the Two Pod, but I've also got a hot single doctor in the Three Pod, and damn . . . I'd definitely let him give me a checkup, feel up, anything if he wants to get up with me." She waggles her eyebrows and does a little shimmy as the lights of the club dance over her.

"You don't understand. I'll give you all my tips. I'll—"

"Is it your ex?" she asks, eyes narrowed and expression surprised since I'm the one girl here who never talks about significant others.

"No. I don't have an ex. It's just—"

"I'm sorry, Vaughn. You know I'd help if I could, but I can't bail on these guys. They pay enough to make my car payment in one tip."

Tears burn the backs of my eyes as I stare at her. "Melissa . . . you—never mind." I shake my head and force a smile as hers widens. With a pat on my shoulder in sympathy, she hustles off to the bathroom before her drink order is up.

With a quick glance over to Ahmed, I take the two shots of tequila he hands me and down them in succession without batting an eye.

One for luck, one for courage. I mutter the toast to myself, remembering it from a book I read a few years back, all the while thinking how damn much those six words are needed right now.

I'll definitely need both to make it through this night.

With the tequila suddenly warm in my belly and soon to take the edge off my nerves, I grab my tray of drinks and head back into the lion's den.

Deep breath. Shoulders straight. Head held high.

I enter the Eight Pod.

CHAPTER FIFTEEN

Ryker

My night just went from shitty—having to put up with my client Ken and wanting to leave as soon as we were done discussing his case—to wanting to sit back and stay awhile.

This place isn't my style. Too loud. Too polished. Too damn trendy.

But her? The woman who just walked back into our private VIP area most definitely is.

Vaughn.

Talk about being shocked to hell when I looked up to see her standing before me. Her black skirt short. Her green top tight. Her heels high. And every part of me remembering what her skin tasted like.

But it was her eyes that fucked with me. Those light blue-green eyes that stared back at me were the same ones that looked at me with tears welling in them the other night. They still held fear, but this time I'm pretty sure it was for a completely different reason.

I wanted to demand answers. Ask her who the hell she really is and make her explain why she is working as a goddamn waitress when she clearly doesn't need to.

None of this makes sense.

Not a goddamn ounce of it.

And yet here I sit, listening to Ken drone on and on about his bitch of a soon-to-be ex-wife and how he can't wait to have the freedom to fuck his way through every single one of the women in this room. All bullshit bravado. The man's going to sleep with a few women and then realize what a good woman he had.

His loss. Her freedom. My retainer replenished.

"Here you go, gentlemen," Vaughn says as she steps toward us, eyes avoiding me at all costs, and sets down our drinks.

"Thank you," I say. *Look at me. Let me see you, Vaughn.*

But she doesn't. Instead she just smiles at Ken. "If you need anything else, I'm your girl. I'll be in and out frequently, but if there's anything you need when I'm gone, make sure you push that button right there," she says, pointing to the button on the wall, "and I'll be here in a second."

"In and out frequently? You want me to push your button when I need you? Are you flirting with me, Vaughn?" he asks playfully as I tense at his shitty line.

"Enjoy your drinks," she says, ignoring his comment.

"Where's the manager?" he asks and pounds a fist on the couch beside him.

Vaughn's head startles. "Is there a problem?"

"Yes. Why can't we have you all to ourselves?" he asks with a mock pout. "What if we don't want to share you tonight?"

Vaughn laughs and winks at him. "I'm a lot to handle."

"And I've got *a lot* to handle."

For the briefest of seconds, my teeth grit at his lame attempt to flirt with her. No wonder I need an escort service for my clients. With lines like that, he'd never get laid.

"Good to know," Vaughn says, patting his arm and taking his come-on in stride, "and I'm sure you'll make one of these ladies in here happy tonight."

We all chuckle at her comeback as she moves to the other side of the table before delivering the rest of the drinks on her tray to the women who Ken invited tonight.

Ken and his financial advisor, Gene, turn back to discussing the documents at hand, but my attention is still on Vaughn.

"Ken. Gene. Are we still partying?" a voice booms to my right.

Ken stands up immediately. "You showed!"

"Do you think I'd let you down?" The voice's owner is blocked from my sight by Ken. "And I brought more women."

"You can never have enough," Ken says and steps back, giving me a clear view of the man.

"Ryker Lockhart, is that you?"

"No shit," I say as I rise from my seat when I meet the eyes of Senator Carter Preston. His clothes are still more expensive than they should be, the women on either side of his arms definitely aren't his wife, and they are both doing a crappy job of pretending not to be with him while secretly vying for first place in the who-will-sleep-with-the-shady-senator-tonight race. Out of duty, I reach out and shake the hand he extends. "Carter Preston. Good to see you. What's it been? A year or two?"

He shrugs. "That's a good sign for me. That means I've been winning the good fight."

"I haven't seen you around at The Club at all."

"Too busy running the country," he says and laughs. *Self-righteous prick.* "Ironic to run into you here, though . . . I've been meaning to call you."

"Not now," I warn, letting him know I'm on someone else's billable hours and hoping maybe he's lost my number. "Give me a call at my office, though."

"Sounds good. I'd like you to meet . . ." He turns to look at the women with him and then shrugs without any apology when their names elude him, before turning his attention to Ken and Gene next to me.

It's in that brief moment that I catch a glimpse of Vaughn from across the space. The drink she's lifting onto the tray stops halfway from the table.

If I thought she was surprised at the sight of me sitting here, she pales visibly when she notices Carter.

The shock that flashes across her face is fleeting but not before I see it, and the minute she realizes I have, she beelines it out of the room.

What the hell was that all about?

But I can guess, and it doesn't sit well with me.

The senator is her client. The fact that he uses an escort service doesn't surprise me, but the notion that he's used *her* eats at my mind and urges me to down my drink so that she can get me another.

Has she slept with him? Was her line saying she doesn't sleep with clients just a bullshit excuse? Is that why she looks like she just saw a goddamn ghost?

I'm pulled into a conversation I don't give a rat's ass about, but it takes my mind off Vaughn, so at least there's that. Maybe I head to the john a few times hoping to run into her in the hallway so I can talk to her. Maybe I lean over the railing and watch the club below to see if I can spot her.

And maybe I should just take what the woman beside me is more than offering with the intentional brushes of her body against mine so I can forget Vaughn. No. Not a fucking chance. I don't need the complications that come with it.

"Do I know you?" I overhear Carter ask.

I pull my attention from the club—and the woman at my side—and turn to see Carter's hand on Vaughn's bicep, his eyes studying her, his body all but saying he wants to fuck her.

Jealousy streaks through me. It's ugly and vicious, and I don't really fucking care because Carter's hands are on her when mine aren't.

But Vaughn's expression stops my knee-jerk reaction. Her wariness of him. The way her eyes glint with steel despite the sugary smile that spreads on her face. And I know there's something between them somehow, even if their connection isn't clear.

"I don't think so," she answers. "I'm always asked that . . . I guess I just have a face that everyone thinks they know. Ordinary."

You are nothing close to ordinary.

Far from it.

CHAPTER SIXTEEN
Vaughn

My stomach churns and nerves rattle.

From the grip the senator has on my arm. From the look in his eyes he's leveling at me that says he doesn't trust my answer. From the fact that Ryker is right beside me, watching this very interaction.

Right now, to Ryker I'm still just Saxony—it's something I can deny and not have to prove—but if the senator makes the connection . . . if the senator realizes I'm Vee, the woman who threatened him the other night in my fury, then my cover with both men is blown to hell, and I'm screwed seven ways from Sunday.

The walls are closing in all around me. My separate circles are colliding in a way I never thought possible. Archer with Lola. The senator with Ryker. Ryker with my personal life. All of them at my work.

And so I do the only thing I can think to break Carter's scrutiny of me. When someone walks behind me, I overreact so that when I jolt forward, the tray of drinks in my hands bumps against the senator's chest and upends down the entire front of me.

I shriek at the cold sting of ice that falls into my bustier and hear the gasps of the crowd behind me.

"Idiot," Carter growls as he jumps back immediately to remove himself from the mess at his feet. The women at his sides pat at the drinks splattered on his jacket and coo niceties to him all the while he growls insults at my incompetence.

"Are you okay?" It's Ryker who steps up in front of me.

"Yes, I'm fine." I don't look in his eyes but rather squat down and begin loading the mess of empty glasses and ice on the floor back onto my tray. Anything to get me out of Carter's line of sight.

"Vaughn." He's beside me now, his proximity flustering me as his hands close over a glass at the same time mine does. Like an idiot, I jolt my hand back instantly, the glass falling again.

But I never answer him.

I never respond to my name, which sounds way too intimate coming from his lips.

"Let me help," he murmurs just above the fray of the music.

"I'll get someone to pick this up. To—"

Ryker's hand closing over my forearm halts my words.

I shake my head and stand abruptly, bypassing the dumbwaiter and heading straight for the kitchen myself. Ice clatters out of my top and down through my skirt as I hurry from the pod and to some privacy that might afford me a moment to process what has happened: I just spilled drinks on myself to get out of one trap and ended up falling headfirst into another one—Ryker's.

Ahmed eyes me as I drop the tray on the counter behind the bar. "Can you get one of the guys to help clean up a spill in the Eight Pod?" I ask. He nods, sympathy in his eyes when he assesses the situation— that I dumped a tray upstairs and am morbidly embarrassed—but I'm already heading toward the locker room before he can ask.

Tears threaten for some reason.

And not because of the ice in my bra but rather the unexpected emotions that streaked through me when Ryker said my name.

Christ, even from his simple touch.

When I shove the door open to the locker room, I sigh in relief that it's empty. But its stoic gray walls and matching lockers mirror the tears that I slowly let slip over and slide down my cheeks.

I just screwed up royally, didn't I?

How have I worked here for two years and never seen either of these men, and yet tonight I saw both—and in the same room?

Lowering myself to the bench in front of the lockers, the emotions get the best of me, and the tears come harder.

I feel like this is all going to topple over. This perfectly constructed house of cards I've been shielding from the wind feels like it's going to be blown over any second by a hurricane of my own making.

It's Ryker's fault.

Isn't he the easiest person to blame? He demanded and I complied, and since meeting with him that night, everything has felt so discombobulated for me.

Before Ryker, I could have handled the senator if he'd been in my pod. I would've shrugged off his scrutiny, worried for a few seconds, but still would have known that no one had seen the real me before.

But with both of them together somehow, it's just too damn close.

My fingers absently play with the string bracelet around my wrist, which matches the one Lucy wears. *Suck it up, Vaughn. You don't get to do this. Being weak is not an option. No matter what it takes, you'll make this work.*

Lucy has no other options.

Suddenly angry at myself for my moment of weakness, I straighten my shoulders and am rising to get cleaned up when the door to the locker room shoves open.

Ryker strides in as if he owns the damn place. The momentary pity I felt for myself turns into anger immediately.

What is it with this man always catching me at my most vulnerable?

"Excuse me?" I say, my hands going up to cover my chest in reflex.

"It's nothing I haven't seen before." He takes a few steps toward me.

"Get out."

"Why?" There's a glint in his eyes. It challenges and dares and holds every part of me captive when all I want to do is tell him to go to hell. When all I want to do is blame him for everything that's happened tonight.

But it's not his fault.

It's not even my sister's fault, when I used to be able to blame her for this mess I'm in.

"Fine, if you won't leave, then I will."

Ryker beats me to the door before I can get there. The lock is flipped, shutting the world beyond out, and within a beat, he has my back up against the wall, his sheer size intimidating me from moving.

"Going somewhere?"

"Yeah. Away from you." I ignore the scent of his cologne. The heat of his body. The gold flecks sparking with anger in the brandy of his eyes.

I try to, anyway.

"Not before you answer me."

"I don't have to answer shit." I sneer, furious at him when I'm not sure why, because it sure as hell isn't fear that's coursing through my body with him standing this damn close to me.

"You know what I can't figure out," he says as he leans in closer so his breath hits my lips and makes my body want things it can't have. "Who you are. Are you Vee the madam? Saxony the escort? Or Vaughn the waitress?" His eyes narrow and never leave mine, but they might as well be opening my soul and asking me about my darkest secrets.

I draw in a shaky breath—my own hands are flat against the wall on either side of me. "It doesn't matter, considering none of the three of them are going to give you the time of day."

"Oh, so you're admitting that you are Vee, then."

Christ. "I didn't admit to shit." I grit my teeth and draw in a deep breath that only smells of him to try to calm my temper. "What do you want, Ryker?"

"What if I want a little bit of all three women?" he asks, his words stopping me in my tracks.

"*What?*"

"When we discussed the services I wanted, you promised that I would have one woman, Vaughn. And only one. You stepped into that role, and now it's your job to stay there." His ghost of a smile is smug.

"That's such a bullshit answer."

"It might be bullshit, but we have a contract, *remember?*" He takes a step toward me. "I'm just collecting on what was promised."

I stare at him doe eyed and blinking, his presence confusing me so much that my need to get back to work has fallen by the wayside. "I don't understand you."

"Don't try. I'm a lot to understand."

"But after what happened—why would—how could—"

"I'll save you the trouble and just lay it out for you. You're going to be mine."

"Excuse me?" Every feminist bone in my body bucks at his claim.

"We have a contract, remember?" There's a chill in his tone, a threat that he's not often crossed, and hell if I don't want to cross everything about him off right now. "And you want me just as much as I want you."

"No, I don't."

"Don't lie to me, Vaughn."

"I'm not."

"I want you." Plain. Simple. No hesitation.

"How's it feel to want?"

"Don't tempt me. I'm not a man who works well with restraint."

"Sounds like something you need to work on."

We stand here, inches apart, with bodies vibrating from the tension—sexual, frustrated, stubborn—neither wanting to back down.

But I do. I have to. "I've got to get back to work."

"Eight thousand a night."

It takes my mind a second to catch up with what he's just said. Is he crazy? "No."

"Nine thousand."

"Must be nice to have money you can throw around."

"It is. Ten thousand dollars, Vaughn. I'm sure that's more than you make working here in a few months."

I grit my teeth and want to wipe everything about the moment from my mind. Everything upstairs. Everything with Ryker—before and now. The fact that my dignity and pride is warring against the mountain of medical bills sitting on my desk at home that $10,000 could put a considerable dent in.

But it's still sex for money. It's still me having to provide it. It's still whatever the hell the memory is inside me threatening to sabotage any chance at it.

"No amount of money is worth my dignity," I grit out between clenched teeth as his body brushes ever so softly against mine.

He leans in, lips near my ear, and murmurs, "Everything has a price, Vaughn."

"Contract's null and void." My voice is strong but barely a whisper as he reaches out and runs the back of his hand down the side of my cheek.

My breath stutters. My heart does too, and my heart doesn't stutter. Ever.

"Maybe I should remind you why it's not."

His lips slant over mine. They coax and tempt and taunt and take in a way that makes me want to resist out of pure principle, but holy hell . . . my lips react without my brain consenting. My body burns bright with a heat I don't want to feel. It's his stubble scraping against my chin. It's his lips controlling my heightened sensations. It's him . . .

"No." I shove against him, duck under his arms framing me on either side, and stride across the small area. My breath is ragged, and every part of me wants to walk back over to him and finish what he just started when I know I can't. When I know that something must be wrong with me to want this, to want him . . .

His chuckle reverberates around the small space, and when I turn back around to look at him, his hands are in his pockets and his back is leaning against the door behind him. "You're incredible."

"No! You don't get to do that!" I shout in response to his stupid compliment.

"I don't?"

"No."

"Why's that?"

"Because it's my body, it's my say, and I say no."

"It was pretty clear your body was saying yes."

"This is not going to happen, Ryker. I am not going to be your plaything to fulfill your needs when you see fit. That's not who I am. I have more dignity than—"

"But it's okay for you to make money from others who do it?"

"Business is business," I assert, cautious and curious why he's standing there looking like he's won this debate that he clearly hasn't.

"If business is business, then I'm sure your girls wouldn't be too thrilled if they knew not only was their boss taking her cut, but she was also taking on clients herself. Stealing clients from them." The muscle in his jaw tics as his eyes challenge me just as fiercely as his words do. "It would be a shame if they found out."

Because he's right. I'd have a mutiny on my hands if anyone found out—Lola especially.

"Are you threatening me?" My voice has turned cold where my body still runs hot. Anger, it seems, is something I feel on the ready when he's near.

His simple shrug tells me he is. "It's not a threat when it's the truth."

"There are a lot of truths out there, Ryker," I say, finding my footing underneath me, pissed as hell that he thinks he can threaten me. "You might want to be careful with what you threaten when your truths aren't always the most flattering."

His eyebrows lift, and a ghost of a smile plays at the corners of his mouth. "You were saying?"

"Roxanne?"

His face shows a flicker of emotion—surprise mixed with annoyance that I know his secrets—before he reins it in, jaw clenched, body tense. "Go right ahead. My dirt would hurt me a helluva lot less than yours would hurt you." He steps away from the wall and moves toward me. "Most people in this city know what a bastard I am. Scruples are something I don't claim to have. Most of them think worse of me than the truth, so spill my secrets, Vaughn. I promise you it wouldn't put a dent in the long list of bullshit I've been accused of."

His eyes glint with a darkness that is frightening and thrilling and begs to be tested. Is he serious? Is he that fearless of the repercussions?

"You're bluffing." He wouldn't tell Lola I took her place, would he? He wouldn't blackmail me with the threat of ruining my business just because I won't?

His smile is anything but warm.

When he steps closer, this time I steel myself for his touch. For the fingers that tuck my hair behind my ear, and for the look in his eyes as he angles his head to the side and stares at me.

"Ten thousand a night, then."

"You're insane."

"Do we have a deal, Vaughn?" he asks, saying my name like a man savoring an expensive scotch on his tongue.

"No." A lift of my chin. A squaring of my shoulders.

"I wasn't asking for permission. I was telling you."

"Thanks for the clarification, but it really doesn't change my answer." I step out of his space to gain some air free of his presence. "It's my body. It's my say. And I say no."

"If it's your body, do you mind explaining to me what exactly happened the other night? Why you spooked worse than a virgin on her wedding night? Because I sure as hell know for a fact your body wanted mine."

I don't know why his sudden mention of the other night hits me so soundly when he definitely has every right to bring it up . . . but it does.

"Don't be an asshole," I mutter.

"It seems to be par for the course . . . especially for a woman who had no problem telling me how inadequate I was." His expression is stone faced, but there's an edge to his voice. "What happened the other night?"

"It's none of your business."

"It is my business when I paid for it and especially after you turned the blame on me when I did nothing wrong."

"Just like a man to defer the blame."

"Nice try, but your bullshit won't work this time around."

"I don't have time for this. I've got to get back to work." When I try to skirt past him, his hand is on my arm and my body is against his. Our lips inches apart once again.

"One woman. My choice. That was the promise you made me. And you're the one woman I choose."

"Fine. Yeah. I'll be her," I say with a sarcastic laugh, finally knowing exactly how to beat him at this game. "But I won't sleep with you. Money was paid up front for companionship and nothing else. You said so yourself the other night."

That muscle tics again in his jaw as he grits his teeth and shakes his head ever so slightly in a way that tells me I'm wrong. I will sleep with him.

"This isn't a game, Vaughn."

"Weren't you the one who said everything is a game?" I fire back.

Someone tries to open the door, and we both jump at the sound as the outside world begins to seep back into our conversation. The door that's never locked but now is may draw some attention.

And just as the thought passes through my mind, a fist pounds on it with a muffled "Is everything okay in there?"

"Yes. Yeah. I'll be right there," I shout to the person and then look toward Ryker. "I've got to get to work. This discussion is over. I'll have your refund deposited in your account by tomorrow morning. I'm sorry Wicked Ways let you down."

I attempt to yank my arm from his grasp, but he holds firm. "Refund the money and I'm calling Lola to let her know that her boss replaced her with a client. Tell me no, I'm calling Lola." The arrogance in his voice makes me want to knee him in the balls. "I expect to hear from you within forty-eight hours on whether I'm calling Lola or I'm planning my next meeting with you." Ryker steps back, and his smile is a lethal combination of arrogance, sex appeal, and threat. "It's up to you."

And without another word, he lets go of my arm, unlocks the door, and walks out of the locker room without looking back.

I stare after the door he went through and wonder how this conversation vaguely mirrors the one I had the other night with the senator—threats and ultimatums and claims over my body—and yet my reaction is so very different. While Carter Preston makes my blood run cold, Ryker Lockhart makes every part of me run hot.

Both men are powerful. Both men can destroy this world I've created for myself. But there's only one man who has been in my thoughts way more than he should be.

"Earth to Vaughn." Melissa's voice shocks me back to the present as she lifts her eyebrows, eyes wide, lips in a shocked smile.

"What?"

"Oh, don't give me the I'm-so-innocent crap. Please tell me you were in here getting it on with hot suit guy!"

"Not hardly," I say with a shake of my head before walking from the locker room to go do my job.

Ryker's threat is heavy on my mind.

The taste of anger and desire on his kiss still creates an ache between my thighs.

How is it possible to hate someone and want them all at the same time?

Bastard.

CHAPTER SEVENTEEN
Vaughn

"I'm not ready to sell yet, Ella."

A rich laugh rings through the connection. "You're ready to sell—you're just not ready to give up the daily income that comes with selling your client list."

"True." I load the dishes from the sink into the dishwasher. "I told you I'd let you know when I was ready to get out."

"In the meantime, you're snatching up all the good clients and killing my business in the process."

"Don't expect an apology for that," I joke, repeating the same conversation we've had every couple of weeks for the past two months. Can't say I'm going to complain that a rival escort company keeps calling about buying out my client list.

That is the endgame for me, when all is said and done, after I pay down my debt enough.

"Then I guess I'll just keep calling you then until you say yes," she says.

"I promise you that one day I will."

When I hang up the phone, I startle to see Priscilla standing at the screen door looking at me.

"Is this a bad time?" she asks with her skeptical smile, her reading glasses perched on her beak-like nose and affixed by a chain of beads that wraps around her neck. She passes judgment on me before I even utter a word.

"No. I'm just tired," I say as I open the screen door. "I had a long shift last night."

Long shift? That's an understatement. Ken requested that I stay on in the Eight Pod, even offered to pay my time if I did. I fought it, told my boss I couldn't, but when another server fell ill, guess who stayed at work until closing time? And of course that meant I had the *pleasure* of spending the evening serving drinks to a very drunk Ken and Gene. Of watching women fawn all over Ryker despite the way he sat aloof on the velvet couch with the weight of his stare following my every move. Of making sure to avoid the senator and his curious glances. The ones where he was trying to figure out how he knew me every time we were in proximity of one another. All of that while silently hating Ryker for his stupid ultimatum and at the same time needing to know if he was interested in any of the women fawning over him.

"May I?" Priscilla asks, her eyes widening, perhaps because I haven't invited her in.

"Yes. Of course."

She walks past me, her nylons making a swishing sound as her white orthopedic shoes thump over the floor and into the house. I watch her study my home. She runs a finger over the rustic red farm table that sits in the dining nook and skirts around its yellow chairs. She angles her head into the door of my office to check it out before heading down the hallway without asking if it's okay. She pushes open the first doorway on the right, takes a moment to see the bedroom I've had made up for Lucy. Its soothing blue walls with light-yellow accents and a bed decorated with Lucy's favorite stuffed animals should be enough to tell her I'm ready for my niece to come home.

Priscilla makes a humming sound of approval and heads to the next bedroom, a quick glance in to make sure there isn't anything she disapproves of before moving on.

Exasperated with these random checks that never lead to any progress, I want to tell her the dungeon where I keep my sex slaves is behind the secret wall but don't think it will go over very well with that stick firmly planted up her ass.

"Everything looks good," she says with a clinical smile as she walks into my living room. She takes in the dusty boxes stacked against the far wall. "Are we doing a project?" she asks benignly, and yet we both know she's sticking her nose in.

"No. My sister kept journals for years. I've only recently had the courage to start going through them."

"That must be hard."

I think of what it's like to see Samantha's handwriting, to hear her voice in my head when I read them . . . and to read the unspoken words between the college-ruled pages that deep down I already know to be true. The truths that I swear led her to take her life because she couldn't live with the demons they brought.

"I'm trying to preserve as much of her memory as possible for Lucy. Little stories her mom might have written about. Dates to remember so I can make a baby book Lucy can look at when she's older. Little things," I lie, knowing that my reading through the journals this time around is solely for me. The need to know what happened and how my uncle James plays into it the paramount reason.

Priscilla looks at the stacked boxes for a second before the TV in her periphery catches her attention.

"Oh, a classic. I love a good classic." She falls silent as Audrey Hepburn owns the screen in *Breakfast at Tiffany's*.

"I do too," I murmur, thinking of the one constant I've always had in my life—the old classic movies my mom used to snuggle up on the couch and watch with us. My source of calm and normalcy. We watch for a few seconds before Priscilla's attention turns back to me. "Yes?"

"You've made a lovely place for Lucy here, and it's obvious she loves you dearly."

"But . . ."

"But your financial status is concerning."

I laugh, but it doesn't hold any humor. "My financial status?" I try to keep my voice calm as frustration and anger bubble up inside me. "My financial status is stressed because I paid for treatments for my sister. Lucy's father sure as hell wasn't concerned about Samantha's well-being. His next high was more important than getting her sober and healthy for Lucy. Psychiatrists and expensive medications to combat the pull of the opioids, and then there was special schooling for Lucy and treatments. That's where my debt has come from and—"

"And it's clear that you're slowly paying it down, but your debt-to-income ratio is so high. What's going to happen when you take this special-needs child in who's going to require additional costly services and appointments?"

"What's going to happen? I'm going to love her. I'm going to do anything and everything in my power to give her the best life possible. I'm going to treat her like she's mine and never let her forget her mother or that her mother loved her with all of her heart. That's what's going to happen," I grit out, exasperated by this never-ending bureaucratic red tape.

"I know you're frustrated—"

"You don't know the half of it, Priscilla." My patience is waning and my irritation is mounting. "How is good ol' Brian?" I ask of Lucy's father. "How's his credit rating and debt ratio? It can't be too great when he's spending every dime on drugs. Beg, borrow, and steal always seemed to be his motto."

"You know I can't discuss other guardians with you . . . but he *is* Lucy's father."

"And my sister said she wanted me to take care of Lucy!" I shout, patience now gone. "She wanted me to. Not her father, because she knew how unstable and uncommitted he was to being a parent."

"Your sister wrote her wishes for you to be Lucy's guardian in her suicide note," Priscilla says, her voice softening with a compassion I swear she doesn't have. "Her state of mind at the time of writing the note is in question. It wouldn't be prudent of us to take her words at face value when she was obviously not in her right mind."

I press my fingers to my eyes and stupidly hope the action will combat the tears I'm fighting. She gives me a moment to collect myself before I look back up to her.

"Brian doesn't want Lucy. He never has cared about her before, and now all of a sudden he cares? Does he know what classes she takes and what teachers and therapists help with which subjects and skills? Does he know her medications and her doctors? No. I'm the responsible one. I'm the one busting my ass day in and day out to pay off the debt I incurred trying to take care of my sister. I'm the one who loves Lucy unconditionally and will provide her with the best life she can have. Not him." My voice breaks, and I don't care because I'm exhausted and worried that this all might be for nothing.

"I know, dear. I know you love her, and I'm sorry for the loss of your sister, but there is a protocol. I'm required to follow it, document everything, and in the end all of the information will allow me to make the best decision for Lucy's sake."

Go to hell.

The thought glances through my mind, but the tight smile on my lips reflects nothing of the sort.

"*You* to make or the *state of New York* to make?"

"I work for the state of New York. All of my actions are on their behalf."

"The state's behalf. Not Lucy's. I got it."

"You are making great progress on paying down your debt," she says, disregarding my snarky comment. "I want you to know your hard work isn't being overlooked." Priscilla moves toward the front door, her pen scribbling something on her clipboard. "That place you work . . . you must earn some great tips there."

My smile is still there, still plastered without sincerity. "That's exactly why I work there." And then I shrug, knowing I need to add something to justify it further. A little extra to substantiate any large payments that don't match my weekly paychecks at Apropos. "Plus I've been trying to sell off some of my jewelry to help pay it down. I have some pieces I've been holding on to—items that have been in my family for years. As hard as it is to part with them, having Lucy is way more important to me."

"Well, I'm noting that, and we'll take a look at your updated finances again next month to see where you're at."

I nod and listen to her clatter on until she finally leaves me alone with Audrey on the TV and sadness in my heart. With a sigh, I lower myself to the couch, sink back into it, close my eyes, and just be.

Ten thousand dollars, Vaughn.

Why did I justify the possibility of such a large payment being made toward my debt if I don't plan on even considering Ryker's offer?

Ten thousand dollars.

I want to kick Ryker's voice from my mind. I want to erase everything about him from this moment, and yet it's still there, still loud, still offering me a quicker way to pay down that debt.

Still giving me a chance to take care of Lucy.

How far would you go to protect the one you love?

I ask myself the question and know I've already lost one of the only two people I love in this world.

The other person is wearing a pink-and-yellow string bracelet like the one on my wrist and is probably wearing a princess dress to match it right now.

How far would you go to protect the one you love?

To the ends of the earth.

CHAPTER EIGHTEEN
Ryker

Rapping my pen against the edge of my desk, I review the demands made by Marty's wife's counsel. Ones that would make me laugh out loud at their ludicrousness and bloodsucking tendencies, but once again, I'm only paying partial attention to Martin and his divorce. Once again, my mind is focused elsewhere.

It's on Vaughn.

I glance at my phone for the tenth time in as many minutes and wonder who's going to fold first in this power play.

Vaughn wants to say yes. She knows it. I know it. And her kiss damn well reflected it too.

But she's stubborn. I'll give her that. Stubborn and sexy and maddening, and fuck if I can figure out why it is I'm chasing a woman when she continually says no.

Is it simply the challenge? Wanting the unattainable? Needing to prove to myself and *to her* that she really does want me?

"Fuck it," I mutter as I pick up my cell and dial.

It rings four times and goes to voice mail, and I hang up without leaving a message. Before I can set my phone down, it rings, Wicked Ways the name on my caller ID.

Fucking woman. Always trying to be in control of the situation. I've got to admire her for it. Maybe I'll even let her think she's just that—in control—for a little bit.

"You haven't issued a refund, so should I assume you're willing to admit that the customer is always right and the terms of their contract should be fulfilled to the best of the owner's ability?"

There's a huff on the other end of the line, and I can imagine her sitting there, that blonde hair pulled up, her full lips pressed in a straight line as she tries to figure out how to concede without feeling like she's giving in.

"Vaughn? You called me—it only seems fair you participate in this conversation."

"Being an asshole isn't exactly the best way to get me to talk."

My grin is automatic, her obstinacy frustrating and appealing all at the same time.

"I'm waiting for an answer. It's a simple yes . . . or no."

I can all but hear her thinking. Sure, I've played hardball with her. Pushed when normally it's not worth the trouble . . . but this woman with her wide eyes full of part fear, part tenacity and her body that has tempted but not satisfied me has gotten under my skin when very little does.

"It's far from simple," she says and then falls silent for a beat.

"Not in my book it isn't."

"Who said your book was right, Mr. Lockhart?" she counters.

"Ryker," I assert. Hell if I won't get her to call me my name at some point. "And I'm always right." Her snort of protest fills the line, and I smile. "Yes or no, Vaughn."

"*No.*"

I end the call without another word and lean back in my chair, smile widening to a grin, knowing she's gripping her phone right now cursing me.

"Let's see how long she holds out," I murmur as I stare at my screen.

And when it rings within seconds, I laugh out loud, its sound echoing around my office.

"Lockhart here."

"You hung up on me," she snaps through the line.

"You said no." Silence. "I don't like the word *no*."

I wait for her to say the word again, just to test me.

"No."

I end the call.

She wants a power play? I'll give her one. *Gladly.*

Ring.

That was quick.

Ring.

Why is her temper so sexy?

Ring.

Why is her need to test me even more so?

Ring.

I let it go to voice mail regardless of how much I want to pick up the phone and push her buttons.

I focus on the Matushek brief—words and ultimatums and legalese that I know like the back of my hand—and ignore the vibration of my cell phone until it stops.

And fuck if I'm not disappointed when she gives up so easily.

The afternoon passes in billable hours, one after another, my mind wandering to Vaughn more than it should and wondering how long she's going to let me have the upper hand in this struggle we've got going.

"Mr. Lockhart?" Bella asks through the intercom.

"Yes."

"There is a Vee Saxony on the line for you."

I fight the twitch of my lips. *Vee Saxony.* Can't say the woman doesn't have an ironclad set of balls. Then again, I already knew that.

"Let her through, and hold my other calls."

"Yes."

My phone rings on my desk, and I push the button to answer the transferred call. "Let's get one thing straight," I say in greeting. "When you're with me, you're Vaughn. Not Vee. Not Saxony. Just Vaughn."

"I can't—"

"Uh-uh-uh," I warn.

"You hang up on me, I'm not calling you back again."

"Then don't say no."

It's as simple as that. How well will she obey? And the tense silence tells me she's struggling with her own damn pride and with giving me what I demand.

"You're the one threatening blackmail here." There's a mixture of anger and disbelief in her voice.

I tsk to fight back my laugh. "*Blackmail* is a very touchy word for a lawyer," I say.

"And threatening exposure is a more-than-touchy word for a woman in my position."

"Then do what I say."

"Do you actually think that will work?"

I bite my tongue to keep from saying no. "I'll ask the question again, Vaughn. *Yes or no?* It's quite simple."

"If you're not blackmailing me, then what exactly do you call this?"

"A negotiation. And that's not an answer."

It's her laugh this time that comes through the connection loud and clear. "A negotiation? That's funny." But I don't respond. I let the silence sit. Let the uncertainty eat at her mind and wait for her to speak. "What's in it for me?"

"Your reputation. Your company. Your livelihood. It'll remain intact, and no one—say, for instance, Lola—will ever know you stole one of your girls' clients right out from under her nose."

"I didn't steal—"

"In their eyes it would appear differently."

Her huff fills the line, but her silence tells me she knows I'm right. "And for you? What's in it for you?"

"Getting what I paid for," I state.

"Nothing's ever that simple."

And fuck if she's not right.

"Not everything has to be that complicated," I counter.

"Mr. Lockhart—"

"Ryker," I reiterate.

"Why are you doing this?" she asks softly, and the sudden change in her tone throws me momentarily.

"I told you. I want you. Can't get any simpler than that."

She laughs, but there's something about it . . . about the way it starts out strong and then fades softly. It's the silence, what I feel is her suddenly doubting herself, that gets to me. And then she speaks. *"Ryker."* It's just my name. Not *Mr. Lockhart.* Just Ryker. The name I've wanted her to call me, and yet when she does, there's a vulnerability to it that does shit to my insides. It makes a man whose heart is cold and dead flicker to life. "What if I can't give you what you need?"

And that's the fucking question of the day, isn't it? That's the reason I'm chasing after this woman when I know sure as hell I could have any other one I want with the dial of my cell.

What is it about her that makes me want to be the one she needs?

She's not yours to fix, Lockhart.

"Are you there?" Where her feistiness is sexy, the uncertainty in her voice, the vulnerability in it, is unnerving to me.

She's yours to fuck.

"Do you want me, Vaughn?" I ask the question full well knowing the answer.

I ask the question maybe hoping she says the words so I have a reason to hang up on her and stop whatever bullshit there is inside me that's not supposed to be there.

I ask the question to gain back the upper hand.

"No."
Goddamn stubborn woman.
"There's that word again."
When I hang up on her this time, I know she won't be calling back.
And I hate myself for it almost as much as I enjoy playing the game.

CHAPTER NINETEEN

Vaughn

I glance down at my text and grit my teeth.

> Your forty-eight hours are almost up. I'll give you till midnight and then I'm calling Lola. It's not a threat. It's a promise.

If I thought he'd fueled my temper earlier today, I was wrong. Dead wrong.

Because seeing his ultimatum written down, seeing the threat clear as day, seems to make it more real somehow.

Seems to make it so I can't pretend they're empty words.

I read the text again and hate how talking to him earlier made me feel. How I stupidly let my guard down when I have to act like a professional regardless of how he makes me feel.

And how the asshole is continually trying to gain the upper hand. Damn it.

CHAPTER TWENTY

Ryker

11:58 p.m.

I watch the clock.

It moves at a fucking snail's pace, and for once I'm okay with it. It needs to slow down. I need to buy time.

I mull over the conference call from earlier tonight and the notes I took on it that are sitting on the coffee table in front of me. Another woman out to screw her husband. Another relationship biting the dust because of lies and betrayal.

11:59 p.m.

My cell rings, and I can't help but laugh. I should've figured she was going to play this game in return.

"Can't stay away from me, huh?" I answer.

"Let's get one thing straight here."

"Giving demands, are we?" I ask, amusement in my voice and my dick getting hard at the defiance in hers.

"I'm a woman of my word. I made an agreement with you, and I'll keep it." I love how she turns this into an assertion of her will versus a concession to my threat. "But I meant what I said. I will not have sex with you."

My laugh is quick and disbelieving. "Yes, you will." Pure male ego has the words falling from my mouth, but her absolute silence has me second-guessing it a minute after the truth is out.

But she just said yes. *Halle-fucking-lujah.*

"No—" She sighs when the word escapes and corrects herself. "That's off the table."

"What happened the other night, then? In the hotel room? Don't I at least get an explanation?"

"The other night has to do with fulfilling the terms of our contract going forward. You don't get to make it about my personal life."

My chuckle fills the line—part amusement, part *you're out of your mind.* "You already made it personal the minute I slipped my fingers between your thighs and felt how wet I made you. The minute you pushed me away and lied about how lacking I was in skill. Your insults—"

"Look—"

"No. That's not how this is going to work, Vaughn. You don't get to lie your way out of giving me an answer. I call the shots. I—"

"How do you know the senator?" she asks, her question throwing me so far off the track that I'm surprised I don't have whiplash, but the territorial feeling over her owns me.

"The senator?"

She's slept with him.

"Carter Preston. The senator."

You'll go mad if you keep asking yourself who she's slept with, Lockhart.

I clear my throat and glance to my pad of paper, where I've just written his name in block letters and underlined it. "He's an acquaintance. We have mutual friends and run in the same circles. I see him occasionally. That's all." *Don't ask the question, Lockhart.* "How do you know him?"

"You're free to make assumptions," she murmurs, and fuck if that doesn't feel like a punch in the gut.

"He's a client, then?"

"My client list is confidential, Mr. Lockhart. I would respond exactly the same way if someone inquired if you were a client."

"The difference is I wouldn't care," I lie.

"My answer remains the same, Counselor." There's a chill to her voice, one that warns I'm pushing too hard.

I don't give a shit. I push again. "Did you sleep with him?"

The need to know burns in my gut. The thought of them together even more so.

"It's none of your business what I do when I'm not with you. If you're so set on adhering to the contract, you should remember the terms you set. One woman who was required when you needed her, but who could do whatever she wanted at all other times. Isn't that right?"

Touché.

"So that's how we're going to play this?" I ask, a smile toying at the corner of my mouth, still hating her lack of response but loving the return of her insolence.

"That's how we're going to play this," she deadpans. "We're on a need-to-know basis."

Oh, sweetheart, there's a hell of a lot I need to know, and for the fucking life of me, what started out as a need to know what your pussy feels like wrapped around me has turned into needing to know a whole lot more.

"And I need to know what happened the other night when we were in the hotel room."

I expect the silence I'm met with. It's deafening to the point of being audible. Another thing about her I can't shake—the look in her eyes and the fear in her voice.

And isn't that what makes me an asshole right now?

Obviously she's gone through some kind of shit, and here I am forcing her to be with me.

Something is wrong with me.

"No sex," I say to break the silence.

Definitely fucking wrong with me when I say something like that.

"What?" Confusion edges her tone, but there's nothing like a little shock value to pull her back into the conversation.

"I said no sex." My dick is already pissed at me for the comment. Already rebelling and hating me since it wants her desperately. But I've learned with witnesses on the stand that the best way to get what you want is to go the reverse psychology route. Change the rules around. Take the offer off the table so it owns their mind.

She'll come around.

No fucking doubt there.

"You're right," I repeat. "No sex."

Her stuttered laugh fills the line. I can all but hear her mind trying to figure out what I'm trying to pull. *Mine's right there with you, sweetheart.*

But I know what I'm doing.

When Vaughn decides to sleep with me, it's going to be because she wants to. Because she needs to. Not because of some damn contract I pushed her to fulfill just so I can have her.

"I don't—"

"I'll send you my schedule later. Where you need to be and when. Or I can always pick you up at your place. I'll just need your address."

"That's personal."

We're going to get a whole lot more personal.

"What's your last name?"

"That's personal, too, and why does my last name matter?"

"Because who you are always matters." I know I've gotten her with that one, and just like a cross-examination in court, I want to leave her with no doubt where we stand. Me in control and her wanting to take it back. "I'll be in touch." And without letting her respond, I end the call.

With lips pursed, I stare at my cell and try to figure out what the hell just happened. I may have just gotten in the last word, but I sure as hell don't feel like I got the upper hand.

Questions circle in my litigator's mind. Why does Vaughn work both jobs? What is the connection, if any, between the club Apropos and Wicked Ways? Why is she petrified of pissing off Lola if I were to follow through with my threat? What is she so intent on covering up besides the obvious illegality of the overall business?

And what the fuck happened to her? A madam who is scared of sex doesn't quite go hand in hand.

I try to connect the dots to the questions I'd typically ask my investigator to find out for me . . . and yet I don't pick up the phone or type an email to Stuart to have him start digging.

Standing from my chair, I skirt around my desk and walk to the wall of windows in front of me. The city buzzes. Taxis litter Park Avenue below, and the street vendors serve food to the people lining up for a quick bite to eat. Everyone on a fast-paced mission to the next meeting, the next event, the next anything—all of them moving with a definite purpose.

What the fuck are you doing, Lockhart?

Paying a woman ten grand for her company without the promise of sex? What if she never gets over whatever her issue is? What if I waste all this time chasing a woman just to be left with my dick in my hand—unserviced and unsatisfied? What if she holds me to what I just said? No sex?

I laugh—long and loud—with a shake of my head.

I wouldn't put it past her to stand her ground simply to screw me over.

Not in the least.

CHAPTER
TWENTY-ONE
Vaughn

The train's horn is in the distance. Its hollow whistle a definite warning for anyone daring to cross its tracks.

The light is dim in our room, but I know Samantha is in here. I can hear her soft snores from where she sneaked in to lie in the big canopy bed beside me. Its shadow on the wall opposite me looks like monsters. Big, scary four-legged monsters that slink into little girls' bedrooms, so they pretend to be asleep when the door opens.

I squeeze my eyes tight to shut out the other monsters lurking in here—real ones—and am thankful for her snores. For how she all of a sudden started wanting to creep into my room at night and sleep in my bed, even though she's cool now and tells her friends she doesn't like me.

But she doesn't come every night. It's those nights that the monsters want in more.

The horn again. *Toot. Toooot.*

The room lights up some as the door creaks open. Glass clinks against glass before the sound of a bottle being set on my dresser. The music is on downstairs again—the kind without words composed by the man with the white wig who played them forever ago. It's fancy music for another party of people who talk way too much about things that make no sense: inflation rates, GDP, capital, depreciation. Things I don't understand but that Uncle James is constantly being praised and awarded for. *Boring.*

But right now I wish I were down there with the boring people instead of up here.

Right now I wish I could go back to sleep and not be scared.

The floor creaks, and I stiffen when the hand slides over my mouth. My body jerks in awareness, in fear, but when I breathe in, I smell the icky smell of the absinthe he drinks mixed with his fancy eau de gross cologne and the cloves of his cigarettes.

It's just Uncle James.

Not a monster.

Just him not wanting me to yelp and wake Sam up.

Just him knowing the train scares me when it sounds off in the middle of the night.

Just him telling me that even with a house full of people, he remembered and came up here to make everything all right.

Toot. Toooot.

But there is no *"Hey, Vaughny, want to come dance to the music with me?"* No *"I have friends over tonight, but I'd rather come snuggle with you."* No *"You know you're my favorite girl?"*

Toot. Toooot.

I open my eyes. It's his face I see. His dark eyes warning me to stay quiet. His hand pressing harder against my mouth. His breath in my ears—harsh and rapid. *Excited.* The weight of his body as he lies partially on me. The scrape of his fingers as he begins to run them up my leg, my nightgown going with it.

The confusion.

Absinthe on his breath.

The churning in my tummy.

Cologne on his skin.

His murmured voice in my ear. "You're beautiful, Vaughny."

123

Cloves on his fingers.

Toot. Toooot.

I jolt awake.

Heart racing.

My room.

Pulse thundering in my ears.

My house.

My empty bed. The same annoying light from the neighbor's backyard trying to blaze through my blinds. And I'm so grateful for that light.

For the visibility to reassure my racing heart that it was all a dream.

Even when my head knows it was much more than a dream.

With one hand clutched over my stomach and the other over my mouth, I fight the bile that threatens. Combat the sudden pressure that's weighing on my chest. Struggle with a memory I just dreamed clear as day but can't remember what happened next.

I'm awake, but it's his eyes I see now. His scent I smell still. The revulsion I still feel just like the other night with Ryker.

My breath is shaky when I draw it in, the sound reverberating around the room and coming back to assault my ears.

It's been twenty years since we lived in that house. The mansion on the hill that overlooked the valley where the train would go by at scheduled times during the night. The one where the conductor would pull the whistle, a secret warning that for those of us on the right side of its track, no one would believe us even if we told the truth.

We may have belonged in that world, but we never fit in.

And I never want to.

I sit in the silent turbulence of my room and try to remember what happened next. Try to fill in the missing pieces when the churning of my stomach already tells me.

But how is it possible that I can't remember?

Was it that bad that my brain doesn't want to remember? And if that's the case, why is it deciding now to bring it back?

On shaky legs, I scoot out of bed. The shower is scalding but a necessity as my mind continues to search its dark recesses and fears them all at the same time. I scrub scents on my skin that are long gone but whose invisible stains still remain.

Sleep evades me.

Every creak of the house winding my imagination into a tailspin of thoughts.

Samantha's journals call to me. Ask me to read them. To listen to her voice again when maybe I missed something the first time around.

So with a blanket wrapped around my shoulders—suddenly chilled in my house when the thermostat says I shouldn't be—I sit on the couch and open one of her boxes at random. I stare at the journals stacked on end inside. My sister's affinity for green is more than apparent in the array of bound notebooks in that hue. The sight of them makes me smile when right now I didn't even know that I could.

Without discretion, I pick up the first one that calls to me. Its edges are broken, the kelly-green fabric frayed to reveal brown cardboard beneath. The dates on the cover showing when it was written make my breath catch. I was ten and Samantha was twelve.

Toot. Toooot.

The sight of her handwriting brings me back instantly. To the words she'd scrawled on the bottom of her headboard that were kept hidden by the tons of pillows placed there. Her *favorites* she called them. Words like *endure, withstand, strength, persist, hope.* All written in black Sharpie, thick letters with doodles around them to help her remember them.

Lost in time, I read through her writing. Most of it is rambling, complaints about things she wanted to do some day, silly things about the kids at school, aspirations she had for our futures . . . but every couple of entries her words make my heart hurt.

"I wish you were here, Mom. Vee and I miss you. I wonder if it's different for her since she had less time with you than I did. I wonder if having more memories is better or worse? More means I miss you because I know what I'm missing out on since we had nine years together . . . but at least I knew you while Vaughn only gets to wonder what you were like. It's just different now. So different. There's no one who . . . never mind. Love you."

I wipe the tears sliding down my cheeks, oddly comforted that we shared similar thoughts about who missed our mom more after her death.

Flipping the pages, being an adult now and seeing her life through her eyes as a teenager is bittersweet. But the entries become sparse for a time before they return with a melancholy edge to them. An edge that one could dismiss perhaps as hormones being in full swing, but that my mind internalizes and connects dots that have been randomly plotted.

"It happened again today. This can't be okay. But if someone found out, what would they think of me? He's him . . . no one would ever believe me."

"Can you make damaged goods whole again? Or once you're damaged, are you broken forever?"

"I told my teacher today. Finally. She laughed at me and told me there's no need to tell lies to get attention. An upstanding citizen like him would never do that. Ever. But little girls who've lost their mom might lie because that's the only way they feel they'll be heard."

"If I ran away, would anyone look for me? But if I left . . . who would take care of Vaughn? There's no way I can leave her here. She's all I have."

That's the last line scrawled on the ending page of the journal, and those words are like a punch to my solar plexus.

I'm unsure how long I sit on the couch, trying to think back, trying to remember the things that seem so foggy to me, as I stare at that line before finally succumbing to exhaustion.

◆ ◆ ◆

"You look like hell."

"Gee. Thank you for that lovely compliment, Joey. You look so refreshed yourself," I say with a roll of my eyes, waving him into my house.

Of course, he's right. I do look like hell: no makeup on, bags under my eyes, my hair a mess . . . but I got to hang out with Lucy, so my day was better just because of her.

"Everything okay?" he asks, tone lowered, expression softening.

"Yes. I'm fine. I, uh . . . just didn't get much sleep last night."

He eyes me for a second, almost as if he's going to ask more, and I sigh with relief when the curiosity fades from his face before he glances over to where Lucy is engrossed in her daily exercises on her computer.

"Did you guys have a good day?" He walks in and takes a seat at the table.

"Of course. Arts and crafts."

"Ah, her favorite."

I motion over to the kitchen counter, where there is a blur of oranges and reds and yellows. "We made some fall decorations for the house and for her room. She said that she wanted us to both have the same thing so that we could pretend we were together." Her words still echo in my ears and cause a pang in my heart.

Joey notices the sadness come across my face but just nods measuredly. "I'll make sure to help her hang them when we get back." He smiles when Lucy giggles out loud at something in her lesson. She looks up and waves animatedly at him before pointing to the computer and returning her attention to the voice speaking to her in her headphones. "You could always come back with us. Tonight's movie night. We could watch the movie, and then you and I could grab a quick bite to eat after. Just to talk about Luce."

My mind immediately shifts to Ryker and our planned date tonight. To my unease over it and my confusion as to why a small part of me deep down is excited at the same time.

It has to be because I'm exhausted.

That's the only way I can reason it.

Looking over to Joey as I move into the kitchen, I smile softly. "That sounds like a perfect night, and as much as I'd much rather be with you guys tonight, I already have plans."

"Then cancel."

"It's not that easy," I say with a shake of my head and the sound of Ryker's threat in my ear. "It's an obligation I have to fulfill."

"So, it's not a hot date you're blowing us off for?" he jokes with a laugh.

"Not a hot date."

His eyes meet mine. There's humor in them and something else I can't quite read. "Then maybe another time?"

"Maybe." I nod subtly. "Working nights makes it hard to do anything."

"It must be exhausting."

"Walking on heels for six hours straight in any job is exhausting." I laugh.

"Do you meet many men?"

"What do you—"

"I mean, you're a gorgeous single woman. What better place to meet a successful man than the überswanky club you work at."

"I'd have to be looking first." I turn on the sink and begin to wash the dishes from Lucy's snack. "And second, most of the guys there are either married or too damn stuck on themselves for me to ever consider giving them the time of day."

"You're not looking? Everybody's always looking," he says through a laugh. It's followed by an awkward silence I'm more than happy Lucy interrupts when she throws her arms up.

"All done!" she exclaims.

She moves across the room and wraps her arms around my waist as is her habit when she's unhappy

"Safety blanket," Joey murmurs in acknowledgment of Lucy's habit of using my comfort as a way to avoid facing the fact she has to leave.

Lucy and I say our goodbyes. Butterfly kisses followed by Eskimo kisses and then a secret handshake that changes every time we share one. A few giggles over jokes we made and a lot of promises about the fun we'll have next time. We collect her decorations, and as Joey grabs her bag, I'm already longing for the next time I get to see her again.

"I really appreciate you picking her up, Joey."

"It's no big deal."

"You know it's not expected, and it's not something you have—"

"I know it isn't . . . but it's on my way in to work, and it's easier on her saying goodbye here rather than at the facility. Besides, we might just have a favorite ice-cream shop that we frequent before we head in."

He winks at Lucy as her face lights up, the prospect of her beloved rainbow sherbet enough to take the sting out of this goodbye.

"Well, thank you. I appreciate it and you more than you know."

Our eyes hold for the briefest of seconds before I give her one last hug and watch them head down the walkway talking animatedly.

CHAPTER TWENTY-TWO

Vaughn

The extravagance of the restaurant is astounding. The exclusive member club is well hidden among the subway stops and endless sidewalks of Manhattan. Even my walk past the mahogany-lined walls toward the tuxedo-clad maître d' gives no hint of what lies beyond the wall at his back.

"Are you here for the event?" he asks, his voice soft, his smile guarded.

Event? He didn't say anything about an event.

"I'm here to meet with Ryker Lockhart."

He eyes me for a second. "So that's a yes. Name, please?"

"Vaughn," I say, realizing that I am not comfortable giving my last name and opening myself up to Ryker knowing it.

"Vaughn?" he asks with a lift of his brows as if he's expecting more, and I just smile sweetly, feeling way out of place.

"Yes."

He makes a humming noise as he looks at the list in front of him and then gives a resolute nod before looking back up and smiling. "Right this way."

He guides me around a wall and into the belly of the restaurant. A cigar lounge is on the right side, its enclosed walls made of glass. Smoke swirls around the small space, and men are leaned back in leather recliners, sleeves rolled up, smiles wide, postures relaxed. On the left is a wine room, racks lining its walls with dark-colored bottles filling their grooved notches.

The room is laid out before us. People mingle here and there, a desirable ratio of men and women wearing expensive clothes and casual smiles. The club is distinguished by its dark decor with chairs in rich blues and its money . . . definitely money. The room reeks of it: in the gold Rolexes dripping from the wrists of the men seated here and there, in the bottles of private label Macallan sitting atop the tables, in the unaffected glances the men in the room give my way. The ones that say if they wanted me, they could have me . . . because that's just how the privilege in their lives has allowed them to live.

My spine stiffens as I walk. My shoulders square and my chin lifts some.

They don't know who I am. All they know now is that I'm here with them.

Not that I'm here because of blackmail.

Then again, it's probably something many of them have done to get where they are . . . just like the man I'm here to meet.

And that single thought causes the subtle anticipation I was feeling about seeing him to spark into defiant anger again.

That spark only burns brighter when I see him. He's leaning back in a chair, a highball glass in one hand, his attention turned toward a few male counterparts standing in front of him. His shirtsleeves are rolled up to his elbows, a dark-gray vest is hugging his torso, and his slacks are hiked up some so that he can sit with his ankle over his knee.

Elegant. Refined. Sexy. Striking.

And the spark of anger ignites into something deeper and darker within me that I'm afraid to acknowledge. I'm physically attracted to him. To his looks and his laugh and his air of superiority that I can't stand but that is somehow seemingly sexy on him.

My thoughts and libido war. Feeling trapped for being here and wanting to be here merely because he does things to my body, to my sensations, in a way that makes me feel a little chaotic, a little out of control, when control is how I've governed every part of my life.

This is not me. Not the woman I know.

But the minute his words stutter to a stop on his lips when he sees me, the conflict in my head burns out, and the fire heats up every other part of my body.

The men he's speaking with take notice of his sudden preoccupation and turn to face me, but it's Ryker who suddenly has my heart leaping in my throat. It's the oh-so-slight lift of one eyebrow as his eyes slide down over me. It's the subtle tic of his jaw that is barely there but that lets me know the outfit I spent forever picking out—the sophisticated pantsuit with the cutouts on the neckline—was the perfect choice. It's the way one side of his mouth curls up into the slightest of smiles.

"Gentlemen, if you'll excuse me," he says to them without breaking eye contact with me, before rising from his seat and closing the short distance.

I hold my breath as he does, and I'm not sure why I do.

"Mr. Lockhart? Ms. Noname for you," the maître d' says. My eyes whip to his while Ryker chuckles.

"Thank you," Ryker says.

"Noname?" I ask.

"Your last name was too personal, remember?" Our eyes hold, an audience of attention weighing our interaction they can't hear as I try to process how to react.

"Still is," I murmur as laughter rings out on the other side of the room, drawing my eyes, but his are still on me when I look back at him. "You can't hang up on me now, so what are you going to do?"

"Cute," he says with a lopsided ghost of a smile.

"I try to be." We stare across the space for a few moments. "An event?"

"Mm-hmm."

"I thought we were having dinner."

"We are."

"Care to elaborate?" There's something about his stare—the one that says he's looking to devour me—that has my throat going dry.

"This is my club."

"Do you have to do something special to join this club?" I ask as he puts a hand on my lower back and guides me to his table.

"Yes."

"This is the part where you actually use more than one-word answers so that I know what's expected of me."

"Just like it's important for you to give me answers too." Ryker smiles at a couple to the left of us as I notice the sly looks others give our way. Either I'm grotesquely out of place or they're not used to seeing Ryker with a woman.

I'm not sure which answer I'm rooting for most . . . because I'm not sure if I want to fit in here.

"I give you answers," I say as he pulls out a chair for me at a quiet table in the corner. Glass windows are on two sides of it, the club high enough to see into the distance—the Statue of Liberty, the lights twinkling—so that it feels like we are on our own island in the sky.

"Like Ms. Noname?" he says with a quirk of a brow and a slight smile. I sigh. "A simple answer is all it requires, Vaughn. Last name?"

I give him the one answer I know will make him stop asking. "Lockhart," I deadpan.

"And Noname is good." He gives a definitive nod while I laugh. He shakes his head as he takes his seat and stares at me across the short distance.

"So the event? The club? Care to tell me if I was supposed to knock three times while hopping on one foot to gain access?"

His eyes light up as he glances at the extravagance around him that he blends into seamlessly. "It's a status thing."

"You're not answering my question."

"Your income has to be at a certain level. You have to give a certain amount annually to charities. You have to—"

"Come from the right bloodline?"

He leans back and brings his drink to his lips while staring at me above the rim. "Why do I get the sense if that were the case that this would all bug you?"

"It bugs me even if it isn't the case."

"Why?"

It's a simple question. One I know the answer to.

But answering would be giving away too much of myself. It would be letting a man who clearly fits in this world too deep into my life.

"More to drink, sir?" the waiter asks as he steps forward and appears out of what I swear is nowhere, only adding to my discord when he solely addresses Ryker and acts like I don't exist.

"Yes, please."

The waiter begins to pour his drink, and the clink of the bottle against the glass has the waiter wincing, and all of a sudden, the churning in my belly again.

"Vaughn?"

The clink of glass against crystal.

"Hmm?" *Focus, Vaughn.*

Absinthe.

"Are you okay?" Ryker asks.

I shake my head as my mind tries to pull itself from the abyss of memories it has been struggling to come to terms with. "Yes. Yeah. Fine."

"You sure?"

I look up and meet his eyes and force a smile. "Yes."

The waiter looks at both of us and reels off the specials for the evening, but I don't hear a word he's saying.

Was that my trigger the other night? Was Ryker pouring his drink from the decanter—the distinct clink of glass on glass—what charged my mind to pull up the memory?

The scent of wealth, the clink of crystal, the air of authority.

Were those the things that helped to blindside me?

"Thank you, Bernard," Ryker says, pulling me from my thoughts.

"So you're ready to order then?"

"Yes, thank you. I'll have my usual, and the lady will have the filet, medium well, a garden salad, the potatoes, and a glass of the Promontory Cabernet Sauvignon 2010."

"Thank you, but I'd prefer the white sea bass with the truffle mac and cheese and a glass of your house rosé, please," I assert, miffed that he thinks he can order for me when he doesn't even know me and ticked off that Bernard started writing it down as if my voice doesn't matter.

And a whole lot relieved to have this fight to pick instead of focusing on the ideas owning my thoughts.

Bury it. Shove it all away. Deal with it later.

"That's a mistake—she'll have what I said."

We wage a visual war of wills, and I don't look away from him when I speak. "No, I'll have the fish, please."

Ryker huffs out a sigh, his eyes boring into mine as the poor waiter stands at the edge of our table and looks from Ryker to me and then back again. "You ate a filet the other night."

"That was over a week ago. A lot of things can make you change your mind in a week's time." I smile tightly at him before turning my attention to Bernard, patiently shifting his feet, uncomfortable from overhearing our spat. "The fish, please."

"Jesus Christ," Ryker mutters under his breath. "At least choose a wine that's worth a shit."

"The house rosé, please, Bernard."

"Very well." Bernard nods and then steps back as if to escape any more of our argument.

I turn to face Ryker's glare. "I'm capable of handling my own order, thank you," I say.

"It's polite for a gentleman to order for the woman."

"It's even more polite to ask the lady what she wants." I lift my eyebrows in challenge. "Desires change on a whim."

"Not for me they don't," he says and lifts his glass to his lips as if to dare me to argue with him.

I look around the room and know this place is so very different from what I'm used to on a date. *Date?* Is that what I'm calling this now? This is more like an obligation.

An obligation with a very handsome man. One who thinks he can order dinner for me. In a very elite club, might I add.

In my need to figure out how I feel about all of this, I think back to the last date I had. God, was it really four months ago? It was Chinese takeout on the Lower East Side with chopsticks that wouldn't work and a good-looking-enough guy who was too handsy, talked too much on his cell phone throughout our dinner, and definitely didn't get laid regardless of how hard he tried.

Ryker hasn't picked up his cell once. Come to think of it, he didn't the first disastrous night we met either. And when I look back at him, his attention is on me—unnervingly so. It's always on me.

Even when I don't want it to be . . . like right now.

A tense silence settles between us that fits his mood—on edge, unsettled, intense.

"What's the event for?" I change topics, hoping to lighten the mood, and his subtle nod acknowledges it.

"It's to raise money for SPD. I have to remember what that—"

"Sensory processing disorder," I say without thought.

The slight lift of his chin says he's surprised by my response. So am I. "Yes, that's it, though I doubt many know that."

"So . . . what? You guys have a big party to socialize, call it a charity event just so you have somewhere to toss your extra money simply because it's a tax donation and you need them?"

His back stiffens some. He can insult his kind, but an outsider, not so much. *So much for easing the tension.*

"If that's how you want to phrase it," he says carefully, his eyes surveying the room before turning his attention back to me. "How do you know what SPD means?"

Lucy's face lights up my thoughts. Her sweet smile. Her absolute freak-outs over socks with seams in them, tags in clothes, and the feel of her panties on her body.

"That's personal," I respond with a purse of my lips as I reach for his drink and take a sip of whatever is in his glass. I'm not sure if it's whiskey or bourbon or scotch, but whatever it is, it's strong and gross and burns my throat, but I refuse to show him any of that.

"Personal?"

"Mm-hmm," I murmur, uncertain how this conversation started out playful and now seems so damn tense. "Where does the money you're raising go to? What does it fund?"

"Why do I feel like you have me on the stand, Counselor?" he asks, eyes narrowing, lips pursing, but I don't apologize.

"Does anyone here even know or care?"

"I can't speak for some of the people in here as it's not my favorite of crowds—"

"Then why are you here?"

He leans in, voice low, eyes glinting from being questioned. "Because sometimes you have to do things you don't want to do, be places where you don't want to be with people you don't know if you really like . . . because that's the best thing for your business. For your reputation. A way to keep the sharks at bay. Even with assholes."

And the way he looks at me—the deep intensity in his gaze—tells me he knows that's exactly how I felt coming here tonight. My hand forced and my curiosity piqued even when I didn't want it to be.

"Even with *the* asshole."

He leans in closer and lowers his voice. "I know what SPD is. I know the charity we're supporting and the R & D it's funding. This club may be stuffy, it might be filled with sharks, but we get together once a month, support a cause, and then go on our merry fucking ways. I realize you think I'm a bastard with money, but that doesn't mean I'm reckless with it."

"You sure about that?" I counter, the $10,000 that was deposited in my account an hour before my arrival time proof to the contrary.

"So much hostility from someone who's a plus-one."

I glare at him again, although his eyes are back on the room, and I grit my teeth at his attempt to put me in my place. "Pardon me—I wasn't aware I was being paid to sit here with my mouth shut."

"And don't forget the 'look pretty' part." His condescending chuckle fills the space as my hands grip the edge of my chair, never more aware of my position in this arrangement we have than now. "It seems to me you walked in here with a chip on your shoulder tonight, Vaughn . . . or is it *Vee*?" There's a smug smirk that plays on his lips and taunts me just like his words do. "If you're going to have a business that caters to wealthy men, then I think you need to come to terms with what pays to butter your bread."

Fuck you.

The words are on my tongue, but I bite them back, cognizant that we are pushing each other's buttons in a game I'm not sure of the point to.

I stand up from my chair abruptly, temper on fire and pride front and center. "I take their money, but I sure as hell don't cater to them," I lie.

"To me, you will."

CHAPTER TWENTY-THREE

Ryker

Temper wars across that gorgeous face of hers, and a sneer mars her lips.

"Is there a reason you glare at every man who looks this way and then get pissy with me as if I invited their attention?" she asks.

"No." I say the word but know she's right. Know that every time a man looks too long her way, I wonder if he's hired her before. She may be the madam now, but she had to start somewhere, didn't she?

"Ryker?"

I look back her way after staring at Darrin and Pete—both men I know who frequent the escort realm—and catch the slight lift of her eyebrow. But there must be something about the look on my face that gives away my thoughts, because sure as shit, I can see the shift in her expression as she makes the realization.

She laughs but there's sarcasm lacing it. "Let's get one thing straight. I didn't show up here tonight so you could spend the whole time wondering who else in this room I might have slept with. *One*, it's none of your business if I have or if I haven't. And *two*," she says, jabbing her finger against the expensive linen tablecloth, "if you want everyone to know I'm yours, then start treating me like I am . . . because right now you're so far off the mark I might as well spend the time I'm forced to be here looking for new clients."

"That's not what I was—"

"Yes, it was," she asserts as she takes a step back before giving a long survey of the room around me much as I was doing. Just the idea of her going home with any one of those fuckers irritates the hell out of me. When her gaze returns to mine, she gives me a quirk of her eyebrow and the snark in her smile I've come to expect, eyes challenging me. "Bernard's slow. I need a drink."

Her words knock the fight momentarily out of me to the point that by the time I have my footing beneath me, Vaughn is striding across the room to the bar. Her hips are swaying and her hair is swinging and fuck if my gaze isn't following her like everyone else's in here is.

Shit. I blow out a breath and down the remainder of my drink. The burn is there but not as potent as the taste of regret.

She's right. Damn right, and I know why my thoughts veered to who she's been with, and fuck if it's not because of Senator Carter Preston.

When he strode into my office earlier today with that stick planted squarely up his ass, my first thought was Vaughn. Vaughn and their strange interaction at Apropos along with the nagging feeling that he's hired her in the past.

That she's slept with him.

To say the idea didn't sit well with me was an understatement. Still is as I watch her walk and know how many guys in this joint would kill to have someone as gorgeous as Vaughn beneath them.

Hell, I've used escorts before. One here and there over time, but after Roxanne . . . after Roxanne I was reminded of the crazy that can come with women and the webs they want to tangle you in—as if having my mom for a mother wasn't enough of a lesson—that I figured I wanted the emotion removed from the necessity and curse of most men: *sex.* I wanted the sex but the hope for more to be nonexistent.

So I was referred to Wicked Ways.

I was good with my decision to use Wicked Ways. The professionalism of Vee. The promises she made that were to my liking. The reputation that had been talked about in some of my circles: the high-boothed whiskey bars where men say they need to go to unwind after a long day's work. The need to have some uncomplicated sex while the whole taste of Rox was washed from my mouth.

But fuck if I know why I'm pushing so hard for Vaughn. For her smart mouth and sweet body. And since when do I care who she's been with so long as her tests are clean and when she's with me, she's mine?

She's a constant contradiction. She looks like she fits in this scene, and yet disdain drips off her. She is sex personified with her gorgeous curves and flawless skin, but I'm not allowed to touch her. I'm paying for her time, yet it seems she wants nothing to do with me.

Maybe because you blackmailed her, you asshole. Threatened to out her to her girls unless she followed through with seeing you.

If you want everyone to know I'm yours, then start treating me like I am . . .

Her words ghost through my mind just as Leland St. Germain strides up to her at the bar.

I'm out of my seat and on the move without thought just as his laugh sounds off and their hands shake in greeting.

"Vaughn?"

Both of their heads startle my way at the sound of my voice. St. Germain's expression is pissed while hers is smug. She just got exactly what she wanted, and I played perfectly into her hand.

"Yes?" she asks, voice innocent, body a temptation to sin.

"Leland, good to see you," I say as he smiles and nods. "I don't mean to interrupt, but I need my date for a second."

Vaughn's eyebrows spark up as her lips ghost a smile. "I'll be there in a minute. I was just making the acquaintance of Mr. St. Germain here."

St. Germain, not Leland. Mr. Lockhart, not Ryker. Her way of telling me she's looking for clients.

Fuck that.

"This can't wait," I assert as I reach out and put my hand on the inside of her arm and all but pull her to go with me. "Leland," I say with another nod and a dose of back-the-fuck-off in my glare.

"What—?"

"In a minute," I say as I lead her by the arm out of the main room toward the front hallway.

People notice.

I'm sure tongues will be wagging. Gossip about how Ryker Lockhart went into a jealous rage when his date was cozying up to his rival and dragged her from The Club.

Something men in The Club don't do publicly, but hell if I haven't heard about their bullshit tendencies privately.

Gossip will fly about Ryker Lockhart, the ruthless shark in court and the stoic, untouchable man outside of it, who just flashed his temper.

Well, let them talk.

Let people outside The Club know.

I don't fucking care.

"What the hell are you—"

My lips close over hers. Her back is against the wall just beyond the dining area, and my hands are twisting in her hair and fuck if I don't take what I want. With lips and tongue and greed I've rarely felt before. She fights against me, hands pushing, head moving, and then it shifts to want, hands fisting, throat moaning—and every single exaggeration that will be thrown out into the gossip mill is worth it.

Fucking hell will it be worth it.

She tastes of wine and resistance. A resistance not to the kiss but to me, and fuck if it doesn't turn me on more.

"Excuse me," someone mutters behind me as they walk past us, and the voice shocks me to my senses. To what I'm doing. To how every part of me knows this is nowhere near enough of her.

I drag my lips from Vaughn's. From the taste and the need and the darkness, and I know now more than ever that this woman is testing my sanity. I kissed her hoping it would sate that need burning inside me, but I realize instead it just threw gasoline on it. Her eyes are wide with an incompatible mixture of mistrust and desire.

"Let's get out of here."

CHAPTER TWENTY-FOUR

Vaughn

I glance in Ryker's direction. His expression relaxed but the tension set in him troubled. His tie is undone and draped around his neck, the collar of his shirt unbuttoned, and he's holding my heels in one of his hands at his side.

Central Park is gorgeous at night.

As a woman, I've never really thought of it as a place to frequent after dark. I'm typically alone, and trouble isn't something I invite. But walking through it right now, with the soft lights casting a glow, the skyline as a backdrop, and a more-than-handsome man beside me, dare I say it feels somewhat romantic? Dare I say I want to close my eyes and memorize the grass beneath my feet, the sound of the laughter floating across the open space, the slight scent of Ryker's cologne?

It has to be because of the wine.

It might have been only one glass, but I never think in terms of romance. I only visit the park to take Lucy to play. I only notice the soft glow of lights to make sure a parking lot is illuminated on the way to my car. And I never look at a man with anticipation and wonder what it will be like when we have sex.

Because that is where this is heading—obviously—I just hope that this time I can do it without the past rearing its ugly head. I just hope that hint of whatever he made me feel that first time returns to make me feel alive again.

"You haven't spoken since we left," I say and recall everything that ensued. The breath-stealing kiss he gave me that prompted us to leave The Club. The utter want and fear that we were heading someplace to have sex. The confusion that followed when his driver dropped us off here—in Central Park, of all places. "Do you want to talk about what's wrong or explain what that was all about or . . . I don't know, tell me why you're in such a foul mood?"

He slides a glance my way, and his sigh is audible as he shakes his head. "Shitty day," he murmurs but doesn't expand.

"So you figured you'd take it out on me?"

"Took on a new client I'm not a fan of."

"Then why'd you take him on? You're big enough, well known enough—I'm sure saying no wouldn't hurt you."

"Mmm." It's the only sound he makes as we pass a group of people sitting on the grass. They're a little intoxicated, and something one of them says makes me laugh even though I shouldn't be listening.

"This new client is a man, I presume?"

"Mmm."

"And why not a woman? Why not add to that status of yours of representing power players and instead opt to defend a wife one of these days?"

He slides me a glance that tells me he thinks I'm crazy, and yet there's something about the look in it that I can't quite read. "Because men are safer."

It's my turn to laugh. "You just keep thinking that." I shake my head and try to focus on the path ahead instead of the man beside me. And it works, for a few minutes—the crunch of his footsteps, his gentle touch to my lower back as he ushers me out of the way of a passing pair of joggers, the silence of our thoughts—until he speaks.

"How did he not know who you were the other night?"

"*Who?*" My mind flashes to the guy at the bar earlier. Is that who he's talking about?

"The senator. He knew you but couldn't place you. Why?"

I open my mouth and then close it, ready to explain but needing to keep the integrity of my word when it comes to my clients, regardless of the fact that Carter Preston is an asshole. "You're the only client I've ever met face-to-face without wearing a disguise."

"Humph." It's the only sound he makes, but I see the tension manifest itself in his posture.

"Ryker?"

"He's a client of yours?"

"No one is a client of mine. They are a client of Wicked Ways," I say, trying to stay afoot on the slippery slope we're treading on here.

"I'm a client of yours," he states, matter of fact, and while he's right, while he's the only client I've ever had, I don't respond. Can't. Because that would be giving too much away to a man who unnerves me and unravels me all in the same breath. "The dark hair doesn't suit you."

My footsteps falter as his words hit my ears. "Dark hair?" I feign ignorance as my heart races.

"The wig you wear. It's sexy but not you."

"Wait. What? You had me followed?" There's a quiet anger in my voice. One that only scratches the surface of the discord his comment created.

"The same way you had me followed. Seems both of us use private investigators." He runs a hand through his hair. "Your secret is safe with me," he murmurs while my mind spins a million miles an hour.

It's safe with you so long as I fulfill your requests.

The second part isn't stated but implied. Just another threat to hang over my head.

I usually only dress up as Vee to meet new girls. They get one face-to-face with me if requested. The only personal touch I provide so that I can look them in the eyes and let them know they can trust me.

As for clients, sometimes I meet with them. Depending on their social and economic station, the personal touch of a face-to-face might bring more business my way. It's something I should have done with Ryker from the start but dismissed.

But I never met him. I never donned the black wig and Vee getup for him. *Shit.* I thought I'd been careful. I thought there was no way possible that someone could figure out who I am—not the police, not social services, not anyone—but his words just proved me wrong.

"How did you know what SPD meant?" he asks casually as if he didn't just blindside me so much so that I'm still trying to process his words.

"What's it to you?"

"There's no need to be snarky."

My chuckle is sarcastic. "Says the man who took the crown in being an asshole earlier?"

Ryker stops and blows out a breath before turning to face me. "Look, I'm sorry. Like I said, shitty day."

"Next time cancel our plans when you're looking for a verbal punching bag. I didn't deserve that." Frustrated, tired, and a little hurt, I grab my shoes back from him and begin to put them on with the intent of leaving.

"Look, I said I was sorry." When I don't look up at him, his hand is on my biceps, his eyes willing me to accept his apology. "It's just . . . I prefer to be in the know on things—"

"You don't own me, Ryker."

"When you don't answer, I don't like it."

"You mean you don't like not knowing if any of the men in the club were my clients."

"I didn't ask that."

"You didn't have to. You sat in that club and wondered if I'd slept with any of them."

"Bullshit. I—"

"That's such crap. It was written all over your face. It was in your posture."

"That's—"

"My sexual history is none of your business."

His jaw clenches as he fights whatever it is he wants to say. There's anger in his eyes, but he reins in his response. I tense when he puts his hand on my lower back. He's just prompting me to walk with him some more, but a part of me bucks at acquiescing to anything he wants when we are having this conversation.

But for the sake of easing the tension, I abide.

And we do walk, both lost in our thoughts as we try to figure out what the two of us are doing here and who the other person really is.

"How did you know what SPD meant?" he asks again.

"I'm sure you could dig into my past and figure the answer out for yourself," I say, still not happy with the invasion of privacy.

"I didn't, though."

"Why not?"

"That's a good question," he muses.

"Then answer it."

"Maybe because there's something about you that makes me want to figure you out all on my own. Maybe because if someone has gone through such great lengths to hide everything about themselves, there must be a damn good reason. And maybe, just maybe, I trust you for some odd reason and want you to be the one to tell me yourself. So do you want to answer my question or not?" Exasperation fills his voice, and I wonder if my resistance to telling him is more because I'm mad about him spying on me or because telling him lets him in a little closer when I already feel like he's too close.

And maybe it's because I care what he thinks about me and know he'll pass judgment over my decisions, even though he doesn't have anything close to the real answers.

"Come on, Vaughn," Ryker says and reaches out to clasp his fingers with mine. "I want to know."

His touch ignites my skin much in the same way his kiss did earlier. These sensations he evokes cause such an explosive reaction within me that it takes a second to line up my train of thought.

"I wanted to be a special education teacher for the longest time."

If I told him I wanted to be an Olympic wrestler there would be less shock registered on his face than there is now. I avert my eyes, needing to look elsewhere to help abate the embarrassment over what my career is now compared to what I had hoped it would be . . . especially in the presence of someone so successful. But at the same time, it feels good to say it out loud. It feels good to talk about me.

"Why?"

"Why what?"

"Why that profession?"

It's a simple question, but a loaded one for me. "Because I think it would be rewarding. Because many people are uncomfortable around those with disabilities, and I'm not. Because . . . I don't know." My voice drifts off as a jogger runs around us, his two dogs stopping to sniff us. "Because it would feel good knowing I'm helping someone, somehow."

"So why do this and not that?"

"Because I have a lot of debt, and this seemed to be the quickest way to pay it off." Simple. Uncomplicated. Partially true.

"But why?"

I open my mouth to tell a lie and then realize this man knows more about me than anyone else, really. And the things he doesn't know I'm sure he can find out.

"Because sex is sex. Nothing less. Nothing more. Everybody wants it. Everybody needs it. So why not sell the one thing that's always in demand, make my share, and then bow out when my time is up."

"Bow out?"

"Yes. Bow out."

"It won't be as easy as you think to walk away from the high life. Money is a powerful thing. Once you have it, it's hard as hell to live without."

I start to protest but then realize he doesn't get it. He knows how much he is paying me. He can conclude that I skim off a percentage of all my girls' income. He sees the expensive clothes and jewelry I have on but has no clue they are from thrift stores and pawnshops.

"I'll walk away."

The chuckle he emits scrapes over my nerves and irritates them. "No, you won't. You're addicted to the power of it. Of knowing you can bring a man to his knees. Of the ability to use your body to get exactly what you want."

"You don't know a thing about me."

But the ghost of a smirk that plays at the corner of his mouth makes me fear he just might. "You don't have to be embarrassed by it, Vaughn. I get off on the same type of power when I'm in court. It's a high. Something once you have a taste of, you only seem to want more of."

"Don't paint your experience on my canvas," I murmur.

"Here we are," he says, pulling my attention to our surroundings instead of to him. We're standing outside the entrance to The Club, and every part of me deflates a little at the thought of having to go back inside with him.

Of having to play more of the part, when this, me getting to be a little more of myself, has been so unexpected and nice.

"Here we are," I repeat.

We stare at each other, the shadows of the night playing over his face and reminding me I barely know this man and that I do, in fact, want to know him more.

"I'd be more than happy to drive you home—"

"But—"

He puts a finger to my lips. "But that's too personal." He steps into me so that we're both in the shadows now on the broad sidewalk.

"It's too personal," I agree as I draw in the scent of him, the feel of his palms as they run up and down my arms. And for the briefest of moments I forget what I'm doing here and that he's paid me for it because all I can think about is him kissing me. All I want is him to.

"Why don't we go—"

His lips close ever so slowly over mine so that I have no choice but to sink into the kiss. A kiss that's soft and tender when every other one we've shared thus far has been raging with a lascivious desire.

But not this one.

My body heats up nerve by nerve. Muscle by muscle. Sensation by sensation.

Until he leans back so his forehead rests against mine and we breathe in the same air.

"Good night, Vaughn."

What?

My head snaps up as Ryker takes a step back, regret owning every part of his expression, including the desire warring in his eyes.

"I don't understand." Flummoxed, I stand where I am and just watch him as he takes another step back and points to the taxi pulled up to the curb at my back.

"Your cab is here." His smile is pained.

"But . . ."

He lifts a hand in silent goodbye before he turns the corner, leaving me staring after him as the taxi driver ushers me into the cab.

Tears sting my eyes as he pulls away from the curb.

Ryker just gave me exactly what I asked for—no sex—and yet every part of me is confused by it.

Because I want him.

And now I'm not exactly sure what I'm supposed to do about it.

CHAPTER TWENTY-FIVE

Vaughn

"You okay?" Ryker's voice comes through the line, his gravelly tone mixed with surprise.

"Yes. Yeah. Um . . ." I walk through my kitchen and sit down on the edge of the couch, now baffled why I thought picking up the phone and calling him was a good idea. "I'm confused about what happened tonight."

"I'm just abiding by the contract."

"What I meant was—"

"Whatever happened to you, Vaughn, you're not ready. You may think you are, because when we kiss it's fucking incredible, but you're not there yet."

"Shouldn't I have a say in that?" I ask, despite slowly melting at his comment and trying to find some of my stubbornness to combat his words just for the sake of it.

Because no one gets to tell me what I want or don't want.

Even worse, I'm scared to find out the answer. I'm scared to know why I want to have sex with him and why I'm petrified all at the same time.

"Yes, you should, but I also know you're stubborn as hell. Sure, as you say, sex is sex . . . but it's a whole lot more than that too."

There's something in his tone that just reinforces what a part of me already knows. Sex with Ryker will be different. I can tell myself it won't be . . . but if his kiss is any indication, it will be.

But I can't think about that. I can't want that.

I change the subject.

"I don't understand. You came to Wicked Ways wanting—"

"Oh, I still want that"—he chuckles—"but in time."

I open my mouth to speak and then shut it as his words, his patience I don't deserve, his kindness I don't expect undoes something in me I can't describe. The silence stretches across the connection as I try to process it all.

"Ryker?" It's a plea, a question, a *don't hang up yet*, all in one.

"Just be grateful you found a man patient enough to let you work through your issues."

"But what's in this for you?"

He's silent until that soft chuckle fills the line again. It warms me. It turns me on. It confuses me because no one has ever been considerate of me before.

"Good night, Vaughn. I'll be in touch."

"There was no one in The Club tonight." I can hear the sharp draw in of his breath. "I've never gone out with a client before. I've never slept with anyone for money." The words stumble out in a flurry of explanation. *"You're the only one."*

More silence that eats at the tension.

"Good night, Vaughn."

And when he hangs up, I sit and stare at the phone, wondering why I just confessed to a man I don't really know.

Why I've opened up to him more than I have to anyone else since my sister died.

Why I want to see him . . .

CHAPTER TWENTY-SIX

Vaughn

The park is beautiful. The sun is out, and people are playing around—tossing a Frisbee, having a picnic, lying on the grass and reading a book. There's laughter and music and the rustle of the breeze through the trees overhead.

I'm content. How can I not be when I'm with the girl I love and outside on a gorgeous day?

"Look, Auntie Vee!"

I laugh when Lucy holds on to the handlebars for dear life but lifts her feet off the pedals of her bicycle. Then I warm from the pride that fills her face at being able to do something so simple, but something we worked on for a few weeks after she saw some other kids doing it.

She's decked out in a princess shirt and brand-new light-up tennis shoes. Her silky brown hair is beneath a helmet that's painted like a unicorn with the tassels on her handlebars matching its colors.

"You're doing awesome! Look at you go!"

"I'm going to go around again!"

"Okay," I say as she makes her way around a predetermined path that I can see the entirety of from where I sit but that makes her feel like a big kid doing it. Independence. It's something I work on with her. No one knows yet if she'll ever be able to live on her own someday, but you better be damn sure that I'm trying as hard as I can to let her live as normal a life as possible.

Just as she turns the first right on the path, I startle at the shade that falls as someone walks up and stands beside me. I look up, and thud goes my heart.

It's the first time I've seen him since I got in the cab last week. No phone calls. No texts. No anything. But it's definitely not the first time I've thought about him.

Nope. Because thinking about him? Yeah, that's happened way more than I'd like to admit to myself.

Ryker's standing before me. He's shirtless, sweaty, and out of breath as he pulls his earbuds from his ears and flashes a smile that does funny things to my insides.

"Hi."

"Hi," I say, my eyes flickering between him and Lucy and back again, all while my pulse speeds up. "You're jogging."

Brilliant statement.

"I am." He's panting. His hair is a mess, his chest is tan, and a dark stain of sweat covers the top band of his shorts.

"You haven't called." And an even more brilliant statement. Especially for someone who isn't supposed to want him to call. Who isn't supposed to check her phone more often than not because she's thinking about him.

"Did you miss me?" Without asking if he can, he takes a seat beside me and blows out a breath, clearly relieved to take a break from his run.

"No."

No. Not now. Lucy's coming.

But yes, please. Sit.

"Liar."

Yes. "No."

"Okay. Back to my run then."

"Wait!" I say, hand reaching out to clasp his forearm as he starts to stand up just as Lucy turns the last corner of her path and heads back toward us.

"Wait?" He cocks one eyebrow and fights the ghost of a smile lighting up his lips.

No.

Go.

Lucy is coming. I don't want him to know about—

"Who's this?" Lucy's grin spreads wide as she stares at Ryker, her helmet askew, a smudge of dirt on her cheek, and a drop of the chocolate ice cream we shared earlier on her shirt.

Ryker turns from me to Lucy, and every part of my body goes on high alert as I watch his expression. His natural smile flashes at Lucy before I see the confusion hit his features, followed by the softening of his smile into a look of realization. "Hi there. You must be the magical unicorn I dreamed about last night. Are you coming to take me to Rainbowville, where there is cotton candy and ice cream for dinner?" he asks, voice comforting, while my insides try to stay on guard but melt at the way he's just put Lucy at ease.

Her giggle electrifies the air as she shakes her head and sits down cross-legged right in front of him. "Ice cream for dinner? That's silly," she says and angles her head to the side as she studies Ryker without shame.

"Ryker," I say, voice shaky, heart stumbling over the fact that now he knows more about me than I'd ever divulge. Now that I've seen a softer side to him that I'd never expect.

Now that he knows the one way to bring me to my knees. My Lucy.

"Mmm?" he says as Lucy picks his hand up and starts to hold it, her fingers running over his in the way she does when she's getting to know somebody. And Ryker lets her. He watches with fascination etched in the lines of his face as she goes through her routine of memorizing his hands, but I can't find the words that were just in my head to voice. It's only when he turns to look at me and lifts his eyebrows as if to tell me to continue that I realize I'm staring at him.

"This is my niece, Lucy."

Ryker's eyes widen for a split second when he realizes his assumption that she's my daughter was incorrect. He nods ever so slowly, his smile telling me he's okay with the unique behavior she's exhibiting with his hand before turning back to her.

"Lucy?"

"Yeah." She looks up and smiles at Ryker. It's big and happy, and I hate that the sight of it—of her being so at ease—causes tears to burn in my eyes.

"This is my friend, Mr. Ryker."

"Friends aren't called *mister*. What's his real name?" she asks as she sets his hand back down on his leg but keeps hers resting ever so gently atop it.

"His real name is Ryker, but we add the *mister* before it. Remember? That's how we show respect."

"How come I can see his boobies? I have to keep my shirt on so no one can see mine."

Ryker stifles a chuckle as I answer. "Because that's just one of those things that isn't really fair. Boys can go shirtless and girls can't."

Lucy stares at Ryker intently as if she's deciding whether it's his fault or not that society has decided this social standard.

"That's kind of stupid."

And before I can correct her on using the word *stupid*, Ryker pipes up. "I was out running, and it got really hot."

"So you took your shirt off?"

"Mm-hmm."

"Then where is it?" she asks, and the laugh he emits says her question caught him off guard.

"Um . . ."

"I like to run too," she says, moving past the shirt topic just as quickly as she broached it.

"Yes, Lucy has one of the fastest times for a lap at her school." She holds her hand up, and I high-five the achievement she's so very proud of.

"You do?" Ryker says, slapping her hand as well. "I bet you're faster than me."

"I am. I know it."

Ryker sputters a laugh, and his smile lights up his face in a way I've never seen before. He's relaxed, without the usual lines of stress that crease his forehead or the calculating scrutiny that typically owns his eyes.

"Is that your bike?" Ryker asks, cutting the debate off and rising to his feet.

Lucy nods emphatically. "Yes. The wheels—the extra ones—have superpowers," she says, referring to the training wheels and my explanation to her of why she needs them. When her hand slides into Ryker's without him even hitching a step, I just draw in an unsteady breath.

How easy it is for her to trust.

How easy it is for all kids to trust.

"Superpowers, huh?"

"Yes. I can ride without my feet on the pedals."

"No way!"

"Yep." Lucy's hands are on her hips as Ryker squats down and pretends to inspect all the parts of her bike.

"Wow. This sure is a cool bike. Do you think I'd fit on it?"

Lucy's giggled "No" floats through the air.

"Well, can I see you ride it, then? I want to see the superpowers."

Lucy's eyes grow big as she looks to me for consent, and when I nod she lets out a whoop, gives Ryker another high five, and then methodically gets on her bike. She starts to pedal, and Ryker walks beside her as she goes. He shouts words of encouragement, exclamations of awe, and the two of them laugh as she makes her way around the path.

I stare at them, my life and my . . . I don't know what Ryker is. *My unexpected?* Because for a man who is determined for me to be his date—his escort—this sure doesn't feel like it.

And I'm scared to admit what this feels like. Normal? Comfortable?

Your mind's running, Vaughn. It's running away to places you needn't dare go. He's a client. He's a ruthless one who not only has threatened your livelihood but now knows about the one thing in your life that you'd give up anything—do anything—for. Your one vulnerability.

Yet as I watch him with her—laughing, joking, playing—I have a hard time seeing that side of him. And an even harder time not softening toward him more than I already have.

"You go around again!" he tells Lucy as he grabs his chest, pretending to be exhausted from keeping up with her before collapsing on the grass at my feet.

Lucy giggles and meets my gaze to make sure I nod and tell her it's okay to go around again. As she starts to pedal, I look down and meet the upside-down face of Ryker.

"Thank you." It's automatic on my tongue with a sincerity I rarely feel. "Most people don't know how to be with her. They say her *specialness* doesn't bug them, but you can tell they are uncomfortable and don't know what to do . . . but you—"

"I what? Treated her like she's a human?" he says with a shake of his head like it's a no-brainer as he pushes himself up to a seated position. "There's no need to thank me for that."

"Still, thank you."

"She's a sweetheart."

"She is." I nod as she turns a corner and throws her head back in laughter. It's so much easier to watch her than to look at him and acknowledge the flutter that being this close to him gives me. "Why are you jogging here?"

"Here?"

"The park."

"Because it's a nice place that has some great lead-in trails," he says as if it's a weird question for me to be asking.

"Do you live around here?"

"No."

"Then why are you here?"

"I just answered that question," he says with a chuckle, but it fades when he sees the perplexity on my face. "Sometimes I want to get out of the concrete jungle. Run where the sidewalks are clear and the horns are quiet."

"But there's always Central Park."

"Yes, and that's a great jog five days out of the week, but . . ." He shrugs.

"So you're a man who gets bored quickly, then?"

He furrows his brow. "Jogging and women are two different things, Vaughn," he responds, negating my innuendo before glancing to Lucy, who waves again at us, and we both put on big smiles and wave back. When he turns back my way, he says, "I come here all the time. Is that a problem? Are you the keeper of the park?"

I eye him skeptically as my mind begins to whirl. Lucy and I come here often, almost every weekend at this time, and we've never seen him. Then, out of the blue, all of a sudden, he's here and sees us?

My spine stiffens immediately.

"I've never seen you here."

"Maybe we've crossed paths before. You ever notice how once you know someone, you see them all the time when you never saw them before?"

I don't respond to him, my fingers picking at the grass and my thoughts veering back to the images he said he had of me from his private investigator.

"Vaughn?" he asks, but I keep my eyes focused on Lucy instead. "Are you implying I'm following you?"

I glance his way but only for a beat as I try to decipher whether I should believe him or not. "I don't know, you tell me. You're the one with an investigator." My voice is reserved, uncertain.

"Seems to me you have one too."

Our wills wage a silent battle. "Mine is for protection. Yours is . . ."

"Mine is for many things," he muses. "And I haven't used him to find out anything about your private life, if that's what you're implying."

I stare at him, wanting to believe him . . . and at the same time doubt myself. It would be one thing if he were calling me and I were avoiding him. Then he'd have reason to find out more about me and seek me out. But nothing like that has happened. In fact, quite the opposite. He's the one who has been ignoring me.

"The last time I talked to you was over a week ago." The words are out of my mouth and sound so needy when I'm not needy in the least.

"Yeah, and . . . ?"

And you haven't called. You haven't emailed. You said that I had to accompany you to events, and there haven't been any scheduled. The words flicker and fade in my mind as I try to come to grips with how this girl who needs no one suddenly wants to be needed by him.

I'm confused by my thoughts. By this sudden whirlwind of feelings that makes no sense and feels so very foreign to me.

Lucy waves, and I return it before facing him. His cheeks are still flushed from his run, his hair is in angry waves from the sweat slowly drying in it, and his brow is furrowed as if he's trying to understand where I'm coming from.

"It's nothing," I say.

"Uh-oh, no. You don't get to say it's nothing after you just went into silent mode with me."

"I said it's nothing."

He purses his lips and shakes his head. "'It's been over a week.' Were those your words?" he presses.

"Just drop it. I shouldn't have expected—anything."

And yes, now I sound like a psycho, crazy person. First, I hate the man's guts, and now all of a sudden I want him to call me.

"You think I was playing you, don't you?"

"No," I lie despite the race-car driver's implied comments coming back to me.

"You think I was ignoring you so you'd wonder and wait and want."

"Not hardly. I don't give you that much credit."

"There you go again," he says. "Every time I hit too close to home with you—anything about you—you insult me. Nice try, Vaughn, but that's not going to work."

"I don't need to be psychoanalyzed."

"And I don't need to be insulted." He leans in closer as I watch Lucy, his mouth near my ear. "I maneuver chess pieces all day long in court. I know their every move and how each one will affect the other. I play with them, toy with them, and then when I spot a weakness, I make my move. But outside of court, I couldn't care less. Hell, if I played games as well as you're insinuating—that I avoided you to make you want me—I'd be awesome at relationships. But I'm not . . . so obviously, I don't play games, Vaughn. I never even try to, and that's part of my downfall when it comes to dating. People only want honesty when it suits their agenda. Every other time they want you to play the game, and hell if I'll ever do that."

I want to believe him. The conviction in his tone. The dark threat underlying it that I've insulted him.

But I return to what I know. To dodge and avert. To turning the heat back to him. "So is that why you use a service?"

His chuckle is a low warning that he's noticed the change of topics . . . back to him. I wait to see if he answers the question or uses my own tactic back on me.

I watch him, and his face lights up when he waves to Lucy and then falls when he turns to look at me. "I use a service, Vaughn, because it's easiest for everyone in the long run. No mess. No complications."

"No attachment."

"Sure."

And I hate the nonchalance in his tone. I hate that all of a sudden I want to matter.

"How often have you used one?"

"What is this, twenty questions?" he asks, and I smile sweetly at him.

"You were the one who was pissed off when you didn't know the answers. Turnabout's fair play." He eyes me, curious but not happy with being on the other end of the inquisition. "Look who you're speaking to . . . it's not like I'm going to judge you because you have." I shrug to make my point, even though inside I'm suddenly wanting him to lie to me and tell me Wicked Ways is the first one he's used. That the number of women he's been with can be counted on one hand.

But even I'm not that much of a masochist to ask a question like that of a wealthy, handsome man like him.

And sounding just like I feel, he blows out a breath and lets the silence fall between us before he answers.

"I've used a service a few times over the years." He lifts his eyebrows but doesn't look my way. "In my line of work, it's important that I reflect a certain image."

"What? The divorce lawyer who has a woman but who isn't married?" I ask, knowing it sounds ridiculous.

"Yes. Men who are going through a divorce want to feel like I understand, like I can relate."

"And you being in a happily ever after marriage mars that for them?" I can understand what he's saying, but at the same time . . . don't completely buy it.

"Something like that."

"So what happens if you fall in love?"

"That won't happen." His words are half chuckle, half sarcasm.

"Why not?"

"Because I've seen enough marriages crash and burn that there's no way in hell I'm stepping into that wreckage."

"I said love, not necessarily marriage."

"Love is even messier than marriage."

"What do you mean?"

"Not all marriages are full of love. Some are just . . . an agreement. But when love's involved, it's . . ." He blows out a breath in exaggeration.

"So the cases you've worked on . . . that's your excuse? Your reason to justify?"

"Believe me. Don't believe me. It is what it is. I am who I am. It's better than pretending I'm something I'm not. That I'm someone I'm not. I've tried that. I've been burned and still have crazy exes out there because of it. So if you want to know why I use a service, it's to avoid all of that."

"I know all about crazies," I murmur, thinking of the strange text I received earlier that I still don't know what to make of. You know we'd be great together. That's all it said. Nothing more. Nothing less. And other than reminding me of a pop song lyric, I wrote it off as someone sending it to the wrong person.

Ryker's exaggerated sigh pulls my attention back to him. "The last woman I dated . . . the last woman who had me thinking there could be something there . . . she never told me she was married. She never thought it was pertinent to let me know that she had a husband who was gone on a six-month sabbatical to try to win a Nobel Prize. You know how I found out?"

"Mmm?" I murmur.

"Her husband came to me wanting to hire me to file for divorce. He thought his wife was cheating on him. We talked, he paid his retainer, and when we went to draw up the paperwork, there she was on his cell's wallpaper where it was sitting beside me on the conference room table."

"Roxanne." The woman from my research on him.

"Roxanne," he says with a nod and then a shake of his head.

"Aren't you afraid he's going to find out?"

"She's already threatened that on more than one occasion. But the minute I found out who she was, *who he was*, that he was now a client and that she'd lied, she and I were over. Besides, she has a caveat in her prenup. If she cheats, then she forfeits her settlement. She can't tell anyone about us, or she risks losing everything."

"Lucky for you."

"It would have been lucky for me if she'd never found me in the first place."

We sit in silence for a bit.

"Lucy," he says as he adjusts his legs and leans back on his hands. "Is she your sister's or your brother's daughter?"

My laugh is quick. "Nope. This is not a tit-for-tat discussion. This is you talking and me listening and nothing more. Remember? Need to know."

"She's your niece. Obviously she's related to you through a sibling. How is that divulging too much information?"

"It just is. End of discussion."

"I was just trying to make conversation."

"You mean you were trying to get answers to the questions you have? Like the other night at The Club?"

"Vaughn," he says, drawing my name out so it's an exasperated sigh. "Not everyone is out to get information to use against you."

"Says the man who blackmailed me into being his sex slave."

It's his turn to chuckle. "Considering that hasn't happened, I think my blackmail techniques need some brushing up on." He leans in, and when I turn to see what he's doing, his lips are closer than expected. The gold in his eyes glints in the sunshine, and the scent of his shampoo fills my nose. "I'm glad I got to see you again, Vaughn. I've had a busy week, and I was trying to keep this professional between you and me.

A contracted negotiation. That's why I haven't called . . . but damn . . . that doesn't mean I wasn't thinking about you." His voice softens to match the expression on his face. "It's good to see you."

Every part of my body aches from his words, from his proximity . . . from wanting him to lean forward so I can taste his lips.

"Auntie Vaughn?"

We jolt apart, hormones buzzing, hearts pounding, and look at her. "Yes, Luce, what's up? You done?" I feel like a teenager whose parents have caught her necking with her boyfriend.

She eyes us with curiosity and a knowing smile. "Were you going to kiss her, Mr. Ryker?"

"Ah, um, uh—"

"Do you want Auntie Vaughn to turn you into a prince?" she asks Ryker.

We both stifle a laugh, and God, I love Lucy and her unfiltered mouth. "She's referring to her beloved fairy tales."

"A prince?" he asks through a laugh as he smiles at Lucy. "Do I look like I need to be saved by a princess?"

"Well . . ." She draws the word out and subconsciously drops her hand to the side of her hip and forms the "hang loose" sign—fingers tucked against her palm, thumb and pinkie pointed out.

The symbol makes me smile. Our little signal that she's telling a little white lie and knows it. Our teaching way to acknowledge that lying isn't good but that she's really joking more than anything and isn't trying to purposely hurt anyone's feelings. Her eyes meet mine to make sure I see the sign.

"Well, what?" Ryker plays along with a fake pout and a cross of his arms across his chest that has me taking notice of his physique.

Who am I kidding? I already took notice.

"You probably look better with your shirt on." She crosses her arms over her chest to mimic Ryker, unicorn helmet askew, and just lifts her eyebrows. "Princes always have fancy shirts on."

"I'll remember that next time I want to feel like a prince." The way they look at each other melts my heart in ways I don't want to acknowledge. Defiance and amusement and challenge and adoration.

"It's important," she says. "All girls want princes."

"Really?" we both say in unison as my mind bucks the notion.

"Really." Matter of fact. Resolute. "Every happy ending has one in it."

I stare at Lucy, developmentally delayed in some ways and so far advanced in others, such as this. "She loves her Disney princesses," I explain to Ryker.

"So do I," he says with so much believability it takes a closer look at him to see he's putting me on but at the same time relating to Lucy.

"Who's your favorite?" Lucy asks.

And this time she's got him. His expression falls for the briefest of seconds before I interject. "I think he's a Moana type. Don't you, Luce?"

Her eyes narrow before her smile widens and she nods. "Me too."

"Moana?" he mouths to me with a bewildered look on his face when she glances over her shoulder to check her bike, and I laugh.

"Do you have tattoos like Maui?" she asks, referring to the hero of the Disney story, now placing her hands on her hips.

"No tattoos." He part frowns, part shrugs. "But I know how to save the day."

"Princesses don't need saving, silly," she says. "They just need someone to take the trash out."

And this time Ryker can't hold it back. His hand goes to his stomach as he laughs loudly, Lucy angling her head to the side and following suit. "You're something else, Ms. Lucy."

"I know," she says, and my cheeks hurt from smiling.

"Well, now that I've been schooled, dare I ask you ladies what your plans are for the day?" he asks, and immediately I tense up. Of course, he notices and just gives me a look—brow furrowed, eyes questioning—and other than telling me to relax, I'm not sure what it means. He can't possibly be hurt because I don't want to share my personal life with him.

I don't know.

But whatever it is, before I can respond, Ryker rises to his feet and dusts the grass and dirt off his hands. He squats down in front of Lucy and holds his hand out. "It was a pleasure meeting you, Ms. Lucy. In fact, I think you just made my day."

"I did?" she asks, beaming and shaking his hand.

"You did."

"I do that a lot. I'm special."

"Not just special," he says. "You're incredible."

Her smile widens and cheeks flush, and I swear I'm watching her get her first crush.

I'm right there with her.

"Do you want to stay and have lunch with us? Auntie usually takes me to the store on the corner with the green sea-witch lady out front, and we have a treat."

"A green sea witch?"

"Starbucks," I interject, always enamored with her imagination.

"Ah, the store that makes America go 'round," he says before turning back to Lucy. "You know what? I'd love to be your guest for lunch, but I don't think your auntie had planned to have me along." Lucy's face falls, and as much as I feel like an ass, I appreciate that Ryker isn't making me out to be the bad guy. "So maybe we can do it another time. Besides, as you noticed, I don't have a shirt, and you kind of need a shirt to go into a store . . . *and* to be a prince."

Lucy giggles and then takes both of us off guard when she steps forward and wraps her arms around Ryker. He hesitates for the briefest of seconds, almost as if he's wondering if it's okay to hug her back, and then he does. He holds her against him and kisses the top of her helmet as if it's the most natural thing in the world.

If I didn't think my heart went thud before, it sure as hell just did now.

Ryker steps back, words warring in his eyes. He starts to say something to me and then stops himself and offers a tight smile instead.

"Vaughn." He nods.

"Ryker."

And with his name still on my lips, Ryker takes a step backward and begins to jog down the path.

I stop myself from calling out his name, confused as to why I want him to stay when in all reality he really needs to go. The thought runs a loop in my mind as Lucy slips her hand in mine, and we both watch him run into the distance.

This was momentous.

This was something I didn't expect, but now . . . now the one thing I would have thought could never happen—my two worlds melding— just did, and the earth didn't stop spinning. It didn't even stutter unless you count the way my heart did watching the ruthless lawyer become a gentle giant with the one person I love more than anyone or anything.

This was momentous.

That's all I keep thinking even when I'm staring at the place where he no longer is.

CHAPTER TWENTY-SEVEN

Vaughn

I rush to the phone when it rings, not wanting the sound to wake Lucy up, only to slow when I see Ryker's name on the screen of my cell.

We crossed over so many boundaries today I'm not sure I want to answer because I fear the next step will to be to go further.

And yet I answer anyway.

"Hello?"

"Hi." That voice. Oh, that voice.

"Is everything okay?" I ask, tone lowered as I look to where Lucy fell asleep on the couch in the middle of watching *Moana*.

"Yeah. Fine. How's Lucy?"

"She's taking a little nap."

"She did a lot of riding today," he says and then falls silent. Obviously his call has a purpose, but what that purpose is, I'm uncertain.

"Ryker?"

"Is she the reason?"

His question unnerves me, and I know he can hear my quick intake of breath in response.

"Reason?" I ask, feigning ignorance.

"The debt. The reason you do what you do?"

"Too personal," I murmur and fight the fact that I open my mouth to tell him more. That I want to tell him more. Especially when she's the one thing I'm most protective about.

"Look, I get it. You run Wicked Ways because it brings in cash quickly. You work at Apropos to explain in some way where your cash comes from." My hand slowly moves to my mouth and covers it, hating and at the same time feeling relieved that someone understands why I do what I do, but knowing I can't talk about it. I can't connect the missing dots for him so he fully understands because that crosses another one of those invisible lines for me. "Vaughn? You there?"

"Mm-hmm." My pulse thunders in my ears because every part of me wants to say it all, tell him the whole story, so someone finally understands me. So at long last I have someone to talk to . . . and yet, it's him. Ryker. The man who finagled this situation that I love and hate all at the same time.

"It makes sense if that's the reason behind it. It's actually really smart if so. As I was finishing my run, the notion hit me, and now I can't get it out of my head. But . . . if—"

"Too personal," I assert a little firmer.

"Why? Because I respect you for doing what you need to do?"

I fight back the tears burning the backs of my eyes. The ones that want to fall because those are the first kind words I've heard from anyone regarding my need to take care of Lucy and the means I'll go to do just that.

And that means he'll be asking more questions. Questions I don't want to answer yet. Ones about where Lucy's parents are. Why I want to adopt her. Why I am how I am. Hell, the last question is one I don't even know the answer to yet.

"Because I do, Vaughn. I respect the hell out of you. I did before, and I do even more so now. Lucy is very lucky to have you—"

"That's enough, Ryker." My voice is calm, my tone even. His praise is hard to hear when it's not something I'm used to.

"I was just trying to get to know you."

"You may have forced your hand with me when it comes to professional stuff, but that's where I draw the line." Being defensive is the only tactic I have to keep him at bay. And by at bay, I mean on the opposite side of the guarded wall around my heart. "Our contract doesn't mean I'm required to give you info about my personal life too."

"When all else fails, mention the contract, right?"

"What's that supposed to mean?" I ask when I'm more than aware what he means.

"At some point your defensive bullshit needs to stop." He sighs and the sound of it—pure condescension—riles me up. Or maybe I'm mad at myself. At wanting to give in and talk to him when I haven't had anyone to talk to since Samantha's death. "Why all the hostility?"

"Because—because . . . I don't want to like you." My voice is barely a whisper as my confession takes both of us by surprise. "Because you represent everything I've always bucked against . . ."

"But I'm so likeable." I can hear the smile in his voice. It's endearing, and I know before we even say another word that I'm going to let him in. I'm just scared. "Even my mom says so." He chuckles.

"And that's the problem." I laugh, nerves tingeing its edges, and look toward Lucy for a moment before damming up my emotions again. "Look, I appreciate you wanting to do the get-to-know-you thing, but it's just better if we keep whatever is between us within the confines of . . . yes, I'm going to say it again, the contract. Somehow we ran into each other today. That wasn't supposed to happen. So let's pretend that it didn't, okay?" I ask, despite the image of Lucy wrapping her arms around Ryker flooding my mind.

"You know I'm a loner too, right? I prefer to do things on my own. To be by myself. I grew up with a mother obsessed with surrounding herself with all the right people so she could keep her status, and I'm the exact fucking opposite because of it. Maybe that's part of the reason I called Wicked Ways in the first place. Maybe it's not." He pauses. "It's one thing to want to be alone; it's another to make yourself an island so that anyone who even tries to approach is pushed away. It has to be a miserable way to live."

"You don't know me."

"You're right—I don't . . . and maybe I want to. Maybe I want to know more about the woman who runs Wicked Ways but who works at Apropos and who also seems to take care of her niece. Maybe I want to figure out why the guard you put up is like a goddamn fortress and why I like the woman I see every so often when it slips. Maybe—"

"Maybe I don't want you to."

"Just like I don't want to think about you . . . *but I do.*" His voice is quiet conviction mixed with a little bewilderment.

I don't want to think about you either, but I do too.

"Ryker." It's just his name, but there is so much uncertainty mixed with need in it that it sounds foreign to my ears.

"It's okay to let someone in, Vaughn."

"Maybe I'm scared to." I let my thoughts slip out, and then I'm blinded with the panic that hits me. "I don't do this kind of thing." I try to correct my error. Cover it up.

"You don't want to, or you can't?"

"I don't know the answer to that." My voice is barely a whisper as I rest my hips against the kitchen counter, one arm wrapped around my stomach, and wonder why I suddenly feel so uncertain. Why there's an unexpected rush to it.

"That's the first honest thing you've said to me." Silence weighs heavily between us as I struggle between wanting to end the conversation and wanting it to continue all at the same time. "Look, we started off on the wrong foot."

I snort, his comment sparking my nerves to life in that single sound.

"Under any other circumstances, we would have met, hit it off—"

"Are you actually implying we wouldn't have been at each other's throats?"

"My turn, Vaughn. This is where I get to speak, and you have to refrain from interrupting until I make my point." I roll my eyes so hard, I'm sure he can feel the draft from the movement through the phone, but I don't speak, and I sure as hell don't agree with him. "Yes, I'm sure there would have been a power struggle of some sort, but I would have asked you out in the end."

"And I would have said no."

"There's that word again." His chuckle sends chills up my spine when I don't want it to. "Why?"

"Because," I assert, spine stiffening even though he can't see it.

"That's not a good enough answer."

"And I'm not on the stand under your cross-examination."

"Christ, you're maddening, woman."

"Thank you."

"And gorgeous."

Those words stun me, when I don't ordinarily get stunned. My mouth opens, but no words come out as I squirm under the discomfort of his compliment.

"I'm not one to be swayed by words."

"I'm more than aware of that . . . but you need to get used to compliments. For a beautiful and intelligent woman, you should be used to hearing them, and it pisses me off that you aren't."

"Maybe I don't get them that often." Patrons of Apropos notwithstanding.

"Then you're hanging around the wrong people."

"Ryker, why did you call?" I ask in frustration, needing to get the focus off me.

"I want you, Vaughn."

His words render me speechless this time. Something has shifted between us. Something has changed. And now when he says those four words, I know it means so much more than to fulfill a contractual obligation.

"How about this?" he continues when I don't speak. "Every time we've met, it's been on my terms."

"Maybe that's because you blackmailed me?" It's so much easier to fall back on sarcasm than to acknowledge the shift here between us.

"True," he muses, "so how about the next time you name where and when."

"What? Why?" My immediate thoughts are out in the form of words before I can hide the fact that the thought unnerves me. *And that I just might want that.*

"Let's just say because that's what I require of you."

"That's bullshit."

"We have a contract, Vaughn."

"Who's hiding behind the contract now?" I ask.

"I'm far from hiding. I'm using it without shame, so I'll say it again. We have a contract, Vaughn."

"Said contract is for me to attend your events, not for me to pick and choose what we do. Not for a date." Panic claws at me momentarily. A panic laced with excitement that he wants to see me without rules or ramifications.

That's what he means by this, right?

"Who said anything about a date? Can't a man and a woman go out together and have a good time?"

"Not this man and not with this woman."

His chuckle rumbles through the line, and I know he can read me. I know he knows that I feel a slight flutter in my belly at his proposition.

"It's your call, Vaughn. Let me know a time and place and what you want to do."

"Or else?"

"Or else it might be some time before I see you again."

"What?"

"Good night, Vaughn."

And he disconnects, leaving me hanging in his biggest power play yet. If I don't give him what he wants, I don't get to see him again.

If I give in, then I will.

He's hedging his bets here that my stubbornness won't win out and keep me from calling him.

Arrogant son of a bitch.

But there's a faint smile on my lips as I hold my cell in my hand and shake my head. He can't be too arrogant, though, since my mind is already trying to think of what I want to do.

I'm not sure how long I stand there reliving the past few weeks and trying to figure out why a man like Ryker—refined, complicated, unexpected—wants anything to do with me, and I jump when the doorbell rings.

My eyes flash to the clock, and I can't believe I've lost that much track of time.

"Auntie?" Lucy calls out to me as she sits up from the couch, groggy but with a smile on her face.

"It's just Joey coming to pick you up."

"Can't I stay? Please?"

"I wish you could. *Soon*. I promise you I'm doing everything I can to make sure that soon you won't have to go anywhere."

She looks at me with a skepticism that breaks my heart as I unlock and open the door.

"Whoa!" I say as I come face-to-face with a large stuffed unicorn. "What's this?"

Joey laughs as he makes his way into the house; seconds later Lucy's screeching in excitement. "It was on the front porch!" he says as Lucy grabs it and wraps her arms around it.

"I love it!" Lucy says, holding it out to look at it before bringing it closer for another squeeze. "Who's it from?"

"There was no name on it," he says and reaches out to tug on her ponytail.

I roll my eyes, well aware that Joey's not allowed to buy toys for his charges—favoritism frowned upon and all that. "The front porch, huh?"

"The front porch. I swear." He holds his hands up to refute it, but the smile on his face has me shaking my head.

"Kind of like how you weren't allowed to buy her that princess doll you did last month but that miraculously showed up in her bag?"

"I have no recollection of what you're talking about." He laughs.

"I bet it was from Mr. Ryker," Lucy says and causes me to choke out a laugh at all of the problems that being true would present to me. First one being that would mean he knows where I live.

"Mr. Ryker?" Joey says with a lift of his brows.

"It's no one. A client from work." I shrug it off.

"Mm-hmm," Lucy chimes in. "He was at the park today. He said I ride my bike like . . . like a guy in the Tour-duh-something."

"Tour de France?" I ask with a laugh, and she nods emphatically.

"Is that so?" Joey emits a low whistle.

I wave a hand his way. "Like I said, *work*. He was jogging in the park today, saw us, stopped to say hi."

"He's my new friend," Lucy asserts and kisses the unicorn.

"No wonder you're in a good mood . . . with a little man on the side," Joey says to me, and I push him playfully out the open doorway.

"Go. Stop being ridiculous."

"Uh-huh," he says with a smile as I pull Lucy into a hug that I don't want to let her out of.

"You have a good time with your dad tomorrow night," I force myself to say, knowing that I'll be worried about her the entire time.

"Mm-hmm," she says into my chest.

"I love you, Lucy Loo." I press a kiss to the top of her head.

"I love you too, Auntie Loo."

"You ready, kiddo?" Joey asks and picks up her bag.

"Yep." She hugs her unicorn tighter.

"Thank you for that," I say with a tilt of my chin to the animal.

Joey just laughs and says, "Not me!" as he turns around and the two of them bound down the pathway to his car.

And I stand there and watch until the waves are all waved out, the kisses are blown, and the car is gone.

CHAPTER TWENTY-EIGHT

Ryker

"You need to go out with your friends more. Get out. Be young while you can."

I stare across the elegantly furnished table at my mother. The restaurant's lights glint off the diamond rings adorning her fingers as the sounds of polished silver scrape against fine china.

"I do go out when I can. Some of us have to represent the men of this world when their wives are divorcing them." I lift an eyebrow, referring to my mother's conversation opener asking me to help her file for divorce.

She huffs and swats at the air. "I told you, you wouldn't understand," she says.

"I'll never understand. I never have."

"Don't start, Ryker, dear. Don't tell me I'm the reason you refuse to settle down and give me grandbabies."

I cough out a laugh. "Grandbabies? Why? So you could tell your assistant what you want her to do with them, let her get dirty, and then step in to take a picture with the final product so you can show all your friends."

Her smile tightens. "I'm not that bad."

I lift an eyebrow. "You have an assistant solely to manage your social calendar."

"Yes, I guess I am."

"It's just how you are." I shrug.

"So any women on your radar? You were talking about that one for a while—what happened to her?"

"It was over before it began." That's all the explanation she needs to know when it comes to Roxanne.

"And now?" The smile on my lips is reflexive when Vaughn comes to mind, and the lift of one of my mom's eyebrows says she noticed. "Is there something you're not telling me, Ryk?"

"I don't ever tell you a lot."

"True . . ." She picks up her wineglass and takes a sip. "But I want to know more about whatever woman in particular brought that smile to your lips."

"It's no one you know."

"But there is someone, right?"

"No one for you to start planning a lavish wedding over," I say with a shake of my head, well aware she wants a wedding so she's back on *Page Six* again. And an excuse to have some more nips, tucks, and fillers—not like she's ever needed an excuse before.

"Marriage is the last thing on my mind, dear." She rolls her eyes dramatically and then waves and smiles coyly at a man across the room, always one to be on the prowl. When she looks back to me, I just shake my head. "What?"

"You never learn, do you?"

"I'm a soon-to-be-single woman, and I refuse to waste away until I am a wrinkled prune."

"You always paint such a picture with your words, Mother."

"Now back to this woman," she says.

"It's nothing. We met. She is far from impressed with me . . . but I think I'm slowly winning her over."

"Wait a minute. You mean she's making you work for it?" She sighs as if she's disappointed. "That's by far the oldest feminine trick in the book—playing hard to get."

"That's not exactly the case with us."

"Oh, so there is an *us* already."

"It's a pronoun." I shake my head, already more than over this conversation. "And no, her playing hard to get is not a game."

"Then what is it?"

"I'm still not quite sure." But I think of Vaughn's smile at the park the other day. The sound of her voice over the phone. The way I get hard thinking about her.

"It's always good when a woman intrigues a man."

I level her with a look that says I'm not buying whatever dating advice she's selling and then breathe a sigh of relief when the waiter slides the check folder onto the table.

"Saved by the bill." I laugh and then look at my watch. "And a meeting that starts in twenty minutes."

"I'm going to get it out of you one way or another."

Spoken like a true woman.

Smoke swirls around me.

The rich scent of Cuban tobacco seduces me as I draw in the taste of fine whiskey.

The meeting that saved me? More like an excuse to go to The Club and relax for a bit.

"That good, huh?"

I glance over to Chuck and nod, not really wanting to be bugged, but respond anyway. "That good."

"So what was up with the woman you brought the last time you were here?"

"She was no one." The less these guys know about Vaughn, the better. The members of The Club are bastards without morals. Case in point, why I can fit in perfectly here.

"No one?" He chuckles and draws on his cigar. "The way you kissed her in the hallway sure made her seem to be *someone* . . . well, unless she was on the clock, of course. Then you and I both know she's a damn good lay who'd suck you dry, swallow it all without complaining, and then you could discard her when you're done with her."

I close my eyes and lean my head back against the leather of the lounge chair in an attempt to let go of what he just said. "Not disposable, not on the clock," I murmur before drawing another inhale on the cigar.

"She could be on my clock then. Or should I say *cock*." He nudges me and laughs that fake laugh of his that says *I'm way too fucking important* when he's riding Daddy's inheritance without a single thing credited to his name.

"Watch it, Chuck," I warn but keep my eyes closed, my tone even.

"I heard Preston was asking about her. Said she looked familiar."

My blood boils instantly at the words. At knowing Carter was here watching from afar and I never noticed him. At wondering what the fuck it is that happened between the two of them.

"Preston's a politician. Everyone looks familiar to him," I say. "His dick's far from discriminating, so let's not insult my date."

"Man, I needed this." Of course, he keeps talking, never one to get a hint. "It's been a shitty week so far. Too many pricks and not enough pussies"—he nudges me *again*—"if you know what I mean."

"Mmm." It's all I trust myself to say because Chuck is high on the list of obnoxious members. Just because I represented him in his divorce doesn't mean I like him. *Not even a little.*

"Hey, Mitch said he saw you with Roxanne . . . uh, Roxanne—" He snaps his fingers as if he's trying to think of her last name while I all but wrap my fingers around his neck to get him to shut his nosy ass up. But rather, I don't look his way because I don't trust myself to not give away anything.

"Flannery," I finish for him.

"That's it. He said he saw you two having dinner at a bistro." The restaurant flashes in my mind. French feel, American food, and Roxanne continuing on with her lies. "If you're hitting that too, dude, you are the fucking man!"

Chuck. Chuck. I don't give a fuck.

I crack an eye open and level him with a glare. "And what business is it of yours?"

He nudges me, and my hand clenches around my highball glass in response.

"You're among like-minded men, Lockhart. We don't spill each other's secrets, and we sure as fuck don't talk outside The Club."

But we do. The fact that he knows about that night with Roxanne says we do, considering Mitch saw me.

I motion for him to lean closer. "The woman the other night is off limits. Roxanne was the wife of a client. I was trying to see what her Mendoza Line is for settlement acceptance," I lie without a flinch or a fucking care. "And while I appreciate you wanting to chat, you're right. It's been a shit week, and I want to sit here and enjoy my cigar and my drink without having to make small talk with you." I offer a tight smile and then lean my head back again, close my eyes, tune him out, and wonder if she'll call.

I turn my cell over in my hand with half a mind to text Stuart and tell him to find out all he can on her. The details I don't know. The answers to the questions I still have.

Because I may know some of it, but I'm sure I don't know the half of it.

CHAPTER TWENTY-NINE

Vaughn

I know you better than you think. We're inevitable. You and me.

I stare at my text again—at the "private caller" for the identifier—and shake my head, confused and curious.

Who is this? I text back.

You know who I am.

The five words send an unexpected chill up my spine. I stare at the text again.

A wrong number, maybe? Or perhaps Ryker giving me a little push to call him back with plans?

Inevitable. That word rings through my mind. Senator Carter Preston. Wasn't that the word he used? This can't be him, can it?

Melissa bumps her hip against mine where I've stood for way too long looking at my phone. "Someone is here to see you."

"Mr. Grab Ass in the Four Pod?" I ask in exasperation.

"No. From what I can tell, he's made some phone calls and he's willing to pay others for the service he wants from you."

"What are you talking about?" I laugh as Ahmed gives me a thumbs-up across the bar top to make sure I'm doing okay. I nod.

"Escorts. Hookers. Whatever you want to call them, the Four Pod is now full of them."

"How do you know they're escorts or hookers?" I ask.

"Honey, I can spot them bitches a mile away."

I all but choke on my next breath of air.

Good to know.

I cover my choke with a cough. "Guess that's good news for me." I flash a smile, and then my scattered brain remembers, "Wait, you said someone was here to see me."

"Yeah. She's down by the locker rooms." She places her drinks on her tray as a new song plays and the lights change from blue to lavender with it. "I can tell her you're busy if you want."

Her?

"No. That's fine."

I walk the few feet to the hallway that houses the locker room and come to a stop when I'm met by a gorgeous woman. Close to six foot in heels, silky auburn hair, and an outfit that's way too expensive even for this upscale club. She appraises me, a disdainful scowl on her face as her eyes scrape up and down the length of me.

"Can I help you?" I ask above the music. It's loud down here but still possible to talk without yelling.

"Not what I expected at all," she murmurs.

"Excuse me?"

"You're nothing like Ryker's type."

"And you are?" And the minute the words are out of my mouth, my thoughts connect. Ryker's report. Roxanne. Red haired.

Oh. Shit.

"How did you even know . . . ?" I ask.

"When you make a scene at The Club like you did," she says with a curl of her lip, "men talk." She studies me and then rolls her eyes ever so subtly. "I suggest you don't get aspirations in your head of becoming Mrs. Ryker Lockhart. He doesn't take love seriously. He doesn't care."

"Neither do I," I say with a shrug and a wide grin as every part of me is shaking in anger and confusion over how she found me and knows the connection between Ryker and me. "We're a perfect match made for each other, then."

Her laugh is loud and dramatic. "He's going to use you and then throw you out."

"Just like he did you, I assume?"

Anger flashes across that cosmetically perfected face of hers. "He loved me. What we had was different."

I angle my head to the side and allow my stare to unnerve her. I can see with each second that ticks by she realizes her veiled threats don't faze me. And then I smile softly and take a step closer. "Different?" I ask innocently.

"Yes, you wouldn't understand."

"Didn't you just say he doesn't believe in love? If that's the case, then how can you say he loved you?" I shrug and take a step back. "Guess that's where you screwed up."

"You're nothing but a—"

"This is where I point out that regardless of what you think I am or am not, I have him . . . and you . . . don't," I taunt.

"You bitch." She lunges toward me, and I jump back.

"I'd rather be a bitch than crazy."

And with perfect timing, Ahmed turns the corner. "Everything all right back here, ladies?"

"Perfectly fine," she says, straightening up, fluffing her hair, and then smoothing down the rumpled fabric of her pencil skirt. "I was just leaving." She takes a step forward and glances around as if she were here for other reasons. "This place has no class."

With a huff, she stalks out, and Ahmed follows her retreat with a whistle.

"What's that all about?" he asks.

"Crazy ex-girlfriend," I mutter.

"You got a man now, Vaughn? Woo-wee. Damn, it's always the quiet ones." He laughs as he takes a step backward before nodding and getting back to what he should be doing—work.

But I give myself a moment and lean against the wall and take a deep breath.

How in the hell did Roxanne find me? Who at The Club told her I was there?

I rack my mind to try to figure out how the connection was made between Vaughn Noname and Vaughn Sanders.

And yet somehow Ryker has made the connection from Vee to Vaughn.

Somehow Ryker found me and took images.

I grab my cell to ask him. To demand to know if he told Roxanne about me in an effort to get her to back the hell off him.

But I slide it back in my pocket without making the call.

The last thing I need in my chaotic life is to be in the middle of their drama. I don't need a crazy ex more pissed off at me than she already is. In fact, I probably should have been smarter in what I said to her than the knee-jerk reaction I gave.

Being drawn into their bad breakup is not what I need. I already know it'll end poorly, and I don't want to be part of the collateral damage when it does.

"Vaughn? You gonna serve your drinks, or do I have to cover for your ass?" Melissa calls down the hallway with a laugh.

"Coming."

CHAPTER THIRTY
Vaughn

"Please tell me my eyes are not deceiving me," I say with a laugh as I cover my mouth and shake my head.

"What?" Ryker asks with his hands out to his side. "You think you can tell a man, 'Meet me at 161 First Street in the Bronx,' and he's not going to know it's Yankee Stadium?"

"That's not what I—" I come to a stop a few feet in front of him, take in his Boston Red Sox hat and T-shirt, and wonder if he's wearing it because he's looking for a fight tonight or he really likes the Yankees' rivals. "You're joking, right?"

His laugh says that he's not. "Only if you're joking with me about being a Yankees fan." But when he steps up and kisses my cheek, I know I'd be any kind of fan he wanted so long as I get that fluttery feeling in my belly again.

"We do live in New York."

"I'm aware." He tugs down on the brim of my hat. "I like this look on you."

My smile is unstoppable right now. "Well, let's hope you get to keep your hat where we're sitting."

"Where are we sitting?"

"Over the Yankees' dugout." I laugh, more than pleased I was able to score a set of always-sold-out tickets. It pays to have a Yankees player on my client list.

"Seriously?" The smile on Ryker's face right now—the one that's every bit little boy in love with the game and nothing like the severe, calculating lawyer I've come to know—does funny things to my insides.

"Seriously." I nod as he reaches out and puts his hand in mine as if it's the most natural thing in the world. "I had a friend who couldn't make it, so he offered them to me." It's close enough to the truth, anyway.

"How did you know I'm a huge baseball fan?"

"I didn't."

"Well, at least we can agree on one thing—the love of baseball. Other things," he says as he eyes my fan gear up and down, "I'm not so sure about."

I bat at his arm playfully and laugh as we start to walk into the stadium. "Dare I ask?"

"What's that?" he asks as the scent of stadium food—popcorn and hot dogs and nachos—and the sounds of "Get your game program right here" assault us.

"It might be a game changer for me."

"Uh-oh," he says and smacks his hands together and rubs them. "Lay it on me, Vaughn."

"Popcorn or peanuts? Nachos with or without jalapeños? Pretzel or churro? Beer or soda?"

He throws his head back and laughs as his arm comes around my shoulder and pulls me against him. "You want to know all of the important stuff, don't you?"

I stop walking, and it halts the both of us. "No. The important stuff would have been knowing you're rooting for the enemy." Someone around us sounds off in agreement with me. "This? This is just to see if you can partially redeem yourself for being a traitor."

That laugh again. The way his hand grips my shoulder. The heat of his body beside me.

"Let's see. Hmm. Popcorn for sure. It's always better if it's caramel popcorn, but beggars can't be choosers. Definitely jalapeños with the nachos. Churro. Always a churro. I have an endless sweet tooth. And what was the other one? Beer. I'm a guy—that answer should have been expected."

I stare up at him. At the amusement in his eyes. At the relaxed smile on his lips.

"You do know if someone throws a punch at you for rooting for the Sox, I won't defend you."

"I do believe those are the most romantic words I've ever heard."

I roll my eyes and slug him playfully . . . but the smile never leaves my lips.

Not when we eat our way through the stadium—arguing over the last bite of churro and which jalapeño was the hottest. Not when he stands up and cheers, arms up, grin wide, when the Sox get a three-run homer to go ahead. Not when I think of bringing up Roxanne's visit to Apropos the other day but realize I don't want to ruin the mood and the lightheartedness of our evening. Definitely not when my Yankees win by one run.

And not now, as Ryker and I sit across from each other in a hole-in-the-wall pub where the light is dim, the beer is darker, and no one cares who is sitting at the table in the back corner except for me . . . because my view of him sure is spectacular.

"So tell me something about you that is unexpected," he says as he tilts his head to the side and just stares at me.

"I'm from Connecticut."

"But you're a Yankees fan?"

I smile and nod, uncertain why I chose this to tell him. "Yep."

My phone alerts with an audible text and vibrates on the table. Ryker lifts an eyebrow when I don't look at it. "That might be a hot date waiting for you."

"Poor guy. Let's not tell him I stood him up for a Red Sox fan."

Ryker belts out a laugh as I glance down to my phone and see a text from Ella. Another request to buy Wicked Ways' client list. Another desperate bid to sell it to her, but I know that I haven't reached my goal yet.

"Please, do tell him. Then he'll stop calling." He reaches out and links his fingers with mine, and that small connection warms me in ways I never expected. "Where were we? Oh, right. I was asking if any of your family still lives in Connecticut?"

"Some of them."

"That's all you're going to give me?"

"My sister and I left and never looked back."

"That sounds like there is a story in there somewhere."

I stare at him. At his easy demeanor and comforting smile, and I answer when normally I'd make an excuse as to why I can't answer.

It's a huge first step for me.

"We lived with my uncle in the Greenwich area. He was a professor, very well known in his field, very well off . . . and not exactly the nicest of people." The words in Sam's diaries flash through my mind. The memories I can't completely recall resurface and make my skin crawl . . . and yet I continue. "Sam left the minute she could and took me with her."

"That sounds very clandestine," he jokes.

"If you're asking if we left in a big hurry in the middle of the night, then yes."

"What was the age difference?"

"Two years. She was older."

"What about your parents?"

191

"My dad left when we were little. His excuse was that he didn't think he'd ever live up to my mom's parents' standards. They were old money steeped in tradition, while he was blue collar without the tradition and pedigree they approved of."

"So he just up and left?"

"Supposedly. Personally, I think it's a BS excuse. If you have kids, you don't give them up for a reason like that. You fight because they matter. You battle because they are everything to you." He makes a noncommittal sound in response. "What's that supposed to mean?"

"Nothing more than you'd be surprised what people walk away from when it comes to their families. Some people have a price that can be named—whether it be money or freedom or I don't know—while others would fight tooth and nail to keep what's theirs. There's never a rhyme or reason . . . and I'm sometimes surprised at which person is the one who fights and which one walks away."

"Does it jade you?"

"You can say that." He chuckles, and there's something that reverberates in the sound of it that tells me *jaded* is an understatement. "What about your mom?"

"She died in a car accident when I was seven."

"I'm so sorry."

I shrug. "It was a long time ago."

"It still sticks with you."

"It does." I take a sip of my drink.

"And your sister? She's Lucy's mom?"

My nod is slow and measured. "She was, yes." He lifts a lone eyebrow at my use of past tense, and when he goes to speak, I stop him. "This conversation is way too depressing. I'm sorry. The topic can be changed anytime."

He reaches out and places a hand over mine and squeezes. "How long has it been?"

"Almost seven months."

"Damn it, Vaughn." He slides his fingers between mine kind of in a backward handhold and stares at our hands before looking up to meet my eyes.

"Samantha committed suicide." The slight tensing of his fingers tells me this isn't what he was expecting.

"I'd ask why, but there's never a good answer to that question."

"She . . . she battled the demons she buried under alcohol and then drugs. Lucy's father did the same. In fact, he pushed her to because he didn't want to be the only one screwing up."

"And Lucy?"

"Besides me, Lucy was the only thing in my sister's life she ever truly loved. Regardless of everything else, that is the one thing I know for sure." He gives me the minute I need to collect myself before I continue. "She was lost in so many ways, and I didn't know how to reach her. I tried—God, I tried—but in the end, no one could save her. In the note she left, Sam made sure to let me know she knew I'd tried to help, and that she'd fought but was so damaged her hope was gone. She said that Lucy was the best thing that had ever happened to her and that her last wish was for me to take Lucy as my own. That she knew I loved her unconditionally and would be the one who could make sure she had every advantage on her side."

"Christ." He orders another round when the waitress stops by and then settles back in his seat and just stares at me for a beat. "And so the business is to help with Lucy's medical bills? Is that the debt you're trying to pay off?"

How did this happen? How did I decide somewhere in this evening's time to let him in? Maybe because it feels way too good to be human—to be able to share things about myself that I never talk about with someone else—when it feels like I've been alone, numb, for way too long.

And so he asks, and I answer.

"The medical bills are from the treatments I tried to get for Sam. The rehab facilities. The counseling. The everything." I thank the server when she slides fresh drinks in front of us and wait until she walks away before I continue. "Those are the bills I have to pay down in order to get a fair shot at getting custody of Luce."

"Wait a minute. You don't have custody of her?"

I shake my head. "Because Sam's wishes were made in her suicide note, her state of mind was deemed questionable, and therefore the state isn't recognizing it as her directive."

"That's such bullshit." He part laughs, part swears.

"Tell me about it."

"Where else would she go?"

"With her father."

"The look on your face tells me that's a bad thing."

"Let's just say sobriety isn't exactly his strongest habit . . . but his family has money. Their support is inconsistent at best. Sometimes cutting off all funds in a tough love gesture, other times giving him money despite his need to stick a needle in his veins. Getting high has always won over everything else. And a stable job and shared DNA does a lot in the state of New York. A lot more than a sister and wishes in a suicide note."

"So you're paying for Sam's medical bills, you're paying for a lawyer to fight for Lucy—"

"It's my sister's last wish, and Lucy's the only thing I have left of her—I'd fight till the end of the earth for her."

"And that's why you started the business."

"Yes."

"How did you . . . how does someone fall into . . . doing this?"

"Everyone has a different path."

His brandy-colored eyes flick up to mine, searching for answers I think he can see I'm not going to give. I've been forthcoming tonight—I've let him in places I swore would always be off limits—but for some reason, I just shake my head ever so slightly and let him know *not this*.

I can see his mind working. The cogs shifting, the gears switching speeds so everything falls into place. "And so you run the business because it's quick money—good money—to pay down the bills, and then work yourself to the bone at Apropos so that there is a paper trail to explain where your income comes from?"

It's a blessing and a curse that he's intelligent. He can connect the dots, figure things out so I don't have to explain everything . . . but what if I don't want everything explained? What if I don't want all of me uncovered?

"Something like that," I murmur into my glass, suddenly more aware than ever I put so much more of me on the line than I ever have. So much more of me to be picked apart and judged.

But the look on his face says anything but that. His expression is as calm as his voice when he finally speaks. "You're pretty amazing."

I blush. I'm sure my cheeks are a deep red, and I avert my eyes because as he knows, the compliment makes me uncomfortable. "Just doing what needs to be done is all."

"Vaughn." His voice is soft, coaxing me to meet his eyes. "Not many people would go to these lengths to get custody of their niece."

"Excuse me. I need to use the restroom." I stand abruptly, and I think he knows I don't need to use the bathroom but rather need a moment to come to terms with letting him in when I'm so damn used to shutting everybody out.

But he lets me walk away without a fight. He allows me a respite to go in the bathroom, lean my head against the wall, and take a deep breath, never more aware how much he listened and didn't give back in return.

Vulnerability eats me whole.

The notion that I just gave him enough information about myself to destroy me if he sees the need to.

"This bathroom is taken," I yell through the closed door when a fist jiggles the lock and then pounds on it. "Occupied."

"Vaughn."

Tears suddenly burn the backs of my eyes, and for the life of me, I don't know why. Is it the sudden feelings I have for Ryker? The ones I thought I'd never be able to feel for anybody but that are here nonetheless? Feelings I thought I was immune to.

It's because you just told him way too much of yourself and feel vulnerable. Just because he listened and was kind doesn't mean you have to like him.

But I know that's not why I like him.

And how screwed up is that? How messed up is the notion that I tried to fill in for Lola, screwed up the sex part with her client, and then he blackmailed me in a sense so that I'd have to see him again, and I'm actually falling for him?

Maybe it's because of that, that you like him.

What normal man would chase after a woman who pushed him off her?

"Vaughn?"

Deep breath.

Open the door.

Those eyes. Brandy colored. Full of concern. Rapt with desire.

"I'm fine."

His hands frame my face, those eyes searching mine for answers I'm afraid he sees even if I don't give them to him. He leans in ever so slowly and brushes his lips to mine. It's the slightest of touches but packs so much emotion in it that when he pulls back, I keep my eyes closed a little bit longer than normal to memorize the feel of it.

When I do open them, he's still there, still patient, with the slightest of smiles turning up the corners of his mouth and desire darkening in his eyes. "Should we get out of here?"

I know before I answer what exactly it is I'm agreeing to. I know that even though he said there would be no sex, there will be.

And a part of me is absolutely terrified and turned on and confused all at the same time.

"Mm-hmm." It's all I say as he links his fingers through mine, and we head out the door.

CHAPTER THIRTY-ONE

Ryker

Who is this woman?

I stare at her as the lights of the subway play with shadows across her face. The quiet confidence she had earlier has given way to nerves. It's in the way she keeps shifting her feet. The way she worries her bottom lip between her teeth. In the soft smile she gives me on the off chance she looks my way and meets my eyes . . . which isn't often right now.

And hell if I'm not more intrigued by and enamored with her because of it.

"You know I had a perfectly good driver who could have taken us back," I say, and her lips turn up in a ghost of a smile. *A perfectly good driver who could have driven you to your house instead of going back across the bridge into the city where I know you don't live.*

"True, but I've already given you shit for being a Sox fan, so it's much more fun when others do it."

"Traitor," the guy across the aisle mumbles and then grins.

Vaughn smiles at him and then finally turns my way and quirks an eyebrow at me. "See?"

"We'll see come playoff time who has the last laugh," I say, glad to see whatever is bugging her lift for a moment before pulling her against me and pressing a kiss to the top of her head.

And we sit there like that—stop after stop—silently watching the people come in and off the subway car. The glares angled my way at my Sox gear. The lovers who don't really care who's watching them kiss. The others obviously in the middle of a fight.

No matter who boards or leaves, it's the woman leaning against me with the summery-smelling shampoo and warm body who keeps my attention.

I don't ask her if it's okay to take her home with me. And I sure as hell don't think twice about the fact that this isn't normal for me. This isn't my usual MO. But there's something about Vaughn *Noname* that makes me want to break the rules.

We get off at my stop.

What are you doing, Lockhart?

She doesn't hesitate; she doesn't question; she just tucks her arm in the crook of mine and follows silently.

Why are you taking her home when you agreed to no sex?

The doorman opens the door for us and nods a greeting.

Why are you going to put yourself through this torture of knowing the bed is so close but not available for use?

The elevator dings the beginning of its ascent to the penthouse.

Because I want her to want me too.

"Your place is lovely," she murmurs when she walks beyond the foyer, as if she's surveying the interior of a cozy brownstone in Brooklyn rather than the 180-degree view of Manhattan beyond.

"Thank you. Would you like a drink?"

"Wine, please," she says as she steps into the great room, her shoes making the slightest of noises as they fall on the hardwood floors.

"Red or white?"

"Whatever you have will be fine," she says as I take in the fifty bottles in my wine fridge and make a decision.

"The balcony is to the left," I tell her as I make my selection. Rosé. I hate the shit, but it's what she asked for in The Club, and maybe I want her to know that I noticed her preferences. Maybe I want her to know that I'm trying. "It's a nice night. We can sit outside if you'd like. I'll meet you out there in a moment."

She murmurs in agreement as she takes in her surroundings, her hand running across the back of the dark leather of the couch.

"Ryker?"

"Hmm?" I look up just as I grab the corkscrew from the drawer and meet the confliction in her eyes.

"Are you drinking it with me, or are you having something else?"

"Umm . . ." There's something about the way she asks that tells me the answer to this question matters. "What do you want me to drink?"

"Nothing. Never mind. Forget I asked," she says, obviously bugged by something, and then turns back to the room, leaving me wondering what it is she needs from me to feel comfortable.

I study her as our evening runs through my mind. Despite the goddamn need owning every part of me right now, thoughts connect and collide. Ones I want to shove away and push aside. Ones that make the man in me who wants to ravage and take slide to a halt when Vaughn's words come slamming back to me.

Her footsteps stop and start beyond my view.

Her sister had demons. They ran away from her uncle. Vaughn's sudden panic attack that first night we were on the verge of sex.

The door of the balcony slides open.

Any intelligent person can draw conclusions, make assumptions about what he did to them, and fuck if I want those thoughts in my head right now.

The faint rush of the city's noise filters up from the street below.

I'm not a fixer. I'm not a man who wants to step in and save the day. Far from it. I'm too goddamn selfish to be that way.

So why am I walking into this knowing there's bound to be complications? Shit, there already have been . . . and yet here I am.

When I round the kitchen counter with two glasses of wine in my hands and look out the windows to the balcony, only one thought races through my mind.

And here she is.

Her back is to me. Her hair playing in the wind and lit up from the city's lights below. Her body the perfect complement to my memorized skyline.

I'm reckless with some things. Calculated with almost all others. And I break the rules every chance I get in my professional life.

But not my personal.

Never my personal.

And yet staring at her, seeing her here, makes me want to break rules I never even knew I had for myself.

How fucked up is that?

I was intrigued by her because she ran away. I chased and threatened because I wanted her in the primal sense. My testosterone-fueled need to have and conquer and claim. And now that she's at my fingertips, now that I can have her, I'm uncertain what's going to happen once I do.

I shake my head as I stare at her. As I want her in ways I haven't wanted a woman in a long time.

If ever.

The rules. No attachment. No getting to know you. Nothing personal.

My goddamn rules.

Maybe it's time I forget the rules and figure out the exceptions to them.

She emits the softest of murmured sighs when I press a kiss to her shoulder. That damn sound is like the permission I was asking for without knowing it. As if I actually needed one more reason to have this woman crawl under my skin and fuck with parts of me I know for a fact having sex with her won't satisfy.

"Thank you," she says as she takes the glass of wine I hand her, but I remain behind her, my front to her back with my chin on her shoulder.

"Thank you for the fun evening."

She's silent for a beat as she takes a sip and we both take in the night around us. Taillights and taxis' horns. Streetlights and the distinct sound of the buses stopping and starting.

"I thought I was going to throw you off tonight. I figured you didn't know how to mix with us little people—"

"You're far from what I'd consider the little people, Vaughn."

"Compared to you, I am." She laughs. "Still, I thought you'd be out of your element at the game."

"Were you testing me?"

"Mmm."

"I'm sorry to let you down. I assure you caviar tastes like shit, hundred-year-aged whiskey doesn't taste all that different from Jack Daniels, and Armani isn't the only thing I wear."

"You sure about that?"

"C'mon," I say as I put my hands on her shoulders and turn her to face me. "Did I pass your test?"

But once the words are out and her body is turned with her lips inches from mine, every part of me that is in contact with her burns with the need to touch her more.

Despite the quirk of her brow, there is the slightest hitch in her breath as she draws it in that tells me she's just as affected by me right now as I am by her. But she doesn't speak. Not as the desire darkens in her eyes. Not as her hands reach out and hook through the belt loops of my jeans. Not when she leans forward and brushes her lips against mine.

She's like goddamn lightning—that's what she is.

She strikes without warning and is going to singe every damn part of me no matter what kind of shelter I try to hide under.

I might as well grab onto something metal and take my chances.

"Tell me you want me, Vaughn. Tell me you want to do this." My voice is strained, everything in me that wants her is being held back by a thread, taut and ready to snap.

Our eyes hold, and even in the dim light, I can see the thoughts and questions race through hers, but she never says a word.

Then she lowers herself to her knees.

And despite every part of me saying I want to hear her answer, I need to know she agrees about what we are about to do here, I stand there silently as her fingers begin to undo my button and zipper. As the cool night air brushes over my cock when she frees it from my pants. Even when her fingers grip around my shaft and then the heat of her tongue leaves its indelible mark as it slides over the tip.

My sharp inhale sounds like a freight train in my own ears as sensations swamp every part of me so that it feels like I can't breathe.

It's been weeks since we were in that hotel. Days of wanting a woman but knowing no other would be able to satisfy me. Hours of thinking about what she'd feel like doing this to me.

And Christ does it feel good. The wet heat as she suctions around me. The way the back of her throat convulses when I hit it. The pressure her tongue adds to the underside of my cock. The way she twists her hand around me to add a taunt to her temptation.

I fight the urge to fist my hand in her hair, to fuck her mouth like I've wanted to do since the first time I set eyes on her in that burgundy dress when she walked across the hotel lobby. Something in the back of my mind, the lone hold I have over my restraint, tells me not to. Somewhere in the fog of pleasure she's seducing me with, I remember my assumption about her past and fight the impulse.

CHAPTER
THIRTY-TWO
Vaughn

My mind has shut down.

My body is on autopilot.

This is what is required to please a man. This is how you render them speechless so they don't ask for more. So I don't have to answer the question he asked me.

This is your get-out-of-jail-free card. Make them come even when they try to push you off so you can't have actual sex. Because when they come, they need time to recoup and get hard again, and that means they usually fall asleep. Bye-bye, sex.

This is your defense mechanism. The way you've survived this far.

No eye contact. No anything. Just do the job and then . . . *but something happens.*

Ryker slides his hand beneath my chin and forces me to look up and meet his eyes while he's still hard in my mouth.

Tell me you want me, Vaughn. Tell me you want to do this.

Something shifts inside me. Emotions. Sensations. Bricks tumble off that wall built around my heart.

Some switch gets flicked deep within me. His words echo and reverberate and spark something in me to life.

"Vaughn." My name is part groan, part plea, but his hands hooking under my arms and hauling me up show no hesitation. They tell me I can't close out the emotion. I can't hide behind this act. Neither does the way his lips crash over mine.

They're hungry and desperate, and they reflect how I feel. How I want him to make me feel.

"Ryker." It's my answer. My consent. My plea for him to do whatever it takes to erase the memory hidden in the depths of my mind.

"Tell me you want me," he murmurs against my lips, asking, needing, wanting with words while his hands are already taking.

With the way he pulls my shirt over my head. With the way his hands skim over my torso and begin to unclasp my bra. With the way his lips kiss a trail down my neckline and then nip the top of my shoulder.

"I want you." The words are out. My confession confessed. My fears and inadequacies now placed on center stage for him to see and take advantage of.

"Thank fuck," he murmurs and then lifts me so that my legs slide around his waist, so that my lips feast with kisses on the underside of his jawline. I hug onto him as we move inside, my face buried against his shoulder as I fight back the bitter wave of panic that threatens to derail us.

But it's wine on his breath. Not absinthe.

There's an ache bone deep from wanting him, not a churning in my belly.

I fight those two warring memories. I push them away. And when Ryker lays me down on a bed that's more comfortable than any other I've lain on before, when his lips meet mine in a tender kiss that hints at how hard he's fighting his own desire to be patient with me, when he murmurs, "Christ, you're gorgeous," they disappear for now.

Ryker takes his time with me. His hands never stop touching; his lips never stop kissing . . . he takes his time but with a consistency that never allows the sensations to ebb long enough for the memories to bubble up.

His mouth closing over my nipples. First one and then the other. His tongue sliding down my stomach to the top part of my jeans, biding its time there until we both fumble and manage to get my pants and panties down and off my legs. Another swear in appreciation as his eyes meet mine from his position between my thighs that sets off a want and need so desperate within me that I'm overwhelmed by it. A lick of his tongue over the top of my slit just as his fingers spread and expose that soft hub of nerves there.

I gasp. Moan. Call out his name as his tongue slides up and down with an appreciative hum in the back of his throat that turns me on in ways I never thought a simple sound could.

No one's done this to me before. I've never let anyone in far enough to trust them like this. And oh my God . . . the ache is so bright I fear it will burn out, but the way my body reacts to the sensations—first molten hot, then tense, then like every nerve ending I have is being teased with a feather—is something I can't describe.

My hands tangle in his hair as he moves. My hips buck up to meet his lips. My body drowns in these feelings that his tongue and his hums and his fingers and his five-o'clock shadow scraping against my inner thighs evoke.

The orgasm slams into me. Those sensations I've only ever been able to create by myself somehow seem a hundred times more powerful at the hand of someone else.

I cry out. Or mewl. Or moan. Maybe all three, and I don't care because my body is so on fire with pleasure that my mind is a mess and my heart is racing so fast it pounds in my ears to match the pulsing of my muscles between my thighs.

For the briefest of moments, I feel like fireworks have exploded inside my body. Little detonations of sensation from a body that has betrayed me for the longest of times. Technicolor in a world that has been black and white for so long.

He groans as I clamp around him. His face above mine, my arousal still a badge of honor around his mouth, his smile so devastating.

And when he leans down and kisses me, when I can taste what he did to me on his tongue, I know I'm ready for him.

I know I want him. *Want this.* I know he won't hurt me.

"I want you," I murmur against his lips as the fist I have in his shirt turns to a frantic scramble to get it off and over his head. As we shove his jeans down and he toes off his socks and shoes. As he positions himself between my thighs, lines up the crest of his beautiful cock at my entrance, and just barely rubs it up and down my slit to let me know what's coming next.

One of his hands links with mine while the other holds his dick, his eyes locked on mine as he makes that slow, deliberate, and restrained push into me.

This time we both moan. This time muscles that normally resist pull him in and tighten around him. This time when he starts to move, he looks down to watch us as I buck my head back into the pillow to feel us.

And feel I do. When he grinds his hips against mine and bottoms out within me. When he pulls out and teases me with just the tip until I'm shoving my hips up begging, asking, demanding that I want more. When he picks up the pace.

Seconds feel like minutes as the ecstasy is shared between the two of us. As he gives it and I receive it and as he takes it when I give it. The minutes stop mattering when we both fall spent and breathless beside each other on the mattress with sweat misting over both our bodies and pleasure hijacking our every nerve.

"Hey, Vaughn," Ryker pants, and I can hear the smile in his voice without even turning my head and looking his way.

"Mmm?" My eyelids are heavy, my body listless, my mind hazy.

"Would now be the time to ask you if you can remember your name?"

I laugh—well, more like chuckle, because it takes way too much effort right now to full-on laugh—at his reference to one of our first conversations.

"Mmm."

"Don't you dare tell me it's too personal"—he places his hand atop my lower belly and pats—"because what I just did to you? What I plan on doing again to you in a few minutes? That's way more personal to me than your last name."

"Noname?" I tease.

"Not gonna fly, Vaughn."

"What if I hold out for more? A girl's got to have seconds in order to make sure the sex is mind blowing enough to give up the goods."

"You're going to give it up, all right," Ryker says as he rolls partially on top of me so his lips can find mine and persuade me with a long, lazy kiss that adds more vibrancy to the Technicolor world he's just found within me.

"I am, am I?"

"Baby, I'm just getting started."

"In that case, then . . ."

A kiss. A slide of his hand over my breast and then back down to my hip. The feel of his cock already swelling back to life.

"Sanders," I murmur against his lips. He pauses ever so slightly as if he's surprised I just let him in.

I'm surprised too.

"It's nice to meet you, Vaughn Sanders." We chuckle. "I think it's time we meet each other in every way possible."

"By all means, then."

And later, much later as the sky begins to turn a muted blue and the city that never sleeps slowly stirs to life with coffee and energy drinks, I stare at Ryker as he slowly drifts off to sleep.

Sated, overwhelmed, and with a soft smile on my lips, I follow soon after him.

CHAPTER THIRTY-THREE

Vaughn

Toot. Toooot.

The room lights up some as the door creaks open. Glass clinks against glass before the sound of a bottle being set on my dresser. The music is on downstairs again—the kind without words composed by the man with the white wig who played them forever ago. It's fancy music for another party of people who talk way too much about things that make no sense: inflation rates, GDP, capital, depreciation. Things I don't understand but that Uncle James is constantly being praised and awarded for. *Boring.*

But right now I wish I were down there with the boring people instead of up here.

Right now I wish I could go back to sleep and not be scared.

The floor creaks, and I stiffen when the hand slides over my mouth. My body jerks in awareness, in fear, but when I breathe in, I smell the icky smell of the absinthe he drinks mixed with his fancy eau de gross cologne and the cloves of his cigarettes.

It's just Uncle James.

Not a monster.

Just him not wanting me to yelp and wake Sam up.

Just him knowing the train scares me when it sounds off in the middle of the night.

Just him telling me that even with a house full of people, he remembered and came up here to make everything all right.

Toot. Toooot.

But there is no *"Hey, Vaughny, want to come dance to the music with me?"* No *"I have friends over tonight, but I'd rather come snuggle with you."* No *"You know you're my favorite girl?"*

Toot. Toooot.

I open my eyes. It's his face I see. His dark eyes warning me to stay quiet. His hand pressing harder against my mouth. His breath in my ears—harsh and rapid. *Excited.* The weight of his body as he lies partially on me. The scrape of his fingers as he begins to run them up my leg, my nightgown going with them.

The confusion.

Absinthe on his breath.

The churning in my tummy.

Cologne on his skin.

His murmured voice in my ear. "You're beautiful, Vaughny."

Cloves on his fingers.

Toot. Toooot.

A tug on my panties, and my muffled protest falling dead against his hand.

Fear. It owns me. Every part of me in a way so very different than the kind when Mommy died.

He's the monster.

Uncle James is worse than the ones who live under my bed waiting to grab my ankles when I run to the bathroom.

"You leave her alone."

His body jerks at the sound of Samantha's voice. At the absolute defiance in it. His weight almost unbearable on top of me now. His hand letting up some over my mouth.

"Get out of here, Sammy." His voice slurs. His body falling off the bed some as he turns to look at her where she stands on the opposite side of the bed.

Her hands are on the gun she holds out, and it scares me. We're not supposed to touch guns. Ever. Where did she get that?

"Whoa, Sam!" Uncle James chuckles as he stumbles to stand upright, something weird pressing against the zipper of his jeans. He holds his hands up for the briefest of seconds before starting to round the bed toward her, his hand motioning for her to give him the gun. "C'mon now. Vaughn and I were just snuggling."

"No, you weren't."

"But you'll never tell anyone because no one will believe you. I'll have no choice then but to kick the two of you out on the streets, homeless and hungry like that bum we saw the other day in the middle of the Village who died. Remember how his body just sat there and people walked around him all day before realizing he'd actually kicked the bucket? That would be a shame, wouldn't it? To die alone and cold and hungry and—"

"Don't you ever touch her again, or I swear to God I'll kill you." She jabs the gun at him like it's a knife, and despite the hatred in her voice, tears I don't understand slide down her cheeks.

But I remember the homeless man. I remember walking past him without knowing, and the image of his bare feet—dirty and blistered—sticks out in my mind. How lonely he must have been. How hungry. And I bite back the sob that I don't want to be like him. I don't want to die like him.

"*God?*" He laughs. "Don't you know God is the reason you were sent here to me?"

Her tears fall harder as he takes a step closer. "I mean it. Don't you touch her."

"Are you jealous, Sammy? You like what I gave you so much that you want more and don't want to share?"

I don't know what that means, but I know it makes Sam even more angry. Her bottom lip quivers, and she shakes her head like she did after we found out that Mommy died. Like she understands what he's saying but doesn't want to believe it. "Do whatever you want to me," she says, every word a sob, "but don't you ever touch her again."

"Sam—"

"Be quiet, Vee," she shouts at me.

"The gun's empty, Samantha." Uncle James straightens up, the crazy look in his eyes gone some.

"I wouldn't be so sure." The hatred in her voice makes my hair stand on end.

"James? Where are you, Jamesey-James?" The singsong voice coming down the hallway makes him freeze. He looks at the open door and then back to Samantha.

"Remember what I said," he threatens.

"And remember what I said. You touch her, I'll kill you."

I jolt up in bed. Startled. Confused. It takes a moment for me to recognize my surroundings. The pale blue of the room and the artwork dotting the walls. The dark wood of the massive bed and the down comforter around me.

And of course the man snoring oh so softly beside me.

I'm sitting in his massive bed, in the place that has brought me more solace and hope than I've had in a long time, suddenly dealing with the crushing weight of my past.

Of the past I finally remember in totality.

Of the nights after that when Samantha and I slept with a gun under the pillow and a chair braced against the bedroom door. Of the nights when she told me she had to stay up to do homework but would slide into bed beside me, hiding her muffled cries in the pillow so as not to wake me. Cries I thought were because she missed our mother but now realize it was for so much more. The bags under her eyes from sleepless nights when she sat awake in bed like she was waiting for something and the sudden red lines I'd find on the tops of her thighs she said were from helping out with the horses but now know were from cutting herself.

I hiccup a sob and then fight back the bile that rises in my throat.

But within seconds I'm moving off the bed and running as quietly as possible to the extravagant bathroom to empty the nonexistent contents of my stomach.

Not because I was molested by my uncle James. He never touched me after that night. But because I know the reason he didn't was because he used my sister instead.

The blinding guilt hits me stronger than the worst panic attack I've ever had.

I have to get out of here.

I need air and time to think and space to move, and . . . I just need to get out of here.

Forcing myself not to look at Ryker sleeping on the bed or to think about the absolute reverence he showed me last night in every way possible, I gather my things and bolt from the penthouse.

And I don't feel like I can really breathe again for hours. I switch from train to train as snapshots from our evening flicker and fade in my mind. Pleasure I've never felt—haven't let myself feel—and finally did. And then the guilt over why I deserve to feel it when Sam never could hits.

I ignore my phone, which rings repeatedly as Ryker calls, I'm sure trying to comprehend why the bed beside him was empty without any explanation when he woke up. The guilt starts again. Over leaving him like that. Over all of the mishmash of emotions I feel toward him when I shouldn't, and then it circles back to Samantha.

Over.

And.

Over.

Not until my feet sink into the sand and the lights and sounds of Atlantic City are at my back do I feel like I can take my first deep breath of air.

I sit on the beach for hours. To the first place Samantha and I ended up when we finally ran away. To where we slept in our car for the first few weeks as we waited indefinitely for the knock on the window by a cop telling us we had to go back.

But nobody cared.

Nobody looked for us.

◆ ◆ ◆

"I have something to tell you, Vaughny."

I looked over to my sister. She was tired, her face gaunt, but the always-constant, assessing eyes were somewhat calmer. "I told Grandma, and she didn't believe me."

"Told her what?"

"About everything."

"What do you mean everything?"

"About . . ." She blinked her eyes a few times as she stared at me. "About Uncle James."

"That he was mean to us? That he . . . I don't know what—Sam, what do you mean?"

"You don't remember, do you?"

215

"Remember what?"

"Nothing. Never mind." She shoved away the tears that slid down her cheeks with the back of her hand and sniffled. *"Just know that Grandma didn't want to help us. She didn't think he was mean, because a brilliantly educated man like him wouldn't hurt us. But he did, Vee. And now we're gone from there, and we'll figure things out. We'll wait a few more days, and then we can go back to the bus station for the stuff I stashed there in the locker. We can sell some of it off to have a place to live for a bit, get jobs . . . we'll make this work."*

◆ ◆ ◆

The waves crash on the beach. The day is dreary like my mood, and the few straggling tourists daring to brave the wind have their hands holding their hats down but only last a short time before heading back to the safety of the casino.

But I pay no attention to them.

Instead I remember the absolute hurt that flashed across Samantha's face when she realized I didn't remember . . . and then the relief that followed soon after that makes so much sense now when it didn't back then.

And my heart hurts because of it.

For the fact that Samantha had to face this all alone, had to find a way to suffer in silence so that she wouldn't burden me with what I couldn't remember. So that I could have a chance at the happiness she spent a lifetime struggling unsuccessfully to find.

I lose hours.

I walk down the strip and stare at the entrance to the first casino that gave us jobs and a room to stay at a reduced rate. So much hope and despair shared in this place. So many memories I'd never take back regardless of how good or bad they were.

Because this was before the drugs took my place in her heart. This was when we depended on each other in this life of nothing, when for so long we had every material thing we wanted at our fingertips.

Everything, that is, except for safety.

Then I continue down memory lane—to where we'd gorge on hot dogs because they were a dollar a dog on Thursdays, and that was all we could afford. We ate like queens on that day and then went back to our rooms with upset stomachs but smiles on our faces. I venture to see if the secret entrance to a rival casino is still there. It was where we could sneak in, sit in the hall, and listen to the live music. We'd close our eyes, pretending we were in the room watching the performance, and then later as we lay on our beds, compare notes over what we thought the musician looked like.

Then my thoughts veer to the first time she brought a man back to the hotel room we lived in. There was nowhere else for me to go at two in the morning, so I had to put a pillow over my head to shut out the noises he made and the tears she cried when she crawled into bed to snuggle with me after he left.

Too many memories of a life I lived but never really understood. Too many recollections of things when I leave here today that I'll put behind me and never look back on again. Too much emotion for a sister I now realize I could have saved if I'd just known what my memory was blocking out sooner.

When I finally leave with the casinos' flashing lights that cut through the moonless night sky, I feel no better than when I came here this morning.

But I'm no longer angry at Samantha for leaving me alone. For leaving me to fight for her now.

Do I miss her? God, yes, with every ounce of my being . . . but I no longer hate her for her decision. I never understood why she'd choose the drugs over me, why she chose death over Lucy . . . and I still don't, but I no longer can blame her for it like I've been doing.

She saved me. She protected me.

The one thing I do know is that now more than ever, I have to somehow repay Samantha for everything she did for me. For the hurt she held on to and for the pain she tried to dim with drugs until she couldn't anymore. For the chance she gave me at having a normal life when she couldn't have one.

I have to fight for Lucy.

That more than anything is crystal clear.

CHAPTER THIRTY-FOUR

Vaughn

Exhaustion is an understatement when I hit my front porch.

The packages sitting there take me by surprise. A bouquet of flowers with a sunshine balloon attached by an orange ribbon. A stuffed pillow that's covered in sequins that spell out PRINCESS sits next to it, and I assume it is for Lucy.

I stare at the items as tears burn my eyes and then win the battle, slipping down my cheeks, and then step past them without picking them up.

The house is cold and empty when I enter, and all I want is Lucy right now. To bury my nose in the sweet spot of her neck that smells like her strawberry shampoo and little girl and breathe her in as she snores softly in the bed beside me.

Feeling like a different person when nothing has really changed, I just stand and stare at the things in my place for a moment, really look at the memories that make up each one and partially feel like a farce. Like I don't deserve them when Sam struggled through so much.

"You get one day for a pity party. Only one," I murmur to myself, more than aware I'm still in last night's clothes, clothes that smell slightly of Ryker's cologne, and that I need a shower. But I plug my phone in, the battery long dead; open the freezer to pull out the gallon of ice cream in there; and start eating it.

Within moments, my phone begins to chirp and alert and notify me of texts and missed calls and voice mails, and the guilt returns again. Over how I left Ryker. And over what exactly I'm supposed to say to him to explain.

How about the truth?

But the truth is ugly and shameful and—

And almost as if on cue, my cell begins to ring. I close my eyes and wish the sound away but know it won't stop. I know that it's Ryker, and even more, I know that he won't give up because he's already proven how persistent he is.

The call goes to voice mail and then within seconds begins again.

Frustrated, high on emotions, and more than embarrassed that once again I ran out on him, I answer the phone with a vitriol he doesn't deserve.

"Just stop!" I shout into the phone. "Stop calling me and sending me things and—"

"Fucking Christ, it's about time you answered your phone!" His anger is valid, but I don't want to hear it. I don't want to hear the worry in his voice and the relief that tinges all of its edges. "What the hell, Vaughn? You just up and disappear? I fucking freaked out when I saw . . . when I thought . . . you know what—never mind."

"When you thought what?" I ask, teeth gritted, pulse racing, a fight just what I'm looking for to take this aimless emotion out on, even though he's not at fault.

"Nothing."

"What?" I shout at him.

"When I got up, the balcony door was open." His voice is a quiet resignation that reverberates within me until it hits me what he thought had happened.

The fuse to my temper is lit.

The fight I was looking for front and center.

"You think that just because my sister committed suicide I would too?" I laugh, but there's no humor in it. Just hurt. Just misery.

"That's not even funny."

"You're the asshole who thought it."

"Christ. Fuck." A frustrated sigh fills the line, and I hate that I can picture him in his house now. I hate that I can see him standing there at the wall of windows, shoulders set with tension, hand running through his hair as he tries to make sense of things I can't even make sense of. "I was worried. Then pissed. Then worried again. Are you okay?"

The raw emotion in his voice guts me.

"I'm fine."

"Did you—did I do something—never mind."

Everything feels too raw. Too real. All of these emotions I feel have been muted for so long they feel like I've just had the earplugs taken out, and they are blaringly loud. Metallica has returned. But in a way that I want to shout out now but can't.

I don't want to care about him. I don't want to feel all these feelings I feel for him when he tells me he was worried about me. I don't deserve the chance to care about him.

You're being crazy. Batshit, certifiable crazy. No wonder he worried that you jumped off the damn balcony.

"Vaughn?" Searching. Asking.

Rein it in. Deep breath.

"Thank you for last night, Ryker."

"You mean two nights ago."

"Yeah. Sure. Whatever." Was it really two nights ago? Has that much time passed? Because I can still feel his lips on my skin. I can still feel where his stubble scraped between my thighs. I can still feel every ache of desire when I should feel guilt instead.

"Atlantic City is a long way to go out of the blue."

221

Mental whiplash hits me suddenly. "Did you follow me?" Every part of me is riled by the idea . . . and yet how . . . ?

"Where did you go?" he demands.

"You already know, so why are you asking?"

Anger bubbles up inside me.

"What were you doing there?" he asks.

"None of your business."

He had me followed.

"You *are* my business," he asserts, the arrogance in his tone only adding fuel to my temper.

He invaded my privacy.

"I'll ask it again: What were you doing in Atlantic City, Vaughn?"

"Don't ask questions you don't want answered," I say, trying to avert and dodge telling him the truth by pissing him off in kind.

"What don't I want answered? What's that supposed to mean? Out and about with another client? Is that what you're trying to tell me?" he asks, his voice suddenly chilled, when moments before it was a mix of concern.

"Need-to-know basis, Lockhart."

"Must have been a big client for you to just up and leave my bed and climb into his."

"Fuck you." There is so much venom in my voice right now it hurts my own stomach. But I did this to myself. I led him down this path so my past stayed private . . . and now I must stomach the fallout that comes with it.

"Mmm." It's all he says. It's all he has to say to tell me he truly believes I might have been with someone else.

I *should* tell him the truth. I *should* hang up. I *should* walk away from this argument where it stands before we say things we can't exactly take back. These are all things I *should* do, but I don't. There's something about Ryker Lockhart that challenges me to defy rationality, and once again he has me there.

"Ryker . . ." *I didn't mean what I just said. I'm scared to open up and tell the truth. I'm scared to want you as much as I already do. I'm—*

"Who's James?"

And it's that word, that name, that stops me dead in my tracks. Is Ryker somehow connected to my uncle? Has this whole thing been a ruse by him to pull me in—his demands and his ultimatums and his blackmail—to get back at me somehow for my uncle?

My mind spins and churns and thinks thoughts that aren't possible.

Are they?

"How do you know that name?"

I feel like I'm going crazy. Like the earth has stopped but my head is still spinning.

"You mumbled it in your sleep."

I fight the sob that I want to emit. I hold it back because if I were in my right mind, I'd know there was no chance after all of these years that he'd come after me—what for, anyway?—but for the briefest of seconds I was petrified. Just like I was that night so long ago.

Get it together, Vaughn.

"How did you know where I was?"

"Isn't there a saying? What is it? A drug dealer never samples the drugs? Yeah, that's it. It seems to me you're sampling, Vee."

"Fuck. You," I grit out again as the hurt robs me of all else.

His chuckle fills the line. It's cruel and condescending. "It seems I already have."

"I didn't sleep with anyone."

"Mmm."

"I didn't. You can believe what you want to believe."

"Do you know what it felt like waking up to an empty bed? Worrying about you? Wondering if whatever happened to you that first time happened again? Calling up Stuart to trace the GPS in your phone so I could make sure you were alive, only to find out you were in

Atlantic City. Then you turned it off, and who knows where you went or what you were trying to hide."

The concern in his voice—real and sincere—eats at me and dares me to want him when I'm so damn scared to. I don't need people. I don't want people. I was so much better in my black-and-white world with Lucy being my only color. I knew how to cope with those limitations.

And now? Now with tears springing to my eyes and emotion swelling in my chest because someone other than Samantha cares about me when it was only her for so very long, I'm afraid to believe it's true.

"You know what? It's better this way, Ryker. You claimed what you thought was yours to conquer. Your contract is null and void. My part is fulfilled." I can't even muster up any emotion in my voice. "We're done here."

"Don't tell me you didn't like the other night. Don't tell me there isn't something there worth exploring. Don't—"

"I didn't."

"You're a goddamn liar," he thunders.

"You should be used to those by now, then."

"So that's all this was to you? Business as usual for you?"

"Yep." It's the only word I can force myself to say.

"If that's all this was to you, then that's how we'll treat this."

And once the words are out there, a little part of me dies. What did I want him to say? What did I want him to do? Fight for me?

Of course I did.

Of course I wanted to feel like all of those feelings he awakened inside me were genuine.

"Vaughn." Something about the way he says my name pulls at me, pulls at the parts of me already dying inside as I try to do the right thing here for him.

"It's just better this way."

"Why?"

"It just is."

"I don't understand."

"Neither do I."

And then I end the call and turn my phone off as I slide down the front of my cabinets until my ass is on the floor. I make no move to wipe away the tears streaming down my cheeks.

I don't even acknowledge that Ryker is the first man to ever really hurt me while at the same time make me feel so alive I'm afraid of what it feels like to really live.

It's fitting, though, because as strange as it sounds given the circumstances, he seems to be the first man who my feet are tripping over so that I don't fall for him.

But I think it's too late.

That's why this hurts so damn much.

CHAPTER THIRTY-FIVE

Ryker

"Goddammit, Vaughn!"

I clench my fist, and it takes every ounce of restraint I have not to throw it into the wall.

You fucking begged, Ryker.

Begged like a man with no shame. Like a woman who was desperate to keep a man.

Like fucking Roxanne.

I slam a fist down onto my kitchen table and sit there with a clenched jaw and an awful fucking pain in my chest to match the one in my hand now that won't go away.

Something is wrong with you, Lockhart.

Something is very fucking wrong.

You don't let them in. You don't let yourself care about them. You don't hire Stuart to chase down GPS signals so that you can make sure she is all right and then fabricate bullshit reasons why she left in your mind and accuse her of them.

"Fuck!" I shout it out into the empty room and then lean back with a sigh as I think about those first few frantic moments I had when I woke up and she was gone.

The fear when I saw the balcony door open and then later the relief when I realized we'd never closed it the night before.

The goddamn woman got to me. Got to me when I swore off women. When I swore that after Roxanne, I was going to put aside crazy for a while.

And yet here I am.

Sitting here pissed off that she's pulling away when normally I'd thank my lucky stars for that. Sitting here with a glass of whiskey in my hands instead of behind my desk looking at all the angles of the senator's situation and seeing if I want to take him on as a client.

That idea just makes me want to pour another drink.

That idea makes me think of Vaughn and try to figure out their connection and then just get more pissed off.

Guess I found my exception to the rules.

Christ if I know what to do about her.

The bar is empty.

The Thursday-night crowd has left already, and only the diehards and the drunks remain.

I don't fit in here, and that's exactly what I want. To slink into the corner by myself and wonder what it is about this woman who's gotten to me.

"Hey, handsome. I'm Sandy. What'll you have?" The bottle-dyed blonde with dark roots and lipstick painted wider than her lips slides onto the stool across from me. She has her notepad in hand to take my order, but I'm pretty damn certain she's not here to figure out what drink to serve me.

"I've got one, thanks," I say and lift my half-full glass up.

A slight giggle that I'm sure is a practiced move to make her tits jiggle with the motion. "I know something that can make you feel a whole lot better than a quick buzz."

"Is that so?" I ask, nowhere near interested.

She crosses her arms on the scarred wood top and leans forward so that her cleavage and the hint of a tattoo that looks more trashy than sexy peeks out above the top of her bra. "Mm-hmm." A bat of her lashes. A lick of her lips. Right on cue. "Let me guess. Wall Street?"

"Trading's not my thing."

"What is?" The innuendo owns her voice.

"Screwing people over," I deadpan with an arrogant smirk that makes her falter momentarily until she sees the dollar signs that might come with it.

"Like who?" A snap of her gum. "The mob?" A twirl of her finger in her hair. "Politician?" A pout of her lips. "An accountant?"

I lean forward, motion to her to come closer, and lower my voice to a whisper, the asshole in me not hard to conjure up. "Women."

Her eyes widen, and then she scoots back abruptly. "Jesus. All you had to say was you were married."

It's my turn to laugh. "Not married. No."

"Then whoever it is has you by the balls and the heart, and I feel sorry for her if she plays with you."

I stare at her for a beat—at the thick blue eyeliner that takes her pretty features and makes them look cheap. "That's probably the truest thing I've heard all day," I say and down the rest of my drink.

The heat of it is gone.

The flavor of it crap.

And the only thought in my head with the waitress's tits right in my face is *I lied to Vaughn.*

All whiskey doesn't taste the same.

Just like all women aren't the same. Just like there are different rules for different ones.

I stare after Sandy as she pats my shoulder on her way to get me another drink, and I know what it is.

In a world of women so ready to play the part, Vaughn doesn't want to. She fought it every step of the way as Saxony. She fought *me* every step of the way.

There's always exceptions.

Always fucking exceptions.

When I stumble out of the bar two hours later, way more worse for the wear, Sandy's tip is big enough to pay her rent for the next month.

It's the least I could do for making me realize Vaughn just might actually be worth the fight.

Then again, if I'm here, I already knew that.

CHAPTER THIRTY-SIX

Vaughn

My shift was long and full of assholes with too much grab-ass and crappy tips. I'm sure my snapping at my customers to get their hands off me didn't help either but . . . just no.

My mood is shitty, my fight with Ryker still front and center in my mind—how much I miss him more so—but my stubbornness is still holding out.

Until I walk up my porch and see the flowers sitting there on my stoop.

"More?" I murmur as if I'm pissed and yet secretly swoon inside. A girl can be mad but still swoon.

I told myself I had to give it a few days before I called him back. A few days to see if I still felt this way—miserable, missing him, ready to tell him the why behind what happened—and then he goes and does this.

More flowers.

Another stuffed animal for Lucy.

I sigh. It's the good kind of sigh—the kind I swore I'd never emit because it's only in stupid romance movies that women forgive and forget when men send them flowers. It's only in romance movies that the woman tells the man she needs space, and he gives it to her. It's only in these movies that the heroine isn't judged when the ugly truths of her past come out.

And still . . . I sigh.

Once in the door and with the high heels off my aching feet, I set the flowers down and open the card.

Sometimes it's the ones you wait forever for who mean the most.

I set the card down next to the other two on the counter and stare at the notes I've gotten from him over the past few days. A soft smile is on my lips despite being bone tired when I drop into the chair at my kitchen table. The bills I have stacked in organized piles flutter from my huff of exhaustion.

"You bastards will have to wait until tomorrow," I mutter to them, because right now I need happy. Right now I don't want to be frustrated or reminded of the burden I undertook to try to save my sister. Right now I just want to hear Ryker's voice.

I pull my cell out of my purse and see the notification from my bank of a deposit being transferred to my account. The notifications pop up often—every time one of my clients transfers money to my account. I take my cut and then send the remainder to the escort they spent time with.

But the amount of this notification more than catches my eye. *$20,000.* I blink at it for a second as I try to recall which girls I had out tonight, and none of them were bringing in $20,000 for one client.

That's ridiculously high. I may try to pretend I'm a big player in the escort business, but on the scale of things, I'm just getting started.

I log into my bank to check the transfer, always wary of suspicious things, always fearful this house of cards I'm holding up on a wing and a prayer will come tumbling down.

But I hesitate to click on the deposit.

A part of me already knows what I'm going to see.

R. Lockhart. $20,000 transferred to XXXX9560

A sickening feeling drops into the pit of my stomach as I stare at Ryker's transfer. Those snapshots that have lived on repeat in my brain come charging back but this time with a skewed observation of them.

One where there was nothing shared between us. No soft moments in the bar. No belly-clenching laughs during the game. No intimate emotions as we shared and pleasured and sated each other's bodies.

Not a single one.

Because it was just Ryker, the client, finally reaching his endgame with me, his escort.

He got precisely what he wanted. The weeks of chasing were done. He took and claimed . . . and now he's paying me to let me know where my exact position is in all of this.

I'm furious and within minutes am back out the door, on the train, and headed to his fancy penthouse to tell him where exactly he can shove his money.

My anger doesn't abate a single bit as I stalk my heels up to the front of his building and wait for the doorman to open it.

"Ms. Noname to see Mr. Lockhart, I presume?" he asks as his gaze flickers over his shoulder to a corner of the lobby area and then back to me. Something in his eyes is a warning I don't want to heed, and so I push past him despite his silent protests.

My heels are loud as I cross the space. Each step more determined than the next, especially when I see the back of Ryker's head. He's in a tuxedo, black jacket, black tie—breathtakingly handsome—and he has one hand holding on to something.

It takes me a second to process the sight once I take a few more steps.

He's dressed for a black-tie event. The woman he's touching is in an emerald-green formfitting dress with her flawlessly styled auburn hair.

It may take me a moment to process what I'm seeing, but it only takes a second for Roxanne to see me, flutter her lashes, and smile in such a sickeningly sweet way.

"Vaughn. So good to see you," she purrs, and even though his back is to me, Ryker's whole body jolts at the sound of my name.

My feet don't stop, though. They sound like thunder on the expensive floor as I stride across the distance. I don't dare look in his eyes. I don't dare show him how goddamn hurt I am right now.

First he pays me for something I thought was truly wanted between us. Something that wasn't forced by contract.

And then he rubs my nose in the fact that I was just his hire-by-night sex by going out with Roxanne—the woman he called crazy—without batting an eye.

Talk about switching bed partners while the sheets are still warm.

"Vaughn." I ignore the broken way he says my name. Drown it out with the sound of my pulse whooshing through my ears.

I take the check I made out for $20,000 while on the train and shove it at him. "I don't want your money any more than I want you." The last word is on a sob, my extended hand trembling as I wait for him to take it.

"Oh, how cute, a lover's quarrel. Don't mind me—I'll just sit here and watch so I know what pieces I have to kiss and make better for Ryker when you're all done," Roxanne says, but Ryker is already moving toward me, hand on my biceps now until he pushes open the ladies' room door of the lobby restroom. He locks the door behind us just as I yank my arm free.

It hurts to look at him. My heart aches just to look at his eyes because for the first time I actually thought something was real, and then . . . and then he let me know exactly where I stand with him.

"What the hell is this?" he shouts as he looks at the check in my hand.

"What the hell was that?" I counter, shoving my finger and pointing at an invisible Roxanne.

"Nothing."

"*Nothing?* Kind of like how you just proved to me I was nothing either?"

"What are you—?"

"You transferred money to my account."

"Yes . . . and?"

I stare at him. At the wide eyes and confused expression and bill it as an act for me to focus on instead of questioning him further about why the hell he went somewhere with Roxanne tonight.

"What happened between us wasn't about money," I grit out.

"Aren't you the one who so plainly stated that it was just business?" He quirks an eyebrow, his eyes and voice both holding a chill.

"Yes," I say out of pure stubbornness and hurt that when I pushed him away, he found his way to Roxanne.

"Then why are you so mad that I paid you for your time as agreed upon in our contract?"

"No, the time agreed upon in our contract was for me to accompany you to events and business dinners."

"Which you have. I'm a man of my word, and I paid you for the time."

"But—that night—the game . . ." Tears burn in my eyes. "It was . . ."

"It was what, Vaughn?" He takes a step closer, anger burning in his eyes, confusion begging me to say that we were more than that. But I don't want to admit it. I don't want to see Roxanne and think about her with him or what her being here means to us. Before I can figure out what to say, he pushes yet another one of my buttons. "Or should I say Vee?"

"Don't be an asshole."

He chuckles, and I can hear the frustration in it. He runs a hand through his hair. "How am I being one? We went out. We had sex. You bailed before daybreak. You're the one who made sure I felt like a client."

"And you're the one who made sure I felt like a whore."

"You can't have it both ways, Vaughn." His lack of a denial is like a punch to the gut.

"I didn't do it for the money," I say, pride front and center when pride shouldn't matter right now. All that matters is getting him back, but I'm so used to protecting myself—to self-preservation—that this is the only way I know how to respond.

That's a lie. I know what I need to do, but I'm too scared to. I've already given more of myself to Ryker than I have anyone else in my adult life, and so opening myself up to more hurt is petrifying.

"You didn't do it for the money?"

"No."

"You sure about that?"

Hurt echoes through me. "What's that supposed to mean?"

"If it wasn't for the money, then why won't you return my calls, Vaughn? Why do you keep resisting—"

"I'm here now, aren't I?"

"Only because you feel insulted . . . not because you want to be."

"That's not true."

"Isn't it?"

He stares at me, and my God, every part of me that wants to believe this is real—that he is standing here wondering the same things I am about where our relationship stands—feels validated. *So then why does it feel like we're an ocean apart?*

The only sound in the room is my phone alerting a text. And then another.

"You need to get that?" he asks with the lift of a brow.

"No," I say as it alerts again.

"Seems to me like someone's in high demand tonight."

The dig is there, noted, but it has nothing on the ache in my heart. "Go to hell, Lockhart."

"Keep the money, *Sanders*," he says, and I swear using my last name is his way of letting me know he got close to me when no one else has. It's his way of reminding me he knows the real me I'm constantly hiding from. "Use it to try to get custody of Lucy. Use it to pay down your debt. Use it to do whatever the fuck it is you need it for . . . we're paid in full."

My mouth shocks open in an *O* as I take in what he's saying. As I try to figure out why I don't want to hear the next words on his lips. As I try to process the fact that he just ended whatever this is between us.

"I don't need your charity."

"Too bad, because I sure as hell need things from you . . . things you're not willing to give." His jaw muscle tics as he stares at me, eyes alive with confusion, body set with tension.

"Like sex without strings? Like having a woman you can discard on a whim and then pick back up when your current lay won't return your calls?" Heartbreak guides my words and dims my rationality.

"And you just proved why it was crazy for me to think we would work in the first place."

"What's that supposed to mean?"

"It means you were so busy trying to justify your own reasons to yourself, you never bothered to see anything else."

"Ryker. What—?"

"Fuck this, Vaughn." He looks at the ceiling for a beat and blows out a breath that drips with both resignation and frustration. "I should've known after that first night this was a disaster in the making."

Panic bubbles up in my throat. My hands tremble. My mind scrambling. He's telling me what I already know . . . that this would never work between us, and yet . . .

"Then why did you pursue me? Why did you threaten? Why—"

"Because you're fucking gorgeous! Is that what you want to hear?" his voice thunders. "Because you were a challenge. A woman who sure as hell didn't play the part like every other woman in my life does. But Christ, Vaughn"—he walks to one side of the small bathroom and back, eyes boring into mine, frustration rolling off him and into me—"I can't keep fighting for someone who doesn't want to be fought for."

"That's not—"

"Because you were the goddamn exception."

"Ryker." It's a soft plea, and I'm not even sure what I'm asking for.

"No. Don't 'Ryker' me. You're the one who ran away. You're the one who—"

"You're the one who paid me like a whore," I sneer, and it stops him dead in his tracks.

"Exactly. And right there is why this whole thing is futile."

We stand so close together but a world apart. Him asking for things I don't know if I can give him. Him saying things that I don't understand.

Me letting the hurt and my fears and my insecurities come between us, but not knowing how to stop it.

The tears threaten, but I refuse to give him the satisfaction of knowing it. I refuse to give him another piece of me when inside there are so many broken ones to give right now.

"You're right—it is futile."

"I'll always be the asshole, and you'll always be the whore, and that's all you'll ever see."

I stare at him, every smart comeback I could have managed numbed by the hurt caused by his words, and nod before turning on my heel, fumbling with the lock, and bolting from the building as fast as I can. When I make it outside, the air is sharp and cold, and as soon as I turn the corner and am out of eyesight of the doorman, I hunch over, hands on my knees. My chest hurts, burns, aches, and every part of me is filled with an indescribable shame and undeniable anger . . . and irrefutable heartache.

Ryker Lockhart could have said anything to me . . . anything at all, but those words cut the deepest. Those words put me in my place and let me know where I stand with him.

Disposable.

Dispensable.

Unwanted.

Just when I was starting to believe I wasn't.

CHAPTER THIRTY-SEVEN

Vaughn

"Vaughn?" Joey's voice is hushed, his eyes wide when he sees me at the entrance of the facility. "Are you okay?"

I shake my head and don't care that I'm still in my work clothes or that my mascara is probably in streaks running down my cheeks or that I look like I've been put through the wringer—because I have. "I came as soon as I saw the texts."

And regardless of whatever I've been through, Lucy takes precedence over everything. Myself. My heartache. My needs.

"You sure you're okay?" he asks as he puts his hands on my shoulders to stop me from bolting down the hallway toward Lucy's room. His eyes fill with concern, and the sight of it has tears welling in mine.

"It's just been a rough night, okay?"

"Your boyfriend?"

A half-hysterical, half-desperate chuckle falls from my mouth. "I don't have a boyfriend." Just saying that hurts, and I run the heel of my hand against my breastbone to try to assuage a pain I know the motion can't ease.

"The Ryker guy?"

"Something like that."

"I'm sorry, sweetie." Joey pulls me in for a quick, comforting hug I don't deserve, knowing Lucy was here needing me while I was fighting with Ryker. And it's a hug I don't want, don't merit, because I just need to see my Luce.

"How is she? What happened?" I whisper. The lights are dim around us, seeing as it's well past two in the morning.

"She had a rough day. She was agitated, combative—"

"That's not like her."

"I know. The day counselor was Jenn—"

"She loves Jenn."

"I know, but Jenn said she was just having a rough time all around. Argumentative. Sad. Fighting everything and with everyone," he says and puts a hand on the small of my back to lead me down the hallway opposite of where Lucy's room is.

"Joey? Where are we—"

"She was screaming, keeping everybody up. Just when we thought we'd calmed her down, she'd start up again." He points to a door that's slightly ajar on the opposite side of the common area than her room. "She's sleeping in there."

"Why?"

"She was too loud in her normal room. We had to separate her from the rest of the kids because she kept waking them up."

And if I thought my heart sank at the notion of Lucy sleeping all alone in this facility, it rips to shreds when I gently push open the door and see her. The room is painted a sunny yellow, but where the walls of her regular room here are covered with the comforts of home—princess posters and pictures of her in fun places and little things to remind her of her mom—this room is stark with vacant walls and nothing familiar to comfort. The bed has a plain white sheet on it compared to her frilly pink ones, and the blanket she has covering her is the only thing that's hers. It's a knit pastel and is the one her mom and I bought her the last time we went shopping together.

Tears sting as I think of the memory. Of swinging Lucy between us as we walked. Of the chocolate ice cream we shared. Of Lucy's excitement over this blanket when she saw it.

It feels like forever ago and yesterday all at the same time.

I go to her. There is no hesitation, only love. The salt from her tears is dried on her cheeks, and her breath keeps hitching every few seconds as a reminder of the hysterics she went through without me here to comfort her.

The door at my back creaks, and I turn to see Joey there. "Was she with her dad last night?" I already know the answer. I already know she was and that she's upset because he reminds her of her mom. His lack of love, attention, and patience often hurts her feelings. It reminds her of the nonstop fighting she grew up with and of the overheard accusations that she was the cause of all of their problems. I'm not sure if Lucy comprehends what he meant by that, but I know the fighting was enough to leave a lasting impression on her. An impression that oftentimes leaves her confused and combative in the following days after their visits.

"You know I can't share that information with you," he murmurs, seeming to forget he often tells me when they are visiting. But that information is divulged when he's picking her up at my doorstep, not here under the ever-watchful eye of the government social workers.

"I'm sleeping here with her tonight," I tell him.

"You know that's not allowed."

"Auntie?" Lucy's sleep-drugged voice fills the room, and even though her eyes are closed and she's probably still asleep, she reaches out and grabs my hand.

I bite back a sob at the ever-present need to protect her and lift my eyebrows when I look back to Joey. "Then I guess you'll have to call the cops and kick me out."

I know he's still there when I toe off my shoes and carefully climb in bed beside her, but I don't acknowledge his presence. My uniform isn't the most comfortable of clothes to sleep in, and my makeup is still on and teeth aren't brushed, but I don't care.

I'm exactly where I need to be.

Wrapping my arm around her waist, I pull her in against me and just hold on tight. The door creaks again, and I know Joey has left me so I can be with my girl. I know he knows I'm what she needs right now.

And despite the exhaustion rioting through my body, I wonder how much heartache the human body can handle in a two-hour period. Ryker's accusations return and hit my ears again. There was more to his words that the hurt wouldn't let me grasp, more to his comments that my self-preservation shut down . . . but he still said them.

And I still have fallen for him.

I sniffle back the tears that spill over, trying not to wake Lucy up. I've already let her down once tonight by not being here when she needed me. I've already proven that my needs don't matter and hers do. She needs to be my focus.

Once I adopt her, then I can think of myself.

With my lips pressed against her temple, I murmur, "I love you, Lucy Loo. I always have, and I always will."

CHAPTER THIRTY-EIGHT

Ryker

Night seeps into the day.

The day screams into the pounding headache I have that the empty bottle of Macallan on my counter can attest to.

And fuck if I'm not all kinds of worse for the wear.

How the hell did this happen?

Because you couldn't get the words out right. Because you're an inexperienced bastard when it comes to shit like this.

I'll always be the asshole, and you'll always be the whore, and that's all you'll ever see.

I dial her cell again, and it goes straight to voice mail.

Goddammit, Vaughn.

CHAPTER THIRTY-NINE

Vaughn

I look like a prostitute.

At least I feel like what I think one would look like.

I'm still in last night's clothes after doing a half-assed job of trying to remove my makeup with hand soap and water, my teeth brushed with my finger and toothpaste, and my eyes puffy and bloodshot from all of the crying last night. The late-morning commuters rushing in and out of Starbucks tell me my assumption is right by their sideways glances and the raised eyebrows they give each other. A few teenagers, late for class, snicker. A couple of mothers pull their children closer or move them to the opposite side as we wait in line.

But I don't care.

Sure, I got to wake up with Lucy and get her off to school, but that doesn't erase the devastation of last night. Of not being there for her and of reeling from whatever it is that happened with Ryker.

Because what it is that happened, I'm still not sure.

I know I'm a hypocrite for justifying taking from women who are paid to have sex, then freaking out when a man tries to pay me for it.

And I know I need a bit of distance from Ryker to clear my head. This all happened too quick and under abnormal circumstances, and I just need to take a step back from it all.

I need to focus on Lucy.

I need to focus on growing my business.

I need to forget about Ryker for a while to make the first two happen.

That's a lot of needs for a woman who usually doesn't need anything.

As subtly as possible, I shove away the tears that leak out as I stand there feeling lost in the middle of Starbucks, coffee in hand, and wondering what I'm supposed to do now.

I've never felt this way before when it comes to a man, and I sure as hell hate every second of it.

When I look up, I'm surprised to see my bartender from Apropos, Ahmed, rising from his seat in the corner, motioning for me to come sit with him. "Vaughn? You okay?"

"Yes. No. I don't know," I mutter, wanting to be alone, knowing he sees the uniform and is making assumptions, but my feet move his way without consent.

"Come sit with me for a second." I meet his eyes for the first time and bristle at the overwhelming amount of compassion in them. He waits until I've sat down and had a sip before continuing. "Late night?"

"Something like that." I lift my eyebrows at him. "Early morning? Didn't you close last night?"

His smile is soft. "Maybe I never went to bed."

"Ah. She was that good, huh?"

"Mmm. She was."

His cheeks flush unexpectedly, his eyes avert down to the cup in his hand, and as much as small talk is low on my list of priorities right now, I'll suffer through so long as the conversation stays on him.

"She from the bar? A customer?"

He smiles and shakes his head subtly. "Contrary to public opinion, the barflies only occupy a portion of my time. The rest of the time it's Sarah Kay and Kate Tempest and Aja Monet." My wide eyes give him a clue that I have no idea who these women are. "Slam poets, Vaughn. There was a huge reading last night in Harlem, and I'm . . ." He shrugs and just leans back, smile widening.

The slam-poet thing takes me by surprise—he's the last person I'd ever think would be into poetry—but there's so much inspiration lighting up his features that it's obvious this is his thing.

"I had no idea."

"Most don't, and I'm okay with that. Poetry isn't very masculine, but it feeds my soul."

"You learn something new every day," I murmur.

"Hopefully." His voice is quiet, introspective, and his head is angled as he studies me for a moment. "Tell me about him."

"What do you mean?" I ask like he's off base when I already know I'm going to talk.

"Is this the same man who had you tied up in knots a few weeks back at the club?" He asks the question, but it's so much easier to look out the window at the people passing by than to acknowledge it. "The same man who had to do with that redhead who looked like she wanted to rip your hair out?"

"Something like that."

My hesitation must speak volumes because he leans forward and places his elbows on the table. "Look, Vaughn. I'm not trying to get into your business. If you want an ear, I have one. If you don't want one, I never saw you here. But sometimes, just getting it out helps."

"Ahmed . . ." Half protest, half twist my arm.

"You are the most private of all of the staff at Apropos. I get that. I respect that. I'm not going to give you advice, but I'm not gonna lie when I tell you I've got a pretty damn good ear for listening. And I'm not going to bullshit you and tell you everything is going to be okay when romance is far from perfect."

Our gazes hold, and I hate that talking to him is just opening me up to letting more people into my already private world, but at the same time, I'm miserable. *And lost.*

This needing-people stuff is for the birds.

I don't trust my voice when I speak, and the waver in it tells me why. "We come from different worlds."

"Isn't that true for all men and women?" he asks, trying to add some levity to the conversation. "Mars. Venus. Whatnot."

"True, but I mean in the sense that he comes from a world where things can be bought, where words can be said without repercussions because he doesn't care what people think of him, and where . . ."

"Where what?"

"Where it seems there's always someone standing in the wings waiting to replace you."

"I find that hard to believe."

"What?"

"That you're replaceable."

"I am." I laugh. "Believe me."

But there's something in the way Ahmed looks at me that has me holding off making any more of my self-deprecating comments.

"Just stop, okay?" he asks with a soft smile. "You're one of a kind, kid. I see it night after night. The men eyeing you. Asking me questions about whether you're single. The ones trying to build up the courage to ask for your number only to be shot down." He lifts his eyebrows. "Without sounding creepy, you're kind of everything a man wants."

I shake my head at the compliment. "I don't want to be that."

"You have no control over that." He laughs. "I think you're looking at this all wrong, though."

"How's that?"

"You need to be looking for the sunset."

"The sunset?" I part laugh, part question, suddenly thinking he needs to go home and get some sleep.

"Yep. *The sunset.* One of the poets last night said something that stuck with me." He takes a sip of his coffee and stares at it for a beat before looking back up to meet my eyes. "He said that most people look for love in the sunrise, when they don't realize for them it can be found in the sunset."

His words hit my ears, and it takes me a second to process their meaning. That so many people look for love from the onset when they meet someone, when for many others it can be found when you think it's almost over, the fire burned out.

I want to tell him that's definitely a different way of looking at things. That it sounds like something a poet would say—romantic, yet unrealistic—and yet when I open my mouth to refute him, nothing comes out.

He takes notice. "See, you're looking at this like a woman when you need to be looking at it like a man."

"And how would a man look at it?" I ask, more than skeptical.

"I'll be the first to admit that for the most part, we're fearful creatures. Scared of fucking everything up. So when we meet someone like you—strong, independent, tell it like it is, and drop-dead gorgeous—well, we get knocked off our stride some and don't know how to react."

I think of Ryker. Of his reputation. Of his own take-no-bullshit attitude.

"I was a challenge." My thoughts tumble out into words I'm not even sure I utter.

"And let me guess—now you're not?"

I eye him. The last thing I need to do is talk about my sex life with Ahmed.

"Here's the thing: men think the challenge is what they want. And maybe it is at first. But with the wrong girl, a guy would get what he came for and then bail faster than fast after he gets it . . . but for the *right* girl. Mmm. For the right girl, he'd be confused over what to do. He'd say words to hurt her and push her away because that's so much easier than dealing with his own bullshit feelings. He'd do things that don't make sense to you but that make perfect sense to him because what he hears in his own head and what comes out of his mouth are two entirely different things."

"I assure you he meant what he did and what he said," I murmur as tears well.

"You wouldn't be as upset as you are if you really thought that was the truth." He nods. "He's just as scared by all of this as you are. He's trying to figure out how you walked into his life and turned it upside down when he swore it would never happen. He's mad at you for it." He holds up his hand when I start to protest. "But madder at himself."

I force a smile and sigh heavily, not feeling any better but possibly understanding a bit more. "I appreciate you trying to make me feel better."

"I'm not trying to make you feel better. I'm just telling you like I see it."

"Thank you. It was sweet of you." I push my chair back to stand. "I should leave you be—"

"No. Sit for a while. I've got to head over to a friend's house." He rises and places the strap of his knapsack over his shoulder. "And, uh, this conversation never happened." He offers me a wink and a smile before turning on his heel and leaving.

I watch the door open, then close, staring after him as he strides away, confused but a little more settled with thoughts of sunsets on my mind.

CHAPTER FORTY

Ryker

"You want to explain why you're being such an asshole to everyone and everything, or should I just hunch over here in the corner and hope I don't get your wrath for breathing?" My glare doesn't faze Stuart as he stands there with his eyebrows raised and hands on his hips. "You forget, I have a tiger mom complete with the thick Chinese accent to boot," he says, mimicking his mother's accent. "You don't scare me."

"What do you need, Stuart?"

"Ah, I get the special treatment? Bella says you're cussing out everyone who comes in here . . . I guess today's my lucky day that you're holding your tongue."

"Stuart?" It's a warning that my tongue will start lashing if he doesn't get to his goddamn point.

"I'm here for you." He drops a stack of files on my desk. "One's a confirmed cheater. One's a fetish freak that made me want to wash my retinas with bleach. And the other . . . she's gorgeous and lonely and hasn't done a thing to deserve her husband trying to fuck her over seven ways from Sunday."

"Hmm," I say as I glance at the files stacked on my desk but don't move to look at them—the evidence I need to use against the wives in court to get them to bend to my settlement offer.

"Hmm? That's all you're going to give me?" He laughs. "No repri-mand for me siding with one of the wives? No *Stuart, I don't need your opinions*. No nothing?"

"I'm fresh out of anger."

He eyes me when I don't want to be studied, and I'm sure he's see-ing the same thing I saw in the mirror this morning. A moody fucker who misses Vaughn and isn't sure what else to do for her other than to try to keep calling her when she won't pick up the phone.

"Out of anger? Then you're definitely not feeling okay."

"You can go now, Stu."

He stands there with his lips pursed, hands in his pockets, and I lift my eyebrows to let him know this conversation is over. He nods his head and then turns to leave.

"Question?" I ask when he reaches for the handle on the door.

"Yeah?" He turns to face me.

"How long do you wait before you call a woman?"

The fucker fights the smile on his lips, and, lucky for him, he wins the battle. "Is this before or after you have sex with her?"

"How about it's after a fight when you said things that . . . fuck it. Never mind." I wave a hand his way and blow out a sigh.

You're asking your PI for relationship advice. And you don't think this has affected you?

And then I hear the word in my own head—*relationship*—and wonder how the fuck I let it get this far.

"So that explains the foul mood. Nothing like a woman to fuck shit up."

"You can say that again," I mutter, while hating myself for this conversation.

"How long ago was the fight?" he asks as I'm mentally fucking myself over here.

"A week."

"A week?"

"Jesus. Don't say it like that."

"A week is a long time for things to rattle around in a woman's mind without them turning whatever it is that happened into an exaggeration of itself."

"What makes you think I said something wrong?"

He just eyes me and chuckles with a shake of his head. "Subtlety isn't exactly your strong suit."

"You can go back to going now," I say.

"Have you at least called her?"

"Yes."

"And?"

"She won't pick up. It goes straight to voice mail."

"So she's blocked you. You must have really been an asshole." He blows out an exaggerated sigh. "You send flowers? Stop by her house? Beg and plead?"

"Stuart."

"This is all new territory to you, I assume, so I just want to make sure you've covered the basics."

"I'm not an idiot."

"Is she worth the hassle?"

I stare at him. "That's the million-dollar question, isn't it?" I ask but already know the answer. My fucking misery is answer enough.

"Give her a few more days, and then return to the beg, borrow, and steal portion of the program. But be creative. Chicks love creative."

"Fucking great."

"You're the sorry sap who put yourself in the situation." He shrugs and heads out the door.

He's right. I put myself in the situation. I set this whole goddamn thing up.

And, it seems to me, I'm the one who tore the whole thing down.

CHAPTER FORTY-ONE
Vaughn

The bills stare at me. They call my name.

Dramatic, I know, but it's been a shitty ten days, and the last thing I want to do is to get even more depressed when I go to check balances and see that they aren't moving as quickly as I need them to.

Yes, I have thirty girls on the payroll so far, but out of that thirty, only ten are high-dollar earners for me. The others are just starting out, just figuring out if this is their thing, or if that crappy feeling in their tummy after they're paid for their bodies, their services, is worth it.

If they're cut out for it, when I sure as hell am not.

And of course, the word *hypocrite* flits through my mind again. It's hard not to when there are flowers on the counter in front of me and on the credenza behind me from a man who I experienced the same thing with.

"Keep telling yourself that, and you might actually start believing it," I mutter as I reach for my planner in its usual place only to find it on the opposite side of my desk. "Bills. I need to pay bills, not think about Ryker." I laugh. "Or talk to myself like a crazy person."

But isn't that how I feel? I put distance between us so I could sort out how I feel, and all it ended up doing was make me feel more unsettled.

And of course I miss him just as much.

The question is, do I miss him . . . or do I miss the idea of having someone to be with, confide in . . . laugh with?

With a deep sigh, I turn back to my spreadsheet and way-too-big balances and figure I need to tackle all of this so I can get it off my table before Lucy comes tomorrow. She's already asked me once what all the papers on my table were.

So did Joey.

"Bills, Vaughn. Focus."

And with perfect timing, the doorbell rings.

Are you kidding me?

I laugh. It's all I can do and hope it's not another delivery, because this is getting quite ridiculous, but my smile fades the minute I open the door.

The man standing before me is a little over six feet tall. He's wiry with dirty-blond hair that's long enough it tucks behind his ears. His cheeks are hollow, his fingers twitching, and his eyes are an unforgiving blue as he stares at me.

All I see is the man who helped my sister end her life. No, he didn't tie the noose, but he sure as hell fueled her depression with drugs and dependency.

If I hated him before, I sure as hell loathe him now.

"What are you doing here?" I ask when what I should have done is slam the door in his face.

"What? No *Hi, Brian, so good to see you?* No *Brian, how have you been since your girlfriend died?* No—"

"Nope. I don't care how you've been." My smile is tight as my blood pumps with fury through my veins.

"You always were a holier-than-thou, little-goody-two-shoes bitch. I shouldn't have expected you to change."

We stare at each other in the entrance to my house, so much bad blood between us, and I know there's only one reason he's here.

"What do you want, Brian?"

"Have you seen my little girl lately?"

"Is it that hard for you to bring yourself to say her name? Or are you so zoned out on your latest high that you forgot it?" Every word I utter to him is pained.

"Dramatic as always." He rolls his eyes. "And I'll have you know I haven't been high in a while."

"What, a few days? Is that a new record for you?"

But I know the answer. It's always been the answer when it comes to Brian.

"Fucking barrel of laughs as usual."

"You have ten seconds to tell me why you're here, or else I'm slamming the door in your face."

"You afraid the people on the street are going to start rumors about how their neighbor with the stick up her ass is finally letting loose with a hot guy like me?" He asks the question, but I can see the signs. The constantly scanning eyes. The violent twitching of his body. The stained fingertips. He's going through withdrawal.

"Does Priscilla know you're using again?" I ask, ignoring his question as I picture Lucy having to live with this, like this, again when it was hard enough worrying about her with my sister. But at least I knew my sister worshipped her. Brian, on the other hand . . .

"Fuck Priscilla."

Please, tell her that. It'll make this process easier.

"I took a hit from a friend. It's the first time I used since . . . since Sammy died."

My laugh is instantaneous. His lie is that funny. But it doesn't matter that he's coming down from whatever it is he took; it only matters if

Priscilla sees it. It only matters if he screws up enough that social services deems him an unfit father.

"Ten. Nine. Eight . . ." I begin the countdown.

"I have a proposition for you."

"I figured."

"Two hundred thousand dollars, and I give up all rights to Lucy."

I sputter out a laugh, and then it slowly fades to disbelief. "Are you fucking kidding me?"

On one hand, this is all it takes to get the jackass out of the picture? On the other hand, that's all he thinks that precious little girl is worth?

And I'm not stupid enough to think that even if I had the money to pay him off, he'd ever stop coming back for more.

But still, if I had the money . . .

"Do I look like I'm joking?"

"You look like a junkie desperate for his next fix and more than willing to sell his daughter for it."

"Hey"—he flashes me a smile that reminds me of what a handsome man he used to be before the drugs ravished his features—"a man has to do what a man has to do."

Tears of anger burn in my eyes as my hands fist, and I fight every inclination I have not to swing out and deck him.

"You know what, Brian? If I could, I would, but I don't have that kind of money."

"Ah, I doubt that. You still work in that fancy club? Can't you get one of the sugar daddies there to front you the cash?"

"You need to leave." My fingers grip onto the sides of the doorframe.

"A fancy place like this, you've got to have some kind of cash lying around."

"A fancy place? I rent it, Brian. I rent it because I'm so busy trying to pay down all of the debt I incurred while trying to keep Samantha alive."

He snorts. "You were the stupid bitch who lifted your credit card up and offered to pay for her."

"It was either that or let her overdose," I shout at him, remembering the frantic calls to facilities to get her into a rehab program after she finally begged me for help. Her confession that she forgot about Lucy and left her at the park alone while she went and got high. How scared she was when she couldn't find Lucy until a neighbor walked her back home. The required up-front fees to even get her admitted. The daily counseling afterward. The medications to combat the urges, the depression, the hepatitis B she'd contracted from sharing needles.

"Overdosing seems like a better way to go than the way she chose."

"Get out!" I scream at him at the top of my lungs as he stares at me with the slightest of smirks.

"I take it that's a no, then?"

"No!" I scream and slam the door in his face, the clicking of the locks accompanied by his chuckle on the other side of it.

The tears flow furiously. The want and need to pay him off, to get him out of our life and secure Lucy in mine is so tempting I can taste it . . . but the stack of bills on the table, the proof that my sister once was alive and fighting the battle he's obviously given up on, tells me it's not possible.

I can't work any harder, do anything more than I'm already doing to try to prove I'm the suitable one to adopt Lucy.

It takes me a few moments to cool down so that my hands aren't trembling and my pulse isn't racing, and when I do, I grab my cell phone.

"Social Service Office, Priscilla Jengle speaking."

"Hi, Priscilla—it's Vaughn Sanders."

"Someone's ears must be burning."

"Excuse me?"

"I just received a very disturbing call from Brian."

Dread drops like a dead weight through me, my mind already assuming the worst before she speaks.

There's nothing I'd put past him.

"Disturbing?" *Deep breath, Vaughn.* "How about the notion that he was just here—at my house. That he offered to give me the right to adopt Lucy in exchange for two hundred thousand dollars. He tried to get me to buy her from him. *Buy her!* I'm not sure if there is anything you can say to me that can top how disturbing that is."

She tsks, and the sound comes through the line in unmistaken disapproval. "Hmm."

"What does that mean?" I ask, trying to rein in my anger.

"It's funny that he was just telling me you made that exact same offer to him."

I burst out in disbelieving laughter without even thinking about how it sounds to her. "You're kidding me, right? What in the hell would I want the two hundred thousand for?"

And then it hits me.

"Well, you are under quite a lot of financial stress. Stress you incurred to try to help Lucy's mother. Two hundred thousand dollars would go a long way to help pay down your debt . . ."

"Are you kidding me? Are you actually implying that I'd sell Lucy to pay down my bills?" *Toe the line, Vaughn. Be calm. She's the one who makes the final decision.* "What about Brian? What about his reasons? You can get a whole lot of drugs for two hundred thousand."

"All of his tests have come back clean."

"Test him right now," I demand. "He was just here. He's going through withdrawals."

"That's not how random drug testing works."

"So, let me get this straight. He comes to my house, propositions me, and when it doesn't go the way he wants to, he calls you to cover his tracks." I blow out a sigh, marveling at his stunt and her naivete. "And you believe him."

"No one said I was taking sides."

Bullshit.

"But since he called you first, you're more apt to—"

"I'm not impressed with your tone, Ms. Sanders."

"I'd like to speak to your supervisor," I say, so far over this it's ridiculous.

"Why?"

"Because I don't think you're doing your job properly. While Brian sits and wines and dines and plays you—"

"How dare you accuse me of impropriety—"

"Exactly. How dare you accuse me of trying to sell the rights to my niece to pay down my debt." I clear my throat and pinch the bridge of my nose to try to calm myself down. "While all of this is going on, an eight-year-old little girl with special needs who needs stability and love and patience is sitting all alone, day in, day out, in a group home."

"They are meeting her needs."

"Meeting her needs is a bullshit way to say she's *in the system*. A system that's broken at best and not skilled to suit her needs in the way that I can. I've been to every doctor's appointment with her when my sister was alive and now that she's gone. I've learned her education protocol. I've taken classes on how to best stimulate and challenge and expand her horizons so that she can grow up to be as independent as possible. I've held her when she cries because she misses her mother and when she lashes out because seeing her dad brings back the dysfunction the drugs created in her house. You tell me which one of any of those things Brian has done. You tell me when he has loved her unconditionally except when showing his cards like he did today, wanting to sell her off to feed that habit of his. The same habit that helped to kill my sister."

"Ms. Sanders—"

"No. Don't 'Ms. Sanders' me. I want the name of your supervisor, and I want it now."

"I'm not allowed to give that out."

My laugh borders on hysteria as I think of the dozens of things I can say to her about how since I help to pay her government paycheck, she damn well can give me her supervisor's name, but I figure I've pissed her off enough.

"I would appreciate it if you would have your supervisor call me at her earliest convenience, please," I say in my most reserved of voices.

Priscilla clears her throat. "I assure you that's not necessary."

"And I assure you it is."

I end the call and lean back against the couch, close my eyes, and try to process how it is Brian continually tries to ruin everything good in my life.

CHAPTER
FORTY-TWO

Ryker

She's stunning.

That's the easiest way to describe the woman who walks into my office. The one who Bella told me needed to see me but wanted her identity kept confidential. She's statuesque and confident, with a power suit on that hints at curves but goes more for sophistication and a purse that could rival my mother's in expense.

Always one to read someone, I watch her take a seat without me offering it first, fold her perfectly manicured hands in her lap, and then flutter those chocolate-colored eyes my way.

Her anonymity aside, this woman knows how to capture the attention of a man.

And most definitely how to use it to her advantage.

I stare at her for a beat, letting her know that while I made an exception to see her without knowing who she is, I'm the one in control here . . . not her.

"How can I help you, Miss . . . ?"

"I hear you're the best there is." Her voice is throaty and smooth, the subtle movement of her head letting me know she's not convinced of what she's heard about me.

"That depends who you're asking." I lean back in my chair. Two can play this game.

"I hear you take risks."

"It seems you hear a lot of things," I counter, and she just lifts a lone eyebrow. "Why do you care if I take risks?"

"Because my being here might end up being a conflict of interest for you."

"Why's that?"

She waits a moment, looks down at her fingernails and then back up to me. "Because I believe my husband has already retained your services."

And now she has my attention.

I exhale evenly and quietly admire the balls this woman already has. "Is that so?"

"Yes." She rises from her seat and moves about my office. Her heels click as she trails a finger over a shelf of my bookcase on her way to the window. She stops with her back to me and stares out at the world below, her hourglass figure purposely on display.

This is a woman who knows how to play her audience.

"And what can I do for you, then?" I ask.

"Take me as your client instead."

My head startles from her statement. A request to go easier on her was what I expected. An explanation of all the ways her husband has wronged her possibly another, but asking me to dump whoever her husband is and take her on instead is so far from what I thought.

When I don't respond, she turns and pins me with her stare. "I'll make it worth your while."

"I'm told that often. I assure you your offer doesn't impress me." *But your gumptions sure as fuck does.*

"Oh, but it will impress you. I'm sure of it." She turns her lips up in the most conniving of smiles, and her eyes glint like she's a fucking witch about to exact her revenge.

"Who's your husband?"

"We'll get to that."

"I think you're mistaken. I'm the one who calls the shots here, not you. When I ask who your husband is, I want to know who he is so as to not jeopardize my relationship with my client."

She makes her way slowly back across my office and returns to the seat across from me, eyes still locked on mine. "And what if I were to tell you, Mr. Lockhart, that by pulling your egotistical bullshit like this, you are jeopardizing your future relationship with me as your client. *And you want me as a client.*"

Jesus Christ. The woman is fearless.

I lean forward and fold my hands atop my desk. "I'm listening."

She puts a hand in her purse and casually slides a fully executed check across the desk in front of me, her finger resting on its top left corner. I glance down and almost choke at the amount it's made out for: $2,000,000. More than triple my typical retainer.

"Are you impressed now?" she asks as my eyes lift slowly up to hers as if I'm not.

"Is it your money or your husband's money?"

"Does it matter so long as I'm a signer on the account?"

"To me it does." Fucking women.

"No prenup. Married young and with nothing." She lifts an eyebrow. "I'll ask my question again: Are you for hire?"

"What's the catch?" I ask. There's always a catch when money comes this easy.

"No catch, just a stipulation."

"Of course there is." I shake my head. "No thanks."

She smiles boldly. "I can't believe a successful man like you is afraid to agree that whatever isn't used of my retainer—whatever the reason may be—will be returned to me."

I meet her stare. Do I really want to deal with another ball-busting female? I'm not seeming to fare too well with the one I've slept with . . . who says I can handle working for one too?

"It's a simple yes or no answer, Mr. Lockhart," she says casually as she removes her hand from the check and leans back in her chair, gaze never wavering from mine.

I glance down at the check, at the names of the account holders in the upper left-hand corner, and know the answer regardless of how much of a disaster I'm creating by doing this.

For the first time in my professional life, I'm going to change my ways.

I'm going to make an exception to my rules.

I reach my hand out across the desk. "I look forward to doing business with you."

CHAPTER
FORTY-THREE
Vaughn

"Is something wrong?" I ask Lola the minute she picks up the phone.

"No, why?"

"I told you I was taking some downtime this week and to only call if it was an emergency," I say, my heartbeat slowing down a bit after freaking out when I saw four missed calls from her. I check the shared calendar I have with each of my girls and see that she's having a slow week. "What's going on?"

"I have a situation, and I'm not sure how to handle it."

"What's that?" I ask, distracted when I shouldn't be distracted, but I can't focus on anything these past few days. That's a lie; I can focus, but just on one person in particular.

The person who's sending me flowers. The one I told myself I needed to keep my distance from to prove to myself I can.

"Remember that client I couldn't meet with when that asshole bruised my face?"

"Which one?" I ask without thought because there were several asshole clients that week.

"The Lockhart guy."

"What about him?" My voice is calm while inside I'm standing at attention.

"He contacted me today."

My heart drops at the sound of his name and more so at the fact that he contacted Lola. The only purpose he would have to do that would be to retain her services.

"And?"

"Relax, Vee—I'm not trying to steal another girl's client," she says in reaction to the tension in my voice, and I can all but hear her eyes roll at me.

"What did he want?"

"It's weird. He says he keeps calling his girl—Saxony was her name, I think. I guess she's not returning his calls."

"Okay . . ." I draw the word out as my pulse gets a little bump and my belly a tiny flutter.

"Is she still working for you?"

"Mm-hmm." I don't trust myself to speak.

"That's no way to build a client list and reputation if she's not returning calls."

"Thank you for the lesson in business, Lola, but I assure you I can take care of my girls," I snap at her.

"Look, he said he keeps calling her. She's not responding. He said he needs her to call him back, or else he's going to have to move on when he really doesn't want to."

Every part of me knows I need to tell her to relay to him to move on.

I try to convince myself it's in my best interest.

But I don't.

"What's your question?" I finally ask when I can find my voice.

"What should I tell him? Can I tell him you're going to have her call him?"

"Are you feeling all right, Lola? Normally you'd swoop in and claim a high-dollar client like him for yourself." I chuckle because it's something I'd normally do—call her out on her ruthless business acumen—when right now I'm so damn thankful she suddenly has morals.

"He said something to me that struck a chord."

"What did he say?"

"He said she made him appreciate the unexpected."

"Oh." It's all I can say, his words making emotion clog in my throat.

"Yeah, oh." She laughs. "Those words gave me pause. I mean, I'm the furthest thing from romantic, but fuck if that didn't make my cold heart thaw a little bit."

"Mine too," I murmur.

"And look, you're right—normally I'd jump all over a client like him, but it's not worth the drama it would cause among the girls. The last place I worked someone did the same shit, and I learned you don't piss in the pool you're swimming in with your coworkers, you know?"

"Uh-huh."

"So you'll call him for me. Get her to call him. However you want to handle it?"

She made him appreciate the unexpected.

"Yes. I'll get in touch with both of them."

"Thanks."

We hang up the phone, and all my restraint is gone. All of the times I had to turn the ringer off on my phone so I wouldn't pick up and the voice mails I deleted without listening to them. Each of the extra shifts I worked so I wouldn't be at home, bored and desperate to talk to him. They all go out the window.

Every single one of them.

Nerves buzz as the phone rings.

"Lockhart."

His voice. That voice. It's all I need to know that I was an idiot. It's all I need to hear to know that me wanting to be with him doesn't make me a bad person because I have interests outside of taking care of Lucy.

"Hello, Mr. Lockhart," I say quietly and secretly pray that he's not going to hang up on me and give me back a taste of my own medicine.

"Vaughn?"

"You never apologized," I say immediately, finally telling him the one thing I've been needing to hear from him.

"You never picked up the phone so I could. And if you had listened to your voice mails, I assure you there were a few in there."

Oh.

Shit.

I guess I neglected to think of it that way.

"Ryker . . ." *I miss you. I need to see you. God, why did I wait so long to call you?*

But I don't say any of those words because I don't want to negate the right I had to be angry at the things he said to me. Sure, I can admit to myself that my stubbornness might have prolonged my misery longer than it needed to be, but I still get to retain the right to deserve an apology.

"I've replayed that night a thousand times while listening to your cell ring and then push me to voice mail. I didn't say things the right way . . ."

"Neither of us did."

"You walked in when Roxanne was paying me one of her I'm-drunk-and-I-miss-you visits—her typical lobby ambush of me. I swear to you nothing was going on—"

"You weren't exactly convincing."

"The last time I saw you was when I watched you while you slept in my bed. The last time we'd talked you'd told me what was between us was strictly business. I was still pissed at you for that, and then to have you walk in while I was dealing with Roxanne . . . I didn't say what I needed to say."

"What did you need to say?"

"That I paid you the money so the debt was settled between us. You fulfilled your end of the contract, and I wanted to follow through on mine."

"But—"

"No, let me finish," he demands. "I let you run away with the conversation before—this time you'll let me finish." When I don't respond, he continues. "What I wanted to say was that I wanted all scores settled so that whatever happened from here on out between you and me, we'd both know there were no ulterior motives. We'd both know it was because we wanted something to happen, not because I threatened you so that you'd be forced to be with me."

And now I want to melt into the biggest puddle on the floor as his words awaken again those feelings I told myself weren't true. The ones that aren't possible . . . because how can you think you're in love with someone when you've never experienced it before and everything between us seems to be in a constant state of turmoil?

"Vaughn, are you there?"

"Yes. Yeah. Yes." I laugh.

"I missed you." There is so much emotion packed in those three words when he says them that this time tears spring to my eyes, and it's for all the right reasons.

"I missed you too." The words are hard to get out simply because every other emotion possible is clouding the way.

"Should I assume you got my message from Lola?"

"Loud and clear." I smile for what feels like the first time in forever.

"When can I see you again?"

Now. As soon as possible. Where are you? I'm coming . . .

"When are you free?"

"My driver is currently en route to your house . . ." His chuckle rumbles through the line. "Is that soon enough?"

"I'd like that," I murmur, thinking how spot on Ahmed was about how men don't always say things the right way. "Sunsets."

"What?" he asks with a laugh.

"Just that I believe in sunsets."

CHAPTER
FORTY-FOUR
Vaughn

My mad dash over the next forty minutes—the one where I pick up the house, change the sheets on my bed, take a quick shower while I silently freak out that Ryker is coming to my house, which is a crackerbox compared to his extravagant penthouse—is chaotic to say the least. Then, after a few moments of stupid doubt, I proceed to fix my makeup so that it doesn't look like I'm trying too hard but still care enough about him to try, spritz body spray in every crack and crevice on my body in the hope that he will explore them, and then pace around nervously because I'm so damn excited to get to see him again.

Every time a car drives by, I rush to the window like an anxious little kid only to be let down. So when there's a knock on the door, I jolt up from the couch, surprised and suddenly anxious.

But that anxiety fades the minute I pull open the door and see him. He looks good—tired, but so damn good. The lines at the sides of his eyes crinkle when his lips turn up into a smile.

We don't speak. I don't invite him in. Instead we just stand there—him on the porch and me in the doorway—and drink each other in like lovers who've gone way too long since they've seen each other.

"Vaughn." His voice. *My name. Hello. I've missed you. God, you're beautiful. I'm sorry.* I never knew my name could say so many things, but when he says it, it can.

"Hi."

I step back and pull the door open wider, and he walks in. He doesn't look around. He doesn't notice the house or the rushed clean-up job or anything else because his eyes never leave mine. It's heady and intoxicating in the most intimate of ways, as if I'm his when no one has ever laid that kind of claim to me.

Reaching out, he twists his fingers with mine as he shuts the door behind us. We both look down—at our fingers intertwined—and for some reason understand that this is the start of something all new for us. It sounds old-classic-black-and-white-romance-movie corny, but I swear to God it's true.

Suddenly bashful, I lift my eyes back up to meet his, and within a beat, he's pulled me into him, and his lips meet mine.

We don't speak, the urgency to smother any doubt either of us has remaining too important. We pour the words we need to say—the apologies, the "never again," the "how can we feel like this when neither of us is this kind of person"—into actions. His lips on mine. His hands touching everywhere on my body and not enough places all at the same time.

It's been thirteen days.

That's all.

But it feels like an eternity.

How do you spend a lifetime not feeling anything so much so that you take pride in being unattached, you build a business on it, only to have someone waltz into your life and make you feel so intensely that thirteen days seems like a damn eternity?

"I missed you," I murmur against his lips as our fingers unbutton and unzip and unclasp as fast as we can.

There is no need to go slow and sweet. To reveal each other through removing one item of clothing at a time. Right now is about pure carnal need.

The need to taste.

The hunger in each other's kiss. The salt on each other's skin. The mint on his tongue.

The need to claim.

His hands mark me everywhere they touch. With sensations. With chills. With an ache so deep it burns bright and fierce.

The need to feel.

The cool wall against my back. The stubble on his jaw as it scrapes over my bare shoulder. The urgency in his fingers as they part me. The feel of his dick hard and ready against my thigh.

The need to hear.

The quick intake of our breaths as he slips his fingers into me. The unmistakable sound of how wet I am just from his touch and anticipation alone, as he slides in and out of me. The groans telling him how much this turns me on.

The need to know.

That he's here. That his touch is real. That with every step forward, we're leaving the drama of the past few weeks behind.

And then, amid all of the fervor, all of the desperation, Ryker slides his hands up to cup the sides of my face and just stares at me. There's an absolute intimacy in the moment. We're stripped raw, down to our basics, just him and me and the act of sharing each other's bodies for pleasure. There's need and greed and pure male masculinity in everything in his eyes, and yet there's something else there. A tenderness. A need to take a second to slow down and understand what this is between us when neither of us is willing to define it.

"Jesus, Vaughn." I turn my cheek into his hand and press a kiss to the center of his palm, my heart flip-flopping in my chest. "Do you know how fucking bad I want you right now?"

I lean up on my tiptoes, press the softest of kisses on his lips, and whisper, "Show me."

It's almost as if I can feel his restraint snap the second my words register. His hands are back on me. Mine on him. Seeking more. Demanding everything. Showing him what I want.

"Bed," he murmurs between kisses. "Or floor." Another kiss. "I'm not picky."

A muffled laugh. A flurry of activity as we move toward my bedroom, all while not wanting to give up a second of touch or taste or togetherness.

And when we make it into my room, we fall clumsily onto the bed. Our laughter rings out and then slowly turns to moans when his lips close over the peak of my breast before making their way up to meet mine as my fingers encircle his cock.

Our lips are touching, our kiss halted as we sink into the feel of each other's actions. We absorb the sensations the other evokes, and then I not so gently pull his shaft toward the *V* of my thighs, desperate for him to fill me. To move inside me. To bring me pleasure and release.

"There's no hurry," he says, his voice sending vibrations against my nipple. And then he laughs when I shift my body beneath him so that I can rub his cock up and down the length of my more-than-wet slit. "Did you want something?"

"Yes, but if you're not willing to give it to me, I'd be more than happy to sit here and do it myself . . . but you'd be forced to watch." My words are coy, my smile even more so, and in a flash his hands have cuffed mine on either side of my head, and he dips down to kiss me.

"As hot as that sounds, watching you get yourself off while thinking of me, we're going to save that for another time . . . because right now I want you, Vaughn." A kiss on my lips. "Right now, I need you." He sits back on his haunches, his eyes locked on mine. He holds his dick in his hand and runs it up and down the length of me so that my sex parts and covers his tip as he teases me with it. "Right now, I'm going to have you."

And with his teeth sinking into his bottom lip, he pushes painstakingly slowly into me. Our hisses fill the room. My eyes close momentarily as I'm washed with pleasure.

"Heaven," he murmurs, prompting me to look back up and watch him. His eyes are watching his dick slide in and out of me. His shoulders are set, his biceps tense from where he holds my thighs, his lips red from mine.

This man wants me.

He could spew a million lies, but everything about his body says he wants me.

And it feels just like he murmured—heaven.

I angle my hips up some as he begins to move. In. Out. In. A grind of his hips as he slides his thumb over my clit before starting the whole delicious process all over again.

Where our first time together was him asking if I was okay through actions and me telling him yes with measured looks and nods, this time is a fire of fury and chaos and desire and passion, and I don't think if either of us protested we'd be able to hear over the absolute desperation that owns every part of us.

We move in unison, like two lovers who've been together for years but with the violent urgency of a couple that's still so new to each other.

Each thrust in a new sensation all its own. Each murmur an added aphrodisiac to the high that we're chasing. Each slide of fingertips over sensitized flesh a seduction like nothing before.

I can feel my climax mounting. It's slow and sweet but burns and aches, and I know my body well enough after so many years of taking care of myself that without doubt this orgasm is going to wreck me.

And it does. It hits me with the ferocity of a hurricane, whipping all of my senses in its fury. My body tenses and my breath holds as the white-hot heat of it slams into me. It races through every nerve, every sensation, every fiber of me before snapping back to the delta of my thighs, where I'm pulsing around him with such fervor that every time he starts to move again, the muscles grip tighter.

"Fucking hell, Vaughn," he murmurs as his body rocks to try to abate his own need to slam into me and take everything he needs. He tries—he does—and hell if the sight of him giving me what I need isn't the sexiest thing on the face of the earth, but when I lift my hips in a cue to tell him to chase his, he does.

His fingers grip into my hips as he sets a bruising pace of hard and fast until his body slams into me. His breath jagged, his body jerking as the ecstasy steals his senses and mutes his reason.

"Holy hell," he murmurs as he collapses on top of me with his head resting on my lower belly, and the rest of his body falls between my thighs.

My hand goes to his head immediately, fingers intertwining in his hair absently as if this is something we do all the time.

It's comforting.

It's normal.

It's exactly what we need right now as our heartbeats slow, our breaths even, and the magnitude of what we just shared hits us.

No contracts.

No ultimatums.

Just him and me.

Because we wanted to.

CHAPTER FORTY-FIVE

Vaughn

Darkness seeps through the half-closed blinds, but neither of us has an urge to move. There's a comfortable silence between us. Two people content to be in each other's space without needing to fill it with sound.

My mind wanders.

Did Samantha ever get a chance to have this feeling? Were she and Brian ever okay before the drugs became their mistress? Before Lucy arrived and made life more complicated for them? Or was my sister always burdened with the secrets of her past?

"Whatever you're thinking about, you probably need to stop thinking about it," he murmurs against my stomach.

"Why's that?"

"Because your body tensed up, your fingers started twitching like you were trying to make a point, and because you're thinking so hard I swear I can hear you."

"Whatever," I murmur and tug on his mussed-up hair.

"You want to talk about it?"

"No." I part laugh, part shake my head.

"That doesn't sound very convincing to me." He turns his head so that his chin is on my belly button, but his eyes find mine through the near-darkness of the room.

"Mmm."

"Does it have anything to do with why you left the other night?" And when my breath catches, he knows it somehow does. He just nods ever so slowly, his eyes compassionate. "Well, I'm just going to turn my head here and face the wall. Maybe if I'm not looking at you, you won't feel so self-conscious, and you'll tell me . . . although you can't get more vulnerable than lying naked with someone, but . . . who am I to say that?"

I can hear the playfulness in his tone. I can appreciate the fact that he's trying to give me a chance to talk to him, to explain the *why* behind all of my actions.

Do I want to tell him and ruin the incredible moment we've shared? No. Absolutely not. But for the sake of whatever this is here between us, whatever I could have sabotaged and ruined with my secrecy, I know I need to.

"I know I owe you an explanation."

"It can wait."

And that simple comment, letting me know I can do whatever I need to do on my own time, is enough that I want to tell him.

"No, it can't. And it's silly that I'm letting it affect me . . . *us*, but when you're slammed with something so unexpected, it kind of messes you up for a bit."

"Mm-hmm." It's all he says, his way of letting me know he'll listen while I talk. He runs his finger over the birthmark just on the inside of my wrist and traces it softly as I build up my courage.

"I told you that my uncle was mean, but I didn't quite understand it fully. Maybe I did. Maybe I just didn't want to acknowledge the truth." I sigh, and his fingers find my hand resting on the bed and link with mine in reassurance. "All I knew was that as soon as we could, Samantha got us out of that house in the dead of night. We rode the bus as far as the Greyhound line would take us with the money we had and a few things we had of his to pawn."

"Where did you end up?"

"Atlantic City." I can feel his body jolt ever so slightly in recognition of where I went that night. "There were things I didn't know, things I couldn't remember, and Samantha opted not to tell me. She tried to protect me from them all. What I didn't realize is what extents she went to in order to do that."

"She loved you."

"She did," I muse. "What you don't understand is that sex has always been mechanical for me. It's always been an unpleasurable necessity. If I thought I liked a guy, I'd have sex with him, not because I wanted to, but because I knew that's what you had to do to keep a boyfriend. It's so hard to put into words."

"I get it," he murmurs. "It's what you thought everyone did, and so you did it because if you didn't, then—"

"Then there was something wrong with me." My voice is barely a whisper.

"Vaughn—"

"No, it's okay." I run my nails through his hair and continue. "There is definitely a lot wrong with me . . . but ironically not the things I thought. You see, that first night in the hotel with you—"

"As Saxony."

"Yes, as Saxony. Do you know how ridiculous that sounds?" I laugh.

"It's not ridiculous if I'm lying here between your thighs talking to you right now."

"True." I take in a deep breath. "There was something about you . . . you made me feel. You made me want. You made me desire. You made me want to have sex and an orgasm. And oh my God, I'm blushing even saying that out loud."

"Don't blush. You're inflating my ego." He chuckles, trying to add levity to my truth.

"Whatever." I tap him on the head, and he kisses my abdomen. "Just as I realized that there was so much more to this sex thing, I had these flashbacks. My uncle's hand on my mouth." Ryker's body tenses, and when he turns to look at me, I keep my hand on his head and murmur, "Uh-uh." I need to do this without him looking at me. "His weight on me. I freaked . . . as you know. I accused you of being a fumbling jerk, and all the while I was racking my brain trying to figure out where these memories came from before I ran from the hotel room. I mean, the dread in my stomach told me what I couldn't remember. It scared the shit out of me and made sense all at the same time. I got home, scrubbed my skin off because I could feel him on me . . . and then I scoured the diaries my sister left behind for any clue to support these sudden memories."

"You should have said something to me when I called. I wouldn't have been so harsh. I wouldn't have been—"

"Yes, you would have," I say with a soft chuckle. "How were you to know? And what was I supposed to say, 'Oh, sorry, I think my uncle molested me'?"

"Something, anything."

"Well, I couldn't remember anything. All my memories and dreams went black at a certain point . . . up until the night we were at your place. We had sex—you made me . . . Christ, Ryker, you made me realize what an orgasm really feels like. You were giving when I expected you to be selfish. You were gentle when I thought you'd be callous. You . . . you . . . I don't know what it was—maybe the fact that you treated me well, that you made me feel . . . whatever it was unlocked the memory for me."

"Christ," he swears, and I realize he thinks it was a bad thing.

"No. No. The memory, it . . . he never laid a hand on me. My uncle . . . he tried to, and Samantha came in and . . ." I retell the story to him. Every part of it. From my sister's ferocious and protective love for me, to my grandmother's refusal to believe the ugly truth about her son. To the guilt over what she endured to save me, to our move and time in Atlantic City. To the night Ryker paid me the money and Lucy had a meltdown I wasn't there for.

Every last detail.

Well, except for the part that I've fallen for him. That part isn't going to be so easy to confess.

And it definitely isn't going to happen right now because I need more time to digest that.

He listens to it all without judgment. He comments here and there to let me know he's paying attention, that he cares, but without interrupting so I know that he knows it's my story to tell.

And when I finish, when I explain why I left that morning without telling him and why I've pushed him away because I didn't feel like I was worthy of his attention, he says, "Can I look at you now?"

I chuckle. "Yes."

He shifts in the bed and sits beside me so that we can look at each other. I'm still thankful for the darkened room, though, still feeling vulnerable some. "A few things."

"Uh-oh, I sense the lawyer coming out."

"Obviously," he says playfully. "I understand why you left, but you didn't have to. You could have told me. I wouldn't have judged then, just like I'm not judging now. I'd figured there was something in your past that was affecting you, but it wasn't my place to ask or assume. Second, I understand the guilt, Vaughn. I understand why you feel it and felt it, but you were kids. She loved you so much she wanted to protect you. To keep protecting you. Just like you continually tried to help and protect her. You both reciprocated the best you could. I'm sure in both of your eyes, it wasn't enough, when it was. You need to know it was."

"Thank you." His words bring tears to my eyes.

"And as for Lucy, she's lucky to have you. She's lucky to have your determination and fierce love. But that doesn't mean you don't get to have a life too. Parents are far from perfect. Fuck, my mom is case in point . . . and I'm sure it's highly debatable, but I think I turned out all right. You can't let your loyalty to her rob you or make you feel guilty to live and be you."

I stare at him for a beat as thoughts and emotions storm inside me, the loudest one being something I've never had before: *someone believes me.*

It sounds so stupid, so juvenile, but sitting here staring at him, listening to him, it's never been more apparent than now how weird it feels to have someone listen to my past, hear my words, and believe me without question.

Empowered.

That single emotion is how Ryker Lockhart just made me feel without even knowing it.

I've lived a life where everyone with power over me has brushed my feelings aside—my uncle James, Priscilla when it comes to Lucy's dad—but then there's Ryker, a man who's powerful in his own right. Not once does he tell me I'm ridiculous or it didn't happen or anything of the sort. Instead he looks me in the eye, squeezes my hand in reassurance, and believes me without any further explanation.

He believes me.

I stare at our hands where they are linked and know that this man has changed me in the most unexpected of ways.

"Thank you for trusting me enough to tell me." He lifts our hands to his lips.

I chuckle. "Well, nothing like putting a damper on some incredible sex, huh?" I say, suddenly nervous with all of the attention on me.

"I did catch one thing you said," he murmurs, shifting to his knees so that my eyes are drawn down to where his cock lies thick and heavy against his thigh. He quiets, and when I look back up, I know I've been caught staring. His eyes are on me, one eyebrow quirked up, an arrogant smirk on his lips.

"I'm sorry." I shrug unapologetically. "I was distracted."

"You were, were you?"

"Mm-hmm," I say, so thankful we can fall back into this easy banter despite the gravity of the past I just divulged. "You were saying?"

"I was saying"—he shifts and straddles my hips, that cock of his now front and center and slowly hardening against my lower belly—"that you said something I caught. Something about me making you want to have an orgasm. Vaughn Sanders . . . have you never had an orgasm before?"

I stare at him, eyes wide and mouth shocked open into an *O*, as I realize I slipped and gave him that very personal information. I squeak out a noise, and my hands fly to cover my face in absolute mortification.

"Vaughn?" he asks as he leans over, his breath feathering over the hands that are covering my face.

"Lalalalala," I say as loud as I can, to which he laughs.

His thumbs rub over my pebbled nipples. "I'm going to torture the answer out of you."

Does he think I'm going to answer him when his type of torture feels so damn good?

He pinches them ever just so, and it's like a main line to between my thighs. I squirm beneath him and garner a chuckle.

"This is just the start. First, I'll work you up so you're just on the edge . . . so you can feel your orgasm just about to hit, and then I'll stop." He teases and taunts with his hand. His dick growing harder a seduction in itself. "Then I'll start all over again."

"This is ridiculous." It comes out in a partial moan.

"Then uncover your face and answer me. Seems simple to me, Vaughny," he croons as his thumbs manipulate my breasts some more so that it hurts so good.

"Fine. Fine. The only orgasms I've ever had were by my own hand before you. Okay?" I shout the words out in frustration, but the silence afterward is deafening.

His hands are static on my body, but I can't see him to gauge his reaction because I refuse to remove my hands from my face.

He surprises me when his lips touch mine through the break in my hands over my mouth. "I don't know why you're embarrassed by that fact," he murmurs against my lips. "It's sexy knowing you know how to get off."

I sigh in response and let the lazy kiss relax me a bit.

"A lot of guys get off on the deflowering-virgin thing," he says when he ends the kiss, both of his hands slowly prying my hands away from my face. "That's not exactly what I'd consider a good time. Look at me, Vaughn," he demands when I refuse to; eventually I acquiesce.

"What?"

"To know I'm the first man who's ever brought you pleasure? Now that? That's a game changer for me." He brushes his lips against mine. "No need to be embarrassed." Another soft kiss with his tongue tracing over my bottom lip. "It's sexy." This time his tongue slips between my lips, and it lasts a little longer. "And endearing." Another kiss. "And I think I want to do it again—right now—just to prove to you that I can . . ." He tugs on my bottom lip with his teeth. "And that you can."

And he does.

It's slower than the first time. Languid and thorough. We explore each other's bodies with our mouths and sensations. We push each other to the brink, pull back, and then start the deliciously torturous ascent all over again.

Then later, just when we're about to fall asleep, Ryker speaks. "Hey."

"Mmm."

"I really missed you, Vaughn."

"Me too."

I snuggle up against him as he tightens his arms around me and breathe in his scent. Breathe in everything about him, really, with my lips pressed against his chest. And with his heart beating beneath them, I'm overwhelmed with how I've let him in. With how much I care about him when I still don't know everything about him.

But I know I want to know everything about him.

A part of me, the part that's not in a sex-satisfied coma, stirs to life, and as much as I want to let my lips travel up to his and start this sensual dance all over again, I also want to memorize what this feels like, to be held safely in someone's arms.

More so, how incredible it felt to have sex with Ryker. To feel him, enjoy him, pleasure him without the ghost of a memory hanging over my head for the first time ever.

CHAPTER
FORTY-SIX
Ryker

"You'd be proud of me."

Vaughn's body jolts to awareness from where she's half-asleep on the couch. She snuggles in deeper where she's lying between my thighs, head turned to watch some god-awful black-and-white classic movie on the television.

I don't think I've ever lain on a couch with a woman in my life when I wasn't fucking her. The thought creeps into my mind, and sadly, I'm okay with this. Perfectly fine, actually, because this woman can wear a man out.

Not that I wouldn't try again if she asked.

But this is nice. Just . . . being together.

Jesus, Lockhart. You sound like a sap.

"Proud? Of what?" she asks.

"I took on a wife for the first time last week." That sounds ridiculously stupid, but she'll understand what I mean.

"That sounds kind of interesting," she says through a laugh.

"A woman client, Vaughn. Client." I tap a hand on her ass. "Get your mind out of the gutter."

"You did?" She twists up and looks at me, surprise on her face and a smile on her lips.

And that smile. Fuck if it doesn't do shit to my insides.

"I did."

"What made you change your MO?"

You.

The answer stutters on my tongue as I realize it's true. Something about Vaughn has given me more respect for women, for some of the bullshit they have to endure.

"Because I wanted to," I murmur and then lean over and press a kiss to the top of her head.

"But why?"

"Because I'm working on being less of an asshole."

"Lucky me," she says and tickles her fingers against my side so that I squirm and hold her tighter.

"Lucky you." I tickle her right back for a second only to get her to snuggle tighter on me. Doesn't she realize that maybe she's the reason I'm working on it?

And just as we settle back down, my eyes on the curve of her ass, she mutters, "Talk about assholes."

"What do you—oh . . ." My words trail off as I see that when we moved, we inadvertently changed the channel to some news network. Senator Carter Preston is on the screen as the newscaster drones on about Carter's nay vote on a Senate bill and the long-lasting repercussions of it.

Your ears burning, Senator?

Prick.

"What is it with you and him anyway?" I ask, even though I'm pretty damn sure Vaughn's not going to say a word.

"He's the reason you and I met," she says softly, catching me completely off guard.

"Wait. What? I'm not following . . ."

Did she just let me in even more?

Vaughn shifts up onto her elbow to meet my gaze again, caution owning her eyes. "Lola."

"Lola?"

"He's the reason she couldn't go out with you that first time."

I stare at her, blink, and try to process what she's saying and what she's not saying. "What do you mean?"

"Read between the lines, Lockhart. I've already said more than I should."

"The prick likes to rough up women?" I ask the question knowing full well she's not going to answer.

But the idea eats at me. The way he carries himself as if he can do no wrong. The way Vaughn was skittish that first night I saw her at Apropos. The fact that any man thinks it's okay to touch a woman other than to make her feel good.

And it eats at me some more as Vaughn flips through the channels. "He's met you face-to-face, hasn't he? That's why you spilled the drinks that night. You were afraid he was going to recognize you."

Her body stills, but she nods ever so subtly. "Someone had to confront him over the bruises he left. Someone had to make him pay for her downtime. Someone had to tell him that's not how you treat a lady."

"And that someone was you, I take it?" I ask, already knowing the answer, but using the question as a means to calm the anger brimming just beneath the surface. Because as much as I love the fact that Vaughn will go toe to toe with the prick and put him in his place, I also hate knowing that she puts herself in situations that could easily escalate out of control.

"I was in my Vee wig and uniform."

"Vaughn." Her name is a warning. An *I don't like this.* "I don't care what you were in. He's—"

"I have to defend my girls, Ryker."

"And who's going to defend you?"

"I have enough dirt on each of my clients. That's all I need to stop most of them in their tracks."

Those words should give me pause. They should make me wonder what—other than Roxanne—she has on me.

But all I can think about is her alone with Carter and the thoughts I'm more than certain were running through his head and itching his fingertips to reach out and take. Of the offhand comments he's made here and there over the years about what he likes to do to his "side" women to get off.

"Stopping most of them isn't good enough, Vaughn. It only takes one of them to hurt you, and fuck if Carter Preston isn't low on the scale of moral compass."

"I'm more than aware."

"If you don't give him what he wants, he'll have no problem going after you to get it."

"Been there. Done that."

"What the hell are you—"

"Don't. Just don't, okay?"

And there's something in her voice that tells me I'm overstepping. That a few nights of sex doesn't mean I have the right to tell her what to do. And fuck if she isn't right, but at the same time, I care about her. "I don't like this one bit."

She shifts so that for the first time since this conversation began, she meets my eyes. "Just like I don't have to love the fact you knew where I lived without ever asking me my address."

She's got me there.

"Vaughn—"

"Stalker," she says with just enough of a smile and roll of her eyes to add some levity to this conversation, and hell if I'm not willing to play along.

"Thank you. I appreciate the compliment," I tease.

"Seriously, though. You used your PI?"

"Just as you've used yours on me."

"You didn't answer the question, Lockhart," she huffs.

"You went missing on me. I was worried. You can't expect me to sit idly by while I think you're in danger or trouble." I figured out a lot more than that, but she doesn't need to know about how I found that uncle of hers.

And how now it's going to be awfully fucking hard not to go and wring his neck for what he did to her and Samantha.

"You're forgiven," she says through a laugh.

"Besides, I figured it wasn't that big of a surprise since I was sending you flowers."

She gives a measured nod. "True . . . but flowers versus just showing up . . . that's two totally different measures of stalking."

"Very true," I say, knowing her forgiveness stands.

"I never pegged you for a flowers-and-gifts kind of guy."

"Mmm." *Maybe because I've never wanted to be that way until you.* But I don't say anything because I'm distracted by her nipples pebbling against her top. My mind veers.

My dick does too.

"Why is it that you always take the husbands and not the wives?"

My laugh is loud as I force my thoughts from her nipples and how hard they get against my tongue when I suck on them. "What was that?"

"Up here, Lockhart." Vaughn directs my chin so I'm forced to look up and meet the desire in her eyes that matches mine.

"I'm quite fond of down there. And even lower too." I flash a grin that hints at all the devilish things I want to do to her.

"Cases. Divorces. Wives. Why do you always side with the husbands?"

Successfully directed back to the topic, I give her nipples one quick appreciative look before responding. "I'm a lawyer. I'm a man." I shrug. *And because women are ruthless.*

"Oh, this is my favorite part," she says, who I represent forgotten as she turns and watches the movie she flipped to. I watch her react to the scene, the emotion playing over her features.

I can't look away.

Goddamn. This woman. The one who watches old classics, cusses without shame, can hold a conversation about almost anything, and has moments like right now where when I watch her, I don't know what to say.

What the fuck is she doing to me?

"Why do you insist on watching this old movie when there are so many current ones with better quality?"

"Because I like them. They remind me of how Sam and I used to fall asleep as kids. My mom would turn one on, and we'd tuck up against either side of her in her huge bed and then drift off to sleep like that."

I can see the memory affects her, and I reach out and rub a thumb over her bottom lip. She offers me a soft smile before lying back down so that her cheek is on my bare stomach and her eyes are back on the television.

"Your turn," she says, throwing me.

"My turn?"

"Tell me something about your mom."

"Let's not." I laugh.

"Seriously, tell me something about her. You can learn a lot about a person from who their mother is."

"You'll hold it against me."

"Don't be silly. Come on."

And of course, I talk. I talk when normally I wouldn't, because she's shared so much, and what does it hurt to say something about my mom?

"There's not much to tell, really, except for her hobby is marrying men, screwing them over, and then going on a search for the next more handsome, wealthier man." I'm matter of fact, no emotion.

"Is that what she did to your dad?"

"Pretty much. He's down in Florida now, living off what he has left . . . and she's moving on to what feels like husband number who knows." I reach for my beer on the table and take a sip.

"Are you close?"

"Close? Not best buds, but regardless of her faults, she's still my mother."

"Mmm."

"Mmm?" I ask.

"Is she why you decided to specialize in divorce law?"

"I don't know? What's the reason you decided to run an escort service?" I ask as my fingers find her ribs and tickle again.

She wriggles against me. "Enough talking, don't you think?" I tickle again. "We've had enough sharing for one day." Another squirm that rubs my dick the right way and awakens parts of me I swore were exhausted from last night . . . and this morning.

"What about show-and-tell, then?"

"Oh," she murmurs as she feels my cock pulse against her. She sits up and runs a fingernail down the line of it straining against my shorts. "I always did like show-and-tell. The question is, who's showing"—her tank top clears her head—"and who's telling?"

"Are you trying to distract me, Ms. Sanders?" It takes everything I have not to look down and appreciate the sight of her pink nipples and the weight of her tits.

I don't fight the half-cocked smirk, though.

"Only if it changes the topic of discussion."

And this time when she teases my cock again, I grab her wrist and pull her into me.

My mouth is on hers in an instant. Her lips are like goddamn candy. Soft. Tasty. Fucking addictive.

We sink into the kiss . . . and jolt when the doorbell rings.

Doorbells are not something I'm used to with a penthouse. I have a doorman. Doormen screen and call and inform.

I don't do unexpected intrusions when I'm about to get laid.

We both groan.

"Don't get it," I tell her, my hands on her wrist as she sits up.

"Let me see who it is."

"Like that?" I ask, lifting my eyebrows at her shirtless torso.

"It's me, Vaughn," a male voice calls through the window near the front door, and I'm immediately curious.

A man who shows up to her house and knows he can call into her window.

"Crap," she says. "It's Joey. What does he want?"

"Joey?" *Who the fuck is Joey?*

"Be right there," she yells to him. Then she whispers to me, "Let me go get a bra on."

"Don't forget the shirt part too," I say.

With a roll of her eyes, she rushes from the room while I stand from the couch. First, I don't like the guy out of principle because he's a guy. Second, I don't like him because now she's putting a shirt on. And third, I'm so fucking tempted to open the door like this—dick hard to make a point, literally, about what was just about to happen.

But it's not my house. It's not my place . . . and by the time I cross the room, my hard-on has died, so I open the door.

"Hi." It's all I say as I enjoy the shocked look on his face. He's a little under six feet, soft in the middle, not bad looking, but the surprise that flashes in his eyes is way worth it. "Joey, I presume?"

Yeah, fucker. I'm in Vaughn's house. It's midday. I don't have a shirt on, and my hair is still fucked up from when she ran her hands through it this morning as we had sex after our shower . . . so I hope you get the point to back the fuck off.

"Yes. Joey. And you are?"

"Joey!" It's Vaughn's singsongy voice as she ducks under my arm braced on the doorjamb. "Is something wrong?"

"No, nothing's wrong." He eyes her and then back to me.

"Have you met Ryker?" He shakes his head. "Ryker, this is Joey—Joey, Ryker."

We shake hands, and the little ghost of a smirk I give is the one I practice for court. The you're-fucked-and-you-don't-have-a-chance-so-don't-even-try smirk.

"Nice to meet you," I say as the three of us stand there in awkward silence for a few moments. My little way of making sure he knows I'm not going anywhere. "Well, I'll leave you two to talk, then." I press a kiss to the side of her head in a show of "she's mine" before I retreat back to the couch to watch them.

Their voices are low, heads bent over, and every few seconds, he glances my way. I meet his look to let him know I'm paying attention. That I'm watching.

And I am. They're familiar with each other. Her hand on his shoulder. Her laugh at something he said.

It's not like I have any right to claim her, but it's not like I'm going to let that stop me.

The longer they talk, the more I know I like this woman. The more I'm glad no matter how fucked it was for me to chase her, it was the right thing.

I've never let a woman consume me before. Always thought they were a dime a dozen . . . but Vaughn Sanders has consumed me.

And I want her to keep consuming me too.

I don't know how long they chat, but it's too damn long in my book. They hug, and when she shuts the door and heads my way, I don't try to hide that I was watching them.

"What was that all about?" I ask.

"He came to talk to me about Lucy." She stops at the edge of the couch and angles her head and stares at me.

"A government employee who makes house calls? Shit. That's a miracle."

"Don't be an ass."

"I don't like him."

She laughs and rolls her eyes. "You're jealous?" she asks as if I'm crazy.

Not jealous. Just making sure he knows what's mine.

"Whatever."

"Well, I don't like Roxanne," she says and folds her arms over her chest.

"That makes two of us. I don't like Roxanne either." I lift my eyebrows and wait to see what her reaction is.

She sits down on the opposite end of the couch. "Joey's harmless and means well. Lucy has been having some issues lately. Things that have to do with some of the visits with her dad. Technically he's not allowed to talk to me about it since she's a ward of the state. If he does and is overheard, he can lose his job."

"So he comes here instead?" I ask, knowing all too well how a man's mind works, and it's far from innocent like she assumes. "He can pick up a phone, can't he?"

"Jealousy is cute on you."

I level a glare her way. "What was the big news he couldn't wait to pay a house call and tell you?"

"Something to do with Lucy's dad, Brian."

"Joey. Brian. Can we stop talking about other men here? That would really help calm me some," I say, part joking, part being serious.

"Oh, poor baby." She crawls across the couch so that she's on all fours, her face so very close to mine, and that bottom lip of hers stuck out in a pout. "Are you feeling left out?"

She leans in to kiss me.

"If I say yes, do I get another one of those from you?"

"You mean like this?"

Another kiss. Sweet and seductive and dick hardening.

We both groan when my cell rings. I pick it up off the table and decline the call without looking at it and toss it without watching where it lands.

"Vaughn?"

"Mmm?"

"I'm sick of being interrupted."

"Then ignore it."

"I'm sick of the distractions."

"Then focus on me."

"Oh, I'm focused all right," I say and move her hand atop my dick so she can see just how focused it is.

"Mmm."

"We need to get away," I murmur as she presses her lips to mine, and her entire body tenses at my comment.

"Away?" She laughs and leans back to look at me.

"No," I groan. "Come back here. You're too far away." I pull her toward me until she's cradled across my lap so she can't escape. "Go away with me. Where there's no distractions, no interruptions. I've been chasing you for months . . . and now that I have you, I want to be selfish."

"You can be selfish right now."

Another kiss.

"Just for a few days. We can—"

"Thank you, Ryker . . . but I don't fit in your world." She rests her forehead against mine.

I start to laugh and then stop myself when I realize she's serious. "I don't care about where you fit in or don't fit in. I just want you with me. I'd never ask you to change to do that."

"Mm-hmm."

There's a disbelief in her murmur that I fucking hate.

And love.

The lack of pretention. An abundance of doubt. A realness to her that I've never gotten from anybody else, and while it's humbling that she can be like this with me, it's also terrifying in all the right ways.

"Vaughn. Look at me." I put my hands on the side of her face and guide it up when I lean back. When she meets my eyes, I see it. Her unease with anyone who wants to treat her right. Her sudden shyness. "It's okay for me to want to spoil you and keep you all to myself."

"You don't need to spoil me. I'm not with you for your money, Ryker."

"I wouldn't be here right now if I thought you were." I suddenly need her alone. I want to show her that the life she wants no part of—my life—isn't all that bad. Not every rich man is her uncle. Not every wealthy person uses others. "I was planning on going away to my house in the Hamptons this weekend," I lie. Anything to get her there. "Go with me."

"But I have to work." I can hear the reluctance in her voice. Can hear the fear that she'll feel out of place.

"Vaughn." It's the closest I get to pleading. "It'll be just you and me. Privacy. The beach. A big bed."

Her lips turn up in the softest of smiles. "I'll see if I can get someone to switch shifts with me."

"There's my girl," I murmur and bring her closer so I can show her my appreciation. "God, I want you."

"What is it you want?" The sound in her voice would make me come in an instant if I were a teenager. Throaty. Sexy. Devastating.

"Oh, I get to make requests?" I remember the feel of her lips closing around my dick. The suction of her mouth. The sight of my come squirting all over her tits.

She leans forward and slides her tongue up the column of my neck, her boobs brushing against my chest, until the heat of her breath is at my ear. "Whatever you ask for, it's yours."

And goddamn if that's not enough to make a man have fantasies for a lifetime.

"Anything?" I murmur as my fingers reach out and start unclasping that bra she just put back on.

"All you have to do is ask."

Oh, I'm going to be asking, all right.

CHAPTER FORTY-SEVEN

Vaughn

"That was fun, but I still don't want you to go."

"I know, Luce." I pull her against me and hold on to her, knowing full well her feelings are hurt that Ryker and I are leaving without her. "But we had fun today, right?" I squat down and place her face in my hands so we're eye to eye.

"Yeah," she murmurs, and the straightening of her posture tells me that Ryker finally found a parking spot and is coming up behind me to say goodbye himself.

If she didn't have a crush on him before, she most definitely has one on him now.

"Hey, speed demon. Next time, I promise you, I'm going to win," Ryker says, trying to distract and divert after seeing how upset she was earlier from feeling left out of our trip.

"No, you're not. I'm Lightning Lucy!" she says and lifts her arms in the air, so damn proud of the nickname Ryker gave her when he let her beat him in a footrace.

"You won't even let me win once?" he asks as he sits on the bench beside me.

"Nope. You have to earn it," Lucy says with a laugh but grabs his hand without thought. She looks at Ryker and then me. "Do you really have to go now?"

"Actually, you're the one who has to go. Your music class is about to start," I explain, knowing how much she loves her music and hoping it will make the goodbye a little easier.

Her sigh is heavy, and as much as it breaks my heart, I think of how awesome Ryker has been today. My only condition to heading to the Hamptons with him was that I had to spend a few hours with Lucy before we left.

Little did I know he was going to make it a jam-packed few hours. Relay races and ice-cream cones and blowing bubbles before going to feed the ducks.

"I promise you we won't have any fun," I say to Lucy, my "hang loose" sign pressed against my thigh. Her eyes flicker there for the briefest of moments before a soft nod of her head, and a smile I know she doesn't feel ghosts her lips.

"And I promise I won't miss you," she says as her own hand mimics mine when she rests it against her thigh.

"And I promise when we get back, we're going to take you to Disney on Ice," Ryker says, eyes darting back and forth between the two of us. And then the minute he notices our two hands, he shoves his hand out onto his thigh in the "hang loose" symbol too.

Lucy giggles, and I welcome the sound because it's so much better than the hurt in her eyes. "He doesn't know, does he?" she asks me.

"Know what?" Ryker questions, confused.

"Nothing." I laugh, knowing how ridiculous the three of us look with "hang loose" signs on our thighs.

"No, tell me."

"Auntie Vee says I shouldn't tell lies. Lies are bad. They can hurt people's feelings . . . but sometimes you have to tell little white lies.

Little white lies aren't great, but . . . but they are better than hurting someone's feelings."

"So we came up with a code," I interject.

"Yep," Lucy says with a big smile and holds the "hang loose" signal up. "This means I'm fibbing, and Auntie knows why."

"We were having some trouble with telling a few too many lies. So much so that we were messing up what was truth and what wasn't," I explain. "So I figured as long as she understands that she's doing it—"

"It's okay!" Lucy says.

"As long as it's not all the time, and it's only done so that she doesn't hurt someone's feelings," I amend.

Ryker belts out a laugh. "So you're telling me that I just told you I was taking you to Disney on Ice, and when I did the symbol—"

"You told me you were lying," Lucy says and giggles.

Ryker pulls his hand off his thigh so fast, only serving to make Lucy laugh harder.

That sound.

It's beautiful.

And now I can head out of town with Ryker feeling a little more at ease over leaving her.

CHAPTER FORTY-EIGHT

Vaughn

I lived in extravagant houses growing up.

Money is something I should be comfortable around, considering my uncle's wealth and the clients I have . . . but when I walk into Ryker's house on Old Town Road in the Hamptons, my breath catches.

The property is gorgeous. With slate-gray exterior siding, manicured lawns, and an ocean view, it looks like something straight out of a designer magazine. The inside is done in crisp white, with a mixture of modern and old world that doesn't sound like it would fit together but somehow does. The kitchen is expansive, the rooms open and airy, and every single wall has a window, so it's impossible to miss the Atlantic Ocean outside. And that has nothing on the backyard's pool, tennis court, pool house, built-in patio with every amenity you can think of, and that's just what I can see from the back door.

"Sorry. I had to check on something," Ryker says as he walks up behind me and presses a kiss to my bare shoulder. "I didn't mean to leave you all alone."

"It's okay. I snooped," I say to abate the nerves that are suddenly fluttering in my stomach.

It's one thing to stay the night with him. It's a whole other one to commit to spending four nights in his house with him.

"Did you find anything good?" he asks. He turns me around and presses a tantalizing kiss to my lips before I can respond.

"Just the broken hearts of your exes swept under the rug."

"Witty," he says as his face breaks out in a smile. His arm slides around my waist and pulls him against my side.

"I've never been here before."

"To the Hamptons?"

I nod as my eyes keep wandering. To the decor and the appliances and everything. When I look back his way, our eyes meet.

"What's going through that mind of yours?" he asks.

"This place is intimidating."

"Only at first." He brushes his lips against my temple. "Once we've screwed on the kitchen island, I promise you'll forget how big the refrigerator seems."

"Funny."

He looks at me with that lift of an eyebrow as if to make me question if he is being serious or not.

"Look, we're here to relax. To have some downtime because God knows we both need it. Stop stressing about everything. It'll be fine. *We'll* be fine."

"We'll be fine," I repeat and blow out a breath, excited and nervous all at the same time over what this weekend holds in its future.

"So . . . the fridge—"

"The massive one I'm supposed to forget about?" I ask, shaking off my doubts.

"That one . . . it's stocked with everything you can imagine. The bathrooms, too, in case you forgot any toiletries. Please, make yourself at home."

"Mm-hmm."

"So, what would you like to do first?"

You.

My grin gives away my thoughts. We stare at each other for a moment, smiles on our mouths and suggestion in our eyes.

"I'd have to agree with your line of thinking, Vaughn, but Rosie is going to be bringing in our bags any moment. While I'm all for kink, having the hired help watch me lick your pussy till you come on my face isn't exactly what I had in mind."

He lifts an eyebrow as I clench my thighs together. "Well then," I murmur, completely surprised and turned on by his frankness.

"Well then." He flashes me a grin and holds out his hand. "Want to take a walk on the beach?"

"That's a good start."

"I promise the licking part will come later."

"Good thing I know you're a man of your word."

"That I am."

"So tomorrow I'm thinking we head into town for a late breakfast, and then we can play tourist since you've never been here before."

"Don't feel the need to for my sake."

"Vaughn," he says, leaning forward and pressing a chaste kiss to my lips. "I brought you here to spoil you. We're going to play tourist. We're going to get lobster rolls and ride our bikes out to the Montauk Point Lighthouse. We'll head to the winery . . . maybe check out the local music scene—"

"All of that, huh?"

"All of that and then some, and you're going to like it," he says with a definitive nod as he wraps the blanket around my shoulder.

He stares at me, the flames of the fire in front of us lighting up his features, and it's the first time I think I've ever seen Ryker Lockhart truly relaxed.

"You look happy," I murmur.

"I am happy."

Where did this come from? This sudden want to be okay with someone, to have someone like Ryker stare across a fire at me and fill me with hope and love.

Love.

There's the word I've been trying to deny.

The word I swore I'd never feel for anybody other than Lucy and Samantha.

But there it is. In my head. In my heart. And I feel it—whatever it is—when I look at him. It's scary and thrilling, and I have no clue if I'm even ready to feel it, but I don't think it cares. I think love is love, and it comes without warning and strikes without caution.

"Thank you for coming this weekend," he says as he refills my glass with wine.

"Thank you for inviting me."

I love him.

"Definitely a good first day."

"A walk on the beach, some being lazy in the pool—"

"Did I mention I was a huge fan of that bikini you were wearing?"

"Only a dozen times or so." I laugh.

"Just wanted to make sure you knew that it's perfectly fine with me if you wear it again."

"I'll keep that in mind."

"Come here," he says, and I shift beside him so that he can put his arm around me with the fire in front of us and the waves crashing on the beach in the darkness beyond.

This feels right. It feels normal. And as much as I can accept it, it also scares the shit out of me.

The thought owns my mind. With each crash of the waves on the beach. With each crackle of the logs on the fire. So much so that

I finally ask the question that's been ghosting in the back of my mind all day.

"Ryker?"

"Hmm?" The heat of his breath hits the crown of my head when he murmurs it.

"What are we doing here?"

"Enjoying the nice night. The warm fire."

"No, I mean . . . what are *we* doing here? You and I?"

His body tenses momentarily, and I suddenly fear that maybe I'm bringing up something he hasn't really thought about. Maybe I'm broaching a topic that is no-go territory for him.

"Why are you asking?"

I fumble for any reason other than the truth. For any reason besides *because I want to know*. I clear my throat. "We're bound to run into people this weekend, and you said yourself that you have a certain reputation to uphold with your job . . . I just didn't want to mess that up for you. I thought maybe you wanted me to have a specific term, or I don't know . . ."

The thumb brushing back and forth on my arm falters momentarily. "The answer is it's none of their goddamn business."

"Oh. Okay." Silence falls again as I decide to let my question die. But I can't. This is all too new to me, too unsettling, too damn perfect. "And what if I were the one asking the question?"

His lips are near my ear. "Then I'd have to give you a better answer, now wouldn't I?"

Jesus. The things the quiet rumble of that voice does to me inside and out. The sudden goose bumps that chase over my skin have nothing to do with the chill in the air.

And completely sidetrack me from my thoughts.

Until he brings them back.

He presses a kiss to my bare shoulder but leaves his lips there so that I can feel them move when he speaks. "Nothing about us has been conventional, Vaughn. Not how we met, not how I pursued you, not even now. We're not people who can be defined by one single term. Not alone and not together. Trust is hard for both of us, but we're trying, so I say we just let whatever this is play out between us. I'm not sleeping with other women, and you're not sleeping with other men, and as long as we acknowledge that, let's just enjoy the now—this weekend—and take everything day by day."

His words stagger me. My blind acceptance of them even more so when I've always bucked anything to do with being with someone.

Trust is hard for both of us, but we're both trying.

He's right. Right when I never noticed it. Right when I lowered my guard and started trusting without ever telling myself it was okay to.

"So no defining, then?" I ask.

"No defining."

"And here I thought you invited me here to make me your sex slave," I murmur, needing humor to abate the overwhelming wave of emotion surging through me.

"Sex slave, huh?" The heat of his breath warms my skin and pulls me to the here and now. "That might have its benefits."

"You're insatiable, Mr. Lockhart."

"Lucky for you."

"Lucky for me," I agree.

And we sit like this with smiles on our lips, completely content and comfortable in each other's silence as we just enjoy being with each other for some time.

"Now . . . about that licking . . . ," I say after a bit.

"Mmm. I thought you'd never ask."

CHAPTER
FORTY-NINE
Ryker

"Vaughn Sanders? Is that you?" The voice catches me off guard, and I know it sure as hell catches Vaughn unaware by her reaction.

"Archer?" Her face lights up in a smile as she pulls the owner of the voice into a bear hug. They look at each other for a second, both grinning stupidly.

"Ryker Lockhart, nice to meet you," I assert and reach my hand out.

The man turns to face me. He's my height, good build, and as polished as money can buy but with a hint of edge to him that screams that he definitely did not do what his mom and dad paid for his Ivy League education to do.

"Oh," he says, looking at me and then back to Vaughn with a lift of his brows. "Archer Collins, and no, I've never dated and have no interest in dating your woman, so you can calm that alpha male thing down some and realize I'm not a threat." He winks and shakes my hand.

He's either gay or blind if he has no interest in Vaughn.

"That makes me like you but question your judgment all at the same time."

"Wouldn't be the first time my judgment's been questioned," he says with a pat on the side of my arm and a laugh.

"You're here?" he says to Vaughn. "You brought her here?" he asks me.

"Yes," Vaughn says. "In fact, I feel like we've been everywhere today."

"Let me guess," he says. "The lighthouse, the winery, a walk on the beach—"

"And now some lobster rolls," I complete for him as I try to make the connection. "I'll go order some while you guys chat."

"Well, aren't you the perfect guy," he says with a flair that makes me shake my head and laugh.

It takes a few minutes for me to order the food and find a table on the busy patio. I can hear Vaughn's laugh every now and again as I wave hello to a few residents I know by name. Others stop by the table and ask how long I'm in town or about my mother, who frequents the Hamptons often.

Just as Vaughn sits down at the table, the food is delivered.

"Perfect timing."

She smiles, and then I watch and wait for her reaction as she takes a bite of the famed lobster rolls. Her eyes fly up to mine, and a moan sounds off deep in her throat.

"Keep making that sound, Sanders . . . ," I murmur as memories of last night and that sound come back instantly.

She smiles at me as she wipes her mouth with her napkin, her cheeks flushing pink.

"Archer Collins. Is he of the Collins Distillery Collinses?" I ask.

"The one and only."

"How do you know him?"

She eyes me and laughs. "He's gay. You don't need to get territorial."

"I'm aware, and I wasn't." I lift a brow.

"Archer and I . . ." She sighs and looks around at the tables near us before staring at the food in her hand.

"That bad, huh?" I tease but hate that she's hesitating.

"Let's just say he helped me set up my company." When she lifts her eyes to meet mine, there is nothing but honesty reflected in them.

"He what?"

She laughs. "I know. You wouldn't think so . . . but we met in Atlantic City. He was there as a salesman for his dad during his dad's *you have to try your hand at real work* phase, and we met. Became friends and stayed in touch. When Sam . . . when Sam fell down the rabbit hole and then . . . you know, he was the one I got drunk with and cried to. He was the one who made a comment about a friend he knew who was an escort and made a fortune."

"No shit?" I'm having a hard time wrapping my head around Party Boy Collins, as he's affectionately known around town, as being the one who helped Vaughn.

"No shit. Anyway, I told him there was no way I could be an escort, but I sure as hell would run their service. It was a joke. But we were drunk, and so our minds ran with it. After several hours, we had a whole world made up where we owned it and everything worked out in the end. Then a few weeks later, he called me. It was right after I'd had a visit from the social worker, and they'd told me my debt was too extensive to be considered to adopt Lucy. I told them it was in the process of being paid down . . . Archer called and . . ." She shrugs.

"So you're telling me you created Wicked—" I stop myself from saying the name as I glance around. "You created a company and all of this within the last year?" Is she kidding me?

"Six months."

"That's incredible."

"Not incredible. It was Archer. He knows everyone who's anyone. All it took was for him to mumble a few recommendations among his circle. Those recommendations turned into word of mouth—some credible, some completely false—and add in the air of mystery, and . . ."

"And then all of a sudden you were being talked about in the most discreet of social circles."

"Exactly. Plus, from paying attention to things his parents have done over the years, he was able to help me set up offshore accounts, scramble things around so that fingers wouldn't point back to me if something went south."

"Protect yourself," I murmur, the curious part of me wanting to understand all of the inner workings of what she's created.

"Fingers crossed it works." She laughs nervously.

"Aren't you ever afraid that he'll tell someone?" I ask.

She laughs like she never gives it a thought. "I asked him the same thing when we were thinking this all up. He told me it wasn't going to be a problem, but just so my mind would be at ease, he had his lawyer draw up a contract. We both signed it."

"Dare I ask what it says?"

"That if he ever told anyone about the business or me or anything, he'd owe me half of his fortune . . . which at the time was close to five hundred million."

And that definitely earned him my respect.

I blow out a whistle. "That will keep a tongue from wagging."

"Exactly." She smiles at me and takes another bite.

I should, too, but my mind's on things other than food at the moment.

It's on her.

I stare at her. At the gold in her hair and how the breeze blows it around her head. At the smile on her face and the color being outdoors has put on her cheeks.

"What?" she asks, suddenly shy under my observation.

"You surprise me more and more every day," I murmur.

"That's a good thing?" she asks cautiously.

"That's a good thing, Vaughn." I take a deep breath and shake my head. "You told me once that when your debt was paid off, you were going to wash your hands of the business." She nods. "I didn't believe you. I thought there was no way a person would walk away from money like that. I was wrong."

Her soft smile tells me she appreciates hearing it. "This isn't me, Ryker."

"I know it's not."

"I just want Lucy. This is all for her. My goal was to build up my book of business, my contact list, and then sell it to a competitor. Pay off my debts and put away any extra for Lucy's future medical needs since she'll have them for the rest of her life. That's all I want."

"Not for you. For Lucy."

"Yes."

"You're incredible—you know that?" And that's an understatement if ever I've heard one.

"Ryker? Is that you?" With a smile I can't help, I stare at her a beat longer before turning to see Ted Talon, media magnate, and greet him. We talk about nothing; all the while my mind is still on Vaughn.

Always seems to be these days.

CHAPTER FIFTY

Vaughn

"This is heaven," I moan as I dip the spoon in the large tub of chocolate chip cookie dough sitting on the kitchen island between us and take another scoop.

"You have your definition of what heaven tastes like," he says with a lift of his brow and a glance down to between my thighs, "and I have mine."

"Is that so?" I ask.

"I did warn you that we'd use this island, didn't I?"

I laugh. "I don't think you had this in mind, though," I say, referring to the fact that we are both sitting atop it, cross-legged, facing each other, with the tub of dough between us.

"Definitely not."

"You were quite the social butterfly today," I say and then finish the bite on my spoon. "It didn't matter where we went—everyone was coming up to talk to you like they haven't seen you in forever."

He takes a bite and then uses the spoon to point at me. "I know. The cat's out of the bag." He chuckles as I furrow my brow, not understanding. "Be prepared for the nosy neighbors to swing by and say hi now."

"What do you mean by that?"

"Being rich is one thing . . . but most people around here are rich and bored, and that only elevates their nosiness to a whole new level."

"Do you not come here often? Is that why they are so friendly?" I ask.

"Not as often as I'd like," he murmurs and takes my glass of wine from my hand and sips from it. "And it's not me they're stopping by to chat with. It's you they're checking out."

"Me?" I sputter. "Great. Thanks for the warning."

"It's true."

"Why would you think that?"

"Why?" he asks as he angles his head to the side and just stares at me with a look that conveys so much that my chest constricts. "Because it's obvious to them."

"What is?"

His smile is soft when he reaches out and tucks a strand of my hair behind my ear. "That I've fallen for you, Vaughn."

The spoon stops halfway to my mouth, the cookie dough forgotten as my heart all but skips a beat. Or maybe it skips like ten beats, because I can't focus on *what h*e just said.

"What?" I ask out of reflex when I know exactly what he said.

He moves the empty bowl of cookie dough from in between us and pulls on my feet so that I slide across the counter until we're knee to knee, no distance between us.

"It's true, Vaughn." He laughs in a way that tells me it's hard for him to believe, too, and thank God for that because I'm still stunned. Still sagging in relief. Still fumbling to believe it.

"What about—I thought—you said we weren't defining—"

"We're not."

"But I don't underst—"

"Neither do I," he murmurs as he presses his lips to mine to stop my protests when I don't want to be protesting. "I thought how I felt was because you were a challenge, but then I caught you. Then I thought it

313

was because I needed to help fix you, but you fixed your broken parts yourself. I was wrong—I just needed you."

That heart that stopped beating? It just sped up.

"You've had me, Ryker. For longer than you know."

"Thank fuck for that," he murmurs and leans forward.

His kiss is slow and seductive. He smells like chocolate and wine and everything I want. Everything I need.

"No defining," he says against my lips. "Just us. Just this."

"Just now."

The tub of dough is moved. The glasses of wine are forgotten.

It's only him I think of. It's only him who can sate this need he's created.

The cool granite of the island is on my back while every other part of me burns bright.

And this time when he lays me down, when he pushes into me moaning how good I feel, when he watches me the entire time we have sex until I fall under the hypnotic wash of pleasure he coaxes out of me, something is different between us.

There's something different every time, actually—something new I learn, something new I feel—but this time it's unmistakable.

This time he shows me how he feels.

This time, I know I'm not alone anymore.

CHAPTER
FIFTY-ONE
Ryker

"Good riddance," I mutter as I shut the door behind me and Vaughn laughs at me.

"Where were we again?" she asks as she steps into me and brings her lips to mine, just as tires crunch on the driveway outside. She laughs against my lips as my balls beg not to be disturbed again. They ache like a sonofabitch after being interrupted more times than I care to count.

"Go away. We don't want any," I shout to whoever is on the other side of the door.

"Maybe someone is bringing more cookies," she teases as I glance over to the kitchen counter with four different baskets of cookies from four different Hamptons' residents.

"I prefer the cookies I ate last night," I say, as every single moment comes back for my own viewing pleasure.

She bursts out laughing. "Every single time that Nancy lady would slide her hand across the island and say how much she loved the granite's texture, all I could think of—"

"Was you sliding over it last night." Legs spread. Mouth parted. My name being moaned. Yep, that was definitely the visual I had when Nancy was droning on about how gorgeous the slab was.

"Mm-hmm." Vaughn's smile is just as suggestive as her voice is husky at the thought.

There's a knock at the door.

"Fuck this," I growl and walk over to where my cell phone has happily stayed unused during most of our time here.

"What are you doing?"

"Ignoring whoever that is." I begin to type a text. "We're having a party."

"A *what*?" She coughs the words out.

"A party. Let them all come. Let them all look. Let them all feed their own damn curiosity about the woman Ryker Lockhart has brought to the Hamptons, and then they'll leave us the fuck alone on our last day here."

"You mean let them define us?" she asks with a lift of her brow and coy smile.

"Their words, baby. Not ours." I pick four names of my neighbors to add to the text and hit send. "Within an hour the whole town will know."

"That's one way to deal with it." She laughs.

"Yep. Let them come. Let them stare at how gorgeous you are and how you're not the least bit enthralled with all of the monetary trappings here . . . and then they can go home and gossip, but I get to stay here and keep you to myself without interruption."

One can hope.

"I like the *without interruption* part."

"Now where were we?" I ask as I pull her against me, my fingers tugging on the tie of her bikini top.

"Oops. I seem to have lost my top," she murmurs against my lips.

"You're about to lose your bottoms too."

"Please and thank you."

CHAPTER FIFTY-TWO

Vaughn

The amount of people here is ridiculous.

"Who knew there were this many people in this sleepy little town," I say to Ryker.

"They'll come out for gossip," he says with a lift of his brows and presses a kiss to the side of my cheek. "You okay?"

"Yes. I'm fine. Go talk to your friends."

"I wouldn't exactly call these people friends," he says wryly.

"You know what I mean."

"I know what you mean." He slides a hand down to rest on my ass and pats it. "You're not going to disappear on me now, are you?"

I stare at him and smile softly. "No. I have my wine. And false courage." I shrug. "You know, the perfect combination to combat nosy, rich socialites."

"I'll make it up to you later, Sanders."

"I'm holding you to that promise."

"Promise?" he asks with a sly smile as someone across the patio calls his name.

I watch him retreat. His broad shoulders beneath his henley, sleeves pulled up to the elbows, and I know that just like I never thought sex could feel as incredible as Ryker has made it feel, he's making love feel just as incredible.

Floating on air, I head over to fill my glass of wine.

"You know she's just here for his money." I freeze when I hear the nasally voice and stop where I am in the shadow of the house and search for its owner. "I mean, I've never heard of her before. *Sanders?* What family is that from?" She's blonde with big hips, thinning hair, and diamonds dripping from her ears.

"Definitely not our pedigree," the taller, dark-skinned woman to her left says. "You'd think by now he'd realize it."

"I heard the Stanleys stopped by today, and they were busy having s-e-x on the other side of the door." This one is brown-haired and petite with a nervous tic of blinking her eyes.

"Well, who wouldn't have sex with him? I mean, come on. He's on my island," says the blonde, mock fanning herself.

"Your island houses every single man with an eight-figure net worth, so that's not saying much," the taller of them says.

"I give her two months. I mean, he likes change. He likes things he can't have. He'll change her oil a few times and then realize she's the dipstick and dump her ass."

Fuck this.

"Excuse me, ladies—is everyone having a great time tonight?" I ask as I step out of the shadows and into their circle. The blonde all but spits out the drink of wine she just took when she sees my saccharine-sweet smile.

"Yes."

"Definitely."

Eyes take me in, scrutinize, judge.

"I'm Vaughn Sanders. Welcome to *our* home," I say, knowing that "our" part will really get them gossiping the moment I turn my back.

"Thank you for inviting us," the brunette says, her eyes flitting to my ring finger to see if she's missed something and we've eloped.

"It wasn't my idea. I figured if people came over, the women would be bitchy and shallow and judge me without ever having met me. You know how females are," I say with a wink. "While the guys would have fun and complain about how all of their wives are sticks-in-the-mud and never give it up . . . but"—I smile broadly—"I'm so glad to see that's not the case."

"No."

"Never."

"Great. That's so good to hear. Well, if you do hear the catty bullshit, just make sure to let them all know they're wrong. I couldn't care less about the money. I've made plenty of my own." I lean forward and lower my voice to a whisper. "I'm just here for the sex. I mean, what woman would turn down a man with twelve inches and a whole helluva lot of skill?" Eyes widen. Lips fall lax. A gasp falls from one of their mouths. "Multiple orgasms. Every. Single. Time."

"Really?" the blonde croaks as if she's talking about china patterns.

"So good," I moan and take a sip of my wine. "In fact"—I look at my watch—"I've got to find him. My alarm's about to go off any second."

"Alarm for what?" the brunette asks.

"What else? Sex this incredible is not to be missed. We like to set alarms on each other's phones without the other knowing. The last person in the bedroom has to give oral first. And let me tell you, his tongue is something I definitely don't want to miss." I walk a few steps and then turn back and smile. "It was a pleasure meeting you. I hope you have a great time."

And when I walk away with a huge smile on my face and their fervent whispers going at my back, I know my job is done.

Serves them right.

I walk into the kitchen high on my victory and all at the same time more than fearful that I made a major mistake in doing that. Bracing my hands on the counter, I draw in a deep breath.

There is the sound of clapping at my back, and I jump when I turn around to see a woman standing there. Her hair is a beautiful silver, her cheekbones perfect, her eyes a light brown. She's flawless in her linen pants and tank top, perfectly accessorized and styled.

"Bravo," she says, her hands clasping together on the last clap. I stare at her, try to place her, but don't say a word. "That was quite impressive what you said back there, putting those women in their arrogant, self-righteous places."

"Thank you," I murmur, still cautious of this woman whose presence dominates the room.

"While I don't believe a word of what you said, they sure did, and rest assured the text chain is suddenly abuzz with your comments."

"Do I know you?" I ask.

"No." She crosses the distance. "I just stopped in on the way to a charity event. I thought I'd say hi and check in on my son." A smile flirts with the corners of her mouth, but her eyes assess. "But after watching your little performance, it seems he's doing just fine." She extends a hand. "Vivian Lockhart."

Oh. Jesus.

Seriously?

Ryker's mom just heard me talk about him having a twelve-inch cock?

Her laugh floats through the room. "We both know you're not shy after what you just said, so don't stand there like you just saw a ghost. I like a woman with a backbone. God knows you'll need it to put up with my son."

I shake her hand. "Vaughn Sanders."

"Everyone around here seems to know. Leave it to the mother to be the last to."

I smile and take a sip of my wine as nerves assault my system.

"Well, it was a pleasure to meet you, but I'd like to find my son and say hi before I leave to fulfill other obligations." She smiles at me one more time. "I'll make sure to let you know how the rumor mill spins that."

"That's not necessary."

"Yes, it is." She winks. "That's half the fun."

And just like that, Ryker's mom heads out the back door to the patio to find her son.

CHAPTER FIFTY-THREE

Ryker

She walks past but doesn't see me.

The music floats in from outside, but her heels clicking on the hardwood floor catch my attention. Her sundress is simple and sexy and calls to me to pull it up and see what it is she's wearing beneath it.

It doesn't hurt that she's fucking awesome.

In every sense of the word.

I might be buzzed, but I sure as fuck know that.

"Hey," I call out to her.

Vaughn startles at my voice, her hand to her chest and a little yelp falling from her throat.

And without thought, I open the door to the downstairs extra bedroom and pull her into it with me. Before I can even shut the door and shove her against it, my lips are on hers.

I take from her. What I need. What I want. And the fact that she meets me match for match is sexy as hell.

We're both tipsy. We're both horny. And where I'm hard she's fucking soaked.

I yank up her dress to find a scrap of lace that just adds fuel to my fire. With my arms wrapped around her, I move her to the dresser opposite us and set her down.

I don't have time to think. Neither of us speaks. The urgency in our desire, the party going on beyond the door, and our greed is all we need as I push into her.

It takes all I have not to come right then. Her hot, wet pussy is heaven and hell and every sinner's paradise in between.

Our hands grip.

Oh God.

Our teeth nip.

Harder.

We both moan.

Faster.

And then groan.

Deeper.

Her fingers dig into my biceps.

Right there.

Her teeth dig into my shoulder.

I'm coming.

And fuck if it doesn't make me lose my breath. If she doesn't make me lose it every damn time.

Our chests heave. Our hearts race. Someone outside somewhere calls my name. Our lips find each other and soften the violent desire we just shared with the tenderness of a kiss.

I lean back and look at her. At what I do to her. Her cheeks are flushed. Her eyes are wild.

She's mine.

I've never said that before and really meant it. Or wanted it.

But she's mine.

A shy smile ghosts on her lips. "Hi."

"Hi." I chuckle.

"Well, that was an unexpected surprise."

"I had to make sure all twelve inches still worked." I wink as her eyes widen.

"Ryker—"

I stop the apology I can see she's about to give by putting my finger on her lips. "That was my thank-you for being so goddamn awesome."

I lean in and kiss her again, and all I can think about is the buzz outside from what she said, how she held her own, and how she turned it around on them.

"We've got to get back," she says through a laugh. "People are going to notice we're missing."

"Good. It serves them right." The women will know she's right, and the men will know she's mine. I slip out of her. "Stay there." I walk to the en suite bathroom and grab a towel and clean myself off. Then I grab one and walk over to where she's perched on the dresser, legs spread, and clean her up. "There you go." But when I glance up, she has that look in her eyes—the one that makes me want to taste those lips again.

"You better get back," she says, the same emotion I feel clogging in her throat.

I take a step toward the door and turn to look at her one last time before unlocking it.

"Vaughn?" Her eyes flash up to me, but the rest of what I was going to say doesn't come.

I love you.

I smile instead and hope she knows.

Because I do.

Fucking Christ, I *am* in love her.

"Yes?" Lids heavy with desire and satisfaction flutter open.

"I—you—*fuck*." I scrub a hand through my hair as I struggle to tell her what it means for her to be here. For her to take hold of my goddamn heart when it's never even been on the damn market. To look at her and see things I never expected to see before.

"I know," she murmurs, smile soft and eyes reflecting the same way I feel back at me. *"No defining, though."*

I chuckle. It's easier than acknowledging how my chest constricts at those two simple words. "Woman, you're beginning to make me want to define things I never imagined before."

"Is that so?" Her question is playful, but the goddamn hope in her eyes makes it hard to swallow.

"It is."

And when we're done, when I open that door and shut it behind me, I'm sober.

Goddamn, Vaughn makes me sober . . . and thank fuck for that, or else I'd miss the high that being with her gives me.

Because I'd take that high any damn day of the week.

CHAPTER
FIFTY-FOUR

Vaughn

I can't help the smile on my face.

Whatever just happened between Ryker and me—not the sex part, because I'd have to be comatose to not feel what he just did to me, but the unspoken part in the look he gave me—expressed all I needed to know about how he feels about me.

I recognize it, because I feel it too.

Screw their definitions.

We have our own.

Hoping to rejoin the party without my absence being scrutinized— well, then again, I am the one who told the ladies I had an alarm set—I open the door.

And startle at the figure standing in the hallway.

"Look at you."

His voice. *That* voice.

"Excuse me—do I know you?" I ask, feigning nonchalance as I try to step around him and out of the corner I'm backed into.

He blocks my exit.

Panic bubbles up.

"I wasn't sure before . . . but I saw you outside. I watched you, and then it clicked." His face is covered by the shadows of the darkened hallway.

"I'm sorry. I'm not sure what you're talking about."

"Oh, come on, *Vee.*" Adrenaline races through my veins at the mention of that name. "Or is it Vaughn? Which name do you make Ryker call you by?"

"If you'd let me by—"

"Why? So you can go con another man out there into thinking you're the real deal when you're obviously on the payroll here?"

Deep breath, Vaughn. You've got this.

Without saying anything, I try to get past him, but he grabs my wrist, yanking it so that he pushes me up against the wall at my back. He steps into me, his body against mine and the whiskey on his breath making my stomach churn.

"You can scream, but there's no one around who's going to hear you."

The hallway's dark. The music outside is loud.

He's right.

And I know it.

"You see, it was this unique little birthmark right here," he says, pressing his thumb against the inside of my wrist where the heart-shaped strawberry birthmark resides, "that clued me in. Sure, your features were similar, but without the wig, it was hard to tell. But this birthmark . . . it sealed the deal for me. Same person. Same bitch trying to fool gullible fuckers. Same female threatening me. Same woman making me hard as a rock."

"I don't know what you're talking about." It's all I've got. All I can think.

"I told you I'd get what I wanted from you one way or another . . . and you have a whole lot of things I want."

My skin crawls as his threat travels over every part of me and lets me know he means it.

I try to find my footing. I attempt to find the sassy woman who doesn't kowtow to threatening senators who dwarf them in size. But too much alcohol . . . too much fear . . . too much of letting my guard down this weekend and I'm frozen in uncertainty.

The bathroom door opens unexpectedly, and a couple giggles as they step out, what they were doing in there without the light on no mystery.

"Leave me alone!" I say loudly enough to get their attention.

"Hey? You okay?" the guy asks as Senator Carter Preston lets go of me with a muttered curse.

"Lovers' quarrel," he says and strides down the hallway and out of reach of the drunk guy's range.

"You sure you're okay?" the woman slurs.

"Yes." *No.*

And where I was just terrified of how dark the hallway was, now I'm grateful because they won't know it's me standing here.

They won't be able to recognize me in the shadows. The woman they all came to see who has caught Ryker Lockhart's eye.

The girl giggles as the guy palms her ass, and I breathe easier when they start walking back toward the party so I can have a second to myself.

What the hell is Carter doing here?

And even worse, he knows who I am.

He can make the connection.

He can ruin me.

CHAPTER FIFTY-FIVE

Vaughn

"Have you seen Ryker?" I ask the first group of people I come in contact with when I make it outside.

"Is everything okay?" Jake, the tech bazillionaire I met earlier, asks.

"Yes." I force a smile. "There's just an issue with something in the kitchen I need to ask him about."

"Last I saw, he was heading toward the pool house," Jake's date says.

"'Kay. Thank you."

I make my way across the grass—frazzled but trying to keep my cool. A few people stop me to talk, but I manage to move on quickly, my eyes constantly scanning for the senator.

But he's nowhere to be found.

When I enter the pool house, the sound of Ryker's voice calms me instantly.

"Think what you will," he says.

He'll know what to do. He'll know how to handle this. He'll help me.

And just as I go to turn the corner, his words stop me in my tracks and knock the wind out of me.

"I only have Vaughn around because of the sex. Nothing more. Nothing less."

I press a hand to the wall to steady myself, not wanting to believe what I just heard. Not wanting to believe that it's Ryker's voice speaking those words.

"Well, you've gone to the right place if it's sex. *Lucky bastard.* Vaughn's a madam and a whore all tied into one neat little bow you get to open up one thigh at a time." The man chuckles, and instantly I know who the owner of that laugh is.

My stomach revolts.

My pulse races.

"You can have her if you want her, Preston. Fuck, I'll even pay for your time with her."

I clasp a hand over my mouth as tears sting my eyes—fury and hurt and disbelief fueling their presence—while I try to fathom what I'm hearing. My thoughts stumble out of control as I strain to make out their murmured words.

Time slows down. Stills.

Ryker just outed me—my identity—to a man whose power and reach can damage me the most.

"You'd pay for me, Lockhart? Why the generosity all of a sudden?"

No, not outed me. Ryker did something even worse. He didn't defend me.

"Senator, even I know when it's time to share the wealth. Besides, aren't you the one who has the most to gain here?"

And despite knowing my past, my secrets, he offered me to a man who gets off on using his power to hurt others.

"You let me down, and then you try to soothe me with pussy." Carter's chuckle rumbles through the air. "A man after my own heart."

"I wasn't aware you had one," Ryker murmurs, followed by the clink of glass against glass.

"What I don't get is how'd you manage to corral her?" the senator asks as I stand paralyzed with an indecision I've never felt before. *Fight or flight.* "She needs a real man to put her in her place. Show her who's boss . . . no offense."

"None taken," Ryker says.

"What'd you do?" Preston says through a laugh, followed by a loud exhale to match the cigar smoke clinging to the air. "Fool her into believing that she meant more to you than a good lay?"

Fight or flight, Vaughn.

Frozen in time, I don't even realize I'm crying until I taste the salt of my tears hit my lips. I was played. He wound me up. He made me believe. And now? And now I know the truth.

"You're a cruel and brilliant fucking bastard," Carter says.

"So they say." Ryker chuckles, and every part of me crumples from its sound.

"You better not be playing me, Lockhart."

"Playing you? Not you, Preston. You'd see right through it. Everybody else, though? Definitely."

Words are exchanged. I can't quite make them out. But I don't need to. The smug laugh Ryker emits is just the twisting of the dagger.

"Like I said, it's the least I can do, given the circumstances."

"Pass the pussy, please," the senator says, and both men laugh as bile threatens in my throat. "How do you know she'll go along with it?"

"Tell me the time and place, and I'll have her ready and willing for you. But first you'll need to give me—"

"Just make sure she's defiant. I love it when they fight."

Fight or flight.

I should walk right out that door and leave and never look back. Gather whatever dignity I have left and flee to salvage what I can of my pride.

Ryker doesn't deserve my wasted breath.

He doesn't deserve anything from me.

But for some reason my feet are moving forward. Toward the voices. When I clear the corner, Ryker and Carter Preston are sitting on stools with their backs to me, cigars in their hands and drinks on the table in front of them.

Fight.

"Not going to happen." Words tumble out of my mouth without thought, and the minute they are in the air, I can see both men tense.

Carter turns immediately, eyebrows lifted and a smug smirk sliding onto his lips as his eyes drag over every inch of my body. Ryker, on the other hand, takes his time turning to face me. He sets his cigar down, takes a measured sip of his drink, and then slowly looks at me.

"Vaughn. Perfect timing. Were your ears burning, babe?" Ryker asks, his eyes meeting Carter's and his silent nod loaded with arrogance, almost as if he's saying *I've got this.*

"Babe?" I ask, my voice breaking but chillingly calm as I rein in the emotions rioting within me. I won't give him the satisfaction of knowing he's affected me. *"Babe?"*

"Yeah." He shrugs, the nonchalance in his tone and indifference in his posture throwing me almost as much as his words.

"I'm not yours to share."

"You took the money, so technically, you're mine to do with as I please." I blink my eyes rapidly as I try to comprehend what he's just said. As I try to come to terms with the fact that I've been played this whole time. Pursued for the sake of pursuit. Fucked for the sake of selfishness. Hurt as a pawn in his egotistical game. "It's not like you'd say no to me."

Our eyes lock, feud, and every question I have is thrown his way, but he doesn't give me any indication that he means differently. His expression is just as ice cold as my voice is.

"I don't—I can't—how . . ." I stumble over words, overconnecting my thoughts, struggling to remain stoic as I stand there and stare at a man I thought I knew but obviously don't. As I try to fathom how I trusted him. How I was so gullible to believe he really cared for me.

How I thought I loved him.

"Did you really think I had changed this much for you?" Ryker scoffs, earning a chuckle from Carter that has tears of humiliation burning in my eyes. Tears I won't give him the sick pleasure of seeing me shed. "Did you really think I want something permanent? Something that can be *defined*? That you were the *exception*?"

And for the slightest of seconds I wonder if I'm misunderstanding something, if I'm walking in on a situation that's causing Ryker to betray my trust.

That has to be the reason.

It has to be.

Ryker wouldn't hurt me like this.

"Ryker?" His name is a plea. A silent appeal to tell me that I've got this all wrong.

Show me the sign.

"You did, didn't you?" he asks, his voice condescending as he looks anywhere but my eyes.

But when I slide my gaze over to his hands, I don't see a "hang loose" sign. I don't see anything other than his subtle nudge to Carter and the arrogant smirk on his lips, which kissed me senseless less than an hour ago.

It's the nudge that does me in. Callous and as if he has ownership over me.

Fight.

That breaks my heart, which finally felt after being dead for so long.

That shreds the trust I'd allowed myself to give someone else.

Dammit, Vaughn, fight.

"Vaughn?" Ryker's voice cuts into the anger silencing my thoughts. Fury I now suddenly feel at both him and at myself.

At him? For obvious reasons.

At myself? For almost wanting there to be an excuse for all of this so I could justify the hurt away. But that wouldn't be okay either. How would Ryker showing a "hang loose" sign validate and nullify the fact that he used me—exposed everything that makes me vulnerable—for his own means?

It wouldn't.

It would just show the kind of man he is: one who exploits others for his own benefit.

Stunned and desperate to understand, I let my eyes flicker from man to man until Carter steps toward me with a crooked smile on his lips and his eyes shining with lust.

Fight.

"No!" It's the only word I can muster. The only thought I can express through the devastation imploding my heart. The only defiance I can give.

And then I run out of there.

Flight.

I don't remember how I get across the backyard and into the house.

Ryker doesn't chase after me.

I don't know how I manage to find my stuff and shove it into the first bag I come to.

Ryker doesn't come to tell me this was all a joke.

I don't know how I can still breathe when it feels like every single thing inside me has been hit with a hammer and then a wrecking ball. He betrayed me in every sense of the word: in outing my identity, in throwing away the trust he worked so hard to get, in manipulating me—and all for his own pleasure. All to gain some kind of favor with an abusive prick like Carter Preston. All to let me know exactly what he thought of me.

Ryker doesn't love me.

I don't recall how I managed to get an Uber and steal out of the house without anyone noticing.

But I noticed.
How he made me trust.
How he made me feel.
How he made me love.
All of those things he made me do when I thought I was broken.
And then broke them when I finally felt whole again.
The Uber driver and I reach the highway.
The tears come. One after another as I stare out the window.
He made me believe.
He made me hope.
And then he crushed me.

ACKNOWLEDGMENTS

I'd like to take a moment to acknowledge a few people who helped me bring Ryker and Vaughn's story to life.

My agent, Kimberly Brower: thank you for scouring thesauruses with me to find titles, discussing plot ideas, and having my back at all times.

My editing team at Montlake—Maria Gomez, Lindsey Faber, Angela Elson, Susan Stokes, and the rest of the crew: thank you for polishing my ideas and words to make the story what it is. It takes a village to publish a book . . . and you're that village.

My helpers—Christy, Alison, Chrisstine, Stephanie, Val, Annette, and Emma: thank you for keeping me sane.

Most importantly, to my readers: I truly hope you enjoyed the first part of Ryker and Vaughn's story in *Resist*. Thank you for trusting me to take you on a journey with every book. Your support means the world to me and keeps me striving to write a better story each time. I race you!

ABOUT THE AUTHOR

Photo © 2017 Lauren Perry

New York Times bestselling author K. Bromberg writes contemporary romance novels that are sweet, emotional, a lot sexy, and a little bit real. She likes to write strong heroines and damaged heroes that readers love to hate but can't help loving.

Since publishing her first book on a whim in 2013, Bromberg has sold over 1.5 million copies of her books across eighteen different countries and has repeatedly landed on the bestseller lists for the *New York Times*, *USA Today*, and *Wall Street Journal*. Her Driven trilogy (*Driven*, *Fueled*, and *Crashed*) is currently being adapted for film by the streaming platform Passionflix, with *Driven* available now.

You can find out more about this mom of three on any of her social media accounts. The easiest way to stay up to date is to sign up for her newsletter (http://bit.ly/254MWtI) or text "KBromberg" to 77948 to receive text alerts when a new book is released.